Mally
the
Maker
and the
Queen
in the
Quilt

Written and Illustrated by Leah Day

Mally the Maker and the Queen in the Quilt.
Text and illustration copyright © 2018 by Leah Day.

Day Style Designs Inc
P.O Box 386
Earl, NC 28038

Email: Support@DayStyleDesigns.com

Printed in the United States of America

First Printing, 2018

ISBN: 978-0-9979011-6-0

First edition

10 9 8 7 6 5 4 3 2 1

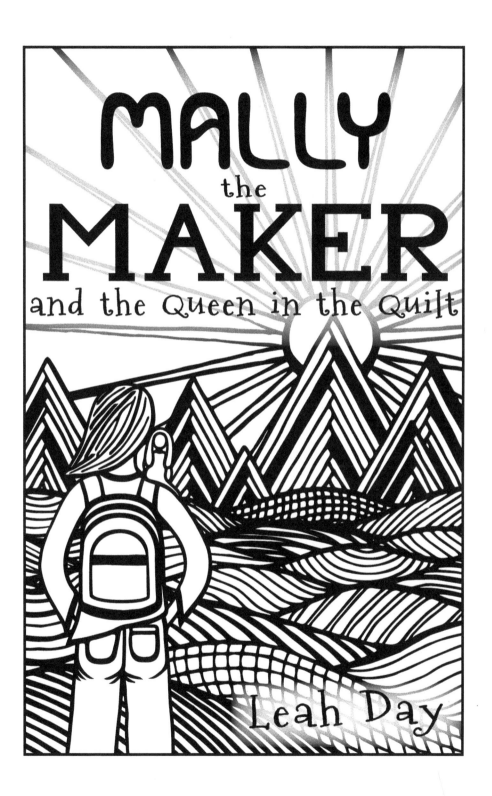

For my grandma,
Mattie Bernice Harrison Gray

&

Ms. Bunny

I miss you both every day.

Contents

Chapter 1

Don't Want to Cry Anymore

"Grandma, why do you make quilts?"

Mally was sitting in her favorite sunny window seat watching Grandma stitch green patches of fabric together. With a thimble on her thumb and forefinger, her wrinkled hands moved fluidly, shifting the fabric over, inserting the needle, then sliding it through to pull the thread straight.

"I suppose I just like it, Mally May. There's something comforting about stitching things together. Sometimes I like playing with the bright fabrics." She winked as she picked up a piece of hot pink material.

"And sometimes I like seeing the pieces come together perfectly." She smoothed out the patchwork on the table and touched the seams where the hexagons came together. "I guess it just makes me feel good."

Mally stretched out her hand to touch the quilt, and stretched and stretched, but her fingertips never reached the soft fabrics. Her fist collided with the wall next to her bed and she sat up with a shriek.

Dream. It was only a dream, Mally thought, holding back tears. *Grandma's gone.* Distantly she heard the rumble of thunder. Happy, sunny days stitching in Grandma's sewing room were a thing of the past.

She searched around the bed for her favorite doll and found her nearly falling off the edge of the mattress. She scooped Ms. Bunny close and laid back down, pulling the quilt up to her chin. The hexagon quilt she'd just dreamed of was spread over her like a comforting hug. She stroked the fabrics where the seams came together as the room around her blurred.

I don't want to cry anymore, Mally thought, even as her mouth filled with saliva and her nose began to run. She had been crying for months and it hadn't done any good.

Ms. Bunny filled the empty space in her arms and Mally imagined what she would say if she could speak. "It's okay, dear. I'm here. I love you. You're going to be fine." She wiped her eyes with one of Ms. Bunny's soft ears and fell back to sleep to the sound of rain pounding on the roof.

*   *   *   *   *

BLEEP. BLEEP. BLEEP.

Mally swung out her hand to hit the alarm. She missed, and it continued to blare in her ear. She gave it another whack and missed again.

"Mally! Are you up yet? Come on, kid, it's an early morning!" Dad yelled from the bottom of the stairs.

She opened her eyes blearily. Her lashes were stuck together with the tears that had dried into crystals around her eyes. She rubbed furiously and finally got her eyes unglued and hit her alarm to shut off the beeping. Still half asleep, Mally rooted around in the sheets until her fingertips brushed a familiar shape. She pulled Ms. Bunny out of the tangled sheets and gave her a hug.

Then she smoothed the doll's pink dress out over her skinny legs and set her on the pillow with her paws crossed on her lap so she could see the room. The doll looked very prim and proper with three heart shaped buttons decorating the front of her calico dress and white lace stitched along the hem and sleeves. Mally smoothed her long ears down on either side of the doll's chest so they framed her tiny body perfectly.

"Have a great day, Ms. Bunny," she said, sliding out of bed. She grabbed the clothes she'd laid out on the floor the night before and made for the bathroom across the hall.

"Snooze you lose, baby." Rose pushed her roughly out of the way and slammed the bathroom door in her face.

"I get the bathroom first! You evil cow!" Mally shouted, pounding on the door. "Dad! Rose stole the bathroom!"

"Mally, there is more than one bathroom in this house…"

"But Rose–"

"Downstairs bathroom, Mally! Get a move on!"

Mally stomped down the stairs to the tiny half bath. She hated this dark bathroom. It smelled funny and spiders were often lurking in the corners. The door tended to stick and there was barely enough space to turn around. Once she'd been startled by a huge spider in the sink only to find she was trapped in the room with it.

She flicked on the light and searched the corners carefully before pulling the door partially closed. She slipped into a t-shirt and sweater then squeezed into her jeans. The fabric fit tight around her waist and the hem came up high above her socks. She'd asked Dad about getting more pants when school started, but he had just sighed and rubbed his hands over his face. She hadn't asked again.

Mally washed her face and checked her reflection in the mirror. Her dark blonde hair was a tangled mess around her head. They didn't keep a comb in this bathroom so she wet her fingertips and tried to smooth it down the best she could. Her hair fell to just below her chin, long enough to blow into her face, but too short to pull back into a ponytail. She could still see gritty tear crystals in her green eyes and washed her face again to remove them.

I have to stop crying, Mally thought. *I have to STOP.* She took a deep breath and left the bathroom, dropping her pajamas in a pile on the stairs. She tried to wiggle her pants into a more comfortable position as she wandered into the kitchen.

Dad was sitting at the table staring into his cup of coffee. His big hands circled around a white mug that said "World's Best MOM" in teal letters. Mally didn't think he'd noticed that he'd picked mama's favorite mug. *Well, it's not like she's going to complain about it,* she thought sourly. *I doubt she'll even notice.*

"Morning," Dad said, not looking up.

"Good morning," Mally answered. She pulled out a box of cereal and shook a mix of flakes and raisins into a bowl. She was pouring milk on top when Rose stormed into the kitchen.

"Have you seen my pink bag?" she demanded.

"No, I haven't seen it," Mally said, tensing for a fight.

"Where is it? What have you done with it?" Rose grabbed Mally's arm and squeezed hard. "I set it at the bottom of the stairs last night and now it's gone. What did you do with it?"

Mally opened her mouth to protest, but Dad beat her to it. "Rose, it's on the couch. I moved it so you wouldn't break your neck tripping on it this morning."

"Fine," Rose muttered, releasing her grip. Mally set the milk back on the counter and turned to pull a spoon out of the drawer. Quick as a flash, Rose snatched a spoon out of the dish drainer and Mally's bowl of cereal and begin wolfing it down.

"Rose! That's mine!"

"Mine now," Rose smirked. Milk dribbled down her wide chin into the bowl.

"Give it back! Dad! Rose stole my cereal!"

A breath of silence descended as Mally waited to see what Dad would do. He couldn't let Rose get away with this yet again… It just wasn't FAIR!

But Dad just sat staring into his coffee cup, and Mally knew he wouldn't do anything.

She turned and poured another bowl of cereal, her hand shaking with rage. This is NOT how the morning would go if Mama still got up with them. Mama would have fixed things. Mama would have made it better.

Mally sat down and glared at her sister across the table, daring her to try something else. Rose had Mama's dark hair and bright blue eyes, but she was built like Dad with big hands and a chunky body. Her chin wobbled as she ate, and more milk dribbled out of her mouth.

Mally caught Rose's eye and mouthed, "Cow." With a small surge of satisfaction, she watched her sister's face flush crimson. But her victory was short lived.

"Baby," Rose mouthed back and Mally jumped as intense pain shot through her shin. Rose had kicked her under the table. Her eyes filled with tears as her sister smirked, finishing off the rest of her cereal with a flourish.

Rose was fourteen and apparently that was the magical age when you turn nasty and become a different person. They had once played dolls together and Mally could remember Rose reading to her when she was little. These days she just wished Rose would go away and leave her alone. Anything was better than being around her.

They finished breakfast in silence, broken only by the sound of water running in the next room. *Mama is up at least. Maybe she will come in and eat breakfast with us*, Mally thought. But as the minutes ticked by it was clear she had just gone back to bed.

"Well, let's get going, girls." Dad rubbed his hand over his eyes and looked like he could use another cup of coffee. Mally slurped the milk from the bottom of the bowl as she walked to the sink, then grabbed her coat and blue bookbag from the bench near the door. Rose pushed past, nearly smacking Mally in the face as she slung a pink duffle, bookbag, and purse over her shoulder.

"Shotgun!" she yelled, flipping her long brown hair over her shoulder.

Mally had the strongest urge to grab her hair and yank her sister backward. Just a fast, powerful tug to trip her and get her back for everything this morning. She resisted the urge as she followed her sister out to the truck. Rose climbed in the front and Mally squeezed into the tiny extended cab in the back, wedging her bookbag between her knees.

The familiar scent of wood shavings and sawdust filled her nose, smells Dad brought with him everywhere. He opened the opposite door and set a wooden toolbox on the seat next to her and three binders on top. Mally saw a beautiful picture of a kitchen with dark cabinets and stone countertops on the front cover. It must be a new job prospect today if Dad was bringing his portfolio.

Her assumption was confirmed when Dad climbed into the front seat and said, "Don't forget you're walking to Grandma's house after school. Rose, please wait for your sister so you can walk together." He started the truck and began to back out of the driveway.

"Dad, no! I don't want to be seen walking with her! She's such a baby – all my friends make fun of her. I can't be seen with her in public."

"I am not!" Mally shouted back.

"Are too! You cry all the time!" Rose turned in her seat to glare at

Mally. "Just like a baby. I bet you're about to cry right now."

As if on cue, Mally's eyes filled with tears. The world went blurry and she felt a familiar pressure in her chest and pain in her throat as she tried to hold it in.

"Enough!" Dad roared, slamming on the brakes. "Rose, you're out of line. Hand me your bag."

"What?"

"Your purse thing. Whatever you keep your phone in. No electronics for a week."

"But Dad! I have an assignment and this thing with Sheila—"

"Bag. NOW." Dad rarely got angry enough to raise his voice, but when he did, it could make windows rattle. Mally felt a nice jolt of pleasure in her stomach at seeing her sister's face crumple for once. She handed over her purse. Dad opened the truck door and threw it on the edge of the driveway.

"Dad! That's outside! What if it gets rained on? I have makeup in there!"

Dad turned to Rose and looked at her for a long moment.

"You should think about the things you value and how you treat them, Rose. When you treat the people around you terrible, you end up looking terrible. I think a few days without makeup or a phone will do you good."

He threw the truck into reverse and they drove the rest of the way to school in silence. Mally felt a bit awestruck and tried not to smile at the thought of Rose's precious phone getting wet, or even better, run over by the mailman.

They pulled up at the high school and Rose snatched her bookbag and pink duffle and jumped out of the truck, slamming the door as hard as she could. She shot Mally a look of pure hatred before stalking off to find her friends.

Mally climbed up between the seats and reached back to pull her bookbag into her lap. Staring out the window at the rain-soaked ground, Mally wished for a second she and Dad could just drive away. Leave Mama to sleep the day away and Rose to be horrible to someone else. Leave it all behind.

They drove down to the elementary school in silence. Dad surprised Mally by pulling into a space in the parking lot rather than the carpool line with the other parents. He put the truck in park but continued looking out the window, the green eyes they both shared staring at the kids lining up.

"Your sister shouldn't treat you like that," he said gently. "But she does have a point."

"What?" Mally couldn't believe what she was hearing.

"If you stood up for yourself, it would be harder for her. She's just looking for buttons to push and you're making it really easy for her."

Mally didn't say anything as Dad's words sunk in. He thought she was a baby too. And here Mally had resisted fighting back because she didn't want to make him look any more sad or tired than he already did.

That's not FAIR, she thought. *I'm trying to be GOOD. I'm trying to make things easy for you. Can't you see that?*

"Just work on the crying thing, baby girl," Dad said softly. "We're all sad, but we can't keep crying about every little thing."

Mally just wanted this conversation to be over. She couldn't believe Dad was actually agreeing with Rose. The insult and injustice of all of it made her eyes brim with tears yet again. She let her hair swing over her face as she slid out of the big truck.

"Just try your best, Mally."

"Sure, Dad." Rushing now, she grabbed her bag and slammed the truck door. She turned and ran up to the school, hoping the cool air would dry her tears before she got to class. Mally joined several kids walking inside the school and inhaled the familiar smell of paper, books, and floor cleaner. She pulled her backpack straps a bit tighter and tried to relax as she walked toward her classroom.

Outside the fourth grade hall she stopped by the bathroom and took a second to splash water on her face. Mally stared into the mirror and saw her cheeks still looked too pink and her eyes too glossy, but it was better than usual. At least her face didn't look like a splotchy red tomato today.

She sighed and walked the last few steps to Mrs. Smith's class. Walking inside was always a bit overwhelming. Her teacher loved color and each wall was decorated top to bottom with colorful drawings, paintings, and even some fabric panels with inspirational words Mrs. Smith had painted herself.

It was mega cheerful, but instead of lifting her spirits, the happy decorations always made her feel like a freak. She stared at a painting of a bright sunshine with the words "Don't Worry! Be Happy!" painted in bright blue. Was it really that easy for everyone else? Could some people just decide not to worry and happy all the time? She wandered over to her desk and began pulling out her notebooks and pencil case.

"Oh Rhet, Rhet! Where shall I go? What shall I do?" Her best friend Audrey threw herself dramatically into a nearby seat, clutching her hands over her heart.

"Frankly my dear, I don't give a damn," Mally replied, mimicking the deep voice of Rhet Butler from *Gone with the Wind*. They had watched the movie during a sleepover and that famous scene had become a standing joke between them.

Audrey laughed. "How you doing, Mally Bally?"

"All right." Mally shrugged as she pulled out her math book.

"I know the perfect thing to cheer you up! My mom is taking me to Renaissance Faire on Saturday and she bought an extra ticket for you."

"Really? Are you sure?"

"Of course, silly! I'd love for you to come. I can't wait to see the gypsies dance." Audrey began dancing around her desk, swinging her hips in a jerky imitation.

Mally's heart constricted as she realized this time last year her mom had put together the exact same trip. They'd had a great day eating roasted turkey legs and screaming their heads off at the joust. Mama had been so happy too.

While Mally and Audrey ran from vendor to vendor, she'd gotten her long brown hair braided into a complicated knot and her face painted with green vines. By the end of the day, Mama looked like a fairy queen, even in her black wool coat and jeans. Audrey had declared that next time they would all dress up and be princesses for a day and Mama had promised to help.

"I'll ask Dad if I can go," she said as Mrs. Smith breezed into the room. Today she was wearing white tights with a neon orange top and a yellow scarf wrapped tightly around her neck. She looked like a walking candy corn and Mally couldn't help smiling at the sight.

The morning passed with normal routine and slowly Mally relaxed. They always started the day with a bit of math because Mrs. Smith believed numbers were "Fundamental to life!" They were working on adding and subtracting fractions which she found surprisingly easy.

She remembered talking through fractions with Grandma last winter and she had helped Mally understand by sewing a quilt block. Mally could still remember adding ¼ inch to all sides of the fabric pieces so they could be sewn together and leave just the right shape behind.

She'd been a bit confused when the block finished ½ inch bigger than needed for the quilt, but as Grandma explained – ¼ inch added to all sides meant the block itself would end up ½ inch bigger. That way it could be pieced to other blocks without getting the edges lopped off.

Crazy quilt math, Grandma called it, but Mally found it helpful today as she visualized the fractions dividing a square of fabric. Thankfully, Mrs. Smith didn't mind her drawing on her papers and Mally found the little diagrams helpful.

At lunch she and Audrey stood in line together. As they stepped into the cafeteria they both breathed in deeply to smell what the kitchen was cooking. "Chicken pie!" they shouted in unison. Chicken pie days were the best.

Mally took in the smell of warm chicken and flakey pastry and it suddenly hit her – she was feeling happy. Almost immediately her throat closed and her chest seized. How could she possibly be happy? How could she be happy when Mama couldn't get out of bed? How could she be happy when she'd never see Grandma again?

The room blurred as Mally wrapped her arms around herself. Audrey was staring at her now and her face burned with embarrassment. They stood in line in silence as Mally fought to hold back a sob. It felt like everyone in the lunchroom was looking at her. When it was finally too much she whispered, "Be right back," and ran to the nearest bathroom.

Locking herself in a stall, she squeezed her arms tight around her chest. *I don't want to cry anymore,* she thought. *I don't want to cry anymore. I don't want to cry anymore.*

But then she thought of everything that had changed and that her Grandma was probably dead somewhere and never coming back. She'd never again have a beautiful day learning fractions in her sewing room or eat her peanut butter cookies or hear her say her name in that funny way she said it.

At this thought, tears trickled down her cheeks. *I don't want to cry anymore*, she thought as she broke down in sobs.

Eventually she was able to catch her breath and found herself on her knees in the stall. Gross. She stood up quickly and unlocked the door. She checked her reflection in the mirror. Great. Her bright red blotchy tomato face looked back at her. She rinsed her face with cold water, then hot water, but it didn't do any good. When Mally really cried, there was no hiding it.

She wandered back into the lunchroom and grabbed a tray, but she didn't feel very hungry now. After paying for her meal, she found Audrey, sat down and began mechanically eating her food.

"So I heard about this vendor at Renaissance Fair that sells corsets and dresses," Audrey said, continuing the earlier conversation seamlessly. "I don't know how much they cost, but wouldn't it be cool to buy a corset and dress up? Remember we planned to do that last year? I think we should check out that vendor and see if they have our sizes."

Then she was off talking through the costuming possibilities. Mally was grateful for the distraction and even more happy Audrey didn't mention her messed up face. She let herself get pulled into the conversation, considering colors and costume designs.

"Wouldn't it be cool to have a costume like the evil queen in Snow White? With that big thing around her head?" Audrey gestured with both hands. "What is that called?"

"A high collar?" Mally guessed. "I wonder if we could make some of the costumes before the weekend. Grandma's sewing machine is still set up at her house. I can ask and see if we can use it. Even if we just made skirts, that's something."

Now that she said it, she couldn't believe she hadn't thought of it before. She hadn't been in Grandma's sewing room in months. It would be so nice just to sit in the sunny window and dig through her favorite scrap basket again. It had been her favorite place to play before Grandma disappeared.

"That would be awesome!" Audrey said. "I've never made anything with a sewing machine before."

"Neither have I. Grandma wanted me to learn how to sew by hand first." Mally gave a weak smile. "I'm sure sewing with a machine is much easier."

They continued talking about different costumes they liked all through lunch. Mally loved the hats the good fairies wore in *Sleeping Beauty*, but she couldn't imagine being able to sew something like that. Audrey liked the villains costumes best and wanted a purple dress with a tall black collar.

"And a cape!" she said, dancing around Mally as they walked back to class.

"Or a cloak," Mally said. "Just in case it rains, it would be nice to have a hood."

"Just don't make it red," Audrey giggled. "Or you'll be Little Red Riding Hood."

Mally shrugged as she sat back down. "I'd rather be Red Riding Hood than the Evil Queen any day."

The rest of the day passed quickly, with reading time, a quick spelling test, and a science worksheet before heading outside for recess. On the playground, Mrs. Smith dismissed the class to play, but added, "Mally, can I see you for a second?"

Mally shoved her hands in her pockets and waited with her teacher as the other kids ran to play. Audrey waved her arms to indicate she'd save a swing for her and Mally smiled gratefully. Mrs. Smith caught her eye and her smile faded. "Am I in trouble?"

"No, Mally, I just wanted to check and see if you're okay."

"Yeah, I'm fine," she said, looking down. She felt embarrassed her teacher had noticed she'd cried earlier. Why couldn't she be normal, like everyone else? For the millionth time that day Mally thought, *I have got to stop crying.*

"I just want you to know that I'm here to talk if you ever need that. I understand you're having a tough time this year. Just let me know, okay?"

"Yes, ma'am." Mally nodded quickly, wishing she could go play.

"I just... Well, I lost my grandparents when I was about your age, Mally," Mrs. Smith said. Mally saw a shadow cross over her face as her teacher adjusted her sunny yellow scarf. She gave her a sad smile and added, "It sucks."

That was the last thing Mally expected to hear. "Thank you, Mrs. Smith." And for a second, she wasn't alone in her sadness.

"That's all I wanted to say, Ms. Mally. You go play now." Mally ran off to find Audrey on the swings.

When the last bell rang Mally grabbed her bookbag and walked out with Audrey to the buses. She waved good-bye to her friend and kept walking up the sidewalk that led to the middle and high school. It wasn't a long walk and the street was lined with trees just beginning to change color for fall. Mally liked looking for the brightest yellow leaves she could find.

When she made it to the high school she slipped through the back doors and wandered through the halls to the front commons. She straightened her shirt and surreptitiously wiped her sweaty hands on her jeans as two tall boys walked by.

Stepping through the main doors, Mally began looking for Rose. She tried to remember what her sister had been wearing that morning, but she couldn't remember anything except wanting to pull her hair out. She wandered through a crowd of laughing students and sat down on a bench to wait. After five awkward minutes, she slipped a book out of her bag to read.

But no matter how hard she tried, she couldn't concentrate. Teenagers lounged over cars and stood together in groups through the parking lot. She felt like a freak sitting on the bench all alone. She kept listening for someone to point out she didn't belong. She glanced over at a nearby group and spotted Rose in the crowd. Mally shut her book, relieved to see her sister.

But then she saw a boy standing behind her sister with his hands on her waist. Rose snuggled into him laughing, then turned to kiss him on the mouth. Right there in front of everyone. Ew.

The guy pulled back and whispered something in her sister's ear. She giggled and nodded, and they walked off into the parking lot hand in hand. Mally watched, dumbfounded, as her sister climbed into the boy's red car. He revved his engine loudly and everyone looked over to watch as they took off, racing out of the parking lot in a cloud of dust and gravel.

Mally didn't know what to do. *We're supposed to walk to Grandma's house together. Dad told us to walk together,* she thought.

She stuffed the book back in her bag and hurried out of the school parking lot alone. She walked quickly along the sidewalk, her heart pounding so loud she couldn't hear anything else. After four blocks she had to stop and catch her breath while waiting for a streetlight to turn.

She knew the way to Grandma's house by heart, but this was the first time she'd ever walked there alone. It felt strange and she found herself questioning which direction to turn more than once. She'd never felt so aware of her surroundings and twice jumped behind a tree when a car drove past.

Mally turned onto Maple Street and walked faster. The houses on this street were older and the one in the middle always gave her the creeps. Rose had told her a ghost was in that house and she'd hated walking past it ever since. It was painted dark gray and the position of the windows and the door made the house look like it was glaring down at her. Mally gripped the straps of her backpack tighter as she practically ran past the driveway.

But soon she was forced to slow her pace. The sidewalk was sunken and cracked in many places and she had to step into the road to avoid the deep puddles left over from last night's rain. Large trees lined both sides of the street, blocking out the sun, and Mally shivered as a cool breeze blew through her hair. She crossed the road and breathed out a sigh of relief as she read the sign for Oak Street. She was nearly there.

Mally turned the corner and squatted down against Mrs. Whittaker's iron fence. She and Rose had taken to running past the old woman's house in a crouch to avoid getting called over for a chat. She crawled along the sidewalk, the waistband of her pants digging painfully into her stomach. She stopped where the fence opened into the yard and glanced at the windows. All the curtains were drawn up tight and no lights were shining from the kitchen.

Thank goodness she isn't home, Mally thought, straightening up. No one was nosier than Mrs. Whittaker. She wouldn't be surprised if she spied on the neighborhood with binoculars from her second story windows. She always seemed to know everything and everyone and made no bones about sharing her opinion whether you liked it or not. The last time Mally had spoken to her, she'd suggested they sell Grandma's house.

Never, Mally thought. The memory of that encounter still made her angry. *We'll never sell Grandma's house.*

She followed the sidewalk around the gentle curve of Oak Street and smiled as Grandma's driveway finally came into view. Her white farmhouse was the oldest on the block, built on top of a small hill and surrounded with dozens of trees for which the street had been named. Mally had always thought the house looked like the queen of the street, standing taller and prouder than all the other houses in the neighborhood.

Her sneakers crunched on the gravel driveway as she ran the rest of the way, up the hill, through the garden, and across the porch to the side door. Mally caught herself on the frame, gasping for breath as she dug the key out of her pocket.

She unlocked the door to the mud room and was greeted by the alarm blasting in her ears. She punched in the code on the panel as fast as she could to silence the noise, then she unlocked the second door and let herself into the kitchen.

Lime green cabinets stretched down the length of the room, covered with a white countertop that had seen better days. The refrigerator hummed loudly in one corner next to a deep kitchen sink.

She shut the door and wandered through the kitchen to the small corner table. There was a much bigger dining table in the next room, but Mally always preferred to sit at the kitchen table to do her homework. Windows ran along the back side of the room, but the curtains were drawn, casting the kitchen into shadow. That curtain was never drawn when Grandma was here. She pulled it open, unleashing a swirl of dust.

Mally sneezed twice as she tucked the curtain into the hook by the window. With daylight shining brightly into the room, things felt better. Back to normal. She could remember so many Saturday mornings sitting here in the bright sunshine while Grandma made pancakes or French toast. Letting the sunlight dance across her eyelids, she imagined Grandma walking in the door with her arms outstretched saying, "There's my Mally May!" The way she always greeted her.

On impulse Mally called out, "Grandma! Grandma! Are you home?" Even though she knew she was being silly, she waited and listened for a response, but of course none came.

The house had a slightly different feel now. Too quiet. Mally felt the hairs on the back of her neck stand up and wished Rose hadn't ditched her at school. She pulled out her books and got started on her homework, trying to ignore the silence pressing hard against her ears.

Just when it felt like too much, she heard footsteps outside and her sister's voice. The door opened and Rose walked in, dropping her bookbag in front of the sink. The tall boy from the parking lot followed, but he stopped short when he spotted Mally. "Oh, this is just my little sister." Rose smiled a bit too brightly. "Mally, this is Rick."

"Hi," Mally said. Her sister looked different standing next to this tall boy. Rick ran his hands through his sandy brown hair and said, "Yeah. Okay. So, um, I guess I better get going."

"No, please stay!" Rose pulled him towards the table. "I'm sure Grandma has some cookies somewhere around here. You've got to try her peanut butter cookies. They're awesome."

Mally's heart pounded as Rick folded his lanky body into a chair next to hers. His arms were muscular with thick black hair running up the back. He wore a chunky ring that he spun around and around his middle finger.

Her sister was acting weird, overly cheerful and chatty as she rooted through the cabinets looking for a snack. When she found the cookies in the freezer she did a little dance, wiggling her hips which made Rick chuckle.

Rose carried the container over to the table and leaned into his side. He wrapped an arm around her waist and pulled her down to sit in his lap. Rose giggled, her back to Rick, as she sent Mally a glare that was impossible to misinterpret: "LEAVE."

Mally had no desire to stick around. Abandoning her homework she announced, "I need to check Grandma's computer," and escaped from the kitchen. There wasn't a computer in Grandma's house anymore, but Rick didn't know that. She just wanted out of the room and away from her sister.

She wandered through the house and up the steep steps to the second floor. She thought about taking a nap. Grandma had set up a guest room for her and Rose when they were little, and it was still decorated to look like Dorothy's journey to Oz, complete with a yellow brick road, the Emerald City, and a scary green witch painted on the walls.

But now that she was upstairs, Mally remembered her plan to sew costumes with Audrey. She walked past the guest room and down the hall to Grandma's sewing room. She tried the door and it stuck a little bit. She pushed harder and the door finally popped open, revealing the special room.

She leaned against the door frame and took a deep breath. The smell of cloves with a hint of lemon filled her nose. Mally looked around and smiled at the familiar arrangement of tables, cabinets, and chairs. A large white table sat under a row of windows with Grandma's sewing machine installed in one corner.

The room curved around a corner of the house and Grandma had once told Mally she'd combined two rooms to create this one space. In the far corner, a window seat had been built into the wall and was covered with baskets of colorful fabric scraps and piles of patchwork quilt blocks. More piles of fabrics, blocks, and baskets dotted the floor.

A green wing-backed chair was tucked along the back wall with a bright lamp close by for hand stitching. Anywhere there wasn't a window on the wall, there was a brightly colored cabinet instead. Mally's favorite cabinet was fire engine red and had over fifty drawers in sizes ranging from smaller than her fist to bigger than a shoebox.

She loved going through all the little red drawers and finding the treasures Grandma stashed there. It was filled with thread of all different colors and thickness, yarns, sequins, buttons, and beautiful bits of fabric Grandma had collected over the years. One of Mally's favorite activities was to pull out all the drawers and rearrange the contents by color, size, and type. Grandma never minded her rearranging so long as she made a new label for the metal frame on the outside of the drawer.

Mally must have made new labels for the drawers once a week at least, especially in the summer when she would spend hours happily digging through the cabinet. She loved pawing through all the beautiful materials. It felt like an endless treasure hunt.

On top of every cabinet were more baskets and bins of varying colors organizing needles, tools, Grandma's massive thimble collection, and a huge arrangement of paper stabilizers and quilting books.

To the left was Grandma's old dining room table, now covered with a special mat to cut fabrics. She'd lifted the table onto risers and Mally loved to play underneath, especially when Grandma was cutting long pieces of fabric that draped off the edges. She liked to imagine she was in a tent in a deep forest filled with monsters, but the fabric would keep her safe and hide her from view.

Mally did a double take as she recognized a familiar box peeking out from under a stack of folded quilt tops on the floor. It was her sewing box! She rushed over and scooped it up, loving the clank the handle made against the metal box.

She opened the lid and found it still filled with sewing supplies. She had a few scraps of fabric, pack of needles, five spools of thread, a tiny thimble, and a special pair of scissors that snapped into a silver chain. Grandma had given her these snips for Christmas last year. Mally immediately looped the scissor necklace over her head.

She made her way to the window seat and sat down with the sewing box on her lap. She pawed through the materials inside and frowned. She could have sworn she'd packed her sewing box full of scraps last spring. She'd never used them, but it was fun to pull out her favorite fabric colors and designs and fold them carefully to fit the space just right with the needles and thread.

She pulled a pink and brown scrap basket over and began digging down to the bottom. The top fabrics were dusty and Mally sneezed as she took out a long green strip. She pulled out more scraps, trying to pick colors she thought Audrey would like. Now that she had her sewing box, she and Audrey could begin sewing costumes together.

When she'd filled her sewing box with scraps, she snapped the latch shut and hugged it to her chest. It felt darker in the sewing room and less energetic. As if Grandma was what added the light and color to the room, not the sunny windows.

She spotted a quilt spread out on the cutting table and walked over, sitting her sewing box on the edge. It had been so long since she'd come in this room, she didn't recognize the quilt at first. Looking closer, she realized it was a landscape quilt Grandma had been working on for more than a year.

Mally touched the fabrics lightly with her fingertips. Rolling green hills filled the bottom of the landscape up to a row of angular purple and blue mountains. A dark brown tree rose below the mountains and she could remember watching the day Grandma had carefully pressed it in place.

The quilt top was spread out flat on the table and it was clear Grandma had only just added two new borders to the sides. A pressing cloth was still spread out on top of the right block. Mally moved it so she could see the entire quilt.

On the left, brown, black, and silver fabrics were pieced to re-semble a closed door on top of a purple rectangle. Mally leaned close and could see Grandma's tiny stitches running along the edges of each piece. A silver button embossed with a simple leaf design served as a door knob. A blue checkerboard block was pieced above the door, blending in with the sky fabric on the landscape.

On the opposite edge of the quilt, another door had been pieced with bright red, blue, green, and yellow fabrics, but it looked very different. This block was pieced with triangles to make the door appear like it was opening inward. Bright light spilled out from the green frame as if someone had just left the room and forgotten to shut the door. The pieces were sewn together messily and long thread tails still hung off the edges.

A black and white checkerboard block rested below the door. Grandma must have been in a very big hurry stitching that block because very few of the seam lines matched up between the pieces.

Mally let her eyes travel over the quilt and frowned. It looked unfinished, as if Grandma had planned to stitch more quilt blocks to the top and bottom edges. Something about the sky was off too. She ran her fingers over the surface and found little holes in the fabric, as if the stitches had been ripped out and pieces removed.

Thinking back, Mally could have sworn the sky had been filled with brightly colored rays of sunshine. Now a flat expanse of blue stretched over the upper part of the quilt with a single reddish orange circle in the center for the sun.

That's weird, Mally thought as she looked closer at the largest purple mountain in the center of the quilt. It could possibly be a trick of the light, but she thought she saw a thin spider web stitched along the side. *I don't remember Grandma stitching that.*

She did remember Grandma stitching all sorts of special threads and thick yarns over the rolling hills and the big tree. She had set the quilt up in a small frame in front of the window and sat with the sun shining on her back as she worked. Mally had watched, entranced as Grandma's wrinkled fingers had added the texture of tree bark and the soft fuzz of grass, one stitch at a time.

While she worked, Mally had imagined a special knot on the side of the tree that could open a door to the Best Treehouse in the World. It would be a beautiful place with a spiral staircase and special nooks to sew and read and even a swing covered in quilts to sleep on. She'd drawn pictures of the rooms and imagined what it would be like to climb up the spiral staircase to the very top of the tree and look out at the pretty world Grandma had created.

She leaned back and gazed at the quilt. Grandma would never be here to finish it. Whatever she planned to add to this quilt would never be stitched. Mally ran her fingertips over the surface once again, loving the feel of the fabrics and occasional bump of decorative threads. She felt a hard lump under her fingers – it was the silver button on the quilt block that looked like a closed door. Mally rubbed her fingertips over the button and sighed.

"Where did you go, Grandma?" she whispered. "Why haven't you come back?" The same question she'd been asking over and over for months. No one had seen or heard from Grace Wright since last April. Mama had searched and searched and even she seemed to have given up hope.

"Why did you leave me?" Mally asked and as if it would somehow provoke a response, she gave the button a sharp twist. A sudden wind blew her hair back and Mally pitched forward over the quilt, face to face with the patchwork door.

The sewing box clanged loudly against her elbow and reflexively she snatched it up in her free hand. The sound echoed unnaturally, gaining in volume until it seemed to vibrate through her whole body. She tried to pull her hand free from the quilt, but she couldn't let go of the silver button.

Then she heard a little "click" and the fabric door pieced on her Grandma's quilt slowly opened before her eyes.

Chapter 2

Welcome to Quilst

Bright light flooded out of the door frame and Mally squinted, barely able to see as the wind grew stronger, whipping her hair across her face.

She kicked out as she felt her legs lift off the ground, struggling against the invisible forces pulling her closer to the quilt. Her fingers were still glued to the tiny button and she tried to shake free, but she couldn't let go. White light wrapped around her until it was the only thing she could see.

Then just as quickly as it had started, everything stopped.

Mally blinked a dozen times. She closed her eyes and counted to three, then opened them again. *Nope. It's still there*, she thought, gazing out at a lush green landscape stretching out to the horizon.

Not just any landscape. It was *the* landscape. Somehow, she was standing inside Grandma's landscape quilt!

Rolling green hills stretched out for miles in every direction, but unlike the quilt top, they were broken up with large rocks, small glittering streams, and a variety of trees from scrubby bushes to massive oaks. Everything appeared to be made from fabric, yarn, and decorative threads. Long green yarn grass waved in the breeze nearby, and what looked like a stream rushed around a little hill carrying strips of blue fabric.

Her hand gripped the silver button that had been stitched to the door block. It had transformed into a full-sized door knob with a leaf shape engraved in the center.

What in the world just happened? Mally thought. She still clutched her sewing box in her right hand and her silver scissors were safe around her neck. *I must be dreaming. I must have fallen asleep back in Grandma's sewing room with my head in a fabric basket or something. Or maybe this whole day has been a dream?*

But the door knob felt so real in her hand. She turned and looked behind her but could see nothing but empty white space filling the door frame. She felt a gentle tug in her stomach that mirrored the feeling when she'd twisted the button on the quilt.

"If this is a dream, why does it feel so real?" Mally wondered aloud.

She took a cautious step forward. The door was set on top of a purple rectangle, exactly as it had been stitched in the quilt. Mally looked closely at the individual threads of fiber woven together to create the black fabric of the door frame. Each seam was outlined with tiny white stitches. She leaned further out to get a better look at the millions of strands of green yarn forming the grassy landscape. Her hand slipped off the door and it began to swing closed.

"Oh my gosh!" She scrambled to catch it. The soft fabric pulled against her grip, as if it wanted to close. She set her sewing box on the ground and wedged it in place so the door couldn't shut. Then she cautiously walked around the door frame, trailing her hands along the fabric. She peeked her head around the back side and gasped. She'd been expecting to see a tunnel or pipe. Something to explain how she'd traveled here. Instead the back of the door was a flat black rectangle of fabric. From this side it looked like a scary modern art sculpture perched on top of a purple platform.

Mally backed away quickly and checked that her sewing box was still holding the door open. It was exactly as she'd left it and a small strip of light glowed from the opening in the door. Taking a deep breath, she walked to the edge of the purple rectangle and bent down to run her hands through the grass. The fibers tickled her fingers. It felt overwhelmingly real.

"Where am I?" Mally said, tugging on a strand of green yarn. "Is this a dream, or am I dead?"

"This place is a little empty for the afterlife, don't you think?" a voice spoke behind her. "I'd expect Heaven to be quite a bustling place these days."

Whirling around, Mally found an orange cat leisurely stretched out on a nearby rock. He closed his eyes lazily, clearly enjoying the warm sunshine.

"Who are you? Where am I? How did I get here?"

It took her a second to realize she'd just asked a cat a question, but he couldn't possibly talk back. She looked around, trying to find whoever it was who had spoken. The cat rolled over, drawing her full attention and spoke in a low, bored voice, "I think you already know the answers to two of those questions." He rested his head on his paws, clearly dismissing her.

"I think I'm inside my Grandma's quilt talking to a very rude cat." Mally shook her head, but she had to admit, it made this place a lot less scary to know she wasn't alone. "Or maybe I've just gone crazy."

"Well, you can always go home and tell Mommy and Daddy all about it. I'm sure they'll make it all better."

"Yeah, right." She knew exactly what her parents would think if she told them about this place. "Imagination Mally," Dad would chuckle, and Mama would tousle her hair and that would be the end of it. They would never believe her. Except now she doubted Mama would want to hear a fun story. She rarely left her bedroom, even for dinner, and Mally hadn't seen her all weekend.

Mally wandered down the hill to the little stream stitched into the landscape. Her heart rate had finally slowed and the water looked so inviting. She sat down and peeled off her socks and shoes. Sticking her feet into the water, she was surprised by the feel of dry fabric against her bare skin.

I guess water isn't wet here, Mally thought. It felt cool and refreshing, but when she pulled her feet out, they weren't dripping. Instead a small strip of blue cloth dangled from one foot. She pulled it off and ran the soft fabric through her fingers. The edges were frayed slightly, and the color was mostly light blue with long streaks of lighter and darker shades. Something about that color brought back a memory of sewing with Grandma.

* * * * *

It was a crisp, cold December day and Mally was sitting in the window seat rummaging through Grandma's scrap basket. She loved running her hands over the fabrics, searching for the perfect colors to knot together. Grandma had several baskets filled with scraps, and this one was made from a braided rope stitched with red and green thread like a Christmas cookie. Mally loved digging through this basket because Grandma had sewn a sachet of spices into the bottom so it always smelled strongly of cinnamon and nutmeg.

Mally could spend hours playing with Grandma's scraps. Sometimes she would braid them together to make a colorful rope necklace. Other times she'd knot the ends to make a chunky wig, so she could pretend she had long, thick hair like a princess.

But on this particular day she wanted to try something new. She'd set Ms. Bunny on the windowsill and covered her lap with a large scrap of purple fabric, but the doll still looked cold.

"Grandma, can I make a quilt for Ms. Bunny?"

"Of course, Mally May." Grandma looked up from her sewing machine. "Pull out the fabrics you like first, then we'll cut them up and I'll show you how to sew them together."

Mally selected her favorites from several scrap bins and carried them over to the cutting table. "Are you making a bed quilt or a doll quilt?" Grandma asked with a chuckle as she spotted the huge pile of fabrics.

"Is this too much? How much do I need?"

"It really depends on your design and how big the quilt is going to be. I think a nine by twelve inch quilt should be just fine for Ms. Bunny. Pull out your three favorites and put the rest back."

Mally did as she was told and after a quick lesson on starching and pressing the scraps flat, Grandma helped her cut the pieces into long, straight strips using her special cutter that looked like a pizza slicer. Mally arranged and rearranged the rectangles a dozen times until the order was perfect: a bright yellow strip in the middle with blue streaked fabrics on either side.

"Now it's time for the best part: sewing your pieces together," Grandma said, sitting down in her green chair with a sigh. She pawed through the drawer of a nearby purple cabinet and pulled out a pack of needles and a small spool of blue thread. She held them up for Mally to see. "I think number nine sharps would be a good choice for your fingers and this thread matches that fabric, don't you think?"

"Yes, but…" Mally was looking over at Grandma's sewing machine.

"We're going to do this by hand first. There's a lot more to it than you think and it's easy to miss certain details when you're just pressing a pedal on a machine," Grandma said as her weathered hands pulled a needle from the paper packet. "Aside from that, I have a cathedral window on the machine right now and it's not going anywhere." She handed Mally the spool of thread and a small pair of scissors.

"Pull out a piece of thread as long as your arm and thread your needle. Then tie the ends in a knot so they'll stay together."

Mally followed her instructions slowly. The eye in the needle was tiny. She licked her fingertips and twisted the end of the string to make a sharp point and poked it through the hole. Then she tried to tie the thread tails in a bow like her shoelaces.

Grandma corrected her, "Hold them together and tie an overhand knot like this." She made a loop, then passed the thread tails through the loop.

"Whew." Mally wiped her sweaty hands on her pants. "This is more complicated than it looks, Grandma." She picked up her fabric scraps and slid them together so the ends were lined up the way she'd seen Grandma do it before. She was impatient to begin stitching.

"We're just getting started. Quilting isn't something to rush, Mally May. Now let's mark the seam allowance on the edges so you have a line to stitch along." Grandma spread out the middle yellow piece on the side table and pulled out a ruler and pen from the drawer. "We measure over from the side a quarter inch." The pen made a scraping sound as she ran it along the edge of the ruler.

"Now you're ready to stitch. Hold the pieces right sides together so the edges are lined up." Grandma pulled Mally down to sit in front of her on the green chair. Mally breathed in her familiar scent of cloves and lemon and felt surrounded by comfort. "Now you take the needle and start stitching right here."

Mally inserted the needle into the upper left corner on the line marked on the fabric. Grandma held the pieces flat in her wrinkled hands so it was easy to take the first few stitches.

"Bring the needle up a little closer. There you go. You don't want monster stitches, Mally May," Grandma said. "If the stitches are too big, it will allow the batting to leak through."

"What's batting?"

"That's the middle layer of the quilt. It makes it puffy and warm, but it's not like fabric so it can come apart if you don't make your quilt the right way."

Mally tried to be patient. She took one small stitch, then another. It was just starting to feel easy when Grandma let go of the fabric.

"It's going to feel different now because you need to hold it all yourself," she said, giving Mally a little push in her back so she could rise from the chair. "Go slow. Just take one stitch at a time." And with that, Grandma returned to her sewing machine and Mally was on her own.

It was instantly impossible. Mally tried holding the fabrics together with her right hand, but the pieces kept shifting away from each other. The needle had felt comfortable in her fingers, but now it was like trying to wrangle a wet fish. Her thread tangled on one corner of the fabric and doubled back on itself creating a wadded mess on the end. She ignored the mess and tried to make a few more stitches, but it only made matters worse.

"OUCH!" The needle jabbed her finger and blood welled. Mally wadded up the whole thing and threw it as hard as she could. The fabrics twisted in the air and landed in an ugly heap on the floor.

The sewing machine stopped and Mally looked up to find Grandma squinting at her over the rim of her glasses. "You're not giving up, are you?"

Mally scooped up the fabrics, and sucking on her bleeding finger, brought them over to Grandma. "I can't do it right without you holding it," she said, tears welling in her eyes.

"Yes, you can. It's not going to feel easy, but you can do this," Grandma said, looking at her messily stitched seam. "You just need to slow down and when stuff like this happens–" she indicated the tangled mess in the corner. "–you stop and pick that out before continuing."

Mally watched in horror as Grandma clipped off the knot and with a tug, removed all the stitches she'd taken. The thread pulled out and the fabrics fell apart. The blue streaked piece fluttered to the floor.

"Why did you do that? I nearly finished that line!" Mally cried.

"You've got to learn how to stitch properly, Mally. No shortcuts.

No sloppy stitches," Grandma said, sternly. "Women used to depend on their stitching for survival. It's a skill to build and you must earn it one stitch at a time. Dry your tears now. There's nothing to cry about. Tie another knot and try again."

Mally scooped up the pieces and stomped over to the green chair. *Why is she being so mean?* she thought, pulling more thread off the spool with a jerk. *I just want to make Ms. Bunny a quilt and we could have it already done if she'd let me use that machine.*

She threaded her needle, managed to knot the end and tried stitching the pieces together again. She instantly made another mess of the thread and fabric. It was like she had three thumbs. She couldn't seem to hold onto everything without something slipping off her lap or falling out of her hand. It had been a relief when the truck horn sounded outside, signaling it was time to leave.

Mally had stuffed the remains of Ms. Bunny's quilt into the bottom of an empty drawer and hurried outside. Days later, she found the strips neatly folded around her needle and spool of thread. Grandma had set it in a corner of the windowsill so she could return to her project.

But she never did. It was too hard, and her hands were just so clumsy. It was so much easier to play pretend or watch Grandma than try to make something herself.

*   *   *   *   *

For the first time since that day, Mally's fingers itched to hold a needle. Maybe it was being inside this impossible quilt land, or seeing the seams holding hundreds of fabrics together. Suddenly, she wanted to sew. She ran back to the door barefooted and picked up her sewing box. Propping the door open with her knee, she dug out a pack of needles and blue thread. She let the door close against the box and returned to her spot next to the stream.

She remembered how to thread the needle and tie a knot in the end. She picked up the blue strip and looked at it closely. *Maybe I could stitch something smaller, like a butterfly.*

With a little "snick" she tugged out the scissors from her necklace and cut the strip of blue fabric into two short lengths. Holding them together firmly, she began stitching along the edge. Her thread snarled up as it had done with Grandma before. She tried to take another stitch and a large knot formed, locking her needle in place.

"No, not again!" Mally tried to pick out the knot, but it was too tightly tangled.

"You're not very good, are you?" the cat's voice called from behind.

Mally glared at him. "This is only my second time stitching anything."

"I can tell," he said, padding over to watch. "Clip that and start over. Don't waste your time trying to pick out that knot."

"Fine." Mally followed his instructions and pulled out a fresh length of thread. "I can never hold the fabric right and the needle feels weird in my hands."

"How many stitches have you made in your life?"

"I don't know. Ten?" Mally guessed. She inserted the needle along the edge of the fabrics.

"Ten stitches does not a Maker make. It'll start feeling comfortable around a thousand stitches."

"One thousand stitches? It would take months to stitch that much!" Mally nearly dropped the blue scraps.

"It adds up quick if you stitch every day," the cat said and Mally paused. She could have sworn that was something Grandma said but couldn't be sure.

She didn't have a ruler to mark the stitching line this time so she just had to eyeball it. Thankfully her thread didn't knot up as she stitched along the edge, but the line was far from straight.

"Have you been drinking, little girl?" the cat asked.

"What? No!" Mally said, tying a knot on the end of the seam.

"I can't think of another excuse for such huge, sloppy stitches."

Mally ignored him and bent to root around in the stream, running her hand through the cool water fabrics until she located the perfect color – white with streaks of silvery gray on the surface. She pulled the fabric out and cut circles to stitch on her butterfly.

Mally had no idea how to stitch the circles on properly, and one ended up much bigger than the other. She trimmed the blue fabric down until the shape roughly resembled a butterfly.

"What in the world are you making anyway?" The cat just couldn't seem to leave her alone.

"I'm making a butterfly, thank you very much. A pretty blue butterfly to enjoy this pretty dream, or whatever this is. Oh!" Mally gasped as the fabric butterfly lifted off from her hand. It was moving! The creature rose several inches into the air, its wings fluttering erratically.

"How is it doing that?" Mally exclaimed.

Before her eyes the stitches holding it together widened. Gaps appeared in the middle of the butterfly's body. *Snap!* The threads broke, and the blue fabrics fell silently back into her hands.

"Wow! I had no idea that would happen. Will everything I make become real here?"

"So it seems," the cat said, a slight frown wrinkling his fabric forehead. "Have you ever made anything before?"

"No, I've never done anything like this before." Mally looked down at her hands in wonder. "This is amazing!" She gripped the scraps of cloth and was suddenly sure this was the same blue fabric she'd picked for Ms. Bunny's quilt last winter. She looked over the stream at the rolling hills rising to mountains in the distance.

Grandma made this quilt. This was her fabric and her stitching, Mally thought as she reached out to stroke the chunky threads that added texture to the ground.

What if...? It was such a dangerous, delicious, wonderfully exciting thought, Mally almost stopped herself from thinking it. *What if Grandma wasn't missing or dead or kidnapped or any of the crazy theories Mama had come up with months ago. What if she was here, in this quilt? What if I can find her?*

"Has anyone else come here?" Mally asked the cat. "An older woman, maybe?

"Makers come and go all the time," he said, standing and stretching his front paws with a shrug. "All quilts connect to Quilst one way or another."

"Quilst?" Mally liked the odd word.

The cat arched one eye as if to say, "Where you are right now."

"So Grandma could be here? Have you seen her? She's about my height with white hair and she usually wears a bright scarf. We think she was wearing a red quilted jacket the day she went missing. It was her favorite and Mama could never find it in her house or car."

The cat flopped back down on his side, clearly unimpressed. He caught his tail with his front paws and looked more interested in that twitching appendage than her story.

Dream or not, Mally was about done with this snarky cat, but she couldn't seem to stop the flood of words streaming out of her mouth

"Her name is Grace Wright. She made this quilt. So that makes her a Maker, right? I saw this fabric in her sewing room and stitched it with her. Have you seen her? She went missing six months ago and no one has seen her since. No one saw her leave the house and the police haven't found anything. It's like she disappeared into thin air. Poof!" She threw up her hands and her fabrics went flying.

"Great Maker, what did I do to earn this penance?" the cat replied, eyes rolling to the heavens as Mally scrambled to retrieve the scraps. "Just a few minutes ago you were convinced you were dead or dreaming. Now you've decided your missing Grannie is vacationing here of all places? I have no idea what you're talking about." He rose as if to walk away and Mally panicked.

"No! Don't go! Please help me!" She dashed forward, her hands outstretched, but he disappeared with a flick of his red tipped tail. She fell to her knees on the ground and began to cry. "Please! I need your help!"

She clutched the blue cloth to her heart as tears coursed down her cheeks. She blubbered on, hoping the cat was still listening. "I really, really need to find my grandma. She's been missing for so long and now something is wrong with Mama and it's all messed up. Everything is awful and it would all be better again if Grandma could just come home. Please help me!"

Her words dissolved into a simple chant, "Please help me. Please help me." Mally wrapped her arms around her chest and rocked back and forth. "Please help me. Please help me."

"Is this what you usually do when things don't go your way? Sit down and cry about it?" The cat asked from behind. Mally whipped her head around and found he was now perched on the hill between the stream and the door.

"I don't know what else to do." Mally sobbed. "Can't you help me?"

"You know, I might've heard a story about a Maker hanging around, but if you're just going to sit there and stain the fabric of Quilst with your tears, I'm not sure I should bother."

"I'll stop crying. I'll do anything, just please help me!" Mally scrambled to dry her face. She considered using the cloth she'd pulled from the stream and thought better of it. She scrubbed her face with the sleeve of her shirt instead. Face clear, she stood up, tucking the precious blue scraps into her back pocket. "I'm Mally Spencer," she added with a shaky breath. "And you are?"

"Very nice to meet you, Mally Spencer," the cat said with exaggerated politeness. "My name is Patch."

"Patch the cat?" Mally asked, cocking her head to one side.

"Yes, it's unfortunately unoriginal. A friend gave it to me, and I didn't want to be impolite." He looked away quickly and shrugged. "A name is a name after all. Who would I be without it?"

Mally looked closer at his body and noticed he was pieced from a variety of orange, yellow, and red fabrics cut in irregular sizes and shapes. None of his seams lined up and some of them looked like they'd been stitched backwards, with the edges of the fabric fraying on the outside of his body.

"Well, Patch, can you help me now? Do you know where my grandma is?" Mally asked.

"As a matter of fact, I believe I do, but I think it's best to leave that story until tomorrow."

"What?! No!"

"Patience, little Maker. You might want to think about taking yourself home. If your grandmother has been gone for months, time has most certainly been passing in your world."

"How much time? How can you tell what time it is here?" Mally asked, looking up at the sky. The sun hadn't moved from its position directly overhead.

"More than enough time for you to be missed, I'd guess."

"Oh no!" Mally scooped up her belongings and hurried up the hill to the door. She didn't think Rose would notice if she disappeared, but she didn't want to give Dad anything else to worry about.

"What about Grandma? Where is the Maker you were talking about?" she asked, shoving her feet into her shoes as she stuffed her socks, pack of needles and spool of thread into her pockets. Patch followed at a slower pace, his tail twitching slowly from side to side.

"Come back tomorrow and meet me there." He pointed at a spot in the distance. Mally could see a gray path at the base of the closest mountain. "I'll tell you everything I know."

"You promise to be there?"

"I swear on every stitch that holds me together."

"Let's shake on it," Mally said, reaching out her hand. The cat stared at her with an odd expression. Slowly he padded forward and extended a soft yellow paw which Mally shook once.

"I'll come back as early as I can tomorrow. Thank you, Patch!" Her eyes filled with tears, but for the first time in a long time, they were tears of joy. "Just think – by tomorrow evening I could bring Grandma back and then everything will be back to normal again."

She stepped onto the purple platform and pulled open the door. Bright light spilled out and a sudden wind blew against her back, pulling her towards the portal. Mally picked up her sewing box and clutching it to her chest, she took one last look over the beautiful landscape.

"I'll see you tomorrow, Patch! Thank you!" Mally called, then she turned and disappeared into the light.

*　*　*　*　*

The return journey was just as odd and unsettling as before. Mally wished her hands were empty so she could grip her head as the wind swirled and a great ringing echoed through her ears. She closed her eyes tight as the light grew blindingly bright. Then just as quickly as before, it all stopped.

Mally blinked and found herself sitting on the floor next to Grandma's cutting table.

Whoa, she thought. *Did that really happen? Or was that all a dream?* She dug into the pockets of her jeans and breathed out a sigh of relief as she pulled out her socks and the scraps of blue fabric from the stream. It wasn't a dream! It was real!

Mally sat and stared at the fabrics, her heart and mind racing at the possibilities. Grandma was alive! She was inside the quilt and Mally just needed to find her and bring her home.

"MAL-LY! MALLORY LAUREN SPENCER WHERE ARE YOU!?" Mally let out a little shriek as Dad's voice reverberated through the house. He was shouting loud enough to wake the dead and Mally could hear his heavy footsteps stomping up the wooden stairs.

"I'm here. I'm sorry!" She scrambled to her feet and snatched the sewing box off the floor. She flung open the door. "Oh my gosh, I have the most amazing thing to tell you!"

Then she came face to face with Dad and Rose at the end of the hall.

"Where have you been?" Dad demanded. "Rose said she looked everywhere and couldn't find you."

"She must have missed me. She might not have been looking very hard." Mally smirked but she lost her smile quickly as she caught her sister's eye. Rose's face was very pale, and she was staring at Mally like she was seeing a ghost.

"I checked every room and you weren't anywhere," Rose said. "Where did you go? Where have you been? It was like Grandma all over again."

Her last words came out in a whisper and Mally was shocked to see tears in her sister's eyes. Rose had never seemed as sad about Grandma's disappearance as Mally or Mama.

"I was just..." Mally wondered if she should tell them about the quilt. Would they believe? What if they took the quilt away? Grandma could be in that landscape right now. It was the first clue they'd gotten in all the months she'd been gone. If the quilt was taken away, Grandma would never come back.

Mally shrugged her shoulders, trying for nonchalance. "I fell asleep reading a boring book from the library. I couldn't hear you all the way back here. That's all."

"So you've been in the sewing room the whole time?" Rose asked. "Because I checked there too. Dad, I looked everywhere after you called."

Both sisters looked at Dad and Mally could see he still didn't believe her. Time to pull out the big guns. Mally crossed her arms and glared at her sister.

"Did you look for me before or after you made out with your boyfriend in Grandma's kitchen?"

*　*　*　*　*

Sometime later Mally lay curled up on her bed, listening to the argument raging downstairs. Dad had blown his top when Mally spilled the beans that Rose had a boyfriend and he had come over to Grandma's house. She hadn't mentioned his car or Rose ditching her at school, but she figured all that would come out eventually.

When they got home, Dad had thrown a frozen pizza in the oven and disappeared into his and Mama's room. They had eaten dinner in silence, Rose glaring at Mally the entire time. When Dad reappeared, he'd ordered Mally to go upstairs and finish her homework. As soon as her door clicked shut the yelling had started.

Mally sighed and pulled Ms. Bunny tighter into her arms. "I didn't want to tell on her, I really didn't, but Rose wasn't going to let it go." She threaded the rabbit's soft cotton ears through her fingers as she told her stuffed friend exactly what had happened that day.

"And I really think she's there, Ms. Bunny! It makes sense. She disappeared, and no one saw her leave the house or anyone come by because she never left the house. She's inside the quilt."

Her mind spun with the possibilities, but the gentle gaze of Ms. Bunny's black eyes always made her feel calm. She squeezed the doll a little tighter and felt the soft cotton squish against her face.

"But why hasn't she come back yet?" Mally asked. "I was able to come back easily. Just walk back through the door and come home. It doesn't even hurt. You'd think it would hurt, wouldn't you? I mean, it feels weird and it's kinda loud, but it doesn't hurt."

She lifted the doll into the air and imagined her flying like the butterfly she'd stitched. "I just have to find her, Ms. Bunny. I'm going back tomorrow, and I'm going to find Grandma and bring her home." She set her friend down carefully on her pillow and was about to tell her about stitching the butterfly when she heard a low laugh from behind.

"Talking to your stuffies again, baby?" Rose stood in the doorway, her thick arms crossed over her chest.

"Go away!"

Rose smirked. "No." She sat down hard on Mally's bed, making it clear she wasn't going anywhere until she wanted to. The bed dipped and Mally scrambled off. She didn't want to be within hitting distance of her sister. She had no idea what was coming but had a feeling Rose was looking to get even.

Rose scooted forward to look at her closely. "So where did you *really* go today?"

"What do you care? You were too busy dancing around for your boyfriend."

Rose narrowed her eyes. "Such a tattle tale. Jeez, when are you going to grow up, Mally?" She picked up Ms. Bunny and twirled the doll in her hands.

Mally fought the instinct to snatch her best friend back. She hated seeing Ms. Bunny anywhere near her sister's hands. As if reading her mind, Rose sat the doll on the bed and began sliding Ms. Bunny's long ears through her fingers, exactly the way Mally liked to do.

"Playing with dolls is just so childish. You'd better be careful your friends never find out. You'll be the class baby. And talking to her? That's just weird." She picked up the doll by her ears and began to swing Ms. Bunny around and around, spinning her over her head like a lasso.

Mally screamed, "No! You'll hurt her!" But it was too late.

Ms. Bunny flew through the air and smashed against the closet door, landing in a heap on the carpet. Rose looked down and let out a surprised giggle. A small piece of brown fabric was still gripped in her hand.

Mally's vision went red and she lashed out with both fists at her sister. She was a head and a half shorter, but her burst of anger more than made up for her size. Time lost all meaning as Mally punched and kicked.

Strong hands suddenly gripped her shoulders and Dad was yelling, "Girls! STOP!"

Mally landed one more smack to Rose's face before she was lifted straight into the air and set on her feet. Rose had a split lip and a series of long scratches down her thick neck. Mally's hair felt like it'd been pulled out by the roots.

"She attacked me! My lip is bleeding!" Rose yelled.

"YOU KILLED BUNNY!" Mally screamed back. Her body shook violently as she heard Rose's giggle play over and over through her mind. *She thought it was FUNNY. I hate her. I hate her. I HATE her.*

"What happened... girls... Mally? What is going on?" Mama stood in the door in her ratty brown bathrobe, looking lost and only half awake.

Everyone went still. Mama looked terrible. She'd cut her hair very short in the middle of the summer and Mally still had to look twice to recognize her. Her face was still beautiful with high cheekbones and a widow's peak crowning her forehead, but it wasn't the same without her long brown hair. Mama's eyes were sunk deep in their sockets and her skin was so pale, Mally wondered when she'd last been outside.

Tears poured down Mally's face as she picked up the ear. "Rose... ripped... her ear off." Her words came in gasps as she held up the scrap of fabric.

"Rose, downstairs, now!" Dad barked.

"It was an accident! She–"

"NOW!" Dad and Mama both yelled. It was a surprise, and Mama seemed to wake up slightly as she added, "You sleep on the couch tonight, Rose."

"What? Why do I have to sleep on the couch?" Rose whined, but Dad had had enough.

"OUT!" He pulled Rose up by the arm and marched her out of the room. Mama bent down and picked up Ms. Bunny from the floor. She sighed and sat down on Mally's bed and held out her hands for the ear. Mally didn't want to see Ms. Bunny's head. What if it was all ripped apart? What if she was broken beyond repair?

Mama took the scrap of cloth and stared at it for a long moment.

"I'm so sorry. I won't be able to fix this as well as your Grandma could." As Mama spoke, tears began running down her face. It didn't matter how many times Mally saw it, watching her mother cry always made her want to cry too.

Mama sniffed and wiped her nose on the back of her hand. "But I'll try my best." She picked up the doll and ear and wandered out of the room. Mally watched her go and wished for the thousandth time that Grandma would just come home. *Please, just come back home.*

*   *   *   *   *

The next morning Mally woke up early to find Ms. Bunny nestled in her arms. She looked closely at her head and the place where her ear was attached and found a row of neat brown stitches holding it in place. Pure relief and happiness bloomed in her chest. Bunny was okay!

She hugged her close and whispered, "I will never let that happen again. I'm so sorry, Ms. Bunny."

She looked at her doll again and met her comforting gaze. She imagined Ms. Bunny saying, "It's okay. I understand. I forgive you." She threaded her soft ears through her fingers and was relieved to find it felt the same as usual. It still didn't make up for what Rose had done, but at least the doll wasn't broken beyond repair.

Mally rolled onto her back and let her mind drift over the events of the day before. Here in her bed, she couldn't quite believe what had happened. The world seemed so normal with cars passing on the street outside and the sun shining in the window. How could there be a whole different world inside Grandma's quilt?

But it had to be real. Mally had slept with the scraps of blue fabric tucked under her pillow. She pulled them out and showed them to Ms. Bunny.

"I'm going back into the quilt today. Quilst, I think that's what Patch called it," Mally said. "And you're coming too." She couldn't stand the thought of leaving her friend behind when she'd only just been stitched back together.

She picked up her sewing box from the floor and dumped the contents on her bed. She sorted through the materials, then jumped off the bed to retrieve the supplies she'd stashed in her jeans pocket yesterday.

Gently, Mally tucked Ms. Bunny into the sewing box and placed the scissor necklace between her skinny arms. She added all five spools of thread, her thimble, pack of sewing needles. Then she tucked in as many fabric scraps around the corners as she could.

It was a tight fit and she apologized to Ms. Bunny for squishing her in. Slipping the box into her bookbag, Mally assessed her situation. Would she need anything else in the quilt? She thought about the door swinging shut and had an idea. Dad would often prop the door to the hall closet open with a plastic wedge when he was organizing tools for a job.

She dressed quickly, pulling on her best fitting pair of jeans and favorite long sleeved red shirt. For once she didn't have to fight Rose for the bathroom. She brushed the tangles out of her hair and washed her face, then raced downstairs to search the closet.

She found the wedge on a shelf near the door and quickly stuffed it into the front pocket of her bookbag. Her hands shook slightly as she pulled the zipper closed. She couldn't wait to return to the quilt, to meet up with Patch and bring Grandma home. Mally would find her. She just knew it.

Heading into the kitchen, she stopped in her tracks as she spotted Dad sitting at the table with his head in his hands. He looked up quickly as she walked in and shifted his hands to grip his coffee cup instead. "Morning."

"Good morning," she said, carefully setting her bag next to the table so the metal box inside didn't make a sound. "Mama fixed Bunny last night. She did a really good job too. I can barely see the stitches."

A strange look passed over Dad's face. "Better make yourself some breakfast, kid. We've gotta get going."

Mally couldn't help but express her newfound hope. "I think everything is going to start getting better, Dad. I can feel it."

He stared at her, blankly. Mally smiled and did a silly little dance and sang, "The sun is coming back today, today. The sun is coming out today!"

He chuckled softly and shook his head. "Gonna need a lot of sunshine to brighten up this place."

Mally felt another burst of joy at making Dad laugh, even just a little bit. She made a bowl of cereal and sat down to eat feeling better than she had in weeks.

Unfortunately, her happy mood faded quickly as Rose wandered into the room. Her long hair was disheveled and it didn't look like she'd gotten much sleep last night. *I will never forgive her,* Mally thought. Ms. Bunny may be fixed, but she would never forget what Rose did.

Rose sat down and Mally shifted in her seat so she was as far away from her as possible without falling off her chair. They finished breakfast in silence and Rose rinsed the bowls in the sink. Her sister's punishment must have been bad because she didn't call shotgun or make a single nasty comment the entire ride to school.

Mally had to jump out of the truck and open the small door to the extended cab to let Rose out at school. Her sister's skirt was pulled up in the back and her thighs jiggled as she tried to tug it down quickly. Mally relished the sight of Rose's bright red face as she struggled to fix her clothes and carry her bags at the same time.

Mally slammed the door shut and just like magic, her happy, hopeful mood was back. She leaned against her bookbag and felt the hard edges of the sewing box press against her back. It felt so good knowing Ms. Bunny was with her and in just a few hours they would be back at Grandma's house.

When they reached her school, Mally leaned over and planted a quick kiss on Dad's cheek. "I love you, Daddy."

He jumped a little, but then a tired smile spread across his face. "Love you too, baby girl. Have a good day."

*　　*　　*　　*　　*

Thankfully, it was a good day and even more thankfully it passed quickly. For the first time since the start of the school year, Mally got through the day easily without even thinking about crying.

It all seemed so silly now. How could she have ever thought Grandma was dead? She was so healthy and active. She'd hopped in her car and driven across two states to participate in a quilting shop hop once with only a day's notice. Someone who did that couldn't just wander off and get lost in their own neighborhood, could they?

The only hard part of the day was when Audrey asked about sewing costumes. Mally wanted to tell her friend everything, but she felt torn. What if she brought Grandma back today? She doubted they would have time to sew costumes before the Renaissance festival. She wanted to tell her friend about the quilt too, but how? It sounded crazy even to herself.

She compromised by showing Audrey her sewing box at recess. Carefully tucking Ms. Bunny deep into her backpack, she pulled out the box and showed her friend the fabric scraps, thread and needles.

"Check out those scissors! Awesome!" Audrey said, carefully lifting the silver chain.

"Yeah, Grandma gave me those for Christmas last year." For once talking about Grandma didn't make Mally feel like crying. "Here, you pick the fabrics and I'll cut out squares."

Audrey selected a strip of pink fabric and a weirdly shaped scrap of teal. Mally hacked at the cloth with the tiny scissors, trying to cut square-ish shapes the best she could. Then she pulled out the spool of white thread, needles, and showed Audrey how to stitch the pieces together.

Sort of. Badly.

"Is it supposed to be like this?" Audrey asked, wiggling her fingers between her huge stitches.

"I don't think so. Does this look right to you?" Mally showed off her seam which was curled up like a tube. For some reason the thread kept looping over the raw edge of the fabrics instead of forming a straight line. Both girls looked at their seams and laughed. Between the monster stitches in Audrey's patch and the snarled edges of Mally's they were a sight to see.

Even though it looked terrible, they kept stitching. Mally cut out more squares and soon the ground around them was littered with leftover bits of thread and cloth. Audrey connected two squares together, then two more.

"Can I do this?" She asked, holding the two pieces side by side so they formed a checkerboard with two squares in pink and two squares in teal.

"Yeah, Grandma did that all the time. Just stitch along the edge the same way," Mally said. "That's a quilt block, but I can't remember what it's called."

"What it's called? It has a name?"

"Yeah, they usually do. Grandma was always piecing new quilt blocks and would tell me their names sometimes. I remember Turkey Tracks and Churn Dash... and that's about it." Mally sped up her stitching to catch up with Audrey. Her last seam was a mess of knots and loops, but by the end of recess they had both stitched four little squares together.

Mally pressed the quilt block flat on her thigh. The seams didn't match up in the middle like Grandma's, but when she spread it out, the patchwork took on a whole different look. "Wow! It looks good from this side."

"Just don't look at the back," Audrey laughed. "I think we need better instructions. That was a lot harder than it looks." She handed her quilt block and needle back to Mally.

"We just need more practice," Mally said, thinking about Patch's thousand stitches. "I'll see if I can bring a book from Grandma's house. Do your Grandmas sew or quilt?"

"Maybe." Audrey crinkled up her nose as she thought about it. "We have one quilt in the closet with red baskets on it or something like that, but my mom never lets me touch it. Both my Grandmas live far away, though, so I don't see them very much."

*   *   *   *   *

The final bell rang and Mally gathered her supplies and stuffed everything into her bookbag. Her heart pounded at the thought that very soon she would be back in Grandma's sewing room, back inside the quilt. Audrey noticed she was walking quicker than usual.

"What's up? I'm not in a hurry to get on my bus."

"I know, I'm just excited about getting back to Grandma's house. I'll find us some more fabric to play with tomorrow."

"Yeah, I think we're going to need a lot to get any good," Audrey said, laughing. She waved good-bye and Mally broke into a run, loving the feel of her bookbag banging against her back.

She made it to the high school in just a few minutes and wove quickly through the halls.

"Watch it!" a cluster of girls snapped as Mally shoved past them through the front doors.

"Sorry!" Mally yelled back as she broke into a run. She was nearly at the parking lot, excitement building the closer she came to Grandma's house.

"Mally, wait up!" She heard a familiar voice behind her, but she didn't slow down. Unfortunately her sister's legs were much longer than hers, and Rose caught up easily.

"Hey, I waited for you today," Rose said.

Mally said nothing. She wanted to shove her sister away, push her down so she would shut up and leave her alone. *Of all the days she could pick to pretend to be nice, why did it have to be today?* She walked faster, ignoring her sister.

"Why are you in such a hurry?" Rose said, laughing now.

She's still laughing about it. She tore off Bunny's ear like it was all just a big fat joke. Mally sped up, running even faster now down the road. She saw the lights starting to change up ahead and had an idea. She slowed down as if she would stop at the intersection and heard Rose's pace match hers.

Then at the last second, she charged across the street. The cars had just started to move as she flashed past. Horns blared behind her, but she made it across and kept running, turning the corner onto Spruce Street.

Distantly she could hear Rose yelling from behind, "Mally! Mally, oh my God, that was so stupid! What are you doing?"

Mally could hear panic in her voice, but she didn't look back as she put her head down and ran as fast as she could up the sidewalk. She got lucky with the lights on Elm and was able to cross to Maple Street without having to stop. She glanced back and couldn't see Rose behind her. Good.

Sweat poured down her back as she hopped, skipped, and jumped her way up the cracked sidewalk on Maple Street. She nearly tripped in front of the spooky gray house but managed to catch herself just in time. She was just turning the corner onto Oak when she heard Mrs. Whittaker calling, "Mally Spencer! Mally Spencer! What are you doing?"

"Sorry, Mrs. Whittaker, I really have to pee!" Mally yelled, not slowing down.

"Oh, go on then, little girl!"

Mally was so shocked she almost stopped running. Mrs. Whittaker had never let her walk past without at least a ten minute chat. *She'll probably catch Rose, though, and she won't have such a good excuse.* She grinned in triumph as she turned onto Grandma's driveway and gravel crunched under her sneakers.

Mally reached the side door in record time and could feel sweat running down her back. She pulled out her key and with shaking hands opened the door. The alarm blared, but she didn't bother entering the code. She unlocked the second door to the kitchen and rushed through the house and up the stairs.

She slowed only as she neared Grandma's sewing room. Mally felt a mixture of excitement and fear as she turned the door knob. *What if I imagined everything?* she thought. *What if there isn't even a quilt on the table?*

She slipped inside the sewing room and shut the door tightly. The room looked just as it had the day before and right in the middle was the cutting table with the landscape quilt spread out on top. She crossed the room slowly, ignoring the sound of the alarm which had just doubled in volume.

The lush green landscape stretched out before her and Mally stroked her fingers over the even rows of green stitches. She barely noticed the line of cut stitches around the sun or the new spider webs stitched along the base of each mountain triangle. Her eyes were focused on the door block pieced to the left edge of the quilt.

Please, please let this work, Mally thought as she reached out to touch the tiny silver button.

Nothing happened.

Mally gasped. Had it all been a dream? She wanted it to be real so badly. And Patch, that snarky, patchwork cat – he had said he would take her to Grandma. Had she just imagined it all?

But then she gave the button just the slightest twist as if she were opening the door. A smile spread across her face as a sudden wind blew through the room, pulling her against the cutting table.

"I'm coming, Grandma. I'm coming to find you," she said as the door clicked open. She leaned into the rush of air and left the real world behind once again.

Chapter 3

Stuck in the Spider's Web

Rolling hills of green yarn grass stretched out for miles. Mally grinned from ear to ear. *I'm here!* she thought. *It was all real! I'm going to find Grandma today!*

Her heart swelled with hope, and she longed to take off her shoes again and run through the field. But first she had to take care of the door. Mally leaned down and pulled the plastic wedge out of her backpack. Jamming it under the door, she checked and double checked that it couldn't swing closed.

Satisfied, Mally took off running across the quilt. She raced up one hill, then another, barely feeling winded as she sprinted over the grassy slopes. She stopped at the top of a particularly tall hill and looked out over the landscape. She loved the variety of colors in the green fabrics and yarns. The hill she was standing on was bright lime green and decorated with a fine green yarn that rose to her knees. The next hill was pieced from much darker fabric with thick rows of chunky yarn stitched to the surface.

Mally couldn't help herself. She sat down and peeled off her socks and shoes. Shrugging off her bookbag, she rolled back and forth on the top of the hill, reveling in the feel of the soft fibers sliding against her skin. She flapped her arms and legs back and forth, then sat up quickly and laughed. She'd made a snow angel impression with wide wings and a full skirt in the grass.

She flopped back down and took a deep breath and held it. Mally knew she could happily spend days rolling down the hills and soaking in the warm sunshine. She let her breath out slowly and got to her feet. It was time to get busy searching for Grandma.

She was just reaching for her bag to stash her shoes and socks when it flopped over. It gave a lurch, then another lurch, and Mally jumped back with a start. It was as if something was inside, fighting to get out.

Her bag gave another lurch and a muffled voice called out, "Mally? Can you let me out please?"

While Mally had not heard the voice before, her heart recognized it instantly. Her fingers moved involuntarily to the top of the bag and she unzipped it as fast as she could.

Out stepped Ms. Bunny.

Mally gasped and stumbled back, and would have probably tumbled down the hill, but with a giant leap Ms. Bunny jumped off the ground and grabbed Mally's hands in her stuffed paws. She was still only around fifteen inches tall, but she was surprisingly strong.

They sat on the hill, staring into each other's eyes. Mally spoke first in a whisper.

"How are you doing that?"

The rabbit smiled kindly. "I'm as surprised as you are, my dear."

That voice again. Mally could have sworn she'd known that voice her whole life, whispering soothing words whenever she was sad or angry.

"But how? Have you always been alive, but you just couldn't speak or move in the real world? How does it feel?" Mally could barely believe her eyes. She poked at Ms. Bunny's arm and shook her head slowly as the doll caught her finger with both paws.

"I think so. I'm honestly not sure," the rabbit said, giving her a squeeze.

Mally sat up and Ms. Bunny stood before her, barely taller than the yarn grass waving in the breeze around them. She looked exactly the same as she had before, her pink calico dress hanging past her knee joints with bits of white lace trimming the sleeves and hem.

The only thing that had changed were her eyes and mouth. Where before her eyes only had a light sheen from black embroidery floss, now they glimmered in the sun with the faintest hint of brown in the center. Her mouth, which had been stitched into a soft pink curve that was neither a smile nor frown, was now moving as she spoke and changing expression.

It was weird, like watching a statue come to life. Mally tried to wrap her head around the fact that her best friend in the world – the creature who knew every secret, every embarrassing detail, every joy, sorrow, triumph or tribulation Mally had ever gone through was alive and talking to her.

"I would suspect it's something to do with this magical place. I've never been able to move or talk before now," Ms. Bunny said, looking around. "As for how it feels... it feels good, I guess." She stretched out her arms and turned in a wide circle. She stumbled and fell backward onto the grass with a little, "Oomph!"

"You've never walked before. It might take a little practice." Mally laughed and rose to her feet. She bent and picked Ms. Bunny straight off the ground by habit. She was just bringing her close for a hug when she froze, staring into the doll's eyes. Ms. Bunny was alive now, not just a stuffed toy she could pluck off the ground whenever she liked.

"I'm so sorry," she said, setting her down quickly. "I guess that was pretty rude. I wouldn't want some giant just grabbing me off the ground."

"It's okay. This is a lot to take in for both of us, I think. How about I ride on your shoulder for right now?"

Mally leaned down and extended her arm, allowing Ms. Bunny to climb on by herself. The doll scrambled up onto Mally's shoulder, then took a second to arrange her dress. She smoothed her ears down around her little chest and Mally felt her heart skip. She had always set Ms. Bunny's ears in the exact same way when she left for school every morning.

"Ready?" Mally asked.

"Ready."

Barefoot, Mally set off walking slowly down the sloping hill. The doll added almost no weight to her shoulder, but it was unnerving to feel her soft paws clinging to her shirt.

As they moved down the slope, Mally remembered Rose. The fight. Ms. Bunny's ear.

"Um, how are you feeling, Ms. Bunny?"

"I don't have much to compare it to, but I'd say I'm feeling just fine. Why do you ask?"

"Well, last night…" Mally trailed off, embarrassed to bring up the incident and her horrible sister.

"Oh, that." Ms. Bunny shrugged. "It hurt more to see you so upset. I don't think Rose meant to rip my ear off, Mally. She comes to me for a hug now and then so she's not quite as tough as she likes you to think."

"Rose hugs you?" Mally couldn't believe it. "So it doesn't hurt now?"

"No, it doesn't hurt at all. Your dad can make some very fine stitches, despite his hands being a bit rough," she said with a half smile.

"What?" Mally stopped dead and stared at her friend. "I thought Mama stitched your ear back on."

"No… She… well… she just couldn't manage it," Ms. Bunny said sadly. "I wish I could have told her it wouldn't matter if the stitches were huge or not. It would have done her good to fix something. It might have helped her sew herself back together a bit. I believe she went back to bed early last night."

A stitch of fear threaded through Mally's heart. What would happen if Mama didn't start to get better soon? All the more reason to find Grandma and bring her home as quickly as she could.

"So we need to get to the path that starts up there," Mally said changing the subject and pointing at a spot in the distance where a gray path began threading its way up the mountain. "That's where Patch said to meet him."

"About that. What did he say, exactly?

"You remember?"

"Anything you told me in the real world, I heard, dear. I'm just not sure I like the sound of this cat."

"He is a bit grumpy," Mally said. "But I think he wants to help. He told me to go home just in time yesterday. If I'd been any later, Dad would have called the police!"

"But have you thought about what we'll do if we don't find your Grandma quickly? I don't know exactly how long we've been away, and the way you left the alarm running…"

"I know, I should have shut it off, but I just had to get back here." Mally swept her arms wide. "Isn't it amazing?!"

"Amazing doesn't begin to cover it, my dear," Ms. Bunny said with a smile.

Mally walked faster, her momentum carrying her down one hill then up the next, in a hurry to reach the spot where Patch had told her to meet him. Ms. Bunny clung to the backpack straps on Mally's shoulder, her skinny legs crossed at the ankle and her long ears streaming behind her head in the breeze.

Mally was relieved when she felt the texture of the stitching under her feet change from soft tufts of grass to hard knots. She looked down and found millions of tiny gray knots covering a narrow strip of dark brown fabric that formed a path up the mountain.

She stopped to put her shoes back on and Ms. Bunny slipped down from her shoulder. She tried out her legs again and was only a little wobbly as she walked in a wide circle around Mally.

"How does it feel?" Mally asked.

"I'm not sure I can describe it. I've seen you walking, running, and doing all sorts of things for years. I guess I had an idea of what it would feel like but never expected to be able to do it myself." Bunny shrugged. "It feels… weird, I guess."

Mally laughed. Somehow the word "weird" seemed odd coming from Ms. Bunny. Shoes and socks back on her feet, Mally stood and looked around. "Patch said he would meet us here and take us to Grandma. I think if we find her quickly, everything will be fine."

Ms. Bunny looked up at the sky and shook her head. "Does it get dark here? We have no way to know how much time has passed. We could always come back tomorrow and search in a different direction. There's always the weekend too."

"No. Patch said he heard a Maker was here. He's going to take us to her." Mally couldn't remember exactly what Patch had said, but she wasn't ready to leave yet.

"Well, he isn't here and I think we should head back. It will take at least that much time to walk back to the door, maybe longer."

"Just a bit further!" Mally protested. *We've come this far*, she thought. *I don't want to give up now.*

Ms. Bunny didn't argue. She trailed behind Mally, slowly but steadily getting her footing. The mountain cast a shadow over the path and the sun didn't seem to be shining as brightly, even though they were closer to the sky than ever.

"Well, well, look what the cat dragged in."

Patch was perched on a rock on the side of the path, the red tip of his tail twitching in time with Mally's footsteps.

"Patch! There you are!" Mally impulsively scooped the cat into her arms. His body went rigid as she hugged him tightly. "Thank you, Patch! Now where is Grandma... or the Maker you were talking about yesterday? Can you take us to her?"

Mally set him back on the rock and laughed at Patch's dazed expression. He shook himself and jumped down to circle around Ms. Bunny.

"Now who is this tasty creature?" he said with a toothy grin.

"Tasty?" Mally exclaimed. "You don't mean you're thinking about eating Ms. Bunny because she's a rabbit and you're a cat?"

"I believe we're based on those animals and have some of those characteristics, do we not?" Patch held up a paw close to his face and slowly extended tiny silver claws.

Mally leaned down, intrigued, and took his little paw in her hands. She ran her finger over his claws and found them surprisingly sharp, even though they were obviously stitched with gray thread.

"That is so cool. Grandma has some silk thread that's almost exactly that color. I've never seen her use it except for really special projects."

"Then I would doubt it's the same thread in my claws." Patch shook himself free and narrowed his eyes at Mally. She reached out to pet his head, but he ducked out of reach before she could touch him. He started up the path at a fast pace and Mally and Ms. Bunny scrambled to keep up.

"You said there was another Maker here? What did you call this land again?" Mally's head was buzzing with questions. "Where has the Maker been hanging out?"

"Yes. Quilst. Around."

Mally was confused for a second, then realized he'd answered her questions in the shortest way possible.

"But where is she? Quilst, you said? This is such a big place! Is this just my Grandma's quilt? Can any quilt do this?"

"I said I'd take you to her, so that's what I'm doing. Take a hint and save your breath. The path is going to get much steeper."

Mally tried her best to be quiet as she followed behind the scrappy cat, taking in the delicate stitches embellishing the purple and blue mountains. Nothing could dim her excitement at the prospect of finding Grandma and bringing her home.

Ms. Bunny trailed behind on the shortest of short legs and Mally occasionally stopped and waited for her to catch up. She offered to carry her best friend, but Ms. Bunny just waved her off, obviously determined to make it up by herself.

The path wound around the base of a blue mountain. Mally remembered watching Grandma carefully cut out the shapes and turn the edges of the fabrics before gluing them in place. She constructed the entire mountain chain in one piece before moving to her machine to stitch along the edges.

"Blanket stitch." Mally said, touching the line of special blue stitches that ran along the folded edge of the fabrics. Grandma had told her the name once of the distinctive stitch and while Mally hadn't really been listening, somehow she remembered that little detail.

"Mally, I think this is far enough," Ms. Bunny said. "I have a bad feeling about this place. I think we should go back." Mally turned and found Ms. Bunny had stopped, her arms crossed firmly over her pink dress.

"But if I don't bring Grandma back, nothing will have changed." Mally kept walking. "We've come this far! Just a bit further!"

"But what about your family? Rose must have called your dad by now and I bet he's really worried."

"If I bring Grandma back it won't matter! Everything will be fine again!" Mally snapped. *I liked it better when she didn't argue with me.*

She wanted Ms. Bunny to support her, not constantly remind her they were on a time limit. Mally sped up, her legs stretching further with each step. She didn't look back to see if Ms. Bunny was following as she rounded a dark bend in the path.

Two mountains loomed on either side of the trail, blocking out almost all light. It was like stepping into a dark, narrow tunnel and Mally pressed her hands to the sides, feeling her way forward.

"Patch? Is this the right way to go?" she called, seeking reassurance, but no reply came. She took a cautious step forward, then another, her eyes straining to see through the gloom. "Ms. Bunny? Are you coming?"

She was just looking back to check on her friend when her hands sank into the wall. She let out a little shriek and whipped her head around, the hairs on the back of her neck standing on end. She couldn't see anything in the dim light, but the texture of the fabric under her fingertips had changed. The woven surface was moving.

Soft fibers slid against her skin as if the threads forming this wall were alive. The sensation tickled up her arms and as she tried to brush the feeling away, Mally suddenly found she couldn't move.

She tried to pull her arms back, but they didn't budge. She leaned back, bending her knees for more leverage, but her legs were stuck too.

"What? Why can't I...? Ms. Bunny!" Mally called. "Ms. Bunny! I'm caught! There's a wall... I... I can't move!"

She listened for a response but could barely hear anything over the pounding of her heart. The scent of cloves and lemon filled her nose, stronger here than anywhere she'd been in the quilt before.

Her eyes slowly adjusted to the dark. She squinted and could just make out the details of the shifting wall in front of her. Tiny white threads were weaving themselves together in a pattern that looked frighteningly familiar...

Spider web.

Mally shrieked, thrashing wildly. But as soon as she'd touched it, the living threads in the web had caught her shirt and pants and begun weaving through the fabrics. She looked down to find row after row of perfectly spaced stitches running through her jeans.

"Mally? What's wrong?" Ms. Bunny's voice called from behind, but Mally was too distracted to answer as a wiggling thread from the wall caught hold of her sleeve. It wove rapidly through the material, in, out, in, out. There was no needle on the end. The tip of the thread burrowed its way through her shirt like a worm, forming a line of white stitches that seemed to glow against the red fabric.

"Mally? What's going on?" Ms. Bunny called again.

"Get it off! Get it off! GET IT OFF!" Mally screamed. The threads made an awful sound as they slithered through her hair, pulling her head into an awkward angle so she couldn't see more than her own shoes. She twisted and shrieked, panicking when she realized just how little she could move.

"Please stop struggling, dear," Ms. Bunny said in her calm voice.

"Can you pull on just one thread with your hand? See if you can break them one at a time."

"I CAN'T MOVE!"

"Calm. We'll figure a way out of this." Mally felt Ms. Bunny climb up her back and tug on her arm. The web bent and bowed with the movement, but Mally remained firmly attached.

"PATCH! Patch! Help me! You'll be able to cut me out with your claws! Please, Patch! I need your help!"

"He's gone, Mally," Ms. Bunny said quietly in her ear. "I don't know when he slipped away, but I don't see him anywhere."

"What are we going to do?" Mally strained against her bonds, even though she knew it wouldn't do any good. "How is this happening? Why would Grandma have made this awful thing?"

She stared down at her shoes and begged her brain to work. *What do I do? What do I do? What do I DO?* She watched as more threads wove around her ankles. So many lines of stitching ran through her jeans, they looked more white than blue. Something about the stitches gave Mally an idea.

"My sewing box! Find the little scissors inside. You can cut me free."

Ms. Bunny's light weight shifted across her back and Mally heard the zipper open. She rooted around in the bookbag and the metal sewing box opened with a click.

Then came another metallic sound, but it came from somewhere in front of her, further up the path.

Snip. Snip. Snip.

Mally froze. "Are you doing that?" she whispered. She couldn't move her head so she squeezed her eyes shut and focused all her energy on listening for the sound.

"No. That isn't me. Is there something coming?" the doll answered quietly. She wiggled around in the backpack and quietly pulled the zipper closed.

Her question threw Mally for a loop. *Who is making that sound? What is making that sound?* Mally hadn't met anyone in Quilst except Patch, but he couldn't possibly be the only animal living in this world.

With dawning horror, she gazed at the spider web stitched right in front of her eyes.

Snip. Snip. Snip.

Mally's mind suddenly filled with the image of a huge spider with giant pincers clicking below a mass of glowing red eyes. A dark shape shifted in her peripheral vision and she panicked.

"It's a spider! It's a spider! *Oh my God, it's a SPIDER!*"

She screamed and kicked, fighting harder than she ever had in her life, but she only became more woven inside the web. Soon her entire body was wrapped up so tight she couldn't move, she couldn't open her eyes, she couldn't even scream. Hot tears slid down her cheeks and her nose began to run. The fibers pressing against her face were soaked with tears and snot, making it difficult to breathe.

Snip. Snip. Snip.

Dread pooled in Mally's belly as the clicking sound drew closer and closer. Without warning, her body rolled forward. Blood rushed to her head as she hung upside down for several seconds. Smoothly, as if she were trapped in the middle of a massive marble, her body rolled up and over again. Mally's head spun and her stomach churned as the rolling motion picked up speed.

Dimly, Mally felt Ms. Bunny press her paws against her back and whisper through the fabric, "It's okay, Mally, we'll figure this out. It's okay, it's all going to be okay."

That was the last thing Mally heard as her body spun into darkness.

*   *   *   *   *

"Mally! Time to get up!" Grandma called. There was nothing like the smell of cinnamon and cloves in the morning. *Grandma must be making pumpkin pancakes.*

"Mally! Wake up!" Someone was nudging her shoulder.

She rolled onto her stomach, reaching out to pull her pillow over her head. But the material brushing against her fingers didn't feel right. It wiggled.

She sat up, suddenly wide awake. She was resting on a cushion in the corner of a strange room. The walls, floor and ceiling were dark purple and the only light came from a square window. Something crawled over her arms and she shrieked, jerking back.

"Shh... it's okay," Ms. Bunny whispered, holding out an orange ball. "See? It's not a spider. It's just a wad of thread." In the dim light, it certainly looked like a spider. Fibers stuck out from its body and wiggled in all directions. The cushion was covered with them.

"Was I just sleeping under that?" Mally asked, scrambling to her feet.

Memories of the day returned and she whipped her head around. "Where are we? What brought us here?" She checked her shirt and pants for signs of the white threads that had stitched through her clothing, but they had all disappeared.

"We're in one of the mountains. I think the purple mountain in the center of the quilt," Ms. Bunny said. Her voice was so soft Mally had to lean close to hear. "I have no idea what trapped you, but... whatever it is... it's bad. I think it's looking for your grandma."

"Grandma? She's here?" Mally didn't wait for a response as she ran to the window. Her stomach lurched. They were hundreds of feet up. The patchwork landscape of Quilst stretched out below, green grass blurring to gray in the distance. She tried to ignore the heights as her eyes skimmed the hills, searching for any sign of movement.

The sun hadn't moved from its spot in the middle of the blue sky. "I guess it doesn't get dark here. That'll make it easier to find her."

"I don't know if your Grandma is here or not. I overheard the thing that took us saying, 'Bring me that Maker' but I don't know..." She shook her head. "Mally, we need to get home. It's been hours since you left."

"But Grandma must be here. If someone else is looking for her, that must mean something, right?"

"Maybe... but that someone has also locked you in a room in a mountain. Unless you can sprout wings and fly, we're going to need a plan to escape." She nodded at the door on the opposite wall. "We're stitched inside. I've tried to open it and it won't budge."

"What if we cut our way out?" Mally ran to her bookbag and pulled out her scissor necklace. She looped the chain around her neck and slipped the scissors out of their case.

Then she stopped, frowning at the tool in her hand. *How can I cut the quilt?* She thought. *Grandma made it. If I cut it, won't that mess it up?*

She decided to make a small cut along the edge of the door where it would be the least noticeable. She widened the hole and looked inside. There was another layer of blue fabric underneath.

She cut again, then again. Each time she snipped, she expected to see something different, but the layers were endless. She cut the hole wider and pulled with both hands. With a loud "RIP," four layers of cloth split from floor to ceiling, but it only revealed more fabric underneath.

"We're never going to get out," Mally said. "It must be dozens of layers thick."

"We might be able to use this material for something else, though," Ms. Bunny mused, pulling at the fabric to test its strength. She gave the blue cloth a sharp tug and four large pieces fluttered to the floor. Mally turned to look at the window on the opposite wall. The seed of an idea was just sprouting in her mind when she heard:

Snip. Snip. Snip.

It was right on the other side of the door. She scooped up Ms. Bunny along with the blue fabric and stuffed her unceremoniously into the backpack. She swung the pack onto her back, so she could make a run for it if there was a chance.

Snip. Snip. Snip.

Mally shrank into the corner, slipping her scissors into her back pocket. She gripped the bookbag straps, preparing to run.

The door fell away suddenly. A bright, flashing light filled the room.

"Don't you like your room?" a high voice asked.

Mally shook her head, trying to squint past the light. She was focusing so hard on seeing the creature, she couldn't understand the question.

"It's one of the best in this mountain, possibly all of Quilst. Is it not good enough?" The voice sounded on the verge of tears.

"N-no," Mally stammered. "It's fine." The figure of a very tall woman emerged, her head nearly brushing the ceiling. Mally breathed out a sigh of relief. It wasn't a massive spider after all. She squinted, trying to see the woman clearly.

She had high cheekbones, a small nose, and brilliant blue eyes stitched over shiny white fabric. A slash of black split one of her cheeks, as if her face had been ripped apart and badly mended. A spikey crown of silver and gold spun around her head. It shone as bright as the sun and filled the room with a strange flashing light.

"Then why were you trying to leave?" she asked, coming closer and closer. The sound again:

Snip. Snip. Snip.

Mally glanced down and gasped. The creature was balanced on the points of two huge pairs of scissors. They lifted her high in the air and walked for her, opening with a soft "snick" and closing with a sharp "snip."

Her body was voluptuous and pieced from black velvet fabrics that seemed to soak up all the light from her crown. Her hands were shaped like mittens – all the fingers fused together, except for her thumb – and she had no feet. Her legs tapered down to sharp points that dangled in the air as the scissor blades propelled her closer.

The shape of her hands and feet reminded Mally of a set of dolls she'd seen at a quilt show with Grandma, and with a jolt she realized that's what this creature must be. *But how did she get here?* she thought. *How is this weird doll in Quilst?*

Snip. Snip. Snip.

Mally's back hit the wall and Ms. Bunny gave a little squeak inside the backpack.

"M-My name is Mally. Who are you?" Mally asked quickly to cover up the sound.

"Mally. Mally. Mally." The woman cocked her head unnaturally to the side and her voice took on a hard edge. "Is that short for Mallory?"

"Um... yes. Mallory Lauren Spencer."

"Ah. Mally May to save the day." The woman's mouth split into a strange smile. "My name is Menda. I am the Queen of Quilst."

"The queen? But..." Mally trailed off as the scissors on the doll's hip twitched. "Pleased to meet you, Queen Menda."

She crossed her legs at her ankles and bowed slightly in her best intimation of a curtsy. She'd seen it in a movie about a princess a few years ago.

"Are you really?" With a snip, the scissors on her hips opened wide and Menda slid down to stand on her pointy legs. She reached forward and Mally shrank back, but she was only holding out her hand to shake.

Mally gripped the strange mitten shape and found the black fabric soft and cushy, but her grip was painfully tight. Mally gasped as Menda squeezed her hand.

The doll reeked of lavender, so strong it made her eyes water. Mally usually liked the scent because it reminded her of the special sachets Grandma packed with her quilts in storage. But the lavender smell coming from Menda was just too strong.

Standing so close, Mally could see the seams holding the creature together. Her stitches were sloppy and so big in places the seams gaped, allowing the stuffing from the inside to leak out. Mally's eyes caught on a particularly wide gap at her elbow. A chunk of gray fiber bulged out from the surface like a massive pimple.

Menda shoved her face closer, gripping Mally's hand. The crown on her head spun faster, flashing like a strobe light through the room.

"What are you looking at? What do you see?" With a faint snick, two pairs of scissors flipped over her shoulders, their sharp tips inches from Mally's face.

"N-N-Nothing," Mally stammered.

The scissors slid back as Menda's face crumpled. "I'm hurt, Mally May. You were trying to leave without saying good-bye."

"No, I wasn't." Mally's head spun as Menda flipped from anger to sadness and back again in seconds.

"Don't lie. You cut the door. You were trying to leave!" The crazy creature buried her face in her hands.

"I'm sorry. I really need to get home. I only meant to come here for a little while, to…" She felt Ms. Bunny shift in the bookbag and decided to leave out any mention of Grandma for now. "But it's been hours. I need to get home."

Snip.

The massive scissors on her hips slid closed with a *snap*, and Menda rose several feet to tower over her.

"Why did you come here? How did you enter Quilst?"

"I… I just wanted to see the world. I came through the door." Mally shrank against the wall as the queen swelled with rage.

"You lie! When you cut the fabric in this quilt, I can feel it." Menda tapped the crown spinning on her head. "You were trying to find the Maker, weren't you?"

"Maker? I don't know what you're talking about."

Menda stormed to the window. With her back turned, Mally counted twelve pairs of scissors in all shapes and sizes secured to the fabric on her back and hips. With a jolt, she recognized several from Grandma's sewing room. The red handled pair was always kept in the cup on the cutting table, while the largest shears were exclusively for cutting dress making fabric.

How does she have those? Mally thought. They were all much bigger than they should be. The shears stretched over four feet long, the metal handles thicker than Mally's wrist.

Menda caressed the side of the windowsill and trailed her thumb over the even row of stitching that held the purple fabrics in place. She sighed. "Such delicate work, when she actually tries. Yes, my lovelies, let's take care of this."

One of the smaller scissors on her back swung around quickly and cut into the seam, breaking the thread. Mally gasped as the seam split. Menda ran her hand over the cut, encouraging the edges of the fabric to fray. The crown on her head spun faster. Menda hunched her shoulders, her face contorting into a grimace of pain.

"Why are you doing that?" Mally cried.

"Because I can," Menda said softly, her eyes closed. She rolled her hand over the frayed mess and a ball of purple thread began to form. Mally watched, her stomach twisting, as three tiny spiders emerged. Broken fibers slid out from their bodies, braided together and became sturdy legs. They scurried up Menda's arm to circle her wrist like a bracelet.

Menda flicked her hand and the spiders on the floor cushion rolled together too, forming a messy ball. It was a horrible cross between a spider and the Blob monster she'd seen in an old movie. Thousands of legs stuck out in all directions and it half rolled, half oozed itself across the floor.

"Aren't my pets beautiful?" Menda asked happily. The crown had slowed its spinning, but her shoulders remained hunched, jutting her head forward at a freakish angle.

The creature rolled to her, then split in half and lifted itself, a hundred thread legs wiggling madly until it found her dark fabric. Mally pressed her fist hard against her mouth as the creature slid up Menda's leg, over the curves of her body and down her arm to rest on her open palm.

The purple spiders on her wrist squished themselves against the thing and they were absorbed instantly. The fibers suddenly knitted themselves together into a roundish shape with eight braided yarn legs.

"Do you not like spiders? Do they frighten you, Mally May?" Menda asked, stroking the monster.

Mally shook her head, gripping the straps of her bookbag tighter. She glanced at the open door, judging the distance.

"Do you ever tell the truth?" Menda shrieked. Without warning, she hurled the giant spider straight at Mally's face.

Mally ducked, covering her head with her arms. The ball just missed her, and she felt it ruffle her hair as it flew overhead. She knew this was her one and only chance to escape. She leapt towards the door.

But Menda was just feet away, standing in front of the window. Two pairs of scissors on her back clicked open and waved threateningly in the air. "Bind her for me, my good pet," she said in a sing song voice.

Something snagged her ankle and Mally was jerked to the ground. Her hands burned as she slid several feet across the room. She glanced back to see what had tripped her. Menda's spider monster had braided itself into a thick rope. One end was wrapped around her ankle and as she watched, tiny threads wiggled out and wove up her jeans. Just like before, Mally was being stitched in place.

"Resourceful, isn't it?" Menda laughed. "My little snarls know exactly what I want them to do and are wonderfully efficient about making it happen. They can become webs and spiders and even those flying things… what are they called?"

Mally ignored her. She twisted her body around, pulling her free leg underneath so she sat in a half crouch, facing the thread monster. Her movement swung the metal case on her necklace hard against her shoulder, reminding her it was there. She pulled the scissors out of her pocket and slashed at the grasping fibers.

She cut through several threads and they immediately stopped moving. Mally hacked at the attacking cords, but the scissor blades were so tiny, she couldn't manage to cut through the entire rope at once. As she sliced, more threads wove into her socks or caught the hem of her jeans. Even her red sneakers were covered with stitches running in all directions in a dozen different colors of thread.

"Stop it! Stop stitching me!" Mally yelled, cutting another bunch of threads attacking her knee.

"Bats! That's what they're called. If you thought my spider web was scary, just wait until you see one of my bats flying through the air." Menda suddenly spun around the room, flapping her black arms.

Mally ignored her. She changed the grip on her scissors, opening the handles wide so she could saw at the rope. It worked. Mally was suddenly cutting faster than the threads could attack. She leaned back with all her weight and found she could move her foot several inches.

"Oh, that won't do, pets," Menda said, twirling to a stop. "She's getting ahead of you. Let's go back to spiders. Itsy. Bitsy. Spiders!" At her words, the braided rope and all the threads stitched into Mally's clothes instantly wiggled out and began rolling into tiny balls.

Mally saw her chance. She jerked her leg free and crawled as fast as she could for the door. A low rumble sounded from behind. Mally was nearly at the door frame. She caught the edge of the fabric and pulled herself up to her feet. The rumble grew into a roar and she couldn't help herself. She glanced back into the room. What she saw made her heart stop dead.

Spiders. The floor was a sea of moving bodies and legs. There was no place to run, and no time to scream. In seconds, the spiders covered her body from head to toe and pulled her back to the floor. The threads dug in, securing her so tight Mally fought to draw breath.

Snip. Snip. Snip.

Menda strutted over and slowly sank to the tips of her pointy legs, then kept sliding down until she was kneeling on the floor in front of her. She grabbed her chin roughly, forcing Mally to look her in the eye.

"Are you ready to stop lying and tell me the truth?" She asked. "Where is the Maker?"

"I don't know what you're talking… uggh!" Mally grunted as the threads binding her chest squeezed tighter.

"They will keep squeezing and squeezing and then you'll go pop!" Menda sang, then her voice turned hard as she demanded, "Tell me the truth! Why are you here? Where is the Maker?""

The queen's face swam before Mally's eyes. "I'm just looking for my Grandma!" she cried. "I don't know anything about a Maker! Please, just let me go find my Grandma!" Tears slipped down her cheeks and into Menda's soft velvet hand.

"Grandma. Grandma." Menda rolled back on her heels, her head cocked at an unnatural angle. "Who is your Grandma?"

Mally pressed her lips closed. She hated how much she'd already let slip.

"Well, based on your name and this lovely set of snips you carry, I can guess." Menda plucked the scissors from her hand. "Grace Mallory Harrison Wright."

The blood drained from Mally's face as the queen's mouth split in a wide grin. "Dear old Granny Grace. My my, how times have changed." She slid the chain off Mally's neck and looped it around her own. "I must say, this was entertaining. Maybe even more entertaining than seeing you in my web outside."

Menda slid the scissors into their case with a little click. "Look at that, you've brought me a new lovely! And I get to wear it in such a fashionable way!" She adjusted the scissor holder to rest in the middle of her curvy chest. "Thank you, Mally May. Now… to business! Where is your grandma?"

"I don't know!" Mally wheezed. "I don't know where she is. She's been missing for six months. I came here to find her."

"I don't believe you!"

"Please! Please, you must believe me! I came through the door and I've been searching for her." Mally stopped to draw breath. "If you're looking for her too, we could look together! I'm sure we can find her!"

"Find her together?" Menda barked out a laugh. "Do you know what I plan to do with Grace Wright when I find her?" All the spiders suddenly released their hold and Mally gasped in relief.

But it was short lived.

Menda's hand lashed out and she lifted Mally by her backpack handle as if she weighed nothing. The scissor blades snicked open, lifting until she dangled several feet above the ground. The queen brought her face so close she could see the individual stitches of blue thread forming her eyes. The smell of lavender was so strong, Mally could taste it in the back of her throat.

"I plan to cut the deepest, darkest hole I can, and then I'm going to drop her in it." She opened her hand and Mally fell into a heap at her feet.

She scrambled away, putting as much distance between herself and Menda as she could. The queen sighed, the crown on her head spinning madly.

"I'm still not quite sure you're telling the truth," she said. She held out her hand and three purple spiders jumped into her palm. She brought her hands together and the threads compressed into a thin sheet. "This will even things out."

The queen walked to the far corner of the room. Mally couldn't see what she was doing, but the air suddenly went ice cold. She wrapped her arms around her knees and curled into a ball. She wasn't being held down by anything now, but she couldn't move. A strange pressure built behind her eyes and across her chest. She struggled to breathe and clenched her fists, fighting back the urge to cry.

"It's okay, Mally May." Menda caressed her cheek. Her sad face was back. "You can tell me anything. Where is Grandma? Where can I find her? You know, I was just joking about dropping her into a hole. I just want to find her to make sure she's okay."

Mally's mouth opened of its own accord. She didn't want to speak, and the words came out in a rasp. "I... don't... know." She choked out the last word and lost her battle with her tears. She pressed her head to her knees and sobbed.

"Uggh." Menda shoved her away in disgust.

Snip. Snip. Snip.

Mally faintly heard her click across the room. She started to pace, talking to herself in a low mutter, "She can't be lying. We're sure of that, my lovelies. But she might be useful. What if the child could draw her out? Make a show of it..."

Mally stopped listening. Flashes of her worst memories began to play in her head. She couldn't see, she couldn't hear, she couldn't feel anything except her heart splitting into a million pieces.

Chapter 4

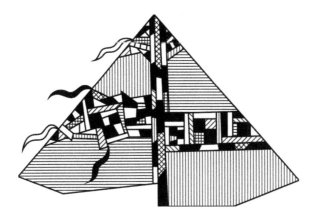

Taking Flight

"Mally! Mally, please stop crying." Ms. Bunny was tugging on her arm. The little rabbit had climbed out of the bookbag after Menda had left the room. "We have to find a way out of here and get home."

Mally tried to answer, but she couldn't form the words. It felt like Ms. Bunny was miles away. She would have to shout so loud for her to hear. And she couldn't shout right now. She couldn't do anything except cry.

"It's okay, Mally. She's gone now." The little doll patted Mally's shoulders, trying to bring her attention back to the room. "What on earth did she do to you?"

"I... can't..." Mally gasped between sobs.

"She must have done something to you. Please, Mally, tell me what she did."

But Mally couldn't speak. She wrapped her arms tight around her chest as a terrible memory filled her mind.

*　　*　　*　　*　　*

She was back in her bedroom at home, playing with her favorite stuffed animals when she heard laughter from behind. Rose had a friend over and they were standing in the doorway, giggling down at her.

Mally ignored them and turned back to the game she was playing with Ms. Bunny, Professor Piggle, and Camping Bear.

"She's still playing with dolls? Doesn't she know how babyish that is?" Sheila asked loudly.

"She doesn't care," Rose said, then raised her voice. "You won't have any friends if they find out you're still playing baby games!"

Mally hunched her shoulders, trying to make herself smaller. *Just go away*, she thought. *I'm not bugging you. Leave me alone.*

But it didn't matter. Rose sauntered into the room and plucked Professor Piggle off the floor.

He was a small rat doll with a long pointed nose and wire glasses that made him look very dignified under normal circumstances. His soft green body was stitched in the shape of a star with a long gray tail Mally liked to wrap around his waist like a belt.

"Give him back!" Mally protested. "Give him back!" She scrambled to her feet, snatching at the doll, but Rose held him high out of reach.

"Not until you say the magic word!"

"Please!" Mally begged, nearly in tears at seeing Piggle being squeezed so tightly in Rose's fist.

"Nope, that's not the magic word! Guess again!" Rose laughed, dancing out of reach.

Without thinking Mally grabbed the nearest object, a clown clock from her bedside table, and threw it as hard as she could. She had been aiming at her sister's chest, but the throw went wide and the clock struck Rose hard in the mouth.

There was a moment of hushed silence as everything stopped. Mally stared at Rose, her gut twisting as her sister's face flipped quickly from shock to outrage.

"You hit me!" Rose screamed. She caught Mally around the waist and they hit the floor in a tangle of limbs. Mally ended up on the bottom and Rose sat down hard on her chest. Mally couldn't breathe. She slapped and kicked, trying to knock her sister off.

Rose still had Professor Piggle in her hand. She smashed the doll against Mally's face. "Like that, baby?! Like your precious rat doll?!"

Mally struggled to get free. She shoved against Rose, managed to suck in a quick breath and screamed as loud as she could.

But no one came to help her. She struggled against her sister, but

Rose just laughed and pressed the doll harder against her face until Mally dissolved in tears. After five agonizing minutes, her sister finally got bored and rose to her feet. She'd kicked Mally in the back and tossed Professor Piggle in the trash can as she walked out of the room.

Mally remembered pulling the doll into her arms and curling up on the floor in a ball. She'd felt completely weak and helpless that day. Her chest hurt where Rose had sat on her and her face was stinging. She'd wanted to fight back, but she hadn't been able to do anything to defend herself.

Weak, pathetic baby.

Painful words chanted through her mind. She didn't notice it was Menda's voice at first, but soon she was saying it to herself. *I'm so weak and helpless. Just like a baby, I can't stop crying.*

* * * * *

In the mountain room, Mally clutched her face and trembled. Her skin felt rubbed raw from the memory. She'd curled up into a tighter and tighter ball and was now rocking back and forth, crying silently.

Ms. Bunny watched her sadly, wishing she could help. She'd tried hugging the little girl and drying her tears with her ears, but nothing she did seemed to help.

She wandered around the room, looking for inspiration. The door had been stitched back in place and they didn't have the scissors any-more in any case. She opened Mally's bookbag and peeked inside. She had books, binders, and a fabric pencil case, but none of that seemed particularly helpful right now.

Ms. Bunny opened the metal sewing box and found several wad-ded up scraps of fabric, a small pack of needles, and five colors of thread. She unwrapped the fabrics and found a beautiful array of colors.

Ms. Bunny had watched Grandma dye many of these fabrics. Mally had propped her up on a chair in the shade and she'd watched the older woman apply red, blue, and yellow dye to the wet fabric. She picked up two strips of bright yellow fabric and on sudden inspira-tion, carried them over to Mally.

"Your Grandma dyed some of these fabrics I think, Mally. I know you will feel better if you can just see them. Look at this beautiful yellow strip. It's so cheerful. Surely that can help you stop crying."

She draped the strips over her hands and sat back hopefully to see if it would help.

But the little girl had fallen into another memory and this one made her shudder with pain.

*   *   *   *   *

She was six and running on the sidewalk with two friends while their mothers talked by their cars. Dread curdled in her stomach. She'd never been able to forget this accident.

They were running and it felt so good to be moving after a long day sitting still in class. The game was to run down the wheelchair ramp, across the sidewalk, up a short set of steps, then back down the ramp. It was kind of a game of tag, but not really. Mally loved racing down the sloping concrete and picking up speed with each lap.

Mally knew exactly what was going to happen next. She screamed at her legs to slow down. She fought to move her arms, but nothing could stop what was coming.

She rounded the bend once more with too much speed. She stumbled.

Mally shrieked in pure terror as she fell, head first down the wheelchair ramp. A flat expanse of white concrete filled her vision. Her knees broke the fall first, slamming into the ground with a sickening thud. Her hands flew forward to protect her face and her palms smacked into the rough surface. But even that wasn't enough to break her fall.

She skidded the rest of the way down the ramp. The gritty sidewalk ripped the skin on her hands, knees, and left cheek to shreds. It'd taken a full thirty seconds for her to remember how to breathe, let alone scream as the pain hit. Every part of her body was on fire.

But this time Mama didn't come running. No soft hands lifted her to cradle or comfort. No one helped her, handed her ice, or whispered soothing words to help her stop crying.

Weak, pathetic baby.

The words were back, but much fainter now. Mally shook her head and opened her eyes. She could just make out the bright yellow fabric covering her hands, but then her vision blurred with tears once again and she was sucked into another terrible memory.

*   *   *   *   *

Ms. Bunny noticed the change in Mally's crying and felt a surge of hope. She had almost pulled free there for just a second. The little doll returned to the pile of scraps and rummaged around. She found a pair of simple four patch quilt blocks pieced with rather questionable stitches, but the colors were very cheerful.

"Mally, please look at this. See these blocks? Did you sew them with a friend from school?"

Mally didn't answer.

Ms. Bunny spread the patchwork blocks on the floor and tried to pick up one of Mally's hands. With great effort she managed to shift a few of her fingers on top of the little block. She remembered how Mally loved to touch the seams of her Grandma's patchwork quilts and hoped it would comfort her.

But nothing changed.

Ms. Bunny made another pass around the room, feeling completely useless. *What good am I moving and talking if I can't help my friend?* she thought. *I might as well go back to being a stuffed doll.*

She was getting more worried by the minute but felt a glimmer of hope when she looked back at Mally. The little girl had moved very slightly, both hands planted on top of the quilt blocks. Delighted, Ms. Bunny grabbed more scraps from the sewing box and draped them over her neck and arms.

* * * * *

But Mally had been pulled into another bad memory. Crystal Ford had stolen her lunch box and was rooting through the contents. Mally jumped, trying to snatch it back, but Crystal was much bigger than she was and had held it high over her head.

She'd pulled out a small bag of chocolate chip cookies and dangled them in Mally's face. "I'll give you the lunch box back, but I get these."

"They're mine! Give it back!" Mally yelled.

The scene suddenly blurred and seemed to go in and out of focus. Mally shook her head once, twice, trying to clear it.

Suddenly she found herself standing in front of Crystal with her fists clenched. She could remember exactly what had happened that day. She'd burst into tears and run to tell a teacher. She'd gotten her lunch box back, but the cookies had been destroyed.

She knew how the memory was supposed to play out, but now she felt something new. She looked into Crystal's laughing face and had no desire to run away.

She didn't feel sad or weak. She felt angry. Without pausing to think, she slapped Crystal as hard as she could.

* * * * *

In the mountain room, Mally slowly lifted her head off the floor. Ms. Bunny eagerly reached out to comfort her.

SMACK! Mally's hand shot out and punched her across the room.

Ms. Bunny was used to flying through the air. She had done it thousands of times as Mally loved to toss her up and catch her while laying in bed. But this time instead of smashing against a wall or the ceiling, her body bounced lightly to a stop.

She looked around and found she was standing, suspended, several feet above the ground on a spider web woven with blue, purple, and black threads that perfectly blended with the wall behind her. She jumped up and down a few times and the strands loosened, then broke and she landed lightly on her feet. She looked up and could just make out the leftover threads clinging to the wall.

"Ms. Bunny?" Mally was sitting up, drying her eyes.

"Mally! How are you?" she asked, hurrying back to her side.

"I'm sorry, Ms. Bunny. I was just so sad." Mally sat back and pulled at her shirt, which was so drenched with tears it was sticking to her skin. "I must have cried a lot."

"I think if you had a competition with Wonderland's Alice, you would've won," Ms. Bunny said, patting the little girl's face with her dry ear. "I believe you were under some sort of spell. Come look at this."

She showed her the spider web and Mally touched the broken threads. She shuddered.

"What is it?"

"It's like ice, and pain, and heartache rolled into one. I think you're right, Ms. Bunny. Menda must have woven some kind of curse into the threads." She shuddered. "I kept going back to the worst days, but it wasn't like a dream. I could really feel what was happening. Worse, I knew what was coming, but I couldn't do anything to stop it."

"But you were getting better at the end. I handed you the four patch blocks from your sewing box and you were able to move at least."

Mally stooped down and picked up the quilt blocks from the floor. "This block is called four patch? I made these with Audrey. I guess that was yesterday now." She stuck her fingers through Audrey's stitches and wiggled them back and forth. "There's something comforting about this. I can feel it just holding these blocks. I feel a bit better, stronger."

"Definitely stronger. You have a mighty backhand," Ms. Bunny said with a smile.

"I'm sorry about that. Everything felt a million miles away." Mally shrugged and looked out the window at the bright blue sky. "You were right about what you said before. I shouldn't have trusted Patch."

"I had a bad feeling about that cat. I could tell he was up to something. I think the most important thing is to get back to the door and return home." Ms. Bunny climbed up the frayed windowsill and gazed down at the landscape of Quilst. "Now, how do we get home?"

"I had an idea about that," Mally said. "Before Menda came in, I was thinking we could sew something and escape out the window."

"What? Like a rope?"

"No, that never works in the movies. They always run out of rope and the bad guy comes in and cuts the end. I was thinking wings. If we stitch them big enough, I should be able to glide down to the ground."

"What will we make it out of?"

"Scraps," Mally explained, holding up the little four patch blocks. "I think it's time we stitch our way out of this mess."

"Anything that gets us home quickly and safely has my vote, dear."

Ms. Bunny hopped down from the window and together they spread out the contents of the sewing box over the purple floor. They had a package of sewing needles called sharps, a small thimble made of leather for Mally's thumb, and five spools of thread. Three spools were filled with normal cotton piecing thread in white, blue, and orange. The other two spools were wound with glittery decorative thread in gold and silver. Metallic – that's what Grandma had called it.

Unfortunately, they didn't have very many fabric scraps. Mally counted a dozen pieces ranging in size from smaller than her hand to bigger than her pillow at home. She spread out the pieces on the floor and her heart sank.

"We don't have nearly enough fabric," she said, sitting back on her heels. She looked around the room and her eyes fell on the door. She dug into her bookbag and pulled out the bundle of fabrics Ms. Bunny had ripped from the door. "What do you think about using this?"

"Looks good to me," Ms. Bunny said, her eyes traveling around the room. "She mentioned being able to feel it when you cut the quilt. What was she tapping when she said that?"

"Her crown," Mally said with a shudder. "It kept spinning around her head. Let's try not to rip anything else or she'll come back."

"But how do we cut the thread? Menda stole your pretty scissors."

"Let me see…" Mally opened her bookbag and sorted through her school books and papers. She dug deeper and found her pencil case and pulled it out. She sorted through all the various pencils and erasers, looking for anything that could possibly be sharp enough to cut the thread. She had almost given up when a flash of silver caught her eye.

"What's this?" she said, pulling out a strange silver blade. It was about an inch long and half an inch wide with a little silver screw running through the middle.

"That looks like something broke in your case."

"I can't think what could break into a piece like this." She felt the edge of the little blade and nearly cut her fingertip it was so sharp. Mally shook her head. It wasn't important where the blade came from. She was just happy to have it.

She set to work pulling out the blue thread and cutting short pieces with the little blade. Ms. Bunny threaded the needles, which was quite tricky because the ends of the threads tended to split and twist.

Mally looked at the pile of fabric and tried to figure out how to make it into wings. She looked down at her arms. She knew she wanted the wings to cover her back and stretch out to reach her wrists.

"Come help me mark a design, Ms. Bunny," she said, laying down on the floor and stretching her arms out.

Ms. Bunny found a pencil and made a mark at her wrist, elbow, neck and back. The pencil mark showed up better than she expected on the purple fabric floor. Mally sat up and began connecting the lines together.

She'd seen Grandma do this before when she'd made her a green jacket in second grade. She had laid down on a huge piece of brown paper and Grandma had drawn the outline of her body, then cut it out. Mally figured marking directly on the floor wasn't too different and now she had a wing shape she was happy with.

She remembered a hang glider she'd seen on a trip to the beach last year. They'd been on the top of a sand dune in Kitty Hawk and the glider had taken off, spun in a slow circle, then glided back to land on a lower dune.

Mally adjusted the pattern to make the wings wider through the middle to be more like her memory of the glider. *Hopefully that will be enough to catch the wind and get us safely to the ground,* she thought.

They arranged the pieces of fabric on top of the wing pattern. Mally started with the largest pieces from the door and spread them out flat to form most of the wing shape. She liked the four patch blocks best so she set each one in the middle, then added scraps all around to fill in the shape and form the tips of the wings.

"There we go. What do you think?" Mally asked, frowning at the makeshift arrangement. Many of the scraps had irregular edges, but Mally didn't want to risk cutting the fabric and calling Menda back to the room. This definitely wasn't like making a quilt with Grandma. She used a special tool that looked like a pizza cutter and could slice through multiple layers of fabric at a time.

"As long as it holds together and we don't crash to the ground, I don't think it matters what it looks like. Purpose instead of perfection, dear."

"Grandma used to say that," Mally said softly.

What would Grandma say when she found her? She couldn't imagine what she could have been doing for the past six months in Quilst, but was sure if they found her there would be a good explanation. What if they found her on the way back to the door? Mally felt buoyed up by the thought.

Unfortunately, her happy mood didn't last long. Stitching the scraps together was a lot harder than she expected. She seemed to have gotten worse since stitching with Audrey on the playground. She kept looping her thread back on itself, causing it to knot up and pull the end of her piece towards the middle. She had to constantly stop and untangle the string when it snagged on the frayed fabrics.

When she managed to complete a stitch, inevitably she would stitch over the edge of the fabrics instead of through the layers properly which made an equally ugly mess. She tried again, pressing hard against the needle to force it through a thick spot and then: "OUCH!"

She stuck her thumb in her mouth to stop it from bleeding on the patchwork. She'd pressed so hard the eye of the needle had pierced her skin.

She watched Ms. Bunny smoothly slide her needle through two fabrics and pull the thread through easily. She didn't seem to be having any issues holding the fabric or stabbing herself with the needle.

"You haven't been able to do this before now, have you?"

"No, dear, I've never been able to do anything before we came here, you know that."

"Then how can you stitch so good?" Mally asked, suddenly jealous and even more frustrated.

"I have no idea. I guess the same way I can talk to you. I've been listening and watching and now I'm putting all my observations to good use."

"Humph," Mally muttered to herself. "She didn't have to take a thousand stitches." She pressed the sides of her thumb to make sure it wasn't bleeding anymore.

"I'm sorry, what did you say, Mally?"

"Patch said I need to make one thousand stitches for it to feel comfortable. But you've never stitched before so he can't be right. You must just be naturally talented at this and I'm not."

"I'm surprised. I actually agree with his advice," Ms. Bunny said, flipping her ears over her shoulders. "I might not have taken a thousand stitches yet, dear, but I'm probably made with double that number so maybe that counts? As for your ability, this is a skill, not a natural talent. The more you practice, the better you will get."

"Well, I'm getting more than enough practice on this project." Mally pawed through the sewing box and found the little leather thimble. She'd never used it before, but it had to be better than stabbing the sore spot on her thumb with every stitch. "Is it really practice if you're making something to use for real?"

"Every time you make something, you're practicing," Ms. Bunny said. "Whether it's just for fun or it's to make wings that will hopefully let us fly home safely, it's all good practice."

Mally watched Ms. Bunny's small paws moving her needle and tried to copy her. It felt awkward trying to hold the needle with the thimble on her thumb. Her next stitches looked more like Audrey's –

so big she could stick her fingers through the holes they made. But at least she didn't make a mess of the thread or stab herself again and that made her feel a tiny bit better.

They sat and stitched for what felt like hours. Mally's hand ached, but when she spread out her half of the wing, she felt a surge of delight seeing all the scraps pieced together.

There wasn't any sort of pattern to the patchwork except the four patch block placed in the center. Blue fabric from the door made up the bulk of the wings, and Mally's bright fabric scraps ran this way and that, fitting together as best they could. Some pieces dangled off the edges. She didn't want to risk cutting any fabric in case it called Menda back to the room.

Ms. Bunny's wing looked much better with an even row of strips circling around the little four patch block Audrey had made. Mally noticed a neat row of stitches running across the top to reinforce the seams. She touched the patchwork, marveling at how the pieces fit together so nicely.

"Time to put it together," Ms. Bunny said. They lined up the edges of the wings and began stitching in the middle of the seam. Mally worked to the right because she was left handed. Ms. Bunny didn't seem to have a dominant paw, so she didn't mind stitching to the left. Working side by side, the center seam was finished in a flash.

"It's done," Ms. Bunny said with a tired smile. "Time to see if we can fly."

Mally flipped the wings over and laid down on top of them, stretching her arms up to test the fit. "It's smaller than I expected," she said, disappointed.

"Seam allowance. We must have forgotten to calculate the extra fabric needed to stitch everything together. I think it will fit, but it may be a bit tight across the arms."

"Well, let's stitch on some straps and see if it will work."

Ms. Bunny picked up the few remaining strips and began stitching them to the back of the wings to wrap around Mally's shoulders, stomach, and wrists. Mally tried to stitch carefully, but she could barely concentrate. Her heart pounded at the prospect of getting out of this room and away from Menda.

To distract herself, she thought about making costumes for the Renaissance Festival with Audrey. How much time had passed? Would they still be able to go? Sewing costumes was probably out, but it would be so much fun to attend and enjoy the delicious food and sweets.

"You know something funny. I haven't felt hungry since we got here."

"Hmmm. Maybe that's just not something you need in this world. I suspect you're tired, though," Ms. Bunny said, not looking up from her stitching.

"Yeah, I wouldn't mind taking a nap once we get out of here," Mally said, rubbing her eyes. She didn't feel very sleepy, but the idea of a nap sounded wonderful. It would be a relief to just sit still for awhile and give her fingers a rest.

"Just a bit more stitching to go. Help me finish this," Ms. Bunny said, nudging her hand gently.

She tried her best to copy Ms. Bunny and slip the needle through the fabrics in short little dips to pick up small stitches, but her fingers and thumb just didn't want to cooperate. At least this time she didn't tangle the threads or loop over the edge of the fabrics. Her stitches formed a jagged line and the size varied from so tiny she could barely see it to wider than her pinky finger.

Then came the sound she'd hoped to never hear again.

Snip. Snip. Snip.

It was coming from the other side of the door. Menda was coming. Mally froze, the needle falling from her suddenly limp fingers. She couldn't complete the last line of stitching to hold her strap in place. She sat, staring at the door, unable to move a muscle.

Luckily Ms. Bunny had the opposite reaction. She sprang to her feet, scooping the tools and remaining fabrics back into the sewing box. Then she turned her attention on Mally. The doll quickly knotted the end of her thread. That strap wasn't as securely stitched as the other side, but it would have to do.

She pushed Mally to stand and helped her into the wings. After a moment of fiddling, Ms. Bunny decided the wings would fit better if the bookbag was on Mally's front. She lost precious seconds helping Mally shift the bag, and rushed to slide the wings back over her shoulders. She was just securing the straps to her wrists when they heard it again.

Snip. Snip. Snip.

Mally watched the edges of the door quiver. Seeing the blue fabric moving and knowing the monster was on the other side spurred her into action. She walked to the windowsill and gripped the opening tightly.

Her mind had gone completely numb with fear. There was a crazy stuffed doll on the other side of the door who wanted to throw Grandma in a dark hole. She had tormented her with her worst memories and tortured her with monster thread spiders.

Looking out the window, however, Mally wasn't sure which was the scarier option. What if they fell straight down? Would the soft ground of Quilst cushion her fall, or would she smash into the fabric and break all the bones in her body? The fear of the potential pain was the worst.

"It's okay, we're going to be okay," Ms. Bunny jumped to the windowsill, clanging the metal sewing box against the wall.

The sound jerked Mally back to reality. She scooped the box and the rabbit into the bookbag, then pulled the zipper closed.

Ms. Bunny's muffled voice shouted from inside. "Mally, all you have to do is climb out of the window. Just climb up on the sill now."

Mally moved slowly, her heart pounding in her throat. She felt like she was moving underwater as she carefully lifted one leg, then the other to the window until she was sitting on the edge. A strong wind whipped her hair in her face and she scrambled to pick it out of her eyes.

Snip. Snip. Snip. Menda was almost in the room.

"What if this doesn't work?" Mally panicked. "What if the wings were a bad idea?"

"It's a bit late to change the plan, Mally,"

"I'm scared! I'm afraid we're going to fall straight down!"

"I know, I know. You're just going to have to trust it."

"But I trusted Patch and he—"

"Trust YOURSELF!" Ms. Bunny shouted over the wind. "You can do this, Mally. Now JUMP!"

Mally closed her eyes, stretched her arms wide, and leapt off the window into the sky. Distantly she heard a terrible shriek, but at the same moment the wind caught her wings and WHOOSH! They were off.

Mally opened her eyes to find the landscape of Quilst stretched out below and she let out a cry of her own. She was flying! They were free!

The rushing wind stung her eyes, but she couldn't stand to close them now. It was so beautiful. Seeing the gorgeous landscape of Quilst from above was almost worth the terrible ordeal they'd just been through.

She held her arms as rigid as she could, the way she remembered the hang glider sticking his arms and legs out at the beach. But he'd been wearing a harness with metal bars to reinforce the glider.

Mally felt the wings pulling her wrists backwards and wished she'd made a parachute instead. It was becoming painful, but she gritted her teeth and stiffened her limbs as the earth sped closer and closer.

Ms. Bunny called from the bag, "Mally? You okay?"

"Fine!" Mally yelled.

It was hard to breathe against the wind and they seemed to be speeding up rather than slowing down. Or maybe that was just because the ground was rushing closer and closer by the second. The air roared in her ears and she struggled to see through her watering eyes.

Blinking rapidly, Mally saw they were flying over a swath of dark trees. She could see some of the branches distinctly below. In between patches of green, she caught a flash of orange, but was distracted by a loud popping sound coming from behind.

She craned her neck around and caught sight of her left wing disintegrating before her eyes. The threads had stretched during their descent, the fabrics bunching together. The stress and strain had held as long as it could, but now the threads were popping one by one, opening a wide gash through the middle of the patchwork.

Off balance, the wind pushed hard against the remaining wing. Mally shrieked as her right arm was wrenched violently backward. She forced her hands together to maintain flight and for a second it seemed to work.

RRRRIIIIIPPPPP!!!!

Without warning, the right wing whipped around and slapped her in the face. She fought against the fabric, but the patchwork had twisted around her head and shoulders tightly.

At the same moment her gut registered the sickening pitch that could only mean one thing: they were no longer flying.

They were falling.

Chapter 5

Where Did Her Buttons Go?

POOMPH!

The impact came, but not from the direction she was expecting. Something crashed into Mally's left side and wrapped around her tightly. It felt like she'd been wrapped in a very thick quilt. Reflexively she tucked her head down and squeezed her eyes shut.

SMASH!

Branches smacked against her back, but the impact was strangely blunted. It was like the time Rose wrapped her in a box with two quilts and rolled her down the steps at home. It still hurt, but the quilts had cushioned the fall. She'd come to a stop at the bottom of the steps, bruised but laughing, begging for another turn.

Down, down they fell, banging against multiple tree limbs until they finally slammed to a stop. Mally's back hit the ground so hard she lost all the breath in her lungs. The sound of fabric ripping filled the air and whatever held her released its grip with a loud groan.

Mally gasped for air, fighting to pull the wings off her face. She finally managed to extricate herself from the fabric and fell back, willing her lungs to fill. A vast expanse of blue sky and curving brown branches filled her vision. She heard a second groan, this time from below. The backpack strapped to her front unzipped and Ms. Bunny poked her head out.

"Are you okay?" The little rabbit looked very shaken, but no worse for the wear. She smoothed Mally's hair out of her face with a soft paw.

Mally managed to suck in a tiny breath and relief flooded her body. Slowly her breathing returned to normal. She sat up and wrapped her arms around the little doll in a fierce hug.

"I'm okay. We're okay," she said, as much to reassure herself as Ms. Bunny. She squeezed her best friend one more time and whispered, "Thank you." They had made it through together and words couldn't really describe how it felt to be free of the mountain.

There was another loud groan and Mally looked around. They were nestled in the middle of a vast orange quilt. How odd. She stretched out her arms and legs. She felt a bit bruised, but nothing felt broken.

Ms. Bunny crawled out of the bookbag and stood, smoothing her ears down her back. She padded down the lumpy patchwork, tilting her head to the side to stare curiously at something Mally couldn't see.

Mally tensed. What now? What was coming next?

She heard another sound, closer to a whimper this time and Ms. Bunny said, "Well, well. Look what the cat dragged in."

Mally sat up quickly and realized she wasn't laying on an orange quilt... it was Patch!

He was no longer the small tabby cat from the first day in Quilst. He had somehow grown to be bigger than Dad's pickup truck with massive paws and a body big enough to wrap around her completely.

But now he looked in no state to wrap around anything. He lay, flat on his back, his huge body wedged between a curve in the hill and several large appliqued trees.

Mally rolled to the edge of his belly and slipped down to the ground. The tattered wings whipped against her legs, but she ignored the flapping fabrics as she ran between the trees to kneel next to his gigantic head.

"Patch? What are you doing here? How did you get so big?"

The cat wheezed softly and rolled over to his side, bringing his huge paws down with a thud that shook leaves from the trees. His eyes were squeezed shut and his ears drawn back tight to his head.

Mally didn't know what to do. He was clearly in a lot of pain and she'd never had to help anyone who was hurt before. That's what parents did. For the first time since she entered Quilst, Mally missed her mother. Before Grandma disappeared, Mama had always known exactly how to make the hurts stop hurting.

Mally patted his cheeks and stroked his ears, trying to help him relax while Ms. Bunny scrambled over his side to survey the damage on his back. The little doll wrapped her thin arms around her body and cringed.

Mally's mind filled with images of broken bones and bloody gashes. She'd seen Jamie Walker break his arm on the playground in second grade. She could still remember the unnatural way his arm bent in the middle, like the bone was split and about to poke through his skin. Even now, just remembering that day made her want to throw up.

Mally took a deep breath and slowly walked around the cat's huge head to see the damage for herself. She had to weave her way around several thread trees, then tuck herself between the cat and the curving hill at their backs. Finally, she made it all the way around and, like Ms. Bunny, she couldn't help but shudder at the sight.

Patch's back was a mess of frayed fabrics and tangled threads. A massive split began near his neck and ran to the base of his tail. His shoulders had clearly taken the brunt of the impact. The fabric had all but disintegrated in that area and his white stuffing littered the ground. While it wasn't as gory as broken bones and blood, it still felt intrinsically wrong. That stuff is supposed to stay inside, and no one is supposed to see it.

Mally ran her fingers down his back, gently pulling the fabrics back together. There was so much damage and her fingers already ached from stitching the wings. Patch lay very still, and the little girl looked at Ms. Bunny for help.

"Do you think we can fix this?" she whispered.

Ms. Bunny looked over the massive cat's back and sighed. "Yes, if you think he bears fixing."

"Of course, we should help him!" Mally said. "He saved us. He must have jumped and caught us as we fell."

"But you wouldn't have been in that mountain room in the first place if it wasn't for him," Ms. Bunny pointed out. "I think it's more important we head for the door, as fast as possible. You need to get home. Everything else will have to stitch itself back together."

"I can't leave him like this," Mally said as Patch let out another shuddering breath. "I have to do something."

She didn't wait for Ms. Bunny to answer. She slipped out of her tattered wings and bookbag and pulled out her sewing box. It was a mess from their hasty exit from the mountain, but she quickly located a needle, the little blade, and a spool of thread.

"I must have packed this spool of orange thread just for you, Patch," she said, cutting off a long length. "I'll be able to sew this up and you won't hardly be able to see the stitches."

"Unless your handwork skills have significantly improved in one day, I doubt that," Patch wheezed.

"Would you rather me stitch you with glittery gold thread instead? I could have you shining like the sun and all my horrible stitches will show all the time."

"No! Please, no glitter," Patch begged. "Orange thread will be fine and I'm sure your stitches will be perfectly adequate, little Maker."

Mally kneeled next to his back and pulled the edges of the fabrics together. She chewed her lip, trying to decide how to stitch the seam. She inserted her needle upwards, but that left the thread tail on the outside. She pulled out the stitch and tried again.

Ms. Bunny suddenly appeared at her side and silently took the needle from her.

"Start like this," she said, and slid the needle down through just the lower ripped fabric to hide the knot and thread tail inside Patch's body. Then she inserted the needle into both pieces, pulling the raw edges tightly together. She repeated the same movement again, stitching through the two ripped fabrics in a downward direction so the thread looped over the seam.

A low rumble sounded in the distance and Mally jerked her head up at the noise.

"You need to get out of here," Patch said in a low voice. "That'll be her snarls. They will find you and make you wish you'd never been made. Go."

He tried to stand, his paws shaking violently, but Mally threw herself across his back and forced him to lay down.

"What is a snarl?" The ground quaked slightly and several large leaves fell from the trees.

"You saw her rip fabric in the mountain?" Patch panted.

"Yes, she made a horrible thread spider and threw it at me. I'll never look at broken threads the same way again," Mally said with a shudder.

"Imagine that times a thousand. Run as far and fast as you can." Patch's face contorted in pain and he shrank to the size of a small horse right before her eyes. His paws, tail, and body deflated like air being let out of a balloon.

"How are you doing that? Can you become any size you want?" Mally asked in wonder, then the reality of what was coming hit her and she focused on the problem at hand. "We can't run fast enough to get away from those things. We need to hide."

"I agree." Ms. Bunny stood staring at the woods surrounding them with her little paws planted on her hips. "You work on that cat and I'll work on this. I think we can add more thread and leaves to these trees and hide right here."

They had luckily fallen against a hill and a small hollow hid them to the back. Several trees curved around the slope, forming a tiny clearing where Patch, Mally, and Ms. Bunny were sitting. The thin tree trunks were luckily spaced close together. Large leaves filled the canopies in all different shades of brown and green. Vines of thickly spun yarn hung from their upper branches.

Ms. Bunny jumped into action, climbing the tree to pull down fabrics and rearrange the vines to fill in the biggest gaps between the trees. The noise sounded in the distance again and the ground trembled.

Mally wiped her sweaty hands off on her jeans and tried to resume her stitching. Menda was already after them. What in the world had Grandma done to make her hate her so much? Why did she want to hurt them? She dismissed those questions for now and set to her task of fixing Patch's ripped up back.

She held the edges of the frayed fabrics with one hand and pulled the needle through with the other. The thread overlapped the torn seam, locking the fabrics together securely. It didn't look very nice because her stitches sloped weirdly to the left. She'd never mended anything in her life, but she didn't think the cat was in a position to be picky.

When she ran across spots where stuffing was leaking out, she gently pressed it back into his body and pulled the fabrics out around it. Patch shifted uncomfortably, but other than that, he remained completely still and silent.

While her stitches still left a lot to be desired, she could see improvement as she worked along the tear. His stuffing also made it easy to see when she'd made a stitch too big. If white fluff stuck out Mally knew that spot needed an extra stitch.

All the while, Ms. Bunny flittered around them, pulling down vines and covering them randomly with large leaves to block off their area. Mally could no longer see anything past the thick curtain surrounding them.

"Of course, you're only made from the brightest, most challenging color to hide," the doll grumbled, turning her attention to covering up Patch's body. She carried over armfuls of green and brown fabric leaves and began spreading them out over his orange patchwork in a single layer.

"Trust me, rabbit, no one hates my colors more than me," Patch said.

"Stop moving so I can cover your head, Chatty Catty," Ms. Bunny snapped and Mally glanced up to see her place the last leaf fabrics over his face. He was completely covered and almost impossible to see, even from Mally's vantage point.

Another rumble shook the ground, much closer now and Mally jumped. Ms. Bunny's ears were on high alert, standing up straight off her head to nearly double her height. If the situation were not so dire, the sight would have been comical.

Mally caught flashes of blue and gray through Ms. Bunny's camouflage screen and she ducked down to hide behind Patch's body. Ms. Bunny burrowed under a pile of leaves nearby.

The ground trembled under her feet and Mally realized the rumbling noise was the sound of threads in the quilt rubbing together, straining under the weight of the encroaching monster. It came closer and closer until it was right next to them, rolling down the hill to their left.

The noises in the woods went suddenly quiet and Mally held her breath. She peeked out from around Patch, but she couldn't see anything past the first row of trees. She heard a strange sound, like a voice whispering, but she was too far away to make out what was being said.

"What's it doing?" Mally hissed.

"Shut up and don't move," Patch growled, and she froze, staring at the spot where she guessed the creature had stopped, less than fifteen feet from their hiding place. Sweat trickled down her back and she had to stuff her hands behind her knees to stop them from shaking.

The ground suddenly lurched and Mally fell against Patch's back. The cat let out an involuntary groan, but the rumble had resumed. The snarl was rolling away. Mally let out a breath she hadn't realized she'd been holding.

"I admit, I'm impressed with your work, rabbit," Patch said, shaking the fabric squares off his face. "I believe you just outsmarted a snarl. That's quite a feat." He was looking at Ms. Bunny with something close to admiration on his face.

"Now that it's passed, you can answer some questions," Ms. Bunny demanded, extricating herself from the pile of leaves. "Why did you lead Mally into that trap, and why did you save her just now? How can you change your size and what was that thing out there?"

Patch looked at Mally and Ms. Bunny for a long moment, then closed his eyes.

Ms. Bunny was incensed. She stood, barely taller than Mally's knee, her skinny arms crossed firmly over her chest, her ears sticking straight up to give her more height.

"I need answers, cat, or I'll just have to draw my own conclusions." Ms. Bunny began pacing the clearing as she listed Patch's offenses: "You tricked us into following you up the mountain. We got trapped by a maniacal doll calling herself a queen and carted off to a prison that we only barely escaped. Care to explain how you fit in with this, or should I guess?"

Patch didn't reply so she continued, "My bet is you work for her. Go on, try to deny it! Are you her pet too?"

The cat's eyes remained closed, and his ears pull back tight against his big head. He held himself rigidly, as if expecting to be hit. He stayed like that for a full minute before Ms. Bunny threw her paws in the air and stalked away in disgust.

Mally looked down at the needle clenched in her fist and at the torn fabric still waiting to be stitched along his back. Patch had saved her. He had also gotten her captured, but he had saved her. That was enough.

Mally pressed her hand to his back and felt him jump slightly, then settle back down as she resumed stitching his ripped fabrics together. She heard Ms. Bunny muttering under her breath, but eventually she cooled down and joined her with a second needle filled with orange thread. They worked silently, slowly pulling the fabrics together and tucking the cat's stuffing back in.

As she stitched towards his shoulders it became harder and harder to pull the fabrics together. Every time she tried to stitch, a clump of frayed threads would break off into her hands. The fabric had split in six directions leaving a massive gap where stuffing leaked out the worst. Ms. Bunny finished a seam curling around Patch's side and she slid down to land with a soft thump at Mally's feet.

"What do I do, Ms. Bunny? The fabric just keeps pulling apart every time I try to take a stitch."

"I think we'll have to add more fabric," Ms. Bunny said, gently pressing against the stuffing to try to bring the edges of the patchwork together. Patch's breathing hitched, but he didn't say anything.

Mally checked the sewing box, but they had used all the fabric scraps she'd brought to sew the wings. She searched the ground and scooped up an assortment of leaves Ms. Bunny had pulled from the trees for camouflage. But only one was big enough to fill in the huge gap. It was unfortunately dark green and clashed badly with his orange fabric.

Mally handed Ms. Bunny the cloth and she spread it out over his back. It was the perfect size to fit the gap, but the color was ugly when paired with orange and yellow. Ms. Bunny moved carefully, tucking the material in place so it covered his exposed stuffing. Almost immediately Patch began to breathe easier.

He shifted as if to stand and Mally grabbed for his back. "Don't get up, Patch! We've just tucked the piece in, but it's not stitched in place."

"You've done enough. We're even. I'll see to the rest," he said, his words coming out in short bursts as he tried to pull himself to his feet. But the gaping hole between his shoulder blades widened and soon he was gasping in pain.

"You made fun of me for asking stupid questions when we first met. Well, now you're *acting* stupid," Mally said. "Lay back down and let me finish the job. I gotta get my thousand stitches in somehow."

The cat had no choice but to obey. He sank down, curling his tail around his body and rested his head on his paws. Mally smoothed the green fabric back in place so it covered his stuffing perfectly.

Then Ms. Bunny showed Mally how to pull the tattered remnants of his back over the green material. The fabrics were so badly frayed, Ms. Bunny had to turn the edges to the inside. She pressed her paws against the orange fabric, showing Mally the crease she'd made.

"See? I watched your grandma applique the mountains and she folded the edges under just like this. She used an iron to crease the folds, but this will have to do. Don't want me to take an iron to your back now do you, Chatty Catty?"

"I'd love to see you try, rabbit."

Ms. Bunny demonstrated how to stitch along the folded fabric, then into the green patch, then back into the fold. It was the hardest thing Mally had stitched so far because you had to insert the needle at a special angle in the fold. She struggled and fought with the fabric and thread, becoming more and more frustrated with every stitch.

"Argh! I can't do it!" Mally said, throwing her hands up as yet again the stitches twisted and the fabrics bunched together sloppily. She squeezed out from behind Patch and stomped off to the edge of their protected clearing.

"Giving up already?" Patch asked. "I'm surprised you lasted this long."

"For someone who could barely breathe without our help, you sure are low on gratitude." Ms. Bunny muttered. "How about encouraging her instead?"

"Encourage what? Her tears and tantrums? I prefer not to reward bad behavior."

"Don't talk about me as if I'm not here! It's really hard to stitch like this and it keeps messing up!" Mally rubbed her eyes furiously. "I just need a break. All I can see is orange and green fabric and my terrible looking stitches."

"That's fine, d–" Ms. Bunny started, but Patch interrupted her.

"Get back to work, little Maker. Between those disintegrating wings and what I can only guess you've stitched on my back, I'd estimate you've made two hundred decent stitches today. You have a long way to go before you're entitled for this to feel easy or even fun."

Mally shot to her feet, her face blazing. "I think you're just a big orange jerk!" she yelled.

Mally the Maker and the Queen in the Quilt

The ground quaked suddenly and Mally lost her balance and fell to her knees. A roll of thunder followed, growing in volume. Another snarl was coming!

Patch's paw shot out, quick as lightning and pulled her into his side. Ms. Bunny snatched up an armful of leaves and scattered them over his face.

They all waited, barely daring to breathe as the monster rolled past. Mally realized Patch's yellow paws were uncovered and practically glowing against the brown trees. *Don't see us, just roll by,* she thought, frantically. *Don't see us, just roll by. Please, please, just go away.*

It must have been listening to her thoughts because it obeyed perfectly. The snarl rumbled off through the trees and Mally let out a deep sigh of relief as the ground stilled.

"That was close," she said, crawling out from between Patch's paws. She met the cat's steady gaze, then looked up to find Ms. Bunny's frightened face peeking over his shoulder. "I'm sorry I quit. I'll try harder, I promise. I never thought there would be anything bad in Grandma's quilt."

"Bad doesn't cover it, little Maker. It's not safe for anyone as long as the Ripping Witch rules," Patch said, closing his eyes with a grimace. "I've seen what she can do, and I know she's after that Maker, your grandma. Take my word for it, you don't want to get in the middle of that."

Mally wanted to ask what he knew about Menda and Grandma, but Patch closed his eyes, clearly dismissing her.

"Time to finish this stitching, dear," Ms. Bunny said crisply, holding up her needle. "Let's fix this cat and go home."

* * * * *

It felt like hours later when she knotted her thread on the last seam. She had struggled through every stitch, twisting her thread, making a mess of the fabric, but eventually she'd gotten the hang of the tricky stitch.

They sat back to survey their handiwork and Mally clapped her hands in delight. Crazy orange patchwork outlined a dark green six-sided star centered between the cat's shoulders. Even with the clashing fabrics, it was beautiful.

"What?" Patch asked, jerking out of a doze. "Is something wrong?"

"We stitched you back together, Patch," Mally said. "And now you have a pretty star on your back!"

The cat rose to his feet slowly. He arched his back and a shiver ran down his spine all the way to the red tip of his tail.

"Ahh…" He crouched down again and shifted his shoulders, trying to see over his own back. "Wait, what is that green thing?"

"We had to add a bit of fabric between your shoulders because the seams split in so many directions. It was the only piece we could find that fit."

The petrified look on Patch's face said it all.

Mally burst out laughing at his expression. All the tension she'd been carrying since the mountain room dissipated as she sank to her knees, laughing hysterically.

"Is it really that funny? Well, another hundred stitches for you, little Maker. Thank you for not giving up," he smiled wryly, patting Mally on the back awkwardly as she tried to catch her breath. "I'd be quite ripped up without you."

"You'd be a leaking pillowcase without her," Ms. Bunny said, her paws full of spools, needles, and a huge pile of fabric scraps. She dumped it all into the sewing box with a loud clang. "It's time for us to go home. Your dad is probably worried sick and your mama…" She didn't have to complete her sentence. Both Ms. Bunny and Mally knew something was very wrong with Mama.

"Yes, let's go." Mally scooped up the sewing box and stashed it into her bookbag. Suddenly it felt very late and impossible to tell how many hours they'd spent in Quilst.

Mally looked around at the beautiful forest. Would anyone believe her? Would they come back inside the quilt with her to find Grandma? But then a more pressing problem crossed her mind.

"Do you know which way to go?"

Ms. Bunny had been pulling on the vines to create an opening and stopped to look around. "Honestly, I have no idea, dear. And there doesn't seem to be a path through these woods either."

"You could just ask me," Patch said, casually inspecting his claws.

"And let you steer us straight into another trap! Do you think I was stitched yesterday?" Ms. Bunny snapped.

The cat sighed dramatically. "Logic, rabbit. If I wanted the Ripping Witch to catch you, you'd be inside one of her monsters right now. I saved you from becoming a bloody paint splatter in the forest, and you saved me from falling apart. We've evaded two snarls, which is nearly impossible, so I'd say we're a pretty good team. But as far as I'm concerned, we're even. That said, I still wouldn't want you wandering off in the wrong direction."

Patch stood, stretched, and began to shrink. His paws deflated like air being let out of a balloon.

"What are you doing?" Mally asked.

"Being big is highly overrated," he said dryly. He'd shrunk to the size of a small tiger and shivered through another full body stretch.

"Can you do that, Ms. Bunny?"

"I don't know. I've never wanted to be any size other than what I am right now," the doll said practically.

Mally chewed her lip, considering. She didn't want to start walking and accidentally wander back into Menda's mountain. She slipped on her backpack and bent down so Ms. Bunny could climb onto her shoulder.

"Fine. You lead the way, and we'll follow. If you disappear again, we'll immediately know to go the other way."

They set off through the trees. Patch padded ahead, his tiger-sized body easily visible against the brown and green leaves. Mally walked warily behind. Vines twisted high into the curving trees, providing a light screen that made her nervous. What could be hiding around the next bend? But they didn't hear any more snarls as Patch guided them through the woods.

They had been walking for perhaps ten minutes when she saw something familiar in a gap between the trees.

"Wait! Is that a big tree in the middle of that field?" She asked, stopping and craning her neck for a better view.

"Yes, but the entire field is littered with Menda's traps. It's best to go around the Great Tree. Everyone avoids it." Patch said, threading a path parallel with the field.

"The Great Tree? Oh, that's the perfect name for it! I remember Grandma stitching it. If she's anywhere in this place, she's got to be there!"

Big didn't do this tree justice. It was massive with a thick trunk and dozens of limbs stretching high into the sky. Grandma had debated for two days whether to trim it down in size to make it more proportional with the rest of the quilt, but Mally had begged her to leave it just as it was.

As she watched Grandma stitch the tree to the quilt, she'd let her imagination run wild. A little knot Grandma stitched on the side with brown threads would be a secret button you needed to push, and that shadow cast by that black stitching was hiding the doorway. Inside the trunk, Mally imagined the Best Treehouse in The World. She'd drawn pictures of a beautiful circular house inside the tree with multiple floors accessed by a giant spiral staircase.

Of all the places she'd been in Quilst, this one seemed the most like home and she felt magnetically drawn to it. Mally stopped on the edge of the woods, gazing up at the magnificent branches and bright green leaves shimmering in the distance. The base was at least fifty feet wide, with massive roots crowning the top of a wide hill.

"Can we go and see it?"

"No. We need to go home," Ms. Bunny said firmly. "Whatever happens here can wait until your family knows you're safe."

"But that's the tree in the middle of the quilt. If Grandma is anywhere in Quilst, that's where she'll be. Can't we go check? We're so close."

Mally stepped further into the field, craning her neck to see it better. Without warning her feet slipped out from under her. A black hole opened wide in the ground as if to swallow her whole. Her stomach lurched and she screamed as her body pitched into darkness.

The next instant seemed to stretch into several long minutes. Ms. Bunny tumbled from her shoulder, spinning end over end in a blur of brown and pink fabrics. Mally flailed her arms, and just managed to grab one of the dolls legs with the tips of her fingers.

There came a jerk from above and Mally was suddenly dangling in the air. Ms. Bunny's leg slipped from her grip. Terror clawed up her throat as the doll disappeared into the void.

"MS. BUNNY!" Mally shrieked.

"I'm okay! I'm okay!" Ms. Bunny called. The doll had wrapped her paws around Mally's belt loops and clung on tight.

"Traps. What part of 'that field is full of traps' did you not understand?" Patch growled from above. He was gripping her backpack and shirt with his long silver claws. With a yank, he pulled them out of the hole and onto solid ground. He must have expanded in size rapidly to catch her because his paws were once again larger than truck tires and he was able to lift her easily with one arm.

Mally collapsed into a heap at his feet and immediately scooped Ms. Bunny up in a tight hug.

"I nearly lost you," she whispered, the dark scene playing through her head again and again. She couldn't believe how close they'd come to disaster. Mally suddenly found she was crying, either in relief or terror at what nearly happened, she couldn't be sure.

"Never," Ms. Bunny said, patting her on the back softly. "I'm the friend you can never lose."

Mally set the little doll down and, meeting Patch's green eyes, she made a decision. She stood and wrapped her arms around his huge neck. The cat made an uncomfortable noise in his throat and patted her back awkwardly with a heavy paw.

"I have no idea why you're helping us, but you just saved me again. You saved Ms. Bunny too. Thank you," Mally said, crying into his bright orange shoulder.

For once, Patch didn't have a sarcastic comeback. A deep rumble rose from his chest as he began to purr. Eventually, she wiped her eyes and bent down to look at the hole in the landscape.

"What happens if you fall through? Where do you go?"

"No idea. I haven't been eager to fall through miles of darkness to find out," Patch said, sounding back to his old self.

The stitching had been cut all along the top edge where one piece of green fabric overlapped another. She folded the cloth back in place and could barely see the thin gap between. It was nearly invisible, even standing right next to it. But when she flipped the fabric over, a four foot gash opened in the landscape.

"Menda did this?" she asked, suddenly furious. "She's ruining Grandma's quilt! I can't even walk across a field to check out the Great Tree. Someone needs to do something about her."

"Mally, we have to go home," Ms. Bunny said. "This isn't your problem or your fight. Imagine how worried your mama and Rose are right now."

Mally shrugged. The idea of leaving the quilt with that monster on the loose was untenable. Even if Grandma wasn't here, the world she created deserved to be saved.

"Think of your Dad then."

That did it. Mally's heart constricted at the thought of Daddy with his head in his hands that morning. He was already so tired and sad. She hadn't meant to make things worse. She just wanted to find Grandma and bring her home.

She teared up again as she thought about this amazing world that was being slowly, methodically ruined. What had Patch called Menda? The Ripping Witch? That was the perfect name for that evil cow. She wanted to attack Menda and slice her into a million pieces. She wanted to rip off her scissors, tear apart her velvet fabrics, and not stop until every stitch of that awful woman was destroyed.

She looked out over the open field at the Great Tree stitched so perfectly in the middle. If only they could reach it, she would bet all the stitching skills she'd learned so far that Grandma was inside.

Mally shrieked as her legs suddenly left the ground. But it was only Patch, scooping her up and neatly catching her on his back. She wrapped her legs around his ribs and leaned forward to rest her face against the dark green star stitched between his shoulders.

Ms. Bunny climbed up and nestled herself in Mally's arms. Patch set off, weaving through the trees, carrying them on his back.

Mally was exhausted, but kept her eyes open, looking back at the Great Tree until it was blocked from view.

* * * * *

Mally jerked awake and opened her eyes. She sat up and brushed her tangled hair away from her face. She was still on Patch's back with Ms. Bunny, but now they were racing over rolling hills covered in bright green yarn grass. Her heart sank. They were nearly at the door and she would have to go home completely empty handed.

She didn't even know if Grandma was here. If Menda was looking for her so hard, why hadn't she found her by now? What if she had just wandered away from the house, or gotten lost or kidnapped? She might have taken off on a six month quilting retreat and simply forgotten to tell them.

Crazier things have happened, Mally thought as she gazed over the lush landscape.

She turned and caught sight of the black door frame in the distance. Patch was headed straight for it, his huge body easily bounding up one hill, then down another. Mally gave Ms. Bunny a squeeze and the little doll met her eyes with a sad smile.

"I know you don't want to leave, dear, but it's the right thing to do. With Menda and those snarls hunting for us, this place is not safe and I know you must have been missed at home."

Guilt twisted Mally's heart. She hadn't meant to scare anyone and she certainly didn't want to make her parents worry. It was supposed to be such a simple thing – come inside the quilt and find Grandma. Why couldn't it have been that easy?

Patch slowed and they walked up the last hill in silence. Finally he stopped and Mally slid off his back, then reached up for Ms. Bunny.

As the doll slid into her arms, Mally scanned the horizon one last time. Rolling hills of soft yarn and beautiful fabrics filled her vision. She could just make out a blotch of dark green that must have been the woods they'd landed in. Purple and blue mountains filled the sky with sharp angles and bad memories.

But even after all that had happened in the mountain room, Mally wanted to stay.

When will I be able to come back? She had no idea what would happen when she returned home, but she could bet on being in lots of trouble for a long time at the very least.

Mally sighed and set Ms. Bunny on the ground and turned to Patch, stroking her hand along his massive patchwork forearm.

"Thank you so much, Patch. I don't know what would have happened without your help."

"You might want to put your good-byes on hold. What did you use to prop the door when you entered this time?" Patch was looking at the door closely, his eyes squinting against the sunlight.

"A door wedge I'd brought from home." Mally turned. She'd avoided looking at the door too closely, but now she noticed the opening looked different from how she'd left it. Instead of propped open against the little gray wedge, it rested flat against the door frame.

"Great Maker help us," Ms. Bunny said, leaping onto the purple platform in a single bound. She pressed her paws to the door frame. "It's sealed shut!"

"Really?" Mally wanted so desperately to stay in Quilst. It would be a cruel trick if the door was still open and just looked closed from a distance. She ran to the door and found the opening shut tight with no sign of the wedge anywhere on the ground. "What happened? Where did the wedge go?"

"What did you do?" Ms. Bunny rounded on Patch. "Did you remove it once we got into this world? Did you intentionally trap us here?"

"Why would I have risked splitting my stitches to get you back here so quickly if I knew the door was shut?" Patch asked with a shrug.

"Who else would have closed it?!" Ms. Bunny demanded.

"Wait," Mally said, derailing their fight. She pulled open her book-bag and began rummaging in the sewing box. Ms. Bunny looked on the verge of exploding when the little girl finally sat back, shaking her head.

"What is it?"

"Plastic." She said, holding up the tiny blade they'd been using to cut fabric and thread.

"Do you care to elaborate or would you prefer to see the rabbit stitch herself into a knot?" Patch was almost enjoying himself.

"I've just realized what this was. I should have recognized it. It was my pencil sharpener, but all the plastic around it has disappeared." She handed it to Ms. Bunny who stared at the little piece of metal on her paw. "I checked my bag and all my plastic pencils are gone too."

Ms. Bunny suddenly pulled at her dress, her face stricken. "My buttons! How did I miss that?!"

Mally was equally surprised. Ms. Bunny had three heart shaped plastic buttons stitched to the front of her dress. She couldn't believe she hadn't noticed they'd disappeared, but then again, they had been very busy since Ms. Bunny came to Quilst. Three small "X's" in white thread now decorated the front of Ms. Bunny's dress.

"So this plastic, what is it, exactly?" Patch asked.

"You don't know what plastic is?"

"Unless it's been stitched into this quilt, I haven't experienced it."

"Maybe that's it," Mally said. "If a material isn't used in the quilt, it doesn't belong. What do you think, Ms. Bunny?"

"I think it's too convenient! That door–" she jabbed a tiny paw angrily in its direction "–was supposed to be open so you could go home. Now what are we going to do?"

"Calm down, Ms. Bunny," Mally said. "There's another door. The door on the other side is wide open. Grandma must have realized her mistake stitching the closed door, so she stitched the open door on the other edge of the quilt." She smacked her forehead with her hand with sudden realization.

"That's why that block was in such bad shape. Grandma must have been in a huge hurry to attach it so she grabbed whatever fabrics were closest and slapped it together."

"Let's hope it's stitched well enough to get you home," Patch said. "I'm not sure I'd trust a portal that's been thrown together in such a hurry."

"But don't you see?" A wide smile was spreading over Mally's face. "This proves Grandma was here! She got stuck in the quilt too and had to stitch her way back out again. If we can just find her, we can go back home and everything will be right again."

"With the exception of the psycho, scissor-wielding witch in the mountain, yes," Patch intoned.

"With Grandma's help, I'm sure we can figure out how to deal with Menda." Mally was brimming with optimism. "I bet she's back at the Great Tree. I knew we should check it out. She's probably been staying there the whole time."

"Surrounded by a field of traps? She may still be gone, just in a way other than you expect." Patch said gently.

"She's here! We will find her!" Mally was almost shouting now. "What do you say, Ms. Bunny?"

The rabbit had been looking hopelessly at the door. She turned, and for a second her face was set in the simple expression she'd worn for years in the real world. Her soft pink smile had always been perfect. On any given day she could be kind, understanding, adventurous, or sympathetic. She was always exactly what Mally needed at any given time.

Then the light caught a glint in the doll's eyes and her mouth twisted in worry. The spell was broken. Ms. Bunny was no longer Mally's toy to drag anywhere she liked. She was alive and able to make her own choices and argue her opinion. Even now, Mally didn't know if she would agree to head back to the Great Tree.

"My goal is to get you home safely. If the only way out is back across this infernal quilt, so be it." She sighed and smoothed her ears down her back. She looked up at the huge cat. "Will you take us back?"

"My dear rabbit, it would be an honor," Patch said, bowing slightly.

"Honor it will be indeed," Ms. Bunny said, crossing her arms in front of her tiny chest. "I have an idea that will significantly speed up this journey. What do you think about flying, cat?"

Chapter 6

Hello Sunshine, Good-bye Sunshine

They began stitching the wings immediately. Mally pulled out the tattered fabric from her bookbag while Ms. Bunny threaded needles and tried to talk Patch into the joys of flight.

"Look at it this way, you'll never be easy prey to a snarl or that horrible Ripping Witch again."

"At the expense of becoming a flying orange and green cat," Patch said, pacing. "I have only ever wanted to be one of those things."

"Clashing colors?" Mally guessed.

"No! A cat! I only ever wanted to be a cat. I want to lay in the sun and sleep all day. I have no desire to get involved with crazy witches or crafty rabbits. And I certainly never wanted to fly."

"Well, you're getting these wings," Ms. Bunny said firmly. "They don't work right on Mally because she's human and I'm not big enough to wear them. You're just the right size and I think with a bit of luck they will work just like real bird wings when stitched to your back."

"You're missing, or simply ignoring the tiny detail that I have no desire to fly. They'll be wasted on me."

"I'm stitching them on anyway. It's up to you to use them." And with that, Ms. Bunny settled herself on a low rock and set to work sewing up the holes in Mally's wing with tiny, even stitches. Mally helped, pulling squares and strips of blue fabric from the nearby stream to reinforce the seams that had ripped during her flight.

Surprisingly, Patch helped as well. As Mally was threading her needle, he reached out and gently took it from her hand. "May I?"

"Of course. I didn't know you could sew. Do you want to help?"

He quirked a half smile and said, "Sure. I know better than to argue with a girl when her mind is made up. If fixing these wings gets us moving again, I'll help."

His paws were huge, but he easily held the needle between his sharp claws and created a line of perfectly spaced stitches through the fabrics. Mally looked at their combined hands and paws stitching the wings and giggled. "I wonder what Grandma would say if she could see us. I'm just not sure she'd believe what she was seeing."

"Yes, we're quite the quilting bee," Patch said softly. Mally could tell he'd meant to be snarky, but it had come out differently, almost wistful.

All the fingertips of her left hand had been rubbed raw from so much stitching, but it no longer felt odd to grip the needle and thread. She still couldn't make stitches as small or neat as Ms. Bunny's, but they were getting better. The thimble on her thumb now felt like a second skin and she rarely looped the thread the wrong way around a seam, which had happened so frequently to her just hours (or was it days?) before.

They sat together stitching in the grass, Ms. Bunny's pink dress spread out over the rock. A breeze ran through Mally's hair and she stopped to tilt her face to the sun. Quilst always seemed to be the perfect temperature and it made her wish they could sit and stitch together forever.

"That's it," Ms. Bunny said, slicing off her last thread tail with the little blade.

Mally stood and held the patchwork up to the light. "What do you think? Do you see any holes?"

"Nope, they're all patched up and ready to go. More patches for Patch," Ms. Bunny said with a grin.

Patch rolled his eyes as he laid down on his belly in the grass so they could position the wings over his back.

"Where do you think they should go? I've seen pictures of gryphons and they're usually somewhere in the middle." Mally said, shifting the colorful wings on the cat's broad back. They played with the arrangement until it felt just right with the fabric positioned several inches below Patch's dark green star. Mally climbed over his back to check the placement and make sure they would work even if she was riding.

"When did I offer to play horsie for the return trip?" Patch grumbled. "Give a girl one ride and she'll expect you to take her everywhere."

"You don't have to carry us anywhere," Mally said, slipping off his back. "I'm just making sure it will work just in case I need to ride, but only if you want to carry me."

"No worries, little Maker. My back can't get worse than it already is. More patches for Patch, indeed." With that, the cat closed his eyes and rested his head in his paws.

Mally and Ms. Bunny set to work. They didn't have pins so they used all the needles in the sewing box to hold the wings in place. Then Ms. Bunny taught Mally how to baste the fabrics together with long stitches.

"See? It's the biggest stitch you'll ever take and it's just to hold the pieces together temporarily. We'll pull this out after we've stitched the wings on properly." The doll demonstrated, sliding the entire needle through the wings, into Patch's back, then back up to the wings, taking a stitch that was nearly an inch long. She used white thread that contrasted sharply with the blue fabric so they could see the stitches clearly.

Mally loved the big basting stitches. Finally! Here was a type of sewing that didn't require tiny, perfectly spaced stitches.

In no time the repaired wings were basted in place securely. Mally and Ms. Bunny knotted their threads at the same time and stepped back. The fabric lay crumpled against Patch's sides and he looked thoroughly content to continue his nap in the tall yarn grass.

"Come on cat, wake up and give the wings a try. See if you can move them," Ms. Bunny demanded.

"I said you could stitch them on, I didn't say I'd use them."

"Patch, we just want to make sure they're in the right place. Aerodynamics and stuff, can you just try?" Mally asked.

"You still don't understand how things work here, little Maker.

If you stitch wings to a creature like me, it doesn't matter where you put them. You could have stitched them to the top of my head and it would still work."

"Oh, that's an idea!" Ms. Bunny started forward, needle in hand, but Patch sprang off the ground and leapt out of her reach.

As he did, the wings billowed out on both sides, expanding to more than twelve feet wide and the little doll was blown backwards off her feet. Ms. Bunny rolled down the hill, coming to rest with her dress pulled up over her head. Mally burst out laughing as she stumbled, trying to get back onto her feet and tug her dress down at the same time.

"I'd say they work, Ms. Bunny! What do you think?" Mally called.

Ms. Bunny finally managed to right herself and fix her clothes. "Yes, I'm sure that was very funny. Come on, try flying one lap around this Closed Door and I'll be satisfied."

"I'm not interested in your satisfaction, rabbit," Patch said, neatly folding the wings and tucking them against his sides. "I'll take them exactly as they are and that will work just fine. I appreciate the extra decoration. Now why don't you both climb on and you can stitch them down properly while I get us out of here. I see darkness on the horizon. That usually means more snarls on the way and there is nowhere to hide in these open fields."

Mally turned to squint in the direction Patch indicated. It looked like a black haze in the distance. Her heart pounded at the memory of Menda's crazy face and her thread spiders stitching her in place.

"We've got to go!" Mally bent and began tossing thread spools and fabric scraps haphazardly back into the sewing box. "Come on, Ms. Bunny. The snarls are coming!"

They set off immediately, Mally and her doll scrambling up the cat's back, but instead of returning the way they'd come, Patch advised a new path, following the streams that bordered the bottom edge of the quilt.

"Let's stay as far from the witch's mountain as we can," he suggested and for once Ms. Bunny didn't accuse him of leading them into a trap. "If we follow the streams through the lower forest we can run along the bottom edge of Quilst and that may be faster."

"The edge? Could we leave the quilt?" Mally asked.

"I don't think we can right now," Ms. Bunny said. She was looking beyond the rolling fields and streams to a strip of black fabric that bordered the quilt. "It just stretches out into darkness. I certainly wouldn't advise wandering off that way. You might get lost and never find your way home."

"I agree, rabbit," Patch said. "This quilt isn't finished, is it, Mally?"

"No, Grandma had only pieced the quilt top. She hasn't sandwiched it with batting or started quilting it." Mally was proud of how much she knew about quilting, even if her stitching still left a lot to be desired. She'd watched Grandma work through all the steps many times and had often helped baste the layers together.

"Maybe when that step is complete, these rips will be less of an issue." Patch said, skirting around a small hole in the quilt that had been cleverly hidden in the shadow of a rock.

"Oh yes, Grandma will fix everything. And if that evil cow rips more holes, it'll just open into the batting once the quilt is a sandwich." Mally scanned the landscape for more traps hiding in plain sight. "Will this path take us next to the Great Tree? We're going to stop and look for Grandma before leaving, right?"

Neither Patch nor Ms. Bunny answered for a long moment.

"Maybe. We'll see." Ms. Bunny offered only the most annoying noncommittal answer in the world. "It will depend on if you can help me sew these wings down properly. It's not going to be easy, especially while riding on his back."

"I'll do it. I'll do anything so long as we can at least go inside the Great Tree." Mally said, pulling out her needle and thread. "Just wait until you see it, Ms. Bunny, if it's anything like I imagined it, it's going to be amazing!"

Patch settled into a steady pace, loping over the rolling hills with a smooth, rocking motion. Mally gripped his back with her legs and watched as Ms. Bunny made a stitch through the center of the wings, into the cat's back fabric, and back up so her needle didn't get lost in his body. It was tricky work, made even harder because Patch was moving.

But she didn't give up or complain. Mally wanted so desperately to see the Great Tree she focused all her attention on forming each stitch. She memorized Patch's movement and was soon keeping up a steady rhythm in time with his paws hitting the landscape. But her stitches weren't as small or as evenly spaced as Ms. Bunny's. There was just no way she could manage it while they moved.

When her friend saw the stitches, she suggested adding an occasional back stitch. "Insert the needle back into that stitch and pull it through again. Now the thread is doubled up over the fabric, which makes that stitch even stronger than before."

Mally gave it a try, and even though it took more time, she felt confident her stitches were secure.

In short order nine parallel lines of thread ran through Patch's wings, locking them permanently to his back. Ms. Bunny began pulling out the basting stitches and Mally giggled as she tied off her thread tails.

"Being laughed at while getting stitched on isn't a pleasant experience. What have you stitched on my back?" Patch asked.

"Just more clashing thread," Mally said, leaning down to wrap her hands around his shoulders for a hug. At some point, she had decided that what Patch needed most was more hugs and she was determined to help with that. "I ran out of thread, so I had to use orange over the blue. Just don't enter any fashion contests!"

Patch grumbled and Mally felt suddenly awkward. "It looks really good, Patch. We stitched long lines so your wings will never rip out like before and I would have matched the color if we'd had more thread."

"I'm sure it's fine, little Maker."

"Would you like to try them out?" Mally asked.

"I'd rather wait. The Ripping Witch has no idea where we are right now. Let's not advertise our location with my great clashing patchwork bu–"

"I agree," Ms. Bunny interrupted. "If Menda sees us take flight, she might feel the need to make something that flies too, and I remember she mentioned something about bats back in the mountain. Just in case we have to walk the whole way I have an idea for getting across the field without falling into another pit."

Mally pulled her bookbag over and Ms. Bunny shifted to sit on Patch's neck. They spread out the scraps they'd collected in the woods and from the stream across his back. The brown, green and blue scraps had gotten very wrinkled from being stuffed into the bag so many times. The doll set to work arranging the fabrics into a narrow strip about twelve inches wide.

"What are we going to make?"

"A path. I think if we piece together a long strip of fabric, we could use it to cover the holes in the field around the Great Tree."

"So it will be like our own Yellow Brick Road?" Mally asked excitedly.

"In a way, but it won't be all yellow. We don't have time to be picky." Ms. Bunny said, looking at the fabrics. "We'll call it the Nature Path. It looks like all we have are green, brown, and blue fabrics from the landscape. How about that?"

Mally loved the idea and quickly grabbed two strips to sew together. Ms. Bunny handed her a threaded needle and said, "We're stitching for speed here, so it doesn't matter how big or awful your stitches are. We'll need to make this as long as we can so let's make it a race."

Ms. Bunny grabbed a threaded needle and began slipping it through the fabric. Up, down, up, down the needle flashed in her paw as she stacked a row of stitches on the thin bit of metal. Then she pulled the needle through and a line of huge stitches appeared, securing a brown and blue strip together. In seconds, she was done and starting on another blue strip. Her stitches were so long Mally could have stuck her fingers through the gaps in the seams.

"But that stitching isn't very secure, is it?"

"No, but that's not the point," Ms. Bunny said. "This is just like the basting we did on the wings. We need the path to be more secure than the landscape, but it doesn't have to be perfect. We're just trying to make something to support our weight one time."

Mally understood and tried to copy her. The stitching she'd done on Patch's back was very different and she kept forgetting what she was doing and inserting the needle in the wrong direction. But it didn't seem to matter. Ms. Bunny had already added six strips to her part of the path before Mally finished her first.

She grabbed a pale blue strip and focused on sliding the fabric up and down to chain the stitches onto her needle. Then she slid the thread through the fabric and found more than four inches secured together. She stacked more stitches and pulled through again and was suddenly at the end of the fabric. She knotted the thread quickly and grabbed a new strip.

Like magic, the stitching method clicked and Mally's fingers flew!

As Patch pounded over the landscape, heading for a dark forest in the distance, Mally and Ms. Bunny stitched their way steadily through the entire collection of scraps. As the Nature Path grew longer, Ms. Bunny rolled it up and stashed the ends into Mally's bookbag so it wouldn't get tangled on the cat's legs.

When their fabric ran low, Mally leaned over the edge of Patch's back and skimmed her fingers through the stream. She pulled out fistfuls of white, gray, and blue strips to add to the path. Needles flashed, and the patchwork grew longer still. She was just shifting to grab another handful of fabric from the stream when Patch slowed his pace.

He was staring pointedly at something up ahead. Mally followed his gaze and found a dense maze of massive trees, tightly packed together. They had reached the lower forest. Unlike the green woods near the mountains, these trees were stitched much closer together and in bright shades of the fall with orange, red, and yellow leaves. The widest open space was the little stream that flowed haphazardly between the giant trunks. But even that gap was no longer wide enough to fit Patch's current size.

"Looks like our taxi ride is over," Mally said, sliding off his back. "Thank you for carrying us this far, Patch."

"I live to serve," Patch said sardonically, but he smiled sheepishly when she wrapped her arms around his neck and squeezed.

Ms. Bunny hopped down. "Let's take some scraps from the trees and stream and keep stitching as we walk."

Mally had been looking forward to a break from stitching, but she didn't argue as the little doll rolled up the patchwork and tucked it into the bookbag, leaving the ends dangling out of the top. Mally pulled the straps over her shoulders, then held out a hand for Ms. Bunny to climb on.

They waded up the stream, following the twists and turns as it wound around boulders and wide tree trunks. Just like she'd found before, the water wasn't actually wet, but it did feel noticeably cool and refreshing. Mally fished around and pulled out handfuls of blue and gray strips from the stream and handed them to Ms. Bunny. When she neared a tree, she collected bright orange and yellow fabric leaves.

As they walked, Patch rapidly shrank in size. It gave Mally a start as they were rounding a tight bend in the stream and both she and the cat were able to walk through the narrow space side by side. Now he was the size of a large dog, his head barely reaching her hip. Surprisingly, the freshly stitched wings shrank too and Patch folded them smoothly at his sides, as if he'd had them his whole life.

"That is so cool, Patch," Mally said. "Does it hurt at all?"

"Pain is all about perspective. It's easier to shrink than grow and only hurts if seams get ripped in the change. Half of the seams you fixed were ripped from growing so fast before I caught you."

Mally was shocked. "I thought all those seams were ripped when you crash landed in the woods!"

The cat quirked up one eyebrow as if to say, "Or so you thought."

Ms. Bunny brought her attention back to stitching by patting her on the cheek with a soft paw. "Here Mally, let me teach you something different for fun. I'll keep working on the path, but I want you to try piecing some triangles."

"Triangles?" Mally sighed. She was exhausted from stitching Patch's back, the wings, and the Nature Path. Triangles sounded hard. Ms. Bunny handed her a rectangle of white fabric and a square of orange. "Where did you find these cut so nicely?"

"From the leaves in the trees. It's lucky because there's no way we could cut these shapes accurately with that pencil sharpener blade," Ms. Bunny said with a laugh. "Now to make this type of triangle, fold the orange fabric in half corner to corner like this," she demonstrated, folding a square of yellow fabric against her dress. "And crease it so you can see a diagonal line on the fabric."

Mally did as she was told, walking slowly and keeping one eye on her hands and the other on the stream in front of her.

"Now put that orange square on top of the rectangle and line it up so it's in one corner. Start stitching on that diagonal line and make small stitches up to the other corner."

Mally followed her instructions and began stitching along the creased line. For some reason this stitching felt easier and she was able to take two careful stitches, then pull the needle through without tangling the thread.

"Look at that! Ms. Bunny, do you see?" she asked excitedly.

"Very good! You're chaining your stitches nicely now. I thought having the line to see might make it easier for you."

Mally continued stitching, pausing when she needed to climb over rocks or navigate through narrow spaces in the stream. Soon she'd finished stitching along the line and Ms. Bunny showed her a better way to tie off her thread so it didn't tangle.

"Now fold the corner of that orange square over."

Mally gasped as a beautiful orange triangle took shape. Her stitches weren't perfect, but once the fabric was folded over, you couldn't see them and the triangle on top looked terrific. She recognized the shape now. It was a patch Grandma used a lot in her quilt blocks and borders, but Mally didn't know what it was called.

"Here's another square for the other side. Do that entire step again and don't rush. I know it's exciting, but you need to take just as much time for one side as the other." Ms. Bunny instructed. "Now toss me a handful of that green fabric there, dear."

Mally scooped up ten strips of mossy green fabric from the base of a tree and handed them up to Ms. Bunny. The doll was making quick work of the path and paused only long enough to stuff the length of patchwork she'd stitched into the bookbag before resuming her stitching.

Mally tried to take her time. She carefully folded the yellow fabric square in half to crease it, then placed it along the other side. But she was so excited, knowing she was nearly done and about to make one of the shapes she'd loved seeing in Grandma's quilts. The fabrics slipped apart, but Mally didn't correct it and continued to stitch along the creased line.

"There! What do you think?" she asked.

"Fold it over and check your work," Ms. Bunny said from her shoulder. "It looks to me like you need to do it again."

Mally folded the yellow square over and found the second triangle a sad imitation of the first. The fabric was distorted across the seam and didn't even reach the opposite corner, making the yellow triangle strangely lopsided. She tried pushing on the fabrics, forcing it to stretch to the other corner, but this only made matters worse.

"Had you not rushed, you'd have a properly finished triangle right now."

"It's fine the way it is. It doesn't have to be perfect," Mally said, stubbornly trying to make the corners meet.

"Perfection isn't the goal, dear. Basic competence and patience is what I'm trying to teach you. Once you master the skill, then you can break the rules and make things intentionally wonky and lopsided. But first you must master the basics. Pick it out and do that side again."

Mally did as she was told, cutting the stitches with the little pencil sharpener blade. As she threaded her needle again, Ms. Bunny pressed her paw to her cheek in a gentle reminder to go slow.

She sat down on a rock in the sunshine so she could focus on taking one small stitch at a time. She pulled on the thread and it tangled instantly into a knot. Mally forced herself to remain calm and gently tugged on the string. Luckily the knot untangled itself and she was able to take another stitch, then another, focusing on each one.

She held her breath as she pulled the last stitch through the fabrics and tied a knot in the end. "There!" she said in relief. She folded the corner of the square over and it formed a beautiful yellow triangle, identical to the first. Now that it was complete, she saw that her stitching had created three triangles: two smaller shapes on either side of a much larger white triangle.

"Very well done, dear," Ms. Bunny said happily. "Ah yes! I was wondering if that would happen."

The patchwork twitched in her hands. The orange and yellow fabrics were fluttering back and forth and, gaining momentum, took flight off Mally's lap. With a little pop, the largest triangle shape expanded into a round white bird with a long neck and an orange wing on one side and a yellow wing on the other.

"What just happened?" Mally asked in surprise.

"Flying geese. That was the shape you created just now," Ms. Bunny said, watching the bright bird flutter around their heads.

"I made a butterfly that first day I came here," Mally said, looking at Patch. "It fell apart instantly."

"Thank the Great Maker you're much less terrible at piecing now," he said.

"Well, they're called flying geese for a reason," Ms. Bunny said. "You can't make just one. Let's continue and keep moving. I want to get you home as soon as possible."

"Yes, but I want to name this one! Could I add eyes and a mouth and see if she will speak to us?"

"You really want to let it talk?" Patch asked.

"Of course! I'd love to make a new friend. Why? Do you think it's a bad idea?" Mally asked as she pulled out the spool of gold thread from her sewing box.

"Oh, don't let me stop you. Just be sure you want to add another voice to the chorus. Once you give it a face, it's rather cruel to rip it off."

"Why would she want to do that?" Ms. Bunny asked. "I think you're just jealous Mally might have made a new orange friend."

Patch rolled his eyes and settled down on a rock nearby to watch.

Mally caught the little bird and held it gently in her hands. She threaded a needle with the glittery gold thread and stitched two eyes on the animal where she guessed they would look best. Her stitches weren't quite as neat because the little bird kept fluttering her wings haphazardly. Once both eyes were stitched, she sat very still, staring at Mally as she finished adding a tiny curving mouth.

Mally was just cutting off the extra thread when the bird shot up into the air. She spun around three times, then let out the most awful, blood curdling shriek.

"AAAAAAHHHHHH!"

Mally jumped and Ms. Bunny toppled backward off her shoulder. She scrambled to hide behind her while Patch crouched low, staring as the little bird fell to the ground, screaming at the top of her lungs.

She landed at Mally's feet and the screaming stopped abruptly. Their ears rang with the sudden silence as they waited for the bird to move. The little girl, doll, and cat all leaned forward, craning their necks to look closer.

"BOO!"

Everyone jumped back and the bird burst out laughing. Then it spoke with a quick, high pitched voice, "Oh my thread tails! You should have seen your faces!"

The trio stared as the bright bird fluttered up to hover at eye level. "Sorry, I just couldn't resist making an entrance. Mally, you did a very good job making me. I love my colorful wings. Wheee!" She went into a fast twirl, blending the colors of her wings together until she became a neon orange blur.

"What did I say about giving it a mouth?" Patch muttered.

Mally caught a funny look on Ms. Bunny's face and had to admit the cat might have been right. The little bird was now darting around like a hummingbird, while a constant stream of high pitched commentary flowed out of her tiny mouth.

"Look how pretty these leaves are! Ah! That's what you used to make me, right? And look at the stream! Go, water, go! I wish I could see my reflection because I bet I look fabulous!"

Mally shook her head, feeling a little dazed. She waved at the bird, trying to get her attention. "Hey! What should we call you?"

"A name? I get a name? Oh, happy day! I get a name!"

"Yes, what do you want your name to be?" Mally asked quickly, struggling to get a word in edgewise.

"Oh, there are so many choices!" The bird seemed to deflate for a second, as if weighed down by all the possibilities. "I could be Sherry or Violet or Pink or Plum! I could be Heather or Purple or Rose or Rachel!"

"Well, this certainly isn't going to take all day," Patch said.

"Yes, I think you'd better pick for her," Ms. Bunny said as she rolled up her progress on the Nature Path and stuffed it in the book-bag. She'd added several yards to the patchwork while Mally stopped to stitch her triangles.

Mally looked back at the bird fluttering around so brightly, the light from the sun flashing off her golden threads. "I know!" Mally snapped her fingers. "Sunshine! Let's call you Sunshine."

"Really? Really? Sunshine? Like sun and shining light all together in one?" The bird thought about it for two full seconds before declaring, "I LOVE IT! I'm SUNSHINE!"

Mally couldn't help but applaud, the little bird's excitement was so infectious. "Hello, Sunshine, it's nice to meet you. I'm Mally, and this is Ms. Bunny and Patch the cat." She said pointing to each of them.

"Yes, yes, I know you all. Hello! Howdy! Hi! Hey!" Sunshine flittered from face to face, vibrating with ferocious energy.

"You already know us?" Ms. Bunny asked, climbing up Mally's arm to resume stitching on her shoulder.

"I was there when you stitched me! Nice job by the way. I love the glitter!" The little bird spun like a disco ball, then sped down to hover in front of Ms. Bunny. "Oh, you're stitching? Could you add something to me? If it's not too much trouble? Please, could you give me some legs?"

"Oh, I'm sorry about that. I guess you can't really stand still if you don't have legs," Mally said. She pulled out another piece of gold thread and Sunshine fluttered down to her hand. As she stitched,

Mally asked, "So you know we're walking to the Open Door and we're going to stop by the Great Tree to see if my grandma's there?"

"Yes! Yes! Yes! I know all about it. And there's an evil bad guy here, or should I say bad girl? Or just baddy? And you were captured and flew out a window and Patch saved you and you've shrunk now," the bird said, pointing an angular wing at the cat.

"But how do you know all that? All of it happened before I made you." Mally clipped off her thread tails and with a little *pop* two tiny clawed feet shot out from the ends of her skinny golden legs.

"No idea! I just know I know so that saves time not knowing, right?" Sunshine hopped from foot to foot, then leapt back into the air to buzz around the rock they were sitting on.

"My head is going to explode. Can you please rip off its mouth now?" Patch asked. "Or better yet, just cut my ears off. That will do it."

"Wait. Do you know what happened before I came into the quilt?"

"Your grandma went missing and your parents are sad." Sunshine deflated like a balloon and came to hover right in front of Mally's face. "Everything is broken and only bringing Grandma back will fix it."

"How can you know everything about me?" the little girl asked in wonder.

"It must carry through the stitching," Ms. Bunny said. "How were you feeling when you were making Sunshine?"

Mally thought for a second as the bright bird fluttered away once again. "Happy, I think. I was really trying hard with my stitches and feeling good that they looked better than usual. And the bird hadn't fallen apart yet when I stitched her eyes and mouth on. So I guess I was feeling excited too."

"Well you must have passed an extra strength, double dose of it to our new featherbrained friend," Patch said.

"I think it's wonderful!" Ms. Bunny countered. "She's so cheerful and she can fly above the trees to scout out our path without giving away our location. That's exactly what we need to help us get home quickly."

"Yes, yes, yes! I can help! How can I help? I really want to help, please!" Sunshine dove in front of Mally and fluttered back and forth eagerly.

"Um…" Mally was unsure about giving orders. She was usually the one being told what to do, not the other way around. "How about you fly ahead to see what is coming next along the stream. Then come right back and tell us? Just make sure to stay out of sight!"

The little bird immediately flew off up the stream. Patch stood and gave a long, lazy stretch. Ms. Bunny stuffed more fabric scraps in the bookbag, then scrambled inside herself. Mally was just pulling the straps over her shoulders when the world suddenly went dark.

It wasn't like the gradual shift from daytime to nighttime. One minute they were standing in bright sunshine and BLINK, they were standing in darkness.

Mally shrieked and crouched low on her rock. She couldn't see anything, not even the tree she was sure was right in front of her. Her eyes strained against the dark, but there wasn't a scrap of light anywhere to be seen. Far off she could hear the rumble of snarls. It wasn't close enough to shake the ground, but it was out there, looking for them. Something brushed against her cheek and she screamed again.

"It's just me. It's just me," Ms. Bunny whispered in her ear. "What happened?" She climbed out of the bookbag to sit on Mally's shoulder, her paws gripping her shirt so tight it pinched.

"The sun. Something must have happened to the sun," Mally whispered back. "I think I heard a snarl, but it wasn't close."

She turned her head left and right, but there was absolutely no light anywhere to be seen, not even a flicker off in the distance. Mally pressed her hands to the rock at her feet. She needed to feel the rough texture and solid shape under her hands to remind her she was still inside the quilt and not falling through endless darkness. She felt bereft, as if she'd lost someone or something extremely special she'd never expected to lose.

"Patch! Where are you, Patch?

She heard a rustling nearby and a low voice, "I'm here," Patch whispered, brushing against Mally's leg. She reached out and ran her fingers along this back. "The witch must have ripped off the sun."

"How are we going to fix this?" Mally cried. "How was she able to rip off the sun? What are we going to do?"

"We should head straight for the Great Tree. It's closer than the Open Door. Any idea on how to move forward? I can barely see a stitch in front of my face."

"I don't know–" Mally said, but Ms. Bunny interrupted her.

"There's a light!"

"What? Where?" Mally turned her head this way and that. Then she caught a flicker through the trees. "What is that?"

The light drew closer and closer. It was dazzlingly bright, but moving so erratically, it was impossible to tell what it was.

Then came a voice through the darkness, shouting on the top of her lungs, "Whoa! Did you see how dark it just got?! I was looking ahead and then WHAM! It went all night time. Did you see that? Why do you think that happened?" Sunshine was back and glowing like a beacon, her golden threads reflecting against her orange and yellow fabrics.

"Sunshine! I don't know what happened. Come down here and let me see you."

The little bird flew low and Mally found the fabric on the insides of her wings and belly were somehow glowing in the darkness. The bird was like a miniature sun and bright enough to illuminate several feet around them. Mally was relieved to see the outline of the trees, the stream at their feet, and the rocks ahead.

"Sunshine, I think you've saved us. We couldn't see anything without you. Can you fly overhead and light up our path?"

"Yes! Yes! Yes! Sure, no problem!" She spun in the air, but the action brought her wings in tight and blocked out her light completely.

Ms. Bunny let out a high-pitched squeak and fell off Mally's shoulder again. "Stop that! Just fly normal, you silly chick!"

"Sorry! Sorry! Sorry! I'll fly better, I promise!" Sunshine opened her wings wide and attempted to hover in place. Her light spread out slightly so Mally could see a few feet of the forest surrounding them.

"That's perfect Sunshine. Try to fly low so the light stays on us." Mally stood and stretched and tried to relax her stiff muscles. "Come and ride on my shoulder, Patch. I don't want to lose you in the dark."

Ms. Bunny scrambled up to her right shoulder as Patch shrank down to the size of a kitten and climbed up her left. Mally appreciated the comforting press of their soft bodies and Patch's deep purr rumbling in her ear.

Mally stepped back into the stream and waded up to her knees in the rushing fabric. She regretted stopping for so long to stitch the triangles, though if she hadn't stopped they'd likely be in an even bigger fix now because they wouldn't have Sunshine.

The tiny bird flew close to their heads, chatting cheerfully about the forest, the stream, and how much closer they were to the clearing with the Great Tree.

"It's a little bit further than we thought. Or you thought. Now I think. That's confusing. Anyway, the trees open up after three more hills. Just a few more big rocks to climb over. Hey, maybe I could help? Maybe I could get bigger like Patch and fly you over there?"

"Let's not push your stitches, Sunshine," Mally said. "You're perfect the size you are right now. Just try to stay a bit lower so the trees block your light. We don't want Menda to know where we are."

Mally continued to whisper. Darkness pressed around them and the beautiful landscape that had once been so open and inviting was now lost in shadow. She felt strangely exposed, as if Menda was looking down from the mountain room right now and could see the little bird and know exactly where they were.

The water fabrics rushed faster past her legs as it flowed from two densely wooded hills. Mally had to pull herself up the slope using the trees on either side of the stream for help.

She tried not to think about thread monsters lurking in the darkness, just outside of Sunshine's glowing light. She couldn't help jerking her hands away quickly whenever she touched something too soft. In the dark, everything felt like Menda's spider webs.

They made it up a particularly steep hill and the ground leveled out slightly. The stream Mally was wading in became deeper and a breeze blew her hair back from her face, bringing with it a soft, swishing sound.

She could sense something moving in the darkness ahead and froze, her hands gripping her bookbag straps. Ms. Bunny was trembling and Patch had just gone completely still, only his tail twitching against her back. "What is that? Sunshine, what's moving?

"Oh, this is my favorite part! I wanted it to be a surprise!" Sunshine flittered off, her light bobbling upward and Mally had to fight the urge not to call her back. She craned her neck and could just make out the faint outline of a waterfall cascading down a high cliff.

"That is so beautiful. Oh, I wish I could see it properly," Mally whispered. The dim light didn't do the area justice as all the fabric colors were faded to a murky gray. Long strips of fabric and thickly spun yarns flowed down the rock face. But unlike a real rushing waterfall, this cloth version made only a soft rustling sound as the fibers slid against one another. Mally waded through the stream and grabbed a thick tree branch to swing herself up to the bank.

Sunshine hovered low, illuminating a rocky cliff face next to the waterfall. Mally reached for a protruding bit of rock and found the surface easy to grip. The fabric squished lightly under her fingers, but it wasn't as soft as the rest of the quilt. *Grandma must have painted the fabrics here.* Mally thought as her hands scraped lightly on the rough texture.

Patch jumped off her shoulder and climbed up the wall easily, his sharp claws digging into the fabric. Once he reached the top, he bent down and snagged Mally's bookbag. He was surprisingly strong for his new tiny size and helped pull her up the rest of the way.

They sat at the top of the waterfall and caught their breath. A faint rumbling sounded in the distance and they all turned their heads to look in that direction.

"Is that coming from where we came or where we're headed?" Mally asked.

"It's impossible to tell," Patch said, climbing back onto her shoulder. "The faster we get to the tree, the better."

"It's just a bit further now!" Sunshine chirped. "Come on! Come on! Don't sit there and worry about those silly snarlie things! Just around that bend and you'll be able to see the Great Tree!"

"Really? We're that close?" Mally scrambled to her feet and followed Sunshine through the forest. She wished yet again she could see this area properly. The texture of each tree she touched was unique. Some were covered with thick yarns and others pieced from silky fabrics. She could feel decorative stitches and funky rough textures that made her wonder how fabric and yarn could be altered in so many ways.

Sunshine's light dimmed as she flew around a particularly large tree and Mally followed quickly. She stepped between two massive trunks and found the bird perched on a low branch.

"There it is! There it is! I found it!" Sunshine called, pointing an orange wing at a faint light in the distance. Mally took a quick step back as she registered where she was standing. They were back on the edge of the clearing.

The Great Tree rose majestically in the middle of the field. The tree crowned the top of a hill, making it look bigger than it really was.

Large roots spread gracefully out around the base, and there was no doubt about it – someone was living inside. Faint light spilled from a large window at the base of the trunk, casting a yellowish glow over the ground.

The sight of the glowing window was enough for Mally. "You see! I bet Grandma has been living in the treehouse this whole time! If only we had stopped here before! We might already be home now."

"Not necessarily," Patch muttered in her ear. Mally glanced over and saw his ears were pulled back tight to his head as he stared at the Great Tree intently.

"And if you hadn't come the way you did, you never woulda made me!" Sunshine said, spinning around their heads.

"That's a very good point, Sunshine. I just want to get Grandma and get back home. I'm so tired of the dark." Mally shivered, her eyes trailing over the vast expanse of sloping land separating them from the Great Tree. The ground rose steadily in small hills up to the tree's roots. Each mound had a potential to be a ripped trap set by Menda. Her eye caught on another light in the distance. "What is that?"

Everyone turned to look at the strange rectangle glowing brightly in the sky.

"That's the Open Door," Patch said. "It's set up high, I think mostly so no one wanders into it by accident. You can usually see it from the middle of Quilst."

"That's perfect," Mally said. "We'll pick up Grandma, then fly straight to the Open Door. Easy peasy–"

"Lemon squeezy!" Sunshine finished with a twirl and Mally laughed.

"Let's just hope this path is long enough to get us there," Ms. Bunny said, tugging the Nature Path out of the bookbag. It fell to the ground with a heavy thud. It was amazing to see how many scraps she'd managed to piece together in such a short time. Patch jumped off Mally's shoulder as she bent down to find the ends.

She handed one end to Sunshine and said, "Fly straight to the Great Tree, but when you feel us tug, drop it and come back." The bird grasped the fabric in her stitched claws and dutifully fluttered off into the dark field.

Mally gripped the other end with both hands as darkness enveloped them. Ms. Bunny curled against her neck, the soft fabric of her ears tickling Mally's chin. Patch circled her legs, pacing restlessly. Soon they would be running across the field, and Mally couldn't help but imagine finding Grandma standing on the other side, her arms opened wide in welcome.

But the field was vast, and their makeshift path had been stitched on a time limit. Mally's heart sank as the patchwork pulled tight. Sunshine had only reached the middle of the clearing and her bright light illuminated a steep hill they would need to climb to reach the Great Tree. At least fifty feet separated the end of the path and their goal.

"It's not long enough," Ms. Bunny announced. "This isn't going to work."

"It will work! We'll get to that point, and then Sunshine can pick up this end of the path and spin it around to reach the tree. Or we'll call to Grandma and she'll figure something out." Mally gave a tug and the patchwork fluttered to the ground.

"I don't think we should do this, Mally," Ms. Bunny said quietly. She jumped onto a nearby tree and scrambled up to peer through the branches. "Patch, is the Open Door surrounded with traps like the field?"

"Not that I know of. This area is one of the worst," he said as Sunshine returned. It was a relief to be able to see again, but Mally didn't like the look on Ms. Bunny's face. She was gazing up at the Open Door, twisting her ears between her paws, clearly forming a new plan.

"No! Don't even think about it," Mally said, crossing her arms over her chest. "I'm not leaving without my grandma! We have to at least check and see if she's here."

There was a moment of total silence while Ms. Bunny stood staring at the Open Door. Her little shoulders rose and fell with a deep sigh. Eventually she climbed back down, but her face was drawn with worry as she let go of the tree and brushed out her dress.

"Okay, we'll do this, but I want a promise from everyone here." She looked particularly at Patch as she spoke, "Whatever happens in that field, I want you to promise you will help Mally reach the Open Door and get home safely." She held out her paw to shake.

"You don't need to–" Mally protested, but Patch interrupted her.

Taking Ms. Bunny's paw, he said, "I promise, rabbit. I'll see her safe." They shook and for once it seemed like they were on the same side.

Sunshine dove down and planted a wing on top of their shaking paws. "Me too! Me too! I want Mally to get Grandma and get home! Now are we going to do this or what?"

"I'll go first." Patch stepped onto the path and padded lightly up the patchwork. As Mally watched, he stopped and swiped at the landscape. A ripped bit of fabric flipped back, revealing a dark slash in the landscape. Patch bounced lightly on the path and Mally sucked in a breath. But the patchwork didn't budge. Even with huge basting stitches holding it together, it was enough to protect them from the rips in the landscape.

"I'd say it's working," Patch said quietly. "Let's go slow."

Mally waved Ms. Bunny to go next. "I'm the heaviest, so I'll come last."

"Just be careful, dear," Ms. Bunny said, giving her leg a squeeze before following Patch. She wobbled a bit on the uneven ground. Sunshine hovered over the little doll and illuminated the path which rose steadily up the hill to the Great Tree. The patchwork had unfortunately bunched up in places as it fell to the ground and occasionally dipped down out of sight, probably where it spanned the ripped gaps in the landscape.

It was also very narrow and Mally wished they'd pieced it just a bit wider as she took her first step. It felt like balancing on a balance beam. Darkness surrounded her as Sunshine bobbled away, following Ms. Bunny. Mally held her arms out to both sides and took one careful step, then another.

It was agonizingly slow. Mally kept her eyes trained on her feet. Sunshine's light dimmed as her friends drew ahead, nearly at the end of the path. She wished she could break into a run and race across the field as fast as she could. Anything would be better than this slow, scary walk balancing over gaping pits in the dark.

A breeze blew across the field, carrying a strong smell of cloves. Mally breathed in deeply and for a second it felt like she was back in Grandma's house. *She's got to be here,* she thought. *Grandma must be in the Great Tree and we'll find her and go home.*

But the wind wasn't blowing from that direction. Mally stopped dead as she realized the scent was coming from the forest at their back. Her friends drew further ahead as she squinted into the gloom.

Her eyes adjusted slowly to the dark and she could just make out a strange luminescent shape partially hidden between the trees. It didn't quite fit with Grandma's stitching or appliqué. It was nearly as tall as the trees twenty feet above and glowing a dull red color.

Without warning, the ground began to shake. Mally wobbled, swinging her arms around wildly to keep her balance. She quickly crouched down, gripping the path with both hands as the boom of thunder sounded in her ears. Another shape rolled up beside the first and Mally's brain finally connected the stitches. *Snarls.*

Time slowed as a third thread monster joined the others, filling the air with its awful noise as it moved into position. Memories of the mountain room filled Mally's mind. Thousands of threads, hundreds of yards of fabric must have been ripped apart to make these creatures. How? Where had all the fiber come from? It looked like half the quilt would have to be ripped to shreds to make something even half the size.

Reddish orange threads swirled across their bodies, casting a strange crimson light over the landscape. The colors finally clicked and Mally realized what Menda had done.

The sun. This was all that was left of the sun.

Chapter 7

Path to the Great Tree

"Mally! Run!" Voices shouted urgently from behind, but she couldn't move. Her mind had gone blank, her eyes fixed on the monsters.

The snarls had stopped moving and seemed to be waiting for something. Their eerie red light shone over the field, bathing the landscape in the color of blood.

Something pressed against Mally's side and she jerked away with a shriek.

"It's just me!" Ms. Bunny said. "Come on Mally! We have to go!" The little doll tugged on her shirt, trying to pull her to her feet.

But Mally couldn't move. "The sun. Ms. Bunny, that was the sun. How are we ever going to fix this?" Tears filled her eyes as all her newfound hope slowly died in her chest. "There's nowhere to hide, Ms. Bunny! What are we going to do?"

"One stitch at a time, dear. Stand up now!" Ms. Bunny spoke in a commanding voice that cut through the fog of fear in Mally's mind. "Get up and walk to the end of the path!"

Robotically Mally followed her orders. She stood and swayed, suddenly lightheaded. The path seemed even narrower than before and she couldn't see through the tears streaming down her face.

Ms. Bunny climbed up Mally's back and into the backpack. She pressed her paws to Mally's shoulders and spoke directly in her ear. "Patch is learning how to use his wings with Sunshine. All you have to do is get to the end of the path. You can do this! Now move!"

Mally bunched up her sleeves in her fists and rubbed her eyes clear. The Nature Path stretched out ahead of her, rising gently up the hillside. In the distance, she could just make out Patch flying, actually flying through the air with the wings she'd helped stitch. The sight gave her a tiny surge of hope and she took one step.

Her shoe sank into a dip in the path and she wobbled wildly to one side. But she didn't fall. Spreading her arms, she caught her balance just in time. She took another step, then another.

"You're doing great! Just keep walking." Ms. Bunny patted her shoulders comfortingly. "Can you speed up, Mally? Just a bit?"

She tried walking faster, her heart hammering in her chest. "How are we going to get out of here? We'll never be able to hide from them. Even if we make it to the Great Tree, what will happen then? Menda is going to capture us again and–"

"Don't give up!" Ms. Bunny interrupted. "We will get through this! See how great Patch is flying?" Mally looked up to find Patch soaring around the Great Tree. Sunshine flittered by his side like a giant lightning bug calling instructions.

"Good! Good! Good! Now beat your wings really hard to fly up, up, up! Like this! Wheee!" She demonstrated and shot straight into the sky.

Patch followed suit and Mally laughed in delight as his scrappy patchwork wings cut through the air. For a few seconds she forgot about the monsters at her back and the traps filling the landscape ahead.

But her joy was extinguished almost immediately.

A deafening roar nearly knocked her off her feet. Mally sank to her hands and knees on the path as the ground trembled.

The snarls were moving.

"Don't look back! Don't look back!" Ms. Bunny shouted as Mally's head turned. "Get up and walk, Mally! Just one step at a time. Just keep walking."

"I'm so sorry, Ms. Bunny," Mally whispered, tears pooling in her eyes once again. She didn't trust her balance on the shaking ground, so she crawled, gripping the patchwork tight in her fists. "I never meant for any of this to happen. I just wanted to find Grandma and fix everything."

"I know, dear. I know."

"I didn't listen to you! I'm so sorry. Do you think Grandma is in the Great Tree? Do you think she's here?"

"I doubt she'd be able to ignore all this noise, Mally," Ms. Bunny said gently. "I don't think she's here."

"So this was all a trap?" But her words were lost as a great rumble of thunder split the air. This time it didn't stop. The sound went on and on growing in volume until she had to stop and clap her hands to her ears.

Mally couldn't help herself. She turned to look back.

The snarls had rolled out of the forest to the edge of the field and were changing shape. Eight ropes, thick as tree trunks, stuck out from their bulbous bodies. The deafening rumble was the sound of thousands of threads splitting and twisting and braiding together.

They were growing legs.

"Spiders! They're becoming spiders!" Mally cried.

"It's time to run, Mally!" Ms. Bunny tugged hard on her hair, pulling her attention away from the monsters. The doll shouted directly in her ear, "You will STOP crying and RUN!"

Mally had never heard Ms. Bunny scream before. The sound was so terrifying she immediately obeyed. She shot to her feet and ran.

The path curved up the hill and Mally swung her arms to keep her balance on the narrow strip of fabric. Her tears dried on her cheeks as the wind pressed against her face. She pounded up the Nature Path, no longer worrying about breaking through the patchwork.

Bright light flashed in her eyes. "Mally! Mally! Mally! I taught Patch how to fly! He's really good!" Sunshine's high voice chattered over the snarl's continued rumble.

A huge shape loomed overhead. Patch was back to the size of a pickup truck, and his new wings had expanded to nearly twenty feet across.

"Arms up, little Maker!" He roared.

Mally stopped running and threw her hands in the air. She stretched up on tip toe, trying to make herself as tall as possible.

"See!? Everything is going to be fine! Let's fly home!" Ms. Bunny shouted, and Mally felt her slide down into the backpack and pull the zipper shut.

Patch's paws were just feet away, stretched out to pluck her off the landscape when a shrill whistle sounded. Something smashed against Mally's head and she pitched forward. Patch tried to catch her but missed. He swerved to the side and crashed into Sunshine. Their wings tangled together and suddenly the bird's light was blotted out.

Mally landed hard on her hands and knees and cried out in pain. Her head felt like it had been split in two. Another whistle sounded and a glowing red rope punched the air just inches from her face. She watched the braided cord pull back slowly into a snarl standing thirty feet below. For some reason the monsters weren't using the woven ropes as legs. Instead they were lashing out with the cords, the frayed ends alive with hundreds of wiggling threads.

She scrambled away blindly on her hands and knees. She didn't register the feeling of soft yarn grass under her fingers until it was too late. Without warning, her hands sank into empty space. A trap!

She grabbed for the edge of the quilt, but missed. Mally screamed as her body tumbled into the pitch-black pit. Air thundered in her ears as she fell down, down, down.

"Mally! What's going on?" Ms. Bunny shouted.

"Trap." Mally could barely speak. "We're falling." She looked up to see the wrong side of the quilt racing away. It looked like a night sky filled with glowing red stars. Then she realized all the red dots were the rips in the landscape, illuminated by the attacking snarls. The gap she'd fallen through was growing smaller and smaller in the distance. She closed her eyes against the rush of wind and darkness, wishing it would stop.

Her wish was granted.

A whistle sounded, and pain shot from her ankles to wrists as she was wrenched out of free fall. The bookbag slipped down her arms and she scrambled to catch the straps just in time.

Hugging the bag to her chest, Mally curled up to find a luminescent rope twisting around her ankles, binding her feet together tightly. Up, up, up went the cord to a glowing hole in the distance. Like a fisherman reeling in a fish, the rope gave a violent yank and she was pulled up a few feet. Blood rushed to her head and she struggled not to be sick.

"Mally! Mally! Mally! Are you okay?" Sunshine was calling down to her from the hole in the quilt. The rope gave another yank and Mally could see the silhouette of the little bird fluttering in the air.

Mally couldn't answer. She felt like she'd left her voice in the fall. Each painful yank of the rope brought her closer to Quilst, but every second gave the fiber more time to weave itself into her jeans.

With a sharp tug, Mally's legs disappeared upward through the gap in the fabric. She cried out as the angle wrenched her hips in an unnatural direction. Something soft and strong wrapped around her shoulders and pulled her straight up through the rip in the quilt. Mally blinked, her eyes dazzled by Sunshine's light and found herself cradled in Patch's massive paws. She rolled to her side, and for a blissful three seconds she pressed her face to the yarn grass and gasped in relief.

Then the rope pulled again.

Mally screamed as she slid down the hill on her back, headed straight for a snarl bigger than Grandma's house. Hugging the bookbag to her chest, she twisted and kicked, trying to break free. But she was no match for the strength of thousands of threads pulling her inexorably into the twisting ball of fiber.

A whistle sounded and two more ropes shot out, aiming for Patch and Sunshine at her back. *No! No! No!* She tried to turn around to see what was happening, but the rope gave another vicious yank and she slid another ten feet down the hill. The distance between her and the snarl was shrinking fast.

The bookbag in Mally's arms suddenly burst open. Ms. Bunny raced down her bound legs, the pencil sharpener blade clutched in her paw. Balancing precariously on Mally's feet, she slashed at the snarl's rope. Threads split and frayed, unable to attack once they'd been cut.

"Cat! Get her out of here!" Ms. Bunny yelled.

"Ms. Bunny! No!" Mally cried, but it was too late. The three snarls advanced, their movement reverberating through the hillside. Mally's vision filled with broken red threads as the largest ball rolled up to meet them.

Sunshine flashed past and Mally could just make out her high-pitched voice calling, "I'll create a distraction! Snarlies! Over here, snarlies!" She fluttered around the monsters, and surprisingly they stopped. Dozens of ropes shot out, but she banked and dived, easily dodging the grasping threads.

Something caught Mally under her arms and she twisted against the new attack, but it was only Patch. "I've got you, little Maker! Hang on!" The cat had expanded in size to be so large his paws could easily wrap around her body twice. His massive wings beat against the ground, lifting her easily into the air.

The snarl yanked against the rope still binding her feet together and Mally cried out in pain. It was like being in the middle of a monster game of tug-of-war. The bookbag slipped out of her grasp as she clutched Patch's paws.

"Almost there!" Ms. Bunny shouted. She'd shifted position so she was balanced precariously on the attacking rope. Her skinny arms were a blur of movement as she sawed through the cord with the tiny blade. "Be ready, cat!"

Mally gasped as she caught sight of the doll's legs. Glowing red threads were weaving through Ms. Bunny's brown fabric and the hem of her pink dress.

"Ms. Bunny! It's stitching you!" Mally strained against Patch's hold, stretching out her hands to reach her friend. "Grab my hand! It's going to trap you!"

But it was too late.

Ms. Bunny's paw swung down one last time, slicing through the threads binding Mally's feet together. Instantly the pressure pulling against her legs released. The rope fell away.

Time slowed as Mally reached for her friend. Just one more inch and she'd have hold of her paw. Her fingertips brushed the soft brown fabric, but she couldn't get a firm grip.

Their eyes met, and Ms. Bunny smiled.

For a second, she was just the pretty doll Mally had been given for Christmas when she was four years old. Then she whispered just loud enough for Mally to hear:

"Go home, Mally. Be safe."

With a mighty yank, Patch lifted her high into the air. Ms. Bunny's paw slipped out of her grasp. Mally screamed as the doll toppled to the ground, "No! BUNNY! NO!"

The landscape sped away below Mally's feet and she twisted around quickly to keep Ms. Bunny in sight. A flash of silver flew through the air.

"She's lost the blade! She can't cut herself free!"

Mally watched in horror as the little doll tried to rise to her feet only to be instantly jerked down by the snarl's rope. Her pink dress tangled around her legs and Ms. Bunny fought to free herself as the cord pulled again. It was reeling her in.

"Go back! Go back! We have to help her!" Mally beat her fists against Patch's grip. Tears poured down her face as she fought to break free. "I can't leave her!"

"It's too late, little Maker. I'm sorry," The cat's voice cracked and his wings faltered as the distance between Ms. Bunny and the snarl shrank rapidly. "There's nothing we can do."

"I'll save her! I'll save her! I've got this!" Sunshine called, speeding across the landscape like a bullet. The bright bird reached Ms. Bunny, but the ball of broken threads was right on top of them. Sunshine hovered, her light illuminating the most horrible scene Mally could ever imagine.

CRACK! The monster split itself in half with a sound like a gun shot. Fibers ripped cleanly down the middle, revealing a dark void in the very center. Mally gagged as the overwhelming scent of cloves filled her nostrils.

Sunshine had caught hold of Ms. Bunny's arms, but with no way to cut the binding ropes, she was powerless to break the snarl's hold.

"They're being pulled inside! We have to do something!"

"There is NOTHING we can do!" Patch roared. "IT'S OVER! Once they split, it's DONE!" With a sweep of his wings, he turned away from the field.

"No! Please, Patch!" Mally shoved against his paws, twisting half out of his grip so she could keep her eyes on her friends. Her last sight was Sunshine wrapping her wings around Ms. Bunny in a tight hug.

BOOM! The two halves of the snarl slammed together.

Sunshine's light went out.

Mally stared at the spot where her friends had been. All she could see was the red glow of the snarl in a sea of inky darkness. Dimly she was aware of a blast of air and noise rushing past, but it all seemed very far away. She kept her eyes fixed on the monster below. It was rolling away through the trees.

Mally leaned out as far as she could over Patch's paws. If she could just keep watch, if she never lost sight of them, then everything would be okay. *I can still save her*, Mally thought.

Then the glowing red ball disappeared.

Mally pressed her face against Patch's paws and sobbed.

*　*　*　*　*

"I'm sorry, little Maker. There was nothing we could do," Patch said, softly. He'd shifted to hold her with all four paws so it almost felt like she was sleeping in her soft bed at home. Except at home, she'd always had Ms. Bunny to comfort her. Her arms were empty and no matter how tightly she hugged herself, it couldn't erase the empty space the little doll usually filled.

Mally had cried herself out and now felt drained and empty. Dully she watched the Open Door growing bigger in the distance without really registering what it meant. Nothing mattered now. Nothing would ever be the same.

I've lost her. It was all my fault, she thought. *I couldn't find Grandma and now I've lost my best friend too.*

Mally glanced down at the vast expanse of emptiness stretching out below. Quilst had been so beautiful the first day she'd seen it. She closed her eyes and tried to remember the lush green landscape, but she couldn't see it. Her mind was filled with images of Ms. Bunny falling and Sunshine's light blinking out. It was all lost.

She rubbed her eyes furiously, trying to block out the memory. She scanned the landscape again, searching for the red light of the snarl carrying her friends.

But they might as well have been flying underground. The only light in the quilt came from the Open Door ahead. There it was in the distance, a green door frame perched on top of a tall checkerboard pillar.

But... wait. There was something new. Mally's eyes caught on a strange reddish glow in the distance. One of the triangular mountain peaks was suddenly visible, silhouetted clearly against the dark sky.

"What is that?" she croaked. Her throat was raw from crying.

"Whatever it is, it can't be good." Patch beat his wings faster and they picked up speed.

Something about the shape was strange. Mally leaned out of Patch's paws, trying to make sense of what she was seeing. The mountain was no longer a perfect triangle. The top was missing, and as she watched, more of the shape disappeared before her eyes.

Where is it going? she wondered. A faint movement caught her eye and she squinted. Great chunks of fabric and thread were spinning in the sky. A sudden wind whipped her hair across her face. She raked it back with her fingers in time to see an ominous funnel shape forming over the mountain.

Tornado.

She'd seen pictures and movies about the cyclones, but nothing could prepare her for the sight. A swirling cloud of broken cloth and fiber churned below. Red and orange threads, obviously more remains of the sun gleamed from the center of the vortex, clearly outlining it against the dark sky.

The air changed, pulling hard against her skin as the whirling sound of a train engine filled her ears. Mally coughed. She pressed her hands over her mouth. Stray bits of fiber and thread buffeted through the air. Everything in the landscape was being sucked into the unnatural disaster.

Terror clawed up her throat. "She's coming for us!" Mally screamed. She clung to Patch as the tornado expanded until it was all she could see. She ducked her head down, burying herself in his paws.

Patch faltered, his wings struggling against the gale. They suddenly plunged out of the sky at a sickening speed. Patch's paws squeezed her body tight as his wings strained to counter the tornado's pull.

"Almost. There," Patch panted. "Get ready!"

They landed much sooner than she expected. Patch's paws hit the ground hard and Mally tumbled out of his grip. She rolled, scrambling for purchase on the soft fabric. She could just make out a black and white checkerboard pattern rushing past her hands, then without warning her legs slipped off a sharp corner and dangled in empty air.

"Patch! Help me!" Mally shrieked.

She just managed to catch a ripped seam between the fabrics and clung on with both hands. The Open Door stood just a few feet away, the green frame rising from the middle of the patchwork platform.

Mally glanced down and immediately regretted it. The flat surface she was clinging to formed a square box on the landscape and at least one hundred feet separated her from the ground below. The smooth sides offered no hand holds, nothing to hang onto if she fell. She kicked against the sides of the platform, the muscles in her arms screaming as she struggled to pull herself up.

RRRRIIIIIPPPPPPPP! The seam she was clutching began to split apart one stitch at a time. Her stomach lurched as she dropped several inches, most of her body now dangling over the edge.

Orange fabric flashed and suddenly she was lifted into the air and slammed onto the checkerboard. Patch gripped her back with a massive paw, shielding her from the tornado.

"You're not going to win this time, witch!" He roared, picking her up again and tossing her at the Open Door. Mally caught the door frame and felt the familiar tug in her stomach with relief. It would take her home.

A furious shriek filled the air. On and on it went, rising in volume and pitch. Menda. Menda was coming.

Mally gripped the door frame and turned back for Patch. He was crouched low on the platform, all his claws sunk deep into the fabric. "Shrink, Patch! You have to shrink or you won't fit!"

"Just go! Get out of here, little Maker!"

"NO! Not without YOU!" Mally glared, refusing to budge.

The wind picked up speed and her ears popped painfully. The door frame rippled and the light shining from inside flickered out for a second, then back on. Mally felt the tug at her back lessen.

"You have to come with me! Please, Patch She's going to destroy it all!"

"FINE!" the cat roared. He sprang for the door, shrinking to the size of a tabby cat in seconds.

The last thing Mally saw was the black and white pieces of the checkerboard block lifting into the air. Then Patch slammed into her chest and together they fell out of Quilst in a swirl of light and sound.

Chapter 8

Hardest thing You've Ever Done

Mally could tell they had left Quilst by the silence that suddenly rang in her ears.

She opened her eyes and found she was back in Grandma's sewing room, both her arms wrapped tightly around Patch. Sunlight filtered through the windows, and she breathed in the familiar smell of cloves and lemon in the room. It was a light scent, nothing like the overwhelming stench Menda's monsters carried.

But it still reminded her of them nonetheless. Tears pricked in her eyes as she remembered the look on Ms. Bunny's sweet face as she fell. Guilt and anger twisted in her stomach as she relived the scene again. *If only I'd gripped her paw better*, she thought. *If only I'd listened and never stepped into that field in the first place.* She hugged the cat hard, trying to pull herself out of the memory.

"We made it home, Patch. We're okay."

But then she registered the strange firmness of his body and looked down. Patch was no longer a slinky, shape-changing, snarky cat. He was a stuffed patchwork doll.

She gasped and dropped him. He made a soft thump as he landed flat on his face on the floor. She immediately scooped him up and apologized.

"I'm sorry, Patch. I had no idea this would happen," Mally whispered. She didn't think her friend would enjoy this experience. In fact, she could imagine exactly what he was saying right now.

"Thank you, little Maker, I always wanted to have my free will, movement, and speech taken away in one fell swoop."

"Well, you'd be an orange streak in the side of that tornado if I hadn't brought you with me," Mally replied, just as if she'd really heard Patch speak. She checked herself, staring at his motionless face. Had he just spoken or not?

"Can you hear me?" she asked.

"Of course. I didn't lose my ears in the process of becoming completely immobile, did I?"

It was so strange. Patch wasn't moving his mouth and was in every way the stuffed doll he looked, but Mally could hear his words in her head just exactly as if he'd spoken out loud.

Something about the expression stitched on Patch's face made Mally glance at the quilt on the cutting table. The entire right edge was a swirling mass of frayed threads. It looked like a rat had started building a nest on top of the Open Door block. She shuddered in revulsion.

As she watched, the area seemed to thicken, with more broken threads churning on the surface. Mally moved without thinking and grabbed the rotary cutter from the cup on Grandma's table. She didn't wait to consider or even set Patch down. She clicked the blade open and pressed it against the quilt.

She sliced along the edge of the tangled mass of threads, severing the destructive tornado from the rest of Quilst. She clicked the cutter closed and set it back in its cup and spread the two pieces of the quilt apart. Then for good measure, she slid the torn and tangled piece off the edge of the cutting table. Better safe than sorry. She hugged Patch to her chest and stared down at what remained of the landscape quilt.

Thankfully the Great Tree was intact, although missing a few branches. It looked like it had escaped the worst of the destruction. Two mountains had been dissolved and she'd just cut off the green Open Door and checkerboard block pieced below it. There was a massive hole in the sky where the sun had once been stitched. Mally leaned close and could see the fabrics had been ripped cleanly away and every stray thread was pulled from the area.

She leaned back, devastated. The quilt looked so different from how she'd seen it the first time. It wasn't even Grandma's quilt anymore. This was Menda's abomination.

Mally glanced down and gave a little shriek. Her jeans were covered up to her knees with straight lines of red stitches crisscrossing in all directions. Her sneakers had been completely encased as well. The snarl's rope! She dropped Patch as she sank to the floor pulling on the threads, desperate to remove the stitches.

"They were cut. They can't hurt you anymore," Patch said gently.

"I can't stand it! I can't stand that witch's rope touching me!"

"Well, yelling about it isn't doing much good. Cut it off if it bothers you so much," he replied.

Mally didn't need telling twice. She pried off her socks and shoes, then jumped back to her feet, wiggling out of her jeans. She spread the garment out on a clear spot on the cutting table and grabbed the rotary cutter again. With a quick slice, she cut her pants off above the knee, removing all traces of the snarl's stitching.

"There! That's better!" She said, slipping on her newly cut-off shorts. She hadn't focused as well on the cutting job this time and one leg was slightly longer than the other. But anything was better than wearing the remains of Menda's monster on her clothes. She threw the ends of the jeans in the trash along with her ruined shoes and socks.

Scooping Patch off the floor, Mally pressed her face into his neck and sucked in a deep, calming breath. *I wonder how long I've been gone,* she thought, wiggling her toes in the carpet. She'd beat Rose back to Grandma's house and returned to Quilst on a Tuesday. *Please don't let it be months and months.* If she could sneak downstairs, Grandma kept a calendar on the kitchen wall and Dad was in the habit of crossing off the days when he checked the house in the evening.

Only then she remembered the alarm. Dad had set up motion detectors on the stairs and around the outer doors to catch anyone moving in the house. If she went downstairs to check the calendar, she'd set off the alarm and he would know someone was here.

Her stomach rumbled and she pressed a hand against her belly. *How long has it been since I ate anything?* she wondered. She walked over to the window seat and pulled back the curtains to peek outside. The sun hung low in the horizon. Whatever day it was, it was nearly over. She wandered back to the cutting table, biting her lip. Her eyes skimmed over the landscape quilt, and she did a double take. Something had changed!

She looked closer and found it was the Nature Path curving gently over the green hills around the Great Tree. Mally stroked her fingers over the tiny pieces and once again the horrible sight of the snarl splitting open behind Ms. Bunny and Sunshine filled her mind. She tried to block out the memory but it was like the scene was etched in her mind. She couldn't close her eyes without seeing it over and over.

What does it matter what day of the week it is? Mally thought, her eyes filling with tears. *I'm the only one who knows about Quilst. Ms. Bunny and Sunshine... what will happen to them? What is Menda doing to them? And Grandma must be there! What is one or two more days missing matter if I can save them all?* Mally made up her mind.

"I'm going to fix this, Patch. I'm going to stitch this quilt back together and I'm going back to Quilst."

"Brave words, little Maker. Now, do you plan to accomplish this feat of extraordinary stitching before or after you stop crying?" He sighed and Mally could have sworn the doll gave her a withering look. "That world is in bad shape and the Ripping Witch wasn't happy we were leaving. This won't be as simple as stitching me back together. This will be the hardest thing you've ever done."

I'm either really tired, or that's just how it works when you bring someone out of Quilst, Mally thought.

Then she remembered the hours of conversation she'd shared with Ms. Bunny. She would tell her everything and she would listen patiently, her black eyes accepting every word. But many times she'd heard the doll's kind voice in her mind, comforting her when she was frustrated, lifting her up when she was sad.

"Or maybe I've been able to hear the entire time, and I just thought I was talking to myself," Mally said out loud.

"Nah, you're probably just crazy." There was no doubt about it, that was Patch's voice speaking clearly in her head.

"So where do I start?" Mally turned in a full circle, her eyes skimming the room. Grandma was a prolific quilter and had stacks of quilts in all stages of progress stashed in every cabinet. But her true passion was piecing quilt blocks. Almost every Friday night when Mally came to stay, they would cut out a new quilt block together before dinner. Grandma liked to cut enough pieces to make two or three blocks at a time.

"Just in case my brain does a flippity flop on me and things don't go quite the right way the first time," she'd explained when Mally asked why they were cutting out so many pieces.

On Saturday morning, after a short stack of the best pancakes in the world, they would head upstairs and Grandma would settle in at her sewing machine and Mally in her window seat and Grandma would piece her blocks.

It would usually take an hour or so, then she'd finish up, cut her thread tails with a flourish, and add the new blocks to one of the various stacks around the room. Grandma didn't seem too concerned with stitching the blocks together into quilts. Neat stacks littered the floor in all shapes and sizes, colors and styles.

Mally wandered over to the nearest pile and found it topped with a bright orange flower block. She stroked her fingers along the delicate stitching that held the flower to the background fabric. Twenty pointy petals surrounded a yellow center circle. *That could also be a new sun block*, Mally thought.

She lifted it off the stack and found an identically pieced block with yellow and red fabrics below. Grandma had made two! She carried them over to the quilt and lined them up in two corners.

The sun rises in the East and sets in the West, she thought as she placed one bright sun block in the upper right corner and the other in the lower left corner. "I'm going to stitch so many suns back into this quilt, Menda won't ever be able to make it go dark again."

"A solid plan. Are you going to fix the hole in the sky she left as well?" Patch asked in her mind.

"Good point." Mally contemplated her options, looking around the room. Her eyes caught on her favorite scrap basket in front of the window. She dug in, looking for just the right fabric for the sun missing from the landscape. She pulled out a deep orange fabric printed with swirls and a larger scrap of solid yellow.

"Which do you think?" She asked, unsure of which looked better on the quilt.

"Either or. They're both sun colors. Did I not mention this would be challenging? There's no hope for us if you can't make up your mind over something so simple."

"Uggh, I was just asking for help picking the color. I can make up my mind!" Mally picked the orange spiral fabric and arranged it over the hole in the sky.

She returned to the stack of quilt blocks and paged through the fabric squares quickly. A small scrap of paper fluttered out and she caught it. "Disappearing Four Patch" was written in Grandma's script.

It seemed to correspond with a strange looking block with squares and rectangles. As Mally browsed through the pile, she found more scraps of paper and sticky notes mixed in with the patchwork recording names like Churn Dash, Turkey Tracks, and Robbing Peter to Pay Paul.

She found several Four Patches with a scrappy checkerboard pattern like the blocks she'd made with Audrey, a few House on a Hill and Sawtooth Stars, and a lot of complicated blocks with curving seams and tiny points with names like New York Beauty and Mariner's Compass that looked off-limits. She didn't want Grandma to come home and be mad about the blocks she used to fix the quilt.

Mally pulled out the ones she liked best and carried them over to the cutting table. She spread out the squares and arranged them around the landscape quilt. But there was still space to fill on all sides. She spotted another pile peeking out from under Grandma's sewing machine table.

Mally slid the stack out and frowned at the top design. It was a weird block with a strange angle pieced in brown and teal fabrics. She rotated the block around and suddenly the shape became familiar – an Open Door!

"Whoo hoo!" She did a little dance and pumped her fists in the air. She had no idea how she would have pieced a new door block by herself, so this was a very lucky find indeed.

In the end she found three Open Doors and two Closed Doors along with two beautifully pieced blocks labeled Moon Over the Mountain that instantly became her favorite. She spread them out with the others she'd picked and now had more than enough to create a border around the quilt.

Mally began arranging the squares around the center landscape. First, she tried all the doors on the top row, but that didn't look right because they would be suspended in sky. Every time she rearranged the blocks, she found something wrong. That block has the same pink color as that one, it would be weird to have that star below the landscape, and so on.

She shifted the pieces again, ignoring the heavy weight of exhaustion that had settled over her shoulders. She longed to lay down and rest, just for a little while. She rubbed her eyes and tried another arrangement. But her stomach had graduated from gently rumbling to making her painfully aware she hadn't eaten anything in a very long time.

She set the blocks down for a second to look out the window behind the thick curtains. Night had fallen, and the street was quiet. The back of her neck prickled and she quickly pulled away from the window. She'd never spent so much time in Grandma's house all by herself, and never at night.

"If I can just get this done, everything will be fine! I just can't make up my mind." Mally said, returning to the cutting table to stare blearily at the quilt.

"How about you try moving those blocks another ten times?" Patch suggested sleepily. His expression hadn't changed, but it seemed like his stitched green eyes were a little less bright. "Do you know what the definition of insanity is? Doing the same thing repeatedly and expecting different results."

"I have to get this stitched back together tonight. I have to save them, but I can't go back until the sun is fixed and..." The fabrics blurred as tears pooled in her eyes.

"You're too tired to do this, little Maker. You need to rest. Nothing you do right now will get you any closer to fixing Quilst. It'll keep for one night and you will see it fresh tomorrow morning."

Guilt twisted Mally's stomach, or maybe that was just hunger. "I feel bad, going to sleep while everything is so messed up."

"Well, look at it this way: You rearranging those blocks another hundred times will not bring anyone home faster."

"Fine." Mally pushed away from the table and scooped the cat into her arms. She snuck down the hall to her special guest room. The floors creaked as she tiptoed in and then shut the door quickly behind her. She knew no one could be inside the house with the alarm on, but it still felt creepy to be here alone.

She tucked Patch into bed and snuggled down under the heavy quilts next to him. She stuck her toes deep into the chilly sheets and felt that perfect combination of weight, comfort and the promise of warmth.

She sighed, expecting to spend hours going over all that had happened in Quilst. But instead she barely closed her eyes and fell instantly into a deep, exhausted sleep.

*   *   *   *   *

Mally awoke and sat up. Sunlight filtered through the window, shining straight into her face. She closed her eyes, drinking in its warmth. She breathed in deeply, taking in the signature smells of Grandma's house, the thick quilts piled up on top of her and something new – pancakes! She shot out of bed and raced downstairs.

At the stove was Grandma, back in her red apron, spatula in hand as she turned over three golden pancakes. Mally loved the way she fried them in hot bacon grease which made a crispy ridge all around the edge.

Grandma turned to hand the plate to Mally. Something was wrong. It looked like she was wearing black gloves and all her fingers were fused together like...

Mally looked up to find Menda's silk face had replaced her Grandmother's soft, wrinkled skin. She smiled widely, her blue eyes flashing. But it was Grandma's gravelly voice that came out of her mouth as she spoke, "Good morning, Mally May. I made these just for you."

Mally jerked awake, screaming. A faint light peeked around the edge of the curtains. It was still nighttime, perhaps an hour before dawn. "It was a dream. It was just a dream."

"I'd say that one had a bit of truth to it, though," Patch said cryptically.

"What would you know? Can you see into my dreams too?" Mally asked. It had been such a delicious dream, so perfect, right up until the moment Menda had taken Grandma's place. Her stomach twisted painfully. She rolled over and tried to forget about the fried pancakes. "It wasn't real. Grandma doesn't have anything to do with Menda. She's evil."

Patch didn't reply, and Mally felt a sudden wave of frustration. Why couldn't they just find Grandma and bring her home? Better yet, why did she leave them in the first place? This was all her fault!

Her eyes caught on the painting on the wall, faintly illuminated by a gap in the curtains. It was the yellow brick road. Dorothy hadn't had a choice in her trip to Oz. She'd been pulled from Kansas and set on the path to defeat the Wicked Witch of the West. Mally had a choice. She could run downstairs, call Dad, and give up this quest right now. But she couldn't leave Ms. Bunny and Sunshine behind.

Her mind swirled with images of the dream. What if Patch was right? Who had made Menda and how had she gotten into Quilst in the first place?

Mally asked the question on her mind, but Patch simply said, "A story for the morning. Sleep, little Maker."

She pulled the cat into her arms. Hugging him tightly, she fell back to sleep.

*   *   *   *   *

"WAKE UP! Come on, Mally! Wake up or we're going to be caught!"

Mally opened her eyes blearily and found them clogged with gritty crystals. She must have cried in her sleep last night. She rubbed her eyes, yawning widely, then froze as the sound of the door slamming downstairs registered in her sleepy brain.

"Someone's here!" She slipped quickly out of bed and pulled Patch down with her. She tucked herself into the narrow space under the bed as heavy footsteps stomped through the house. She glanced up and her heart rate doubled as she saw the edge of her purple quilt dragging the floor.

"The bed is a mess!" she whispered to Patch. "I have to fix it or they'll know I'm here."

She wiggled out from under the bed and jumped to her feet. She made the bed faster than she ever had in her life, pulling the sheet up with a jerk, then the layers of quilts. Thankfully Grandma didn't care much for perfectly made beds. So long as the quilt on top was smooth and flat, that was good enough for her.

Mally had just smoothed out both sides when the footsteps started up the creaking staircase. She ducked back under the bed and pressed herself flat to the cold floor.

Years of playing hide-and-seek finally paid off. Mally knew to keep her head down and not move a muscle. What gave you away was movement and the glitter of your eyes in the dark. She'd caught her younger cousins so many times because they always wanted to see the seeker coming.

Mally squeezed her eyes shut as the bedroom door clicked open. She resisted the urge to move her legs and tuck her feet in closer to her body. She heard a loud sigh and knew it was Dad standing at the door.

Guilt wrenched her heart as he sighed again. It would be so easy to be found. She could tell him what happened and maybe he would help her piece Quilst back together again.

"Highly unlikely," Patch's voice echoed in her head. "If you get caught now, you won't be fixing anything for months. You'll never get a chance to be alone long enough to return."

But he sounds so sad, Mally thought. *It's my fault, and I could fix it. Shouldn't I fix this too?*

"No," Patch replied. "Where is all your 'save Quilst' spirit from last night? Do you remember what you decided? What is a day or two if it means you can save everyone and fix everything at once?"

The floor creaked as Dad turned and closed the door. It felt as if he'd made the decision for her. Mally let out a breath she hadn't realized she'd been holding. She remained motionless on the floor as her stomach suddenly doubled over in knots.

Ow! Ow! Ow! Mally yelled in her head. She was beyond hungry now.

She tried to distract herself by focusing completely on Dad's footsteps. She closed her eyes and tried to imagine where he was in the house. She listened to him opening each door and knew when he entered the sewing room. He seemed to pause longer in that room than the others. Did he notice the quilt on the table had changed?

For several agonizing minutes she waited for him to start yelling, "I know you're here! Come out now!" But he didn't. He shut the door quietly and was walking back down the hall to the stairs when his phone rang. She and Rose loved to change his ringtones to the most outrageous rings and right now it sounded like cats meowing to the tune of *Jingle Bells*. Mally bit her lip, trying not to laugh.

"John here. What? Slow down, what did you say? Yes, I'm on my way." His footsteps were suddenly pounding down the stairs. The back door slammed loudly and seconds later the truck roared to life.

"What was that about?" Mally whispered as the sound of the engine faded in the distance. Even though she knew the house was empty, she continued to speak quietly. She waited a full minute to see if he would come back.

The house remained still and silent. Mally slipped out and, tucking Patch under one arm padded down the stairs carefully. She hadn't heard Dad reset the alarm. It always made an awful shriek you could hear through the entire house until it fully armed.

She slipped into the kitchen and checked the panel. A green light on the bottom told her it was disarmed. She breathed out a sigh of relief. Time to eat!

Grandma's house had been empty for six months. After she'd been missing three weeks, Mama had cleaned out her refrigerator and emptied it of everything perishable. But since Mally and Rose still came by sometimes after school and Dad checked on the house every day, they'd left a lot of food in the cabinets.

Mally found peanut butter, graham crackers, and a half full honey bear. She quickly buttered a cracker to make a peanut butter sandwich and stuffed it into her mouth. She moaned with pleasure at the taste.

She poured herself a tall glass of water from the sink and drank it down, then poured another. She ate her way through the entire package of graham crackers and dug back into the cabinet for more.

"I think this gorge fest should be taken upstairs." Patch said from where she'd set him on the kitchen table. "We have a job to do."

"You mean I do. You can't stitch anything right now." Mally said, as she slathered another cracker with peanut butter, this time topping it with a squirt of honey.

"Yes, yes, you don't need to remind me I can't move. But if Daddy returns in a hurry, won't it be easier to hide upstairs than right next to the door?"

"Good point." Mally put the rest of the crackers on a plate and filled her glass again. She scooped up Patch under one arm and made to leave the room. She paused, glancing at the calendar next to the door.

"Patch... I've been gone five days." Little black "x" marks scratched out each day.

"Maybe six. He might have forgotten to mark today," Patch mused. "As you said, what does another day matter, when you're already up to your neck in trouble?"

"Just so long as we don't get caught before we finish fixing the quilt. I'm sure Mrs. Whittaker is watching the house too. We'll have to be very careful."

Mally walked slowly upstairs, trying not to slosh water on the carpet. She had a glass in one hand, her full plate of peanut butter, honey, and crackers in the other, and Patch tucked under one arm. She elbowed the sewing room door open and felt instantly at home. Even with the curtains closed, the room was filled with light and warmth. She set her food down on the window seat and returned to the cutting table to look at the quilt.

She frowned at the blocks arranged around the landscape. She'd fussed and debated over their placement for at least an hour last night, but now she couldn't see what she'd been agonizing about. She fiddled with an Open Door block, lining it up against the right edge of the landscape. Who cared about the exact placement of these blocks if it got Grandma and Ms. Bunny home?

"Exactly what I was saying last night," Patch said in her head. "Stitch it together and get the job done."

Several hours of tedious hand stitching followed as Mally added a border of twelve quilt blocks and stitched a new sun in the middle. She considered using Grandma's sewing machine, but since she had no idea how to even turn it on, she stuck with the hand stitching techniques Ms. Bunny taught her in Quilst.

Sitting in Grandma's comfy green sewing chair, she cut the scrap of orange fabric she'd set aside the night before into a rough circle and placed it over the hole in the sky where the sun had been. She had no idea how to turn the edges under neatly the way she'd seen Grandma make the original sun. The edges frayed a bit as she stitched the scrap in place, but at least the world would have sunshine again. Her stitches were far from perfect and many times she had to stop to pick out knots when her thread became tangled.

Whenever she began to feel frustrated, she'd close her eyes and see Ms. Bunny and Sunshine disappearing inside the snarl or imagine what Menda was doing to them right now. Whatever they were going through had to be much worse than this.

Slowly she stitched the quilt blocks together one by one and then secured the pieced borders to the edges of the quilt, just as she'd seen Grandma do many times before. She also stitched on new buttons – doorknobs – to the three Open Door and two Closed Door blocks she was adding to the borders.

"Will these doors open underground?" Mally asked as she secured a red and white striped glass button to a hot pink door that was destined for the bottom edge of the quilt.

"Use your imagination, little Maker. I think a large cave would be convenient."

"But caves are dirty and dark," Mally protested. She'd visited Appalachian Caverns with her family when she was little and vividly remembered descending into the cold, dark cave.

"It can be as pretty or as ugly as you like. It's your imagination so make it whatever you want."

So Mally attached buttons to the doors and imagined a different sort of cave with white rock walls. She'd flipped through Dad's countertop catalogs enough times to know many different types of rock by sight. Quartz and marble were her favorites.

This cave will always have light, Mally thought as she ran her fingers over the seams of a pale gold Sawtooth Star block pieced between the two doors. It was weird to put a star underground, but now it made sense. There would be long passageways leading to the surface of Quilst, but the patchwork doors would open into a massive cavern with the star shining in the center.

For the top border, Mally pieced a House on a Hill block in between the door blocks and stitched an extra thin strip of gray fabric on the bottom edge of all three. She imagined the gray fabric acting like a thin cloud layer, hiding the doors and house in the sky. *It will feel squishy and soft to stand on*, she thought as she secured the fabric strip in place. *But it won't be big like the cave. Just a narrow little space for the doors and house so we can easily fly up to it whenever we're in trouble. Menda will never find it.*

While she stitched as fast as her small fingers could manage, Patch rested in the window seat. But he was far from idle. Almost immediately he began questioning exactly how they were going to return to Quilst and achieve their goals. At first, Mally had no answers, but soon she could see the value of having a plan, and a backup plan, and a third plan because Patch insisted she think through all the worst possibilities.

While they talked, Mally occasionally stopped to pull out materials or tools from nearby cabinets and add them to the yellow bag at her feet. She'd lost her backpack and sewing box during the snarl attack, so she'd rummaged through Grandma's drawers and found a small yellow shoulder bag to hold supplies when they returned. She was just adding a spool of white thread when she thought of Menda and the spider web on the mountain path.

"I need to ask you something, Patch."

"I'm listening."

"The day we got trapped, you led us up to Menda's spider web. You led us there. Now we're planning to go back and take her on together and I just need to know. Can I trust you?"

He was silent for a long minute, then sighed.

"I am very sorry for my earlier actions. I thought... well I thought I could fix a wrong with another wrong, but that never works out, does it? But I swear on every thread that holds my orange hide together that it won't happen again. You can trust me."

"But how do I know that for sure?" Mally said softly, rolling the spool through her fingers. She shivered at the memory of the spider web locking her in place and the horrible threads worming their way through her hair.

Patch didn't answer directly, "Did you see any other animals in Quilst, other than me?"

"No. I only met you on the first day. I haven't met anyone else except Menda"

"There were lots of animals before the Ripping Witch came. Sheep, skunks, deer, racoons and dogs. My best friends were a horse and an owl." He chuckled and Mally could hear wistfulness in his voice. "She took them all. Some she would push into those pits in the landscape. I have no idea what happened to them. But their fate was probably better than what happened to the rest."

"What did she do to them?"

"The worst was turning them into snarls. She'd rip them down to pure fiber, then command it, and they had to do whatever she asked, but you can still hear them inside. That's the whispering. You heard it in the woods when you were fixing me. That's the animals inside calling for help. It drives her crazy she can't shut them up. She can rip us apart thread by thread, but she can't erase us completely."

"But why? Why did she rip them apart? Why is she so determined to find my Grandma and destroy Quilst?"

"I have no idea. Maybe it makes her feel good," Mally knew if Patch could move he'd be shrugging. "All I know is it's the crown that does it. I've never seen anyone else be able to control things like her, but she has to rip living things apart first. She can't make new things. Like you, making Sunshine – she can't do that. Whatever she is, she's not a Maker."

"But how did she get into the quilt? She's a doll, right? Like you and Ms. Bunny. But who made her? Who would make something like that?"

"Time's a wasting and you have a lot more seams to stitch. How about you focus on your needle and I'll worry about the Ripping Witch."

His tone closed the subject completely, but Mally had a feeling there was a lot more he wasn't telling her.

Sometime later Mally stood and stretched. She bent her fingers back and groaned as her knuckles popped. She'd attached rows of blocks to the top and right edge of the quilt. She only had one more long line of stitching to go along the bottom of the landscape.

"What do you think?" she asked, holding up the quilt to show Patch.

"You're doing great, little Maker. I'm sure it's already making a difference in Quilst."

"Because of the new Open Door blocks?" Mally asked, stroking her fingers over the delicate door frame pieced in brown fabric.

"And the, what? Three suns? You'd notice it if there were suddenly three new suns in the sky, wouldn't you?"

"Good point. Do you think I should change it?"

"No, definitely not. The more you add, the better off we'll be. Are there any other blocks that might be useful in these stacks?" Quilt blocks surrounded Patch on the window seat and he sounded supremely annoyed he couldn't move to look through them himself.

Mally joined him at the window. It was a relief to not be stitching, even if it was only for a short break. She scooped up a stack of blocks and sneezed as a cloud of dust filled the air. Sitting down next to the cat, she slid her hand across the top blue block. It was composed of four large squares surrounded with tiny triangles. Bears Claw was written on bit of paper pinned to one corner. Mally flipped through the stack and found four more Bears Claw blocks, then a slew of Turkey Tracks, which were pieced almost identically.

"Do you think this could become a turkey?" she asked Patch, thinking of Sunshine. She had been a patchwork unit with a special name. What had Ms. Bunny called it? Flying bird? Flying goose? She began separating the blocks into stacks organized by their types. She grabbed another pile from the floor and the name suddenly came back to her.

"Flying geese! Sunshine was a flying geese unit and she started flying. Do you think these might turn into bears and turkeys and birds?"

"I would suppose so. I was hoping you'd find something along the lines of a battle ax or sword block. I don't suppose we'd be so lucky as to have a traditional Evil Witch Instant Death quilt block?"

"But what if they could help us?" Mally said, ignoring his sarcasm. "There's dozens and dozens here! Look – Cats and Mice!" She held up a red and green quilt block with a square surrounded by twelve small triangles. "The mice could help us find Menda and you wouldn't mind another cat to hang out with, would you?"

"Another kitty to compete with your affections? I suppose I could deal with that. We'll need some bigger animals too."

Mally quickly sorted the blocks around the window, stacking them up by the animals they corresponded with. Frogs, monkeys, dozens of different bird blocks, game cocks, hawks, turkeys, ducks and ducklings, and hens and chicks. She ran around the room scooping up more piles from the floor.

Unfortunately, most of the quilt blocks Grandma had pieced weren't animal blocks. "I don't need more Churn Dash!" Mally shouted as she found yet another stack of the iconic block.

"Unless you plan to butter the Ripping Witch to death, no, those won't be helpful."

"If only they were named Throwing Star or something like that, they would be a lot more useful. I wish she'd made more Bears Claw blocks, and we only have one elephant." Mally said, placing a large stack of blocks they couldn't use on Grandma's sewing machine table. "I have no idea what a Toad in a Puddle or Honeycomb could help us with, but I think we should bring them just in case."

"Anyone or anything that can come alive has my vote," Patch said.

Mally surveyed the stacks spread over the window seat. "We have about a hundred blocks here, Patch, and who knows how many birds this Birds in the Air block will make." She ran her fingers over a complicated block that had thirty-six smaller triangles pieced between four larger triangles. "We may end up with a lot more animals than quilt blocks."

"I agree. If they become real, we'd have quite an army at our backs."

"An army?" Mally asked.

"You are going into battle, little Maker, are you not? We have to destroy the Ripping Witch," he said sharply. "I've tried to ignore it. I've tried to run from it. But there is no other way."

"But does it have to be a war?" Mally's heart raced as she picked up the quilt to resume her stitching. "I just want to save Ms. Bunny and Sunshine and find my grandma."

"And hang everyone else?" Patch growled. "This isn't just your family and friends on the line here, little Maker. The Ripping Witch has destroyed the sun once and she will do it again. She's taken more lives than you can know and she's a danger to everyone and everything in Quilst."

"I know! I hate her for taking them! She's horrible and crazy, but I don't see what I can do against her. She's armed with twelve – no – thirteen pairs of scissors and she's so strong!" Mally's hand shook. "What can I possibly do against her? I'm only ten!"

"Your age has nothing to do with it!" the cat roared in her head. "Can you think? Then you can plan. Can you breathe? Then you can fight! I told you this would be the hardest thing you've ever done, and you thought I meant fixing that quilt, didn't you? I meant the battle to come. The Ripping Witch will never give up and you'd better be ready to wage war against her because that is what it's going to take."

Mally's vision blurred and she struggled to thread her needle. She was silent for a long moment. "I'm scared."

"I know," Patch sighed. "You don't have to do this alone. See all those animals? You'll have plenty of help and you've also got me. And I promise you, little Maker, come stitch or rip, I will always have your back."

Mally dried her eyes and returned to her stitching, and together they plotted their return to Quilst. There was much more on the line now, and the weight on her shoulders felt heavier than ever.

But all she could do was take one stitch at a time.

One stitch led to the next until all the blocks were pieced together and the quilt was whole once more.

By the end, all the fingertips on her left hand were bleeding, her thumb thimble was very worn in, and the light shining against the curtains had begun to fade. Mally had eaten all the food she'd brought up from the kitchen and was wondering if she could sneak back downstairs for some more.

She went to the bathroom to refill her water glass. When she glanced into the mirror, she was startled to see her reflection. Her face was flushed and her hair was a tangled mess around her head, but something had changed in her eyes and the set of her mouth. She couldn't quite put her finger on it until she smiled at herself. Then she realized for the first time in ages, she felt happy.

She was going to save Grandma and Ms. Bunny and Sunshine and with luck she'd be back home by this time tomorrow. Menda would never haunt her dreams again and the world of Quilst would be safe. "We will win," she said to her reflection with a determined smile. She skipped back to the sewing room, and found Patch waiting for her by the window.

"Ready to save the world, Patch?"

"Look who stitched herself up a notch," Patch said. "Ready and waiting, your majesty."

"We're going to save them today," Mally scooped the cat up into her arms and spun around, hugging him tight. "We're going to save everyone! Then I'll come home and everything will be perfect again!"

Mally set the patchwork cat on the edge of the cutting table, then danced over to the window seat and quickly stacked up all the animal quilt blocks. She pulled open the bottom drawer of a nearby cabinet and found Grandma's huge green and purple vegetable sack.

It was big enough to hold a bushel of tomatoes and had thick purple handles to sling over her shoulder. Mally slipped the stack of quilt blocks inside, then she pulled the handles over one shoulder and tested the weight. The blocks were bulky, but thankfully they weren't too heavy.

She'd already packed the yellow shoulder bag with needles, over a dozen spools of thread, and three metal seam rippers. She'd considered bringing the rotary cutter and a small pair of scissors she'd found in a drawer but thought better of it. Menda didn't need any more blades to play with.

She stuffed the smaller bag into the tote and found there was still a lot of space left. She scanned the room and spotted the scrap baskets on the window seat. "You can never have too much fabric," she said, upending the contents of three scrap bins on top. Grandma's sack overflowed with scraps of all shapes and colors and she pushed and tucked to pack it all in.

She slung the sack over her shoulder and grabbed the quilt top off the sewing chair and hauled it all over to the cutting table. She spread Quilst out flat and stared at the surface. Even with the twelve blocks added, it still wasn't a very large quilt.

The row of mountains looked bigger on the horizon. Mally frowned, unable to tell if they were bigger, or it just appeared that way with the new border surrounding the landscape. The largest purple mountain in particular seemed to stretch higher into the sky. Mally did a double take as a dark shape in the middle caught her eye.

"Is that the…" She leaned closer to peer at a dark blue square in the middle of the triangle. "Yes! It's the mountain room where Ms. Bunny and I were trapped. And there's a tiny orange triangle below. It's showing up here on the quilt and I know it wasn't there before."

"She might have made it bigger. Bring me closer, let me see it."

"There's something else. An orange triangle." Mally said, scooting Patch over. "Wait, you don't think that could be Sunshine, do you?"

"A very good possibility. That wouldn't be the first time that evil witch has stitched someone to the side of a mountain to send a message."

"That's horrible! Stitched? She's tied her there with a spider web?"

"Exactly. Do you see anything else? Any sign of the rabbit or your grandma?"

"No… wait! There's something else! The Closed Door block I went through the first time. Uggh! It's surrounded with gray balls of fluff," Mally said, pulling on a tangled bird's nest of broken threads that had appeared on the landscape. The threads stretched off the quilt and she was just reaching for something to cut them free when Patch yelled in her mind.

"That's a snarl! Let it go!"

Mally immediately released the tangled ball. "What? Shouldn't I cut it off? It's right next to the door like it's waiting for us."

149

"Don't cut it. That might be a friend of mine. Remember what I said about the Ripping Witch? If you pull it off the quilt, there's no way we can repair the damage. That's if we can ever figure out how to fix someone that's been shredded to pieces," he added as an afterthought.

"But what about the tornado? I cut off a big chunk of the quilt yesterday. Won't some of your friends be lost now?"

"Maybe. We'll need to save that piece and bring it back into Quilst later if this plan works. Let's use another door. Hopefully she hasn't noticed the extra blocks you added yet."

"I sure hope not. Which door do you think? Up in the sky or underground?"

"I vote for underground. We need to stay completely out of sight until we're ready to attack."

"Good idea," Mally said, running her fingers over the green fabrics. She hadn't had time to repair the rips in the landscape and she could easily see the cutting mat through several holes around the Great Tree.

"I'm worried about these rips Menda made in the quilt. I think layering it with batting might fix the holes. I helped Grandma baste lots of quilts and I don't remember it being too hard."

"Sounds like a plan," Patch said. "I'd help, but you know, I can't move. So I'll just sit here and watch."

Mally searched the sewing room for more fabric and batting. She found a large piece of light blue material that looked bigger than they needed. *Thank goodness! That's one thing I don't have to stitch,* she thought.

Grandma kept packages of batting piled up under the cutting table. She was just checking the size printed on the plastic wrapping when she heard the familiar sound of Dad's truck pulling up outside.

Mally froze, her hands gripping the batting so tight the plastic popped and air hissed out. What if he found her now? They were so close to returning to Quilst. Her mind whirled. Had she cleaned up her crackers in the kitchen? She couldn't remember and suddenly she felt completely terrified. What if he came storming up the stairs?

"Move! Mally, spread out the fabric and batting. NOW!" Patch's voice cut through her terror and she rushed to follow his instructions. She jerked the quilt top off the table and spread out the piece of blue fabric as quickly as she could. It was so big it draped over the edges on all sides.

The truck door slammed loudly outside. Her hands were shaking as she ripped open the package of batting. It was also much too big and seemed to fill the room as she shook out the folds and spread it over the table. A white cascade of fluffy material fell to the floor. If Dad checked this room, he would notice this change. *Will he move the quilt? Will he call the police?* A swirl of questions she couldn't answer danced around her head.

She heard the porch door open downstairs as she scooped the quilt off the floor. She lifted her arms high to snap out the wrinkles and brought it down gracefully in the center of the table. It was perfect. A total of fourteen patchwork quilt blocks ringed the center landscape. Mally wished she had more time to look at it as she quickly ran her hands over the surface, smoothing out the wrinkles

She jumped at the sound of heavy feet pounding up the stairs. "MALLY!" Dad yelled. "Mally, are you here? Mally Lauren Spencer, answer me!"

There was no time to secure the layers of the quilt together with pins or stitching. Just being layered like this would have to be enough. She pulled the heavy tote bag over her shoulder and turned to snatch Patch off the table. Tucking the doll securely under her arm, she twisted the button on the new Closed Door block pieced to the bottom edge of the quilt.

For an agonizing moment she didn't think it would work. Grandma hadn't attached this block to the quilt after all. What if it was something about her, or the button, or maybe magical thread that opened the portal to Quilst?

But she needn't have worried. Just like before, a rush of wind and sound filled her ears as the tiny patchwork door clicked open. She could just make out the sound of Dad shouting and the sewing room door rattling as her bare feet lifted off the floor.

"I'm sorry, Daddy," she whispered. "I'll be right back." She closed her eyes and once again disappeared into the world inside the quilt.

Chapter 9

Never the Same Again

"We're back," Mally whispered. She hugged Patch to her chest as she stepped into a vast chamber with glowing white walls stretching as far as she could see. "At least I think we are. I've never seen this place before."

Mally let Grandma's heavy sack slide off her shoulder. It hit the ground with a resounding thump, and she stretched out her arms in relief. She squinted up at the ceiling and could just make out the Saw-tooth Star quilt block suspended high above like a giant patchwork chandelier.

The pink door she'd traveled through swung shut behind her with a faint click. She turned to find a new Open Door and Closed Door stitched side by side into the white rock wall. She was reaching out to touch a thin vein stitched in the rock when Patch twitched in her arms. First his paws moved, opening and stretching and extending his claws. Then he began pressing his paws rhythmically against her arm.

"Patch! You're making biscuits!" Mally laughed, setting him gently on the floor. Mama had loved it when their old cat Lucy made biscuits for a good hour before settling down for a nap. "We're in the cave, Patch, and it's not dirty or dark at all. I wanted it to be light and clean and perfectly hidden from Menda in every way."

"Hmmph…" Patch's face scrunched in a comical expression and she laughed with relief.

"Yes, I'm sure that was very funny," Patch said. He stood and stretched, shaking out each leg and his tail. He unfurled his wings with a flourish, then he closed his eyes and tripled in size in seconds, back to the size of a small horse which seemed to be his favorite. "I have to commend you on the accommodations, little Maker. You're right, this is a lot better than the cave I would've imagined."

They moved to investigate the walls that seemed to stretch on and on forever. Mally touched the rock. It felt just like the marble countertop her dad installed in someone's kitchen, except it felt warm instead of cold. "Is this fabric or really rock? I honestly can't tell."

"It must be fabric. We're in Quilst after all." Patch swung his head around. "Can you hear that?" A faint, high pitched noise sounded behind them. Mally turned to look but couldn't tell where the sound was coming from.

She noticed Grandma's tote bag had flopped over on its side and she went to turn it the right way up. The noise built as she drew near, a growing rumble reminiscent of Menda's snarls. The bag suddenly swelled and Mally shrank back in alarm. The green fabric stretched, the seams screaming in protest as the sack inflated like a miniature hot air balloon, growing rounder and rounder every second.

With a sound like a gunshot, the sack exploded in a cloud of fabric and frayed threads. Birds burst out of the bag flying in all directions. Mally threw up her hands to shield her face as scraps of cloth shot across the room. The cavern was suddenly filled with so much color, noise, and movement it was like being back in the middle of the tornado.

Patch pressed against her side, unfurling his wings to wrap around them both. Mally peeked around the edge of the blue fabric and watched as colorful animals streamed out of the remains of the bag by the dozen. Triangular birds in all shapes and sizes flew as high as they could before swooping down to circle the cave. Mice ran in all directions, followed by cats in coordinating colors. A swarm of turkeys went berserk, rushing one way, then another, gobbling furiously.

"Looks like part one of our plan worked!" Mally shouted.

"There goes the neighborhood," Patch replied.

"You said we needed an army! I can't believe the blocks made so many animals."

Most of the quilt blocks created several creatures at once. Fluffy hens in every color of the rainbow clucked madly as four matching baby chicks ran in circles around their legs. Mother ducks and ducklings followed, waddling as fast as their webbed feet could manage. Tall roosters flapped their wings and crowed, adding their voices to the cacophony. Foxes, frogs and a single toad leapt out of the way as a huge butterfly shot into the air.

With a deafening roar, a bear rose on his hind legs and stretched his massive blue arms high overhead. Four more bears emerged, sending the mice, chicks and ducklings scrambling to get out of their way. Mally thought the bears were huge, but then the elephant took shape. Unlike most of the animals in the room, her body was a patchwork of different colors, all except her ears which were pink on one side and purple on the other.

Mally was awestruck. The cavern which had seemed so vast when she arrived now felt filled to the brim. Hummingbirds raced overhead with a sound like helicopter blades, followed by a swarm of bees which must have sprung from the honeycomb blocks she'd found under Grandma's sewing table. Finally, the flood of new animals seemed to slow as a band of monkeys emerged one by one.

They moved a bit slower than the rest so Mally could get a better look at them. Their bodies were pieced from whatever fabrics had been in their blocks, which were mostly two solid colors.

Each had a Monkey Wrench quilt block pieced to their chest, paws, face, or back like a birth mark. Unlike Sunshine who hadn't had eyes, feet, or a mouth when she first came alive, all of the animals in the room were fully formed and they were all talking, shouting, and laughing as loud as they could.

I must have imagined them as real animals this time, Mally thought dazedly.

Something tickled her bare leg and she let out a little shriek. But it was only a tiny yellow mouse with a white Cat and Mouse quilt block pieced to her back. The mouse was trying to get Mally's attention, pressing her little paws against her bare feet.

Mally bent down and held out her hands and the mouse leapt onto her palm. Standing up on her hind legs, the mouse spoke in a surprisingly loud, clear voice. Mally had been expecting a high-pitched squeak.

"Mally Maker, I'm Goldie, First Mouse. We are assembled and prepared to scout ahead. We plan to find the exit to this cavern, then split into groups to search the mountains for Ms. Bunny and Sunshine and the wider reaches for your grandma."

"Oh, okay!" Mally said, slightly taken aback by how fast everything was moving. "Perfect!"

"Where shall we send our reports?"

"Um…" Mally looked at Patch and he shrugged. "I guess send information here for now. Just make sure everyone knows to stay out of sight, and don't rip a single stitch of this world. Menda will immediately know we're here if anything is broken."

Goldie gave a crisp salute and vaulted off Mally's hands. She landed in the middle of a veritable swarm of mice. They immediately shot for the far end of the cavern. The sound of their tiny paws hitting the floor echoed through the cave, like a steady drumroll and the ground trembled lightly under Mally's feet.

"That's a lot of mice," Patch said.

"Yeah, I would hate to see what happens to the cat that chases them." Mally smiled.

"Might we beeee of service?" A swarm of honey bees buzzed over, speaking in unison. "Weeee can fly up to the mountain to check the triangle you saw. Single file, weeee will beeee very hard to seeee. Then weeee will send word, one beeeeeee to the next beeeeeee."

"Yes, please!" Mally said, and the bees buzzed away immediately, following the mice. The crowd had gone quiet, watching the animals leave. Suddenly the patchwork elephant stepped forward and bowed to Mally. Her ears flapped, stirring the air enough to send several chickens and their matching baby chicks tumbling across the floor. Her regal head rose slowly, her long trunk towering over Mally and she spoke with a soft voice just barely over a whisper.

"Mally the Maker, I am Thimble, and on behalf of all the animals you've created, I offer our sincerest thanks for making us real."

"But I didn't make you," Mally said, confused. "Grandma stitched the blocks–"

"But you brought us through the door. You imagined us being real and here we are, able to walk and talk and laugh and play. You are our Maker."

Mally's face flushed as Thimble bowed her head again. With a great rustle of shifting bodies, all the creatures in the cavern followed suit. Bears, monkeys, turkeys, foxes, chickens, ducks and frogs lowered their heads. The birds in the air suddenly swirled into a tight circle. Flying in unison, they nearly blocked out the light from the star in the ceiling.

"I... I don't know what to say," Mally pressed her hands to her mouth, completely awestruck. Then she remembered the words Mama drilled into her head constantly when she was little. "Thank you. Thank you all so much."

With a great rustle of wings, the birds broke formation and light flooded the cavern once more. The animals rose silently to their full height. All eyes remained fixed on Mally and she had to clench her hands together behind her back to stop them from shaking.

"I guess we should start with why you're here?" Mally asked nervously.

"We're here to save Ms. Bunny!" four purple ducklings called from a few feet away, perched on the back of a coordinating pink and purple duck.

"Sunshine! We're here to save her too!" the birds in the air chanted.

"Your grandma is also missing," Thimble said. "The Maker of Quilst needs to be found."

"There's an evil witch to destroy!" a giant black and white bear roared and several animals broke into applause.

"And a world to repair." A small green monkey stepped forward, carrying the yellow bag Mally had packed with supplies.

"Oh, thank you! Yes, there are lots of seams to mend." Mally slipped the strap over her shoulder and unzipped the bag. She pulled out several spools of thread and a pack of needles and handed them to the monkey. "Please share the needles and thread and fix any ripped seams you find. I brought a lot of scraps with me and they're all over the floor so gather them up and use them any way you need to."

A murmur ran through the crowd and suddenly Goldie was back. Mally held out her hands and the small mouse easily vaulted off the back of a teal fox and landed with a flourish on her open palm.

"We have found the exit, Mally Maker. The cave extends fifty feet and narrows into a tunnel. The tunnel continues for approximately one hundred feet, then emerges behind the waterfall."

"Oh, that's perfect! Is the entrance hidden?" Mally asked excitedly.

"Yes, the opening is concealed completely. One additional note, it is growing dark outside. I personally climbed the cliff to check the sky myself."

"Getting dark? How? How could Menda rip off all three Suns already?" Many of the animals shifted nervously and a swarm of baby chicks scurried to hide under a handful of fluffy hens.

"No, two moons are rising in the east over the original Open Door. The three Suns are setting in the west," Goldie said, gesturing with her tiny paws to illustrate the change in Quilst.

"We have nighttime now?" Mally glanced at Patch and he shrugged.

"It might be that you pieced both blocks in one quilt, or it could be where you placed them in the border. It's to our advantage, little Maker. I know it will throw the Ripping Witch for a loop and it will be much easier to move undetected while it's dark."

"I guess that means it's time to go," Mally said as Goldie jumped back to the ground. "I want to start with the triangle on the mountain first."

"If you think that's the best place to start. Personally, I think it's a trap," Patch said.

"It may beeee a trap, but that is Sunshine." A single honey bee had returned. "Mally the Maker, weeee formed a beeeeeee train and flew to the mountain. It is Sunshine. All beeeeeees confirm it."

"That settles it." Mally climbed onto Patch's back, shifting the yellow bag so it fit comfortably against her hip. She gripped the green star she'd help piece between his shoulder blades. Her heart raced wildly in her chest, but her voice came out steady as she spoke loudly to the crowd, "We're going to save Sunshine. It's getting dark outside and this is the perfect time to cut her free and learn what we can about Menda and what she's planning."

"But won't the Ripping Witch find out we're here?" a turquoise cat called.

"That's a risk I'm willing to take. I wouldn't leave any of you stitched to the side of a mountain if I could do something about it. I have to save her, and I need your help." Mally looked up at the massive flock circling overhead. "Can the birds pieced from the darkest colors come with us? If you fly around Patch and me, that might hide us from view." Immediately the purple, blue, black, brown, and dark green birds broke away from the rest and soared to the far end of the cavern.

"But we want to help too! How can we help?" voices called in all directions.

"You can all help!" Patch roared. "We need information, and the more the better. We need to know where the Ripping Witch is and what she's doing. Mouse?" He searched for Goldie in the crowd.

"Take all the mice up to the mountain. With night coming and so much altered in Quilst, I'd bet that crazy witch is holed up inside. Sneak in and whatever you do, don't get caught. She can and will slice you to ribbons so don't give her a chance. Stay in the shadows and keep out of sight. Send reports with the birds so everyone knows what's going on."

"It will be done," Goldie declared and with a flick of her tail, she was gone.

Mally caught Patch's line of thinking. "It would be good to know where the snarls are and how many. Can the rest of you scout the landscape?"

"It will need to be the darker colors," Patch pointed out. "Anyone who can move silently and is pieced in black, purple, brown or blue can leave the cave.

"But what about the brightest and biggest of us?" A hot pink bear called from the back. "Do you want us to just sit and twiddle our claws?"

"There is always a solution if you're creative." With that, Patch closed his eyes and began to grow. Mally gripped his back tightly as his body quivered and suddenly Patch was back to the size of Dad's pickup truck. "If you are too big, think small thoughts. If you are too small, think big thoughts. If your colors are too bright, ride on the back of someone darker. If you want to be useful, you can find a way."

The animals stared with wide eyes as Patch gave a lazy stretch. His wings snapped wide, then straight up into the air and Mally smiled to see him showing them off. You'd never know he didn't want those wings stitched on to begin with.

"We'll send word with the birds! Good luck!" Mally called. She'd been itching to move since they'd stepped through the door. Patch must have been feeling the same because he brought his huge wings down in a sweeping arc and suddenly they were in the air, soaring through the cavern. Mally let out a *whoop* of joy. No more waiting. No more stitching. It was time to save her friends!

The cave stretched on and on for what felt like miles. As the space narrowed, Patch shrank in size until he was back to the size of a horse.

"This way Mally Maker!" A red and green mouse was waving at them from the ground.

Patch landed lightly next to the mouse and they followed him through a tight tunnel that twisted and turned so many times Mally wasn't sure it would ever end. They were rounding yet another switchback when she picked up a faint rustling sound in the distance. Patch hunched down to wiggle through a tight bend in the tunnel and suddenly the end was in sight.

Silvery light peeked through the waterfall. Patch carried her to the edge of the tunnel and Mally stuck her hands into the stream of rustling fabrics. The fabric strips flowing over her palms felt cool and refreshing, but like all the water in Quilst, it was not actually wet.

"It seems I'll never be able to enjoy this waterfall in proper light. The last time I saw it was after Menda had ripped off the sun. And now it's nighttime!"

"Something to look forward to, little Maker. Now, where is the exit?" Patch asked the mouse.

"Just climb through here to reach the top of the cliff." Mally followed his pointing paw and found an even tinier tunnel angling to the right.

"I have a better idea. Hang on!" With that, Patch sprang through the middle of the waterfall, sending fabrics flying in all directions.

Mally laughed as the soft cloth brushed past her face. She caught a few scraps as they broke through the barrier, then looked back to watch the waterfall shrinking rapidly below.

She stuffed the scraps into her bag as Patch took them higher, soaring up above the trees. Goldie had been correct. Two moons hung in the sky over the Open Door, casting a silver glow over the landscape of Quilst. Miles of green hills and dense patches of trees stretched out before them, leading up to the largest purple mountain in the distance. With a rush of wings, a flock of dark birds surrounded them.

"Hi, Mally Maker! Night Company at your service!"

"We're the best flyers in Quilst!"

"And we're going to save Sunshine! Wheee!"

It seemed many of the birds shared Sunshine's cheerful personality, but they were all business when it came to hiding them from view.

One by one the flying geese landed on Patch's back and wings and pressed their dark fabrics over his bright orange body. Soon the cat looked like he'd been covered in a triangle patterned slipcover. Mally tried not to laugh as a handful of geese attached themselves to his tail, their points lined up perfectly end to end.

A few birds landed on her shoulders and expanded in size to block her hair and face from reflecting the moonlight. They angled their wings so she could still see clearly in all directions.

Not that there was much to look at. More birds surrounded them in tight rings until she could barely see anything except dark triangles against the even darker sky.

A black and blue bird fluttered down to land on her shoulder and spoke clearly in her ear, "Hi Mally Maker, I'm Midnight. I'm going to perch here on your shirt just in case something goes wrong. It's always good to have a backup plan, right?"

"Right," Mally said nervously.

A faint buzzing sounded in her ear and she whipped her head around to find three tiny honeybees hovering nearby. "Mally Maker, weeee bring a warning. Threeee beeeeeees have entered the mountain and not returned. This may beeee a trap."

"Exactly what I was saying," Patch grumbled, his ears pulling back against his head.

"What can you tell us? How is Sunshine?"

"Weeee cannot tell. Sheeee is stitched in place. Weeee saw two lines tying her to the mountainside. You will neeeed to cut her freeee."

"Then Menda will know we're here." Mally bit her lip, considering. "You said the bees have disappeared? Where? What happened?"

"The beeeeeeees entered the window in the purple mountain. Beeee careful Mally Maker. Weeee will beeee close by if you need us."

"Thank you!" Mally whispered as they disappeared into the night. She watched the purple mountain slowly growing closer and closer with each beat of Patch's wings. She could just barely make out a tiny orange triangle in the middle below a dark blue square.

The sight of the window in the mountain made her stomach twist.

She'd risked her neck jumping out of that window, and she had no desire to go anywhere near it again. But it also broke her heart to think of Sunshine stitched in place and unable to move.

"What's the plan, little Maker?" Patch asked. "Any chance we can avoid flying straight into a trap?"

"Easy for you to say. You're not lashed to the side of a mountain!" Mally countered.

"If I might make a suggestion," Midnight broke in. "If we fly in low and don't attract any attention, we might be able to cut Sunshine free without anyone knowing we're here."

"Perfect!" Mally said. She rooted through the yellow bag at her hip and pulled out a silver seam ripper.

"That's assuming nothing goes wrong." Patch angled his wings to take them into a dive. "Ever heard of Murphy's law?"

Mally ignored him. Her heart beat wildly in her throat and she found it difficult to breathe against the wind rushing in her face.

The mountain was suddenly upon them, purple fabric glowing strangely in the moonlight. Patch flew so low Mally felt the yarn grass on the landscape brush against her toes. Then with another sweep of his wings, they were soaring back up once again, flying nearly parallel with the side of the mountain.

Mally gripped her seam ripper tightly, her eyes on Sunshine. The bird had been stitched facing the mountain, the light from her body blocked by the purple fabric. Patch spread his wings wide and stopped about twenty feet below the bird.

"Show time, little Maker," Patch whispered. "I'll take you up slow and steady. Be ready to rip those stitches."

They rose in small flutters, completely silent now. Midnight squeezed her shoulder. Mally rose to her feet and balanced on Patch's back with difficulty. The dark flying geese camouflaged his orange fabrics so perfectly she could barely tell where he ended and empty air began.

Another small flutter of wings and the bottom edge of Sunshine's triangles were finally within reach. Mally barely had time to take in the line of crude zigzag stitches lashing her friend to the mountain. She set the tip of the blade against Sunshine's wings and pulled straight across.

ZZZIIIPPPPP! The stitches split easily down the line.

Blinding light suddenly flooded the darkness as the air filled with an ear splitting screech. Sunshine thrashed against the mountain. The top edge of her wings was still firmly attached. She twisted and bucked, her bright little body flashing like a strobe light.

"SHHHH! Sunshine! It's me!" Mally whispered loudly, but the bird couldn't possibly hear her over the racket she was making. She tried pressing her hands to her friend's back, but it only made matters worse. Sunshine hollered louder than ever, her glittery legs kicking viciously.

Mally had just caught hold of her wings when she felt something huge emerge from the window in the mountain. It brushed past her hair as it passed and she ducked, releasing Sunshine.

"Gig's up! We've got company!" Patch roared. Mally's stomach plummeted as they dropped out of the sky. Time slowed as she hovered in that place between falling and flying, still standing upright on Patch's back. He pulled out of the dive long enough for her to scramble down and hook her legs in front of his wings, and then they were off, diving away from the mountain.

Mally craned her neck to keep Sunshine in view. Instead she caught sight of the creature pursuing them. It had wings like a bat, but a huge circular body that was strangely flat when she caught sight of it from the side. Light from the two moons reflected off the round pink body and all the hair on Mally's arms suddenly stood on end.

"Web! It's a spider web with wings!" she yelled, gripping Patch's back tightly. Her skin crawled with the memory of the wiggling threads weaving through her clothes. If it got hold of them, there would be no escape.

"That's a bat! Hang on tight," Patch said. "Focus on Sunshine. Birds, protect the Maker at all costs."

His wings beat fiercely, taking them high into the air. He abruptly banked to the left, changing direction so rapidly Mally had to wrap her arms around his neck to keep from falling off. The bat had smaller wings and couldn't change course as quickly.

The birds flanking them immediately fell back and formed a solid wall with their dark wings. Midnight squeezed Mally's shoulder and whispered, "He's working around for another pass. Be ready to rip her free."

Mally nodded, focusing on Sunshine's bright shape. They were nearly there when a strong gust of wind blasted in her face. Her hair whipped across her eyes and a violent squawking filled her ears.

"What happened?" She clawed her face clear and turned to look back. Dozens of flying geese had vanished from the sky. Only a handful remained, beating their wings quickly to catch up with Patch.

"On your left!" Midnight shouted, jerking her attention back to the mountain.

"Sunshine! It's me, Mally! Hold still!" Mally yelled. Patch slowed the tiniest amount, but they were moving too fast to properly rip out the line of stitches. On impulse Mally stabbed the blade into the purple mountain, then angled it quickly to cut a long gash in the surface.

RRRRIIIIIPPPPPP!

A horrible, piercing scream split the night air. It was coming from the mountain room. The sound made the hair on the back of Mally's neck stand on end. It was the same sound she'd heard before the tornado destroyed the Open Door. Menda was here.

She gritted her teeth and tried to angle the seam ripper to cut the line of stitching locking Sunshine to the mountain.

She missed.

The blade slid smoothly through the purple fabric and across the top edge of Sunshine's wings. The bird shrieked in pain, smacking Mally in the face so hard, she dropped the seam ripper. It bounced off the side of the mountain and spun out of sight.

Everything was happening too fast. Mally just barely had time to grab hold of the little bird before they were past the mountain. Patch carried them up into the sky in a climb so steep it made Mally's ears pop.

Sunshine was wriggling in her grip. She lashed out with her beak, biting at Mally's hands.

"Sunshine! It's me, Mally! You can't fly! I cut your wings, I'm so sorry!" But nothing she said did any good. Dimly she was aware of their pursuit and Patch's erratic flight, but her attention was entirely focused on the little bird, now screeching on the top of her lungs.

"Can't you shut her up?" Patch roared.

"She won't stop! It's like she doesn't know who I am!" Mally cried desperately.

"Hold her down then! Cover up her infernal light!"

Mally pulled Sunshine into a tight hug, muffling her cries against her shirt. The bird continued to struggle, her light flashing like a beacon in the darkness. Midnight let out a short cry and three flying geese lifted off Patch's back and wrapped their wings around Mally's shoulders. Their dark fabrics blocked Sunshine's light completely and darkness enveloped them once again.

As her eyes adjusted, Mally was suddenly aware of how fast they were flying. The landscape raced by at a sickening speed. Patch abruptly changed direction and sped between two mountains.

Mally looked back to find the bat monster still on their tail, and worse yet, it had grown bigger. Moonlight reflected off the creature's body which had expanded to fifteen feet across at least. The spider web in the center had turned black and nearly blended into the dark sky.

Mally frowned, wondering how it could have grown so large so quickly. That particular pink color reminded her of something too, but she couldn't put her finger on it. As she watched, one of the birds perched on Patch's back took flight. It joined with the remaining birds in the air and together they attacked the monster's wings.

It appeared to work for a few seconds and the distance between them grew. But then a thick rope shot out and whipped through the air.

"Watch out!" Mally called, but it was too late. The frayed ends of the cord caught the bird's wings and like all the ropes Menda made, immediately wove through their fabrics. The birds struggled, fluttering helplessly as they were pulled inexorably into the center of the spider web. The black area in the center of the monster expanded and Mally understood.

"It's eating the birds!" she screamed, horrified.

Midnight squeezed her shoulder. "We need a place to hide. Quick!"

"The house in the sky! Patch take us up!"

"Not with that monster on our tail! We have to lose it first," the cat argued, diving for the ground. "I have an idea. Just keep that bird quiet and her light off!"

Patch was heading straight for a small blue mountain. Mally squeezed Sunshine tight as the dark peak rushed closer and closer. She tucked her head, ready for a crash.

At the last second Patch changed course. His left wing skimmed the side of the mountain as they swung in a tight arc around the patchwork. He changed course again, flying even closer to the next mountain.

"Get ready! Hold on tight!"

Patch pulled out of the dive abruptly and they slammed to a stop on the side of a dark blue mountain. Mally gasped as the bones in her body rattled with the impact. But she didn't let go of Sunshine. She clung to Patch's back and hugged the little bird even tighter to her chest. The flying geese already covering Patch silently expanded their wings to cover her completely.

"Don't make a sound," Patch breathed.

Mally squeezed her eyes shut and thought, *We're invisible. Just fly past. We're invisible. You can't see us. Go away! Go away! Go away!*

A gust of wind blew past her hair and she resisted the urge to turn and look. A faint sound reached her ears and she had to clamp her jaw shut to stop from retching. It was the same sound the spider web threads had made as they wormed through her hair. The sound faded into the distance, returned for a time, then faded into the distance again.

Sunshine twisted in her grip, still fighting furiously to break free. Mally pressed the little bird firmly against her shirt, ignoring the digs from her sharp claws.

Several long minutes passed. No one moved or spoke.

Without warning a high pitched shriek cut through the silence, making them all jump. The sound was coming from far away, but it still made Mally's heart race wildly in her chest. Menda was out there, furious and vengeful, and she knew they were back in Quilst.

Mally was so distracted by the thought, she missed the faint buzz of bees until they were right next to her ear.

"Weeee bring news from the mount–"

Mally gasped, shaking her head reflexively to knock the bugs away. She caught herself just in time and didn't move her hands. Sunshine remained locked tight in her arms.

"Sorry!" she whispered as loud as she dared. A few birds had been dislodged with her movement and she'd sent the bees tumbling in all directions as well.

They buzzed back to her and quickly gave their report. "Weeee saw the bat return to the mountain. Menda has retreated inside. The skies are freeee."

"Oh, thank goodness!" Mally let out a gasp of relief.

"We still need a place to hide," Patch spoke quietly. Birds were still pressed over his face so only his eyes shone in the moonlight. "Sunshine's wings need work."

"The house in the sky?" Mally suggested.

"That will work. Bees keep watch and let us know if anything changes."

"It will beeee done."

They took flight at once. Patch was clearly not taking any chances on another bat attack. He flew as high and as fast as he could, and Mally kept her eyes peeled for any sign of movement. But they met no monsters and saw no other sign of Menda as they rose through the air.

The mountain peaks had shrunk to the size of pinpricks when Patch's wings finally changed rhythm. Mally was relieved to see the little orange house nestled between the new set of door blocks, exactly as she'd pieced the top border of the quilt. The flight had seemed endless and she itched to be *doing* something. Anything was better than hiding, sitting still or thinking about all the ways that rescue had gone wrong.

Patch landed heavily on a narrow strip of gray fabric. In a rush of wings, the flying geese shielding them rose into the air and flew in a tight circle around the house. Mally shook her head gently. It felt like she'd been wearing a hat and now missed the light weight on her head.

Midnight fluttered off her shoulder too. "Mally Maker, we need to inform the others that Sunshine has been rescued, and that the Ripping Witch knows we've returned."

"Oh… okay. Thank you so much for your help tonight." Mally gazed at the birds still circling the cabin. There were only two dozen dark flying geese left. "I'm so sorry. We lost so many."

Midnight closed his eyes for a long moment, then he lifted his head and spoke quickly, "I'll leave Night Company with you for when you're ready to return. Send any messages with Twilight or Evening and I'll return with news from Quilst as soon as possible." He rested a wing briefly on Sunshine's back, but the bird flinched away, her angry shrieks muffled by Mally's shirt.

"You might want to try a smaller size," Patch suggested as Midnight prepared to leave. "I know the bees said the witch retreated, but you can never be too careful."

With a quick nod, Midnight took to the air. He shrank to the size of a moth in seconds and disappeared into the night.

Mally slipped to the ground clumsily, her arms still locked firmly around Sunshine. She paused to take in the new patchwork doors rising on either side of the little house. She wished she'd imagined the squishy gray ground stretching a bit further. They had barely six feet of space to stand before the fabric ended abruptly. If you weren't paying attention, you could step right off the edge into empty air.

Patch let out a long sigh of relief and slowly began to shrink. She caught his eye as he settled into the size of a great dane. He looked as exhausted and sad as she felt.

"Do you know what's wrong with her?" Mally asked, indicating the bird still struggling in her grip.

"I have a pretty good idea. Let's get inside."

They entered the cabin and Mally instantly felt at home. Soft chairs were arranged around a crackling fire on the far side of the room. A small table and more chairs were nestled under a window she was sure would be filled with warm sunshine in the daytime. A ladder led to an overhead loft and Mally longed to explore every nook and cranny of the comfortable space.

But it was time to help her friend.

"Hi Sunshine. It's me, Mally," she spoke quietly as she set the bird on the table.

Sunshine immediately lashed out at her hands, slapping and kicking.

Patch's paw shot out and caught hold of one wing. Sunshine twisted against his grip and let out an ear piercing screech. Mally grabbed her other wing and stared at her exposed belly. Words were stitched there in black block letters that seemed to glow against the white cloth.

SHE WILL NEVER BE THE SAME AGAIN

"What? What is this?!" Mally cried. "She stitched this onto you! Oh, Sunshine, I'm so sorry!" Tears poured down her face as Sunshine continued to thrash against their hold.

"That's a curse web. Classic Ripping Witch entertainment." Patch growled, his ears pulled back. "She won't be herself again until you rip it out, every last stitch."

Mally nodded. She wiped her eyes with the back of her sleeve and pulled out a new seam ripper from her bag. Patch gripped Sunshine's wings as Mally carefully removed the letters one stitch at a time. The thread she ripped free was cold to the touch and Mally felt her own mind wandering down a dark path as she held a long strand in her hand. *This is all my fault*, she thought. *At least a hundred birds were killed tonight because of me. Sunshine is in pain because of me.*

Patch flicked his tail, smacking her arm hard and she dropped the thread. Suddenly her head was clear again.

She pulled the remaining threads free and wadded them into a ball. Without giving it a second thought, she ran across the room and threw the ball into the fire. She wasn't sure if it would burn, but as soon as the fibers hit the flame, they went bright white and disappeared.

There was a sob from behind and Mally turned to find Sunshine curled into a ball on the table, her wings wrapped tightly around her tiny body.

"Sunshine? Are you okay?" She asked gently. "You should feel better now, I ripped all those bad stitches out."

But it seemed removing the words had had the reverse effect on her friend.

"No. No. No," she moaned, rocking back and forth. "Oh, Mally, no."

"What is it? What's wrong?" Mally said desperately.

"There's nothing you can do." Sunshine lifted her head to look straight into Mally's eyes. "I watched it all and it was the most horrible thing. She made me. She made me watch her ripping."

"Who?" Patch demanded. His voice made Mally jump. She hadn't realized she'd been whispering.

"I wish I could have done something, but I couldn't. I'm so sorry Mally. I felt so terrible and she stitched my head so I couldn't move and had to see it all."

Mally looked from Sunshine to Patch, a cold understanding starting to sink in. "What? What is she talking about?"

Sunshine answered. "She ripped Ms. Bunny apart. She's in pieces. She'll never be the same again."

Chapter 10

Battle for Quilst

Mally found she had very scattered memories of what happened next in the house in the sky. She must have stitched Sunshine's wing and come up with a plan with Patch, but all she could remember clearly were the words stitched in block letters: She. Will. Never. Be. The. Same. Again.

She couldn't escape this curse. Despite the stitches being ripped away, she kept seeing them, and worse she could hear Menda's voice whispering them in her head.

The only saving grace was a tiny hopeful thought in the back of her mind. What if this could all be a trick? What if Menda cursed Sunshine into seeing something that didn't happen? Then Ms. Bunny would be fine, right? Menda had made that awful spider web in the mountain room and Mally had relived all her worst memories again, so that must be something the witch could do to everyone.

But then she'd see the words again and couldn't be sure. All she knew is she had to find her best friend, and fast.

*   *   *   *   *

They set off as soon as Sunshine's wings were repaired. Mally pulled the door shut, thinking that under any other circumstance she would have loved to sit by the fire and explore the little cabin. But she only wanted to leave this place and the memories it held as fast as possible.

She turned to find Midnight waiting with Patch on the strip of gray fabric. The cat had expanded his size once again and the Night Company had already covered his body and wings.

"We'll see you at the meeting?" Midnight was asking.

"Yes, we'll be there," Patch replied, and the bird dove off the gray strip of fabric and disappeared instantly into the night.

Sunshine perched on Patch's neck, her wings still wrapped tightly around her body. She had barely spoken a word after revealing what she'd seen and now she stared at the two moons in the distance with a blank expression that made Mally want to cry.

But the time for tears was over. Mally joined them, unzipping the yellow bag at her hip. She picked up the little bird and gave her a hug.

"It'll be okay. We'll find her and fix everything. I promise," she said.

Sunshine ducked her head. "I didn't want my light to give us away. I know I can fly, I just don't want her to see us."

"That's fine. You can ride inside my bag and rest." Mally said, holding it open so Sunshine could settle herself inside.

"So where to next, little Maker?" Patch asked.

Mally zipped the bag shut with a jerk. "I think you know exactly where we're going." She slid the strap gently over her shoulder and crossed her arms.

Patch raised one scrappy eyebrow by way of a reply.

"What? It's dark. We'll sneak in. She won't be expecting a counter attack this soon."

"Maybe, but maybe not."

Mally sighed. "What's your point, cat?"

"I'm not going to sugar coat it for you. We took a beating tonight and we're lucky everything worked out as well as it did. We might not be so lucky next time."

"I know, I just can't stand it, Patch!" Mally cried. "Is it true? Is Ms. Bunny in pieces, or was that just the curse web?"

"I honestly don't know. Look, you just released an army of soldiers, scouts, and spies." Patch said. "Midnight returned twice with updates and things are looking good for us. There's a meeting planned. Let's at least hear all they've found before rushing straight into the witch's lair."

Mally scanned the landscape far below, her eyes searching for the largest mountain in the center. *Ms. Bunny is there*, she thought. *I have to save her.*

Then she thought of the beautiful flock of birds that had joined them to save Sunshine. Less than twenty-four remained. How many more animals would be lost if they went into battle against Menda? Would anyone survive?

"You won't do Ms. Bunny any good if you get caught too," Patch said quietly, as if he could read her thoughts.

"Thank you, Captain Obvious."

"This isn't a joke, little Maker," Patch growled. "If you get caught, there isn't anyone else who can do this. We have no idea where your grandma is, no one knows you're here, and Menda can shred through anything made of cloth with a single thought. All the animals you've created, every last bird, cat, and bear could be gone by this time tomorrow if we make the wrong move."

"Fine," Mally snapped, climbing onto his back. "But no matter what they say, I'm going back to the mountain tonight."

A rush of wings ruffled her hair as the remaining flying geese settled over Patch's face. Three birds arranged themselves over Mally's head and she suddenly wondered what they were thinking. Were they angry all those birds were torn apart? Did they blame her? Guilt twisted in her belly as Patch dove into the air.

As they soared over the landscape Mally searched for any sign of the spider web bats. She almost wanted it to attack.

Come and get me, she thought, gripping a seam ripper in each hand. It was so much easier to feel angry than guilty. *I'm going to rip you all apart.*

They met nothing on the flight. Mally was surprised to see the huge branches of the Great Tree, silhouetted against the bright moons.

"Why are we meeting here? Why not the Cavern?" she asked.

"Midnight and Twilight said most of the animals are still scouting the landscape. They didn't find any sign of the Ripping Witch here so this seemed like a good place for the leaders to meet."

"Did they find Grandma? Was she inside?" Even after everything that had happened, Mally found she was still holding onto a thread of hope that Grandma was here. If only she could help her find Ms. Bunny and repair all the damage Menda had done.

But his answer wasn't surprising, "No, there hasn't been any sign of her."

Patch circled the enormous trunk as they descended, then landed with a soft bounce on the end of the Nature Path. With another rush of soft wings, the Night Company birds detached themselves from Patch's fabrics and soared off to circle the Great Tree.

"Thank you!" Mally whispered, waving to the birds that had covered her hair. She slipped to the ground and her chest immediately constricted. Just a few feet away the path was bunched in a messy knot. Her mind flashed back to being pulled down the hill by the snarl's rope. That was where Ms. Bunny had saved her. That was the last place she'd seen her friend.

Her heart pounded as she searched the landscape and the edge of the trees for any sign of movement. A flash of silver glimmered on the ground nearby. Mally bent down and found it was the little pencil sharpener blade Ms. Bunny had used to cut her free. It was such a small thing, but knowing Ms. Bunny was the last person to touch it made Mally feel closer to her somehow.

"Come and look at this, little Maker," Patch called as she tucked the blade into her back pocket.

He'd shrunk to the size of a leopard and was pressing his paws against a ripped seam on the landscape. A tuft of white fiber glowed in the moonlight between the frayed fabrics.

Mally squatted down to look closer. The stitches had been ripped cleanly between two hills, but now squishy batting filled the gap. She pressed against it and her hands sank several inches into the ground.

"It worked," she said. "You can't fall into these traps anymore."

"One less thing to worry about," Patch said. "But this could still trip you up if you weren't paying attention."

"But it's a lot better than falling into an endless pit of darkness. Trust me – I know," she said, rising to her feet. Side by side, they walked up the hill to the base of the Great Tree. Mally couldn't help contrasting this easy stroll with the last time they were here.

Almost everything was different this time. Instead of total darkness, she was walking up a hill bathed in the light of two moons she'd stitched on the quilt herself. Hundreds of birds nested in the tree

174

branches above. Their angular bodies stood out against the soft curves of the appliquéd tree.

The light emanating from the tree had changed as well. All the windows blazed so bright she had to shield her eyes with her hands as they drew near. A dark shape was silhouetted against the strong light and an unfamiliar voice growled.

"Mally the Maker?"

"Um, yes?" Mally said. A massive black bear stepped out of the darkness, the top of his head nearly brushing the lowest branches of the tree. A white Bears Claw block blazed across his broad chest.

"I am Seam, sentry of the Great Tree. All of the First Made have assembled and are ready to report. Come inside and the meeting can begin."

The bear pressed a knot in the tree trunk and a door opened. They stepped inside and Mally gasped. She wasn't sure what she'd been expecting. Maybe another large room like the Cavern, but with wooden textured walls instead of rock. What she found was shocking. It was the Best Treehouse in the World, exactly as she'd imagined it more than a year ago.

The inside of the tree was hollowed out forming a huge circular room. She craned her neck to look up, way, way up, and could see the trunk open to the night sky. In the middle, a braided spiral staircase rose majestically to the upper floors. Brightly colored birds in all shapes and sizes illuminated the walls. A flock of ducks and ducklings skittered through the room, nearly blinding Mally as lights flashed from every direction.

"I hope you don't mind," Seam said. "We needed light and those ducks found the glitter thread. I'm afraid they went overboard decorating all the birds, but at least we're not sitting here in the dark."

"Of course I don't mind," Mally said, shaking her head slowly in awe. "It's exactly the way I imagined it." She touched the railing of the spiral staircase. It was braided from dozens of brown yarns with two golden threads woven through the middle. She loved the texture each little bump of fiber made in the chain and how the surface felt both strong and soft at the same time.

Mally unzipped the bag at her hip.

"Sunshine, why don't you join these birds?" she suggested gently.

"Okay, yeah, that sounds good." Sunshine hopped out of the bag and flew up to a nearby wall to nest between two pink flying geese.

Seam wasn't exaggerating. The birds really had gone overboard with the light, but it was glorious to see every nook and cranny of the huge space. It was hard to believe everything here from the square tiles on the floor to the tree rings stitched on the ceiling had been made with fabric and thread. The furniture looked like it was crafted from solid wood. She had to examine it closely to find the grain line was actually embroidered on the surface.

She'd imagined this big central room split into little nooks, each space flowing seamlessly into the next. She'd drawn cutaway pictures with a comfortable place to sew in front of a wide, curving window. There it was, a beautiful alcove filled with soft armchairs and low cabinets to hold sewing supplies. She wandered over and pulled open a red drawer. It was packed with thread in every color of the rainbow.

The sewing space flowed smoothly into a reading area with a large chaise lounge and pillows piled up on the floor. Next came the resting nook. Mally pushed the corner of a bed suspended in the air with thick green ropes. A quilt with pink flower blocks was draped messily over the surface. It looked like the perfect spot to take a nap.

She froze. The fabric on the quilt was pink calico with small white dots, the same fabric as Ms. Bunny's dress. Her brain made another sudden connection. It was exactly the same color as the monster they'd met in the night. She jerked her hand from the swing as if it burned.

The last nook was dominated by a massive table. When she'd first imagined the inside of the Great Tree, she'd wanted this table to be big enough for her whole family including all her cousins, aunts, and uncles.

Yeah, I think it's big enough. Mally thought, her eyes widening at the sight.

Dozens of patchwork animals surrounded the table. Monkeys, cats, frogs, bears, and birds of every variety sat, crouched, or stood in chairs, or on the table itself, all watching as she approached. With a flutter of dark wings Twilight soared past and perched on the back of a chair next to Midnight.

Mally wrapped her arms around her chest, suddenly unsure of herself. Something nudged her in the back.

"Move, little Maker. Sit down so the meeting can start," Patch said under his breath.

"But there's only the chair at the head of the table left." Mally whispered back. She'd never sat at the head of a table, ever, except if you counted Thanksgiving when she sat at the narrow end of the kiddy table with her cousins.

"Yeah, that's yours. Sit."

Mally's face burned as she awkwardly slid out the remaining chair and sat down quickly. She twisted her fingers together in her lap to stop her hands from shaking as everyone continued to stare at her.

"I, Seam, sentry of the Great Tree, call this First Meeting of Firsts to order." Seam roared, making Mally jump. He clapped his huge paws together three times, then retreated to his post by the door.

"First Meeting of Firsts?" Mally asked, confused.

"The first you made, Mally Maker," Thimble said softly. The elephant filled the opposite side of the table, her colorful body standing out against the brown walls. "We are the first of each type of animal you created. I am an Only Made because there is only one of my kind. Many have brought their Seconds and Thirds as well."

"What about the birds? There are so many here and outside in the tree? Mally asked.

"Sunshine is the First Made bird so they are hers to command," a dark blue turkey with an orange block blazing on his cheek replied sharply. "It's almost impossible to keep them in line so I hope she's ready to take the lead."

"She will lead when she's ready," Midnight replied. "Until then, I can command the birds in the air."

Mally frowned. Her older sister would love being in charge just because she was first born. She was suddenly very glad Rose would never be setting foot in Quilst. She took a deep breath and forced her brain to focus. "Menda. I want to know about Menda. Where is she and what is she doing? We heard her scream and the bees said she retreated into the mountain."

A familiar yellow mouse scampered up the table, a large piece of fabric rolled up and tied to her back. "Great Maker Mally, the mice split into three groups to search as you instructed. Gray Company and the Christmas Gang have been sending in regular reports.

We can't infiltrate as seamlessly as the bees, but we've been able to learn quite a lot. Menda is indeed inside the center purple mountain. Her fortress is vast, but fortunately for us, very rudimentary in design."

"Oh! Thank you!" Mally said as Goldie slid a beautifully illustrated map into her hands, breaking down the mountain into a series of tunnels and rooms.

"What do you know about Menda? What is she doing?"

"She spends most of her time here." Goldie said, pressing her paw to a small room on the map. "It's the only room with a window and she stands there for hours at a time. As for what she does…" the mouse shrugged "she mostly talks to herself and… rips things apart."

A chill ran down Mally's spine. "That's the room I was trapped in before and where I think she was tonight. How do we get inside?"

Goldie traced a route on the map through a maze of twisting halls that emerged on the side of the mountain.

"Perfect! Thank you, Goldie," Mally said.

"I am Spool, representing the turkeys." The grumpy turkey cleared his throat loudly. "We also divided into groups and confirm the mice reports. Menda holds close to the mountain and her snarls do not stray further than the upper wood. However, we did see signs of new creatures, especially concentrated in the mountain passes and open landscapes. They are not of our flock."

"You mean they're new animals? Where did they come from?" Mally asked.

"I can shed light on that," A blue bear at the opposite end of the table stood. "I am Pattern, speaker for the Bears. We encountered a half dozen such creatures and questioned them all thoroughly. They are no friend to the Ripping Witch, but have no knowledge of you either. It seems they have another Maker."

"Yes, that makes sense," Mally said. "They must all have been animals like Patch, original to the quilt, so their Maker is Grandma."

"Where have you found them? Where are they now?" Patch asked.

Spool shuffled through his notes with a blue wing. "Many were found near rips in the landscape. Areas where the Inside can be seen."

"Oh, they must be coming out of the holes Menda cut in the fabric!" Mally said, looking at Patch. "What if they can climb out now? Your friends could come back!"

Patch nodded, his brow furrowed.

"What shall we do with them?" Spool asked. "I have two dozen turkeys at my command and with the bears and monkeys at my disposal, we can round them up before dawn."

"Round them up?" Mally's head was suddenly spinning. "Why?"

"They're unknown elements." Spool ruffled his orange tail feathers impatiently. "They could join with Menda and we could find ourselves fighting a war on two fronts."

"What? I thought you said they're no friend to the Ripping Witch?"

"I think what Spool is trying to say is we don't know them," Pattern spoke up. "They might change sides and fight against us. Is that a chance you're willing to take?"

"What do you think?" Mally asked Patch. The cat had gone strangely still and silent throughout the exchange, as if lost in thought.

"The originals are no threat to our cause," Patch said quietly. "I doubt they will be in any fit state to fight anything or anyone at this point. Leave them be. They've suffered enough."

The crowd around the table shifted and Mally watched several animals exchange worried looks. Spool rolled his eyes impatiently and even Thimble looked concerned.

Mally squared her shoulders. "I trust Patch completely. If he says the animals Grandma made are no threat to us, then I believe him. I think we should send out a search party. My grandma might have also fallen into one of Menda's traps. That could be where she's been this whole time."

A dark shape moved from the corner. A purple hawk with glowing yellow eyes shifted into the light. She met Mally's eyes and gave the slightest of nods.

"Done."

With a majestic unfurling of wings, she took flight straight up from the table. Mally lost sight of her as she soared out through the opening in the center of the Great Tree. Mally hadn't expected her suggestion to be taken seriously, or to be carried out so quickly. She fiddled with the map in her hands to give herself time to think.

The sheer volume of rooms within the mountain was surprising. Did Menda make this herself, or had Grandma imagined a castle as she stitched that purple triangle onto the quilt? And where was Ms. Bunny?

"Have you seen…" Mally couldn't bring herself to finish the question.

"We haven't been able to locate her." A small green monkey said with a sad shake of his head. "I'm Pin, leader of the monkeys. We searched every room from top to bottom. We haven't seen anything that matches Ms. Bunny's appearance. We did find this, however." He held out Mally's blue bookbag.

"Oh, Pin! Thank you so much!" Mally took the bag and immediately pulled open the zipper to check the contents. "Where did you find it?"

"Seam found it in the field outside during the first sweep of the area," Pattern replied.

Mally wouldn't have thought she'd miss her silly school bag so much, but it made her eyes prick with tears to find her books and papers and red sewing box still tucked inside. She hugged the bag to her chest and took a deep breath.

"I lost this the night Ms. Bunny and Sunshine were taken. It's silly to be so happy I have it back, but I am." She closed her eyes and tears leaked out between her eyelashes. She took a deep breath and met Midnight's dark eyes.

"I'm sure you've all heard we saved Sunshine tonight, but we lost so many birds in the attack. I don't know what will happen if we go up against Menda again. I understand if you don't want to fight."

She scanned the table, looking at each animal in turn. "I don't think Menda can kill me because I'm human, but she can easily end all of you. Patch reminded me of that tonight." Mally caught the cat's eye and he nodded grimly.

Thimble stepped closer to the table, her long patchwork trunk lifted high. "Our home is Quilst, Mally Maker. If you take us back through the door to the outside, we will go back to just being quilt blocks again. We accept the risks. The only way for us to live is to fight."

She brought her long trunk down with a *smack* in the middle of the table. With a great rustle of fabric, every animal followed suit, pounding their paws and wings against the surface as they shouted in unison, "We will live! We will fight!"

"Okay," Mally said, shakily, her heart swelling with hope. She set her bookbag on the ground and pressed her hands against the table too. "Let's get to work!"

* * * * *

Mally spread her arms wide. Wind rushed past, pulling her hair back from her face and for a second she felt like she was flying. Instead she was riding on Patch's back with a dozen smaller animals from the meeting, including Goldie and Pin. They were charging, low to the ground, through the woods and over the hills between the Great Tree and Menda's purple mountain.

An army of patchwork animals surrounded her on all sides, seamlessly keeping up with Patch's huge strides. Each animal stood out with distinctive squares, diamonds, and triangles forming patterns on their backs, faces, or paws. It was like looking at a colossal, moving quilt. Mally loved the sound of their paws hitting the soft ground. Individually they didn't make much noise, but several hundred animals together created a thunderous drum beat that resonated through her body and made her heart swell with excitement.

The meeting in the Great Tree had lasted so long, she'd wondered if it would ever end. But after hours of strategizing and debate, every detail of the plan was meticulously crafted and every animal at the table was satisfied.

The assault on Menda hinged on getting into the mountain as quickly as possible. The longer Menda knew they were back in Quilst, the more time she could prepare her defense. Thankfully all the First Made had agreed the best strategy was to attack as soon as possible.

A tiny sliver of sunlight was peeking over the edge of the horizon. All at once, the sky filled with birds. A great rushing of wings sounded along with cheerful shouts Mally could just make out far below.

"Let's go! Form up! In a line now, geese!"

"Flying Geese to save the day!"

Rows upon rows of flying geese filled the sky. At some point during the meeting, Mally had realized they would need more birds and she'd pulled out her sewing box to stitch more triangles as they planned their attack. Every animal at the table had followed suit, and it had been the strangest sight watching mice, bears, frogs, monkeys, hens, roosters, turkeys, cats, ducks and even two polka dotted baby chicks hand stitching together. So long as Mally completed the last stitch on the two triangles, the flying geese unit would come to life, flapping its wings happily.

It was worth it. Edge to edge, triangle to triangle, the birds filled the sky in every color of the rainbow. Weaving in between the ranks she watched one bright bird flying harder and faster than the rest, yelling encouragement on the top of her voice.

"We can do this! Yes! Yes! Yes! We're going to get her! Take that evil queen! Today is your last day in power!"

Sunshine was back to her old self again. Mally had called her over during the meeting and asked if she would like to lead the birds to the mountain. As Spool had pointed out, she was the First Made and should be in command. Mally hadn't been sure what she would say, but the little bird immediately perked up and began calling orders and running drills. Now she flew beautifully, her body glowing brightly as she shouted cheerfully to the other birds.

Mally closed her eyes and Grandma's face swam through her mind. But she wasn't sure if her memory was accurate anymore. It felt fuzzy, as if Grandma was blurring out of focus.

She had found many beautifully stitched projects in progress in the Great Tree along with half of Grandma's collection of threads, needles and her favorite thimbles stashed in cabinets in the sewing nook. Seeing the supplies had made her tear up again, but not in sadness.

It had made her furious. Clearly Grandma had been living in the Great Tree, and she must have come back home to get more supplies. Why didn't she check a clock or go downstairs to see the calendar? Couldn't she have left a note at least?

And now where in Quilst was she? Had Menda caught her and dropped her into the deepest, darkest pit she could find, as she'd threatened in the mountain? The hawk that had left to search for her hadn't returned.

As she watched Sunshine the words *SHE WILL NEVER BE THE SAME AGAIN* flashed through her head, and she clenched her fists. *It has to be the same again*, she thought. *I will prove her wrong. I'm going to save Ms. Bunny and Grandma and I will make that evil witch pay for what she's done.*

She was pulled out of her thoughts abruptly as Patch slowed his pace, then stopped. They were only a few yards from the largest purple mountain. A low rumble sounded from deep below the ground.

"What is that?" She asked, scanning the landscape.

"I think we're about to find out." Patch said. He hunched his shoulders, digging his paws into the fabric as the landscape suddenly shifted. The material under their feet buckled as the rumble grew to a roar.

RRIIIPPPP!

The ground split open less than twenty feet away. Mally watched as a deep gash cut across their path, circling around the mountain. The earth quaked again and something emerged from the break in the cloth.

Blue and purple threads shot up from the ground and began weaving themselves together. Ten feet tall, then twenty. In just a few seconds, a thick barrier formed, casting the landscape into shadow. Mally pressed her hand over her nose as the overwhelming scent of cloves hit her full in the face. The stitches were large and haphazard, but the pattern they made was unmistakable.

"It's a spider web! Everyone, back up! Don't let it touch you!" Mally yelled and her call was picked up and repeated, but it was too late.

The chorus of stampeding paws abruptly changed as the animals in the front halted, digging their claws into the landscape. But everyone in the back was still pushing forward. The air instantly filled with screams. Mally saw a red hen and her four chicks struggling against the press of bodies. The chicks bobbed easily between the legs of the other animals, but the hen was trapped. She squawked, flapping her wings frantically as she was pushed closer and closer to the wall.

A pink rooster rushed to the rescue, shoving the hen away from the spider web, but his momentum carried him too far. His wings hit the wall and immediately blue threads wove through his body, locking him tight to the surface. Mally watched, horrified as his fabrics were pulled apart, the threads unraveling one by one. Soon only a blotch of pink fiber remained, spreading slowing in a spiral pattern across the wall.

A deafening screech sounded overhead. The birds in the air weren't fairing any better. The wall had caught hundreds when it first formed and seemed to grow bigger with every animal it ate.

"Back up! Get away from the wall! We'll find another way in!" Mally ordered.

Patch crouched low trying to open his wings, but the press of bodies was too close. Mally shifted her legs to give him more room, but nearly lost her balance as a knotted rope, thick as a tree trunk, lashed out from the wall. It punched through the crowd, capturing a dozen animals at once. Then with a yank, it pulled them back into the spider web. Panicked screams filled the air as animals fought to save their friends.

"Patch! What do we do?" Mally yelled.

"There's nowhere to go! We're stuck!"

She scanned the field desperately and watched as another rope shot out nearly thirty feet long. Mally bent down and held out her hands so nearby animals could scramble up her arms and onto Patch's back. With more space to move, the cat spun and leapt away from the wall.

Another rope shot out, catching the red tip of his tail and they jerked to a stop. The world spun wildly as Mally flew off Patch's back. Too fast. It was all happening way too fast. The ground rushed up to meet her and she spread out her hands ready for the crash.

Something grabbed her around the middle. It was Pattern, speaker for the bears. Without a word, he slung her onto his back and bounded back to Patch. The cat's head was down and all his claws were sunk deep into the landscape, but he was still slowly sliding backward into the growing monstrous wall.

Mally leapt off the bear and landed squarely on Patch's back. Pulling a seam ripper out of her pocket, she raced down his body to his tail. Several mice and monkeys were trying to help free him, but they couldn't break the attacking fibers and were becoming ensnared themselves.

"Watch out!" Mally yelled.

She cut through the threads binding Patch and they fell away. The entire rope extending from the wall fell flat on the ground and stopped moving. That was all she needed to see. She jumped off the cat's back and ran along the wall, cutting every cord she could reach.

But for every rope she sliced, ten more took its place. Mally slashed directly into the spider web. A long rip formed and the edges curled inward. She cut again, and again and a hole began to form. She stepped closer, but dangling blue threads caught her shirt and immediately began weaving through the fabric. She sliced herself free and backed away quickly.

"Mally! Mally! Mally!" Sunshine called from above, surrounded by a flock of flying geese. "What do we do? We can't get past this wall!"

"I don't know, Sunshine!" Mally shouted. "I've started a hole, but I can't get through." She gestured at the opening she'd cut into the wall. Patch suddenly appeared at her side, a small group of animals on his back. Pattern followed with more mice and two frogs clinging to his head and shoulders.

"We must retreat. She won this round. We'll have to find a new—"

Sunshine interrupted, "I have an idea! Yes! Yes! Yes! Mally, start ripping! Cut that hole in the wall and keep cutting. Don't stop until it's big enough for all of you."

"Okay!" Mally turned and slashed through the threads above her head and down to the ground. The hole widened, but she couldn't cut again without risking her shirt getting stitched. She turned and met Sunshine's brilliant eyes.

"You have to get Menda!" the bird said urgently. "Mally, you must take her crown! Please! Please! Please! You have to take her crown! Promise me!"

"I promise, Sunshine. I'll take it." Mally said, quickly, not really sure what she was agreeing to.

"Good!" Sunshine nodded once, instantly doubled her size and flew straight into the spider web. She pressed her wings against the surface and instantly purple and blue threads wove over her bright fabrics.

"No! Sunshine, what are you doing?" Mally cried.

"Keep cutting, Mally! You have to get thru —" Her last words were cut off as her body was engulfed in the hungry wall.

"Sunshine!" Mally pulled out her second seam ripper and slashed with both hands, but it was too late for her friend. Suddenly she saw what Sunshine's sacrifice had accomplished. While the wall was busy ripping apart one fabric, it couldn't attack another. With Sunshine's help, she could cut deeper into the spider web.

She hacked at the wall viciously, ripping through as many threads as she could reach with every pass. The hole widened, then lengthened, turning into a tunnel.

Wings fluttered against her back and two more flying geese pressed themselves against the spider web. Mally's vision blurred as the animals slowly dissolved around her. She kept cutting, tearing deeper and deeper into the tangle of fibers. She soon found a rhythm: cut vertically then horizontally, step forward, cut vertical, cut horizontal, step forward.

She felt the wings of more birds at her back and kept count as she slashed through layer after layer of the spider web wall. She'd counted to one hundred, twenty-three when she brought the seam ripper down and suddenly there was nothing to cut.

She'd slashed all the way through the spider web and was now standing in the narrow space between the wall and the mountain. The light of the suns was filtered strangely by the spider web, and for the first time in Quilst, Mally felt cold.

She turned and cut the hole wider so Patch could fit through the opening. More than two dozen tiny mice, monkeys, and even a pint-sized pink bear rode on his back. More animals emerged one by one and Pattern squeezed through last. They stared at one another in the dim light. Less than forty patchwork faces stared back.

"Is this everyone?" Mally asked, dreading the answer.

Patch nodded sadly as the animals scrambled off his back. Goldie rushed up the path and gestured frantically for them to follow her.

"Maker Mally, we're very close to the entrance of the tunnels. Let me guide you inside." She darted around the purple mountain and stopped by a small hole in the ground.

"It will be completely dark for the first hundred feet. Just keep crawling and it will get easier once we get into the upper tunnels."

Mally slipped her seam rippers back into her pocket and crouched down on her hands and knees. Her bookbag felt awkward on her back, so she shifted it quickly to her front before crawling into the dark hole.

It was a tight squeeze, but surprisingly comfortable. Fabric pressed against her on all sides. It was like being in a very squishy, soft tube. She wiggled forward, following Goldie as she heard Patch grumbling behind.

"I may be able to change my size, but for the record I am neither a mouse nor a ferret."

Mally smiled to herself. Then she remembered the battle outside. *How many animals were just ripped apart? Will I be able to fix them? Why did Sunshine make me promise to take Menda's crown?* A swirl of unanswerable questions churned through her mind.

After a hundred feet of wiggling and squishing herself through the tight space, the tunnel widened out and Mally was able to crawl easier on her hands and knees. Light shone from the end of the tunnel and she could see the openings to other passages running in different directions.

"This way, Maker. The halls branch off so you must follow me carefully. You don't want to turn the wrong way," Goldie whispered.

Mally followed the little mouse through a maze of twisting tunnels. It felt like they were sloping upward as well as angling towards the center of the mountain. The tunnel curled around a tight bend and suddenly the path opened onto a wide hall with purple walls and blue doors spaced every few yards. It was lit with yellow fabric stretched across the ceiling that reminded Mally of the old fluorescent lights in her dentist's office.

The smaller animals shrank against the wall and, being made of fabric, were able to tuck themselves so tightly into the soft cloth they disappeared. That same trick wouldn't work for Mally so she rose to her feet. She slipped her bookbag off and stretched in relief.

She glanced behind and caught Patch's eye. He'd expanded to the size of a great dane and after a long stretch, tucked his wings neatly at his sides. Clearly he wasn't shrinking into the wall, either.

And they weren't alone. The pink bear stood behind Patch, growing quickly to match Mally's height, and Pin, the green monkey came next. Pattern rose slowly to his feet at the very back and she looked to him for a nod that he was ready.

"Let's go," she whispered to Goldie.

Without a word they darted out to check if the path was clear. Mally leaned against the wall, wiping her sweaty hands on her jeans. Seconds later, the little golden mouse scurried back and wiggled her tail. The group turned the corner to find an empty hallway. Mally crept after the mouse, straining to hear anything above the pounding of her heart.

They turned a corner, then another, each twist taking them deeper into the mountain. The empty halls blurred together in a monotonous stream of purple.

At one point Mally bent down and whispered, "Is it usually this empty? Do you think she knows we're inside?"

"It's always like this. The only one who lives here is the Ripping Witch, Maker Mally. She is always alone," Goldie replied and for a sliver of a second Mally felt sorry for Menda. It seemed very lonely to live in a mountain castle all by yourself.

Then she remembered what Menda had done. There was a reason the witch was alone. She was a monster, pure and simple.

They seemed to be getting closer as Goldie advanced slowly and tucked herself into the walls to turn corners. Several of the rooms had no doors and Mally glanced inside as they passed. Each room was empty. Purple fabric stretched from floor to ceiling, and there wasn't a scrap of furniture, decoration, or embellishment anywhere she could see. It was barren, and more to the point: boring.

They crept down two more deserted hallways. With a squeak that had everyone scrambling to hide against the walls, three mice and a tiny cat emerged from the opposite direction. They had a short exchange with Goldie, wiggling ears and whiskers in an improvised sign language.

Mally crept down the hall and stuck her head around the next corner to see what was going on. It was yet another purple passageway with more open doorways on all sides. It felt like she'd walked down this hall at least a hundred times now.

Something caught her eye in the next room. Directly opposite the door, a familiar square window was cut in one corner. It was the room. *Her* room. Unconsciously she stepped closer, her eyes locked on a strange shape in the middle of the floor. She didn't hear the warning squeaks of the mice behind her.

All Mally could see was a small bundle of brown fabrics and stuffing piled in the middle of the room.

A square of pink calico lay crumpled on top.

Chapter 11

The Queen in the Quilt

"Ms. Bunny!" Mally rushed into the room. She sank to her knees and grabbed for the little bundle.

"Mally, no!" Patch leapt in after her. He knocked her out of the way, expanding in size instantaneously to block the doll's pieces from view.

"What are you doing? She's right there!" Mally cried, shoving past him. Then she froze, staring at the spot where the open doorway had been just seconds before. A thick spider web woven from purple and pink threads now filled the space completely.

They were trapped.

"Well, well, look who the cat dragged in," the voice from Mally's nightmares floated out of a dark corner of the room. Menda stepped into the light, all her teeth showing in a wide smile.

Mally took an involuntary step back, pressing against Patch. The witch had changed dramatically since the last time she'd seen her in this room. Her shoulders hunched and her head craned forward at an unnatural angle. The scissor necklace she'd stolen from Mally hung from her crooked neck. Her crown was spinning so fast around her head it was heating the room, filling the space with a sickly odor of lavender and singed fabric.

But the worst change was her face. The silk fabric on her head had been smooth and flawless but now was streaked with burn marks and deep wrinkles. Every expression Menda made was exaggerated as the stitches forming her eyes and mouth bulged against the distorted material.

"I was so sad you left so quickly the last time." Like a switch had been flipped, Menda suddenly sounded on the verge of tears. She clutched her black hands together at her chest and looked genuinely heartbroken, but Mally couldn't be fooled again.

Mally reached into her pockets for her seam rippers, but her arms were suddenly wrenched backwards. Patch gripped her backpack with his teeth and wasn't letting go. She glared at him, struggling in his grip. Then he winked, so quick and sly she almost missed it.

A cold chill ran up her spine and she twisted, trying to hide her fear with anger. "What are you doing? Let me get her!"

"Yes, I'd love to see you try to 'get me' when you've just waltzed in the room with one of my most loyal subjects," Menda laughed, all traces of sorrow in her voice vanishing in an instant.

Mally froze. "What are you talking about?"

"You may find in life that it pays to be a little less trusting. Not everyone handing out lollipops just wants to give you sweets. Not every orange cat really wants to be your friend." Menda sauntered over, her wide hips swinging jauntily and stroked Patch's head with her strange mitten shaped hand. "You can let her go now, my pet."

Patch yanked the bookbag straight up. With a loud rip, the seams on the straps gave way and Mally landed in a heap on the floor. She scrambled to her knees as he spat the broken bag into a corner of the room.

"Thank the Great Maker that's over," the cat said, rolling his eyes. "I believe that was the dullest ruse I've ever endured. Can you please find me a smarter plaything next time?"

"Oh, I will," Menda said, planting a kiss on his cheek with her bulbous lips.

"You lied to me," Mally whispered. "I thought you were my friend."

"Like I said, boring and stupid. Why are those two traits so often found together? Like chocolate and strawberries. But not nearly so sweet," Patch said.

"You're the idiot if you think she's on your side. She's evil! You call her the Ripping Witch!"

With a snarl of rage, Menda grabbed Mally's arm and yanked her to her feet.

Snip. Snip. Snip.

The witch dragged her to the window. She gripped her chin and forced her to view the landscape below.

"See your army? See all the creatures you brought into this world? I'm going to make you watch as I slaughter them. I am the Queen of Quilst and I can destroy everything you make," Menda spat in her ear. Then her grip suddenly slackened and her next words came out in a sob, "Why do you keep attacking me? I just want what's best for this world, and you keep messing it all up!"

For a second, Mally couldn't make sense of what she was seeing. The spider web wall had grown nearly as tall as the mountain. Only a few animals remained clustered together in a tight group as thick ropes surrounded them. Thimble was still on her feet lashing out with her huge trunk to shield the others. A handful of flying geese were trying to distract the tendrils, but every time a bird swooped down, it didn't return to the sky.

With an ear splitting rip, a gap opened in the wall and five massive snarls rolled out. The ground trembled with their movement and Mally could feel it even in the middle of the mountain. The fabric the monsters rolled over disappeared instantly, leaving a wide stripe of batting exposed. As they ate the quilt, the monsters grew even bigger and they were headed straight for the small band of animals trapped on the field.

"No! Flying Geese, tell them to run! Get away!"

Menda whirled, jerking Mally away from the window. She caught her hand and gripped it so tight Mally felt her bones grinding together. She twisted, trying to pull away, but Menda just tightened her hold. Mally's tiny scissors flashed in the witch's hand and she began to sing:

"There is no running Mally May.

You cannot, cannot save the day.

Let's see what happens when YOU fray."

Menda slashed the blades against her palm. Mally stared at her hand, dumbstruck as blood welled around the cut. Then the pain registered and she cried out, struggling to get away, but Menda wouldn't let her go. The witch held tight as she brought the scissors down a second and third time.

Mally screamed, crumpling to the ground as Menda finally released her. The blades had cut deep, but the pain was nothing to the fear filling Mally's mind. Her vision blurred as blood trickled between her fingers and dripped on the floor.

"Oh dear. You're bleeding on the quilt." Menda clicked the scissors into the metal case on the necklace and swung the heavy end back and forth, watching gleefully. "You know how much Grandma Grace hates that. Mally May has ruined the day. I wonder what Grandma will say?"

Mally looked up at Patch, tears pouring down her face.

"Help me! Please Patch! I thought you were my friend!" But the cat just smiled down at her with a strange mix of pity and scorn on his face.

"Why would he help you? Why would anyone?" Menda pondered the question for a second. "I know! The only creatures that really love you are the ones you've made yourself. Pathetic. You have to stitch your own friends." She wandered back across the room and gave a little kick to the bundle of brown fabrics on the floor. Mally flinched.

"So much like Grandma Grace. She didn't know what to do with herself when she was lonely. She stitched all manner of things when her heart was torn in two after pathetic David died."

"What? What does my Grandpa have to do with anything?"

"He has everything to do with me!" Menda snarled, rising to the tips of her largest scissors to tower over Mally. "You *must* have realized by now, Mally May, the only way I could be here, the only way I can exist is if Grace Wright made me herself."

"No! She would never —" Mally stopped speaking, suddenly unsure. The Great Tree had been filled with fabrics and threads. Grandma could have been living in Quilst this whole time and Menda even smelled like the lavender sachets Grandma packed her quilts in for storage.

Snip. Snip. Snip.

Menda drew close, her face curious. "How well do you really know dear old Grandma? You didn't exist when I was being stitched by her hand. You have no idea who she *really* is."

"Yes, I do and she's nothing like you!" Mally shouted.

Menda caught hold of her face and tilted it to one side. "I see some of us in you. Do you want to know why I love ripping things apart?"

Mally shook her head slowly, closing her eyes to block out Menda's twisted face. But the witch squeezed her chin painfully until she met her gaze.

"It fills the void." She whispered and Mally knew exactly what she meant. Ever since Grandma disappeared and Mama stopped caring it was like she had a hole in her heart. No matter what she did, no matter how much fun she was having with friends, the empty place was always there, begging to be filled.

"No." Mally whispered, then with more force. "NO!" She jerked her face free of Menda's grip. Swiping the tears from her eyes, she glared at the witch towering above her. "You choose to be like this. You could make this place pretty, but you don't. You could make friends, but you don't! You choose to be ugly and horrible!"

Menda stepped back and swung her arms wide. "Pretty? Friends? Who needs that when you can have all this!? I'm the Queen of Quilst and I don't need anyone, I'm perfect the way I—"

But her words were cut short as Patch lunged at her back. Menda landed flat on her face, and the crown flew off her head in a wide arc. The witch screamed, her arms flailing, desperately trying to reach it. The scissors fell flat against her back with a deafening clang.

Mally scrambled out of the way just in time. Two blades crashed into the floor where she'd just been sitting, their sharp points sinking deep into the floor. Then something very unexpected happened. Right before her eyes the blades began to shrink.

"No! No! Not my lovelies!" Menda shrieked.

"Rip her now," Patch growled. He held Menda down with all four paws, his claws extended through her fabric and into the floor.

Mally pulled a seam ripper out of her pocket and rose to her feet. The cuts on her palm throbbed so badly she nearly dropped the tool. She switched hands, wiping the blood off her palm onto the front of her shirt.

"No! Please Mally, please don't hurt me," Menda cried. Her blue eyes were wide and pleading. Without the crown spinning around her head, she looked frail and helpless, like a bald baby bird.

Mally approached the witch slowly, then she closed her eyes and sank to her knees. She'd imagined this moment so many times. Ever since Menda had first trapped her in this room, she'd wanted to rip her to pieces. But wanting to hurt her was one thing... actually cutting into her fabrics felt very different.

"You don't want to do this Mally! It was all a misunderstanding! I swear I never meant to hurt anyone!"

Mally ignored her. She slipped the seam ripper blade into Menda's shoulder seam. The witch shrieked and bucked, but Patch spread his wings wide and pressed all his weight against her back. Mally gripped the tool tightly and pulled it quickly through the stitches holding the fabrics together.

In her imagination, this never worked. Her worst fear was that Menda's fabric would be indestructible and her blade would bounce off, or worse, break against the witch's body. But fabric is just fabric, and thread is just thread, and the seams split wide as her blade passed through the stitches.

She held her breath as she leaned over Menda's head and ripped her second shoulder seam. The blade slid easily through the gaping stitches and stuffing immediately leaked out between the fabrics.

She was about to pull away when she spotted the silver chain of her necklace still looped around the witch's neck. She pulled it off and double checked the scissors were still locked inside. She pulled it over her head and scrambled away from the witch as quickly as she could. Menda's eyes were on her as a wide smile crept across her face.

"What? That's all you got? You're not going to cut my head off? Why not rip off my arms and legs? It was so much fun playing with your little —" Her voice cut off as Patch pressed her face flat to the floor.

"The crown," he said. "Take it."

Mally followed his gaze to a scrap of gold and silver fabric on the floor. She walked over, tucking the seam ripper into her pocket and found it was the most beautiful quilt block she'd ever seen. Squares and triangles pieced together to form an elegant circular pattern.

"No, Mally, don't touch it!" Menda shrieked, her eyes bulging madly as her arms scrabbled against the floor. "It will hurt you! It will split your skull in half. Look what it's done to me!"

"You've done this to yourself, stupid witch," Patch said. "Take it, Mally. You promised Sunshine you'd take it!"

Mally picked up the quilt block.

A crash of cymbals sounded. She threw up her hands, pressing the fabric against her ears to block out the sound, but it didn't do any good. The noise was ringing inside her head, inside her skull, resonating in her blood.

Faintly, she could hear Patch yelling, "Mally? What's going on? Mally? Speak to me, little Maker!"

But she couldn't answer him. She was being pulled into light, far from the mountain room, far from Quilst. The clang of cymbals was changing, mellowing, ringing. Now it was music, a glorious music, that filled her heart and made her eyes well with tears. She blinked and suddenly found herself standing in the middle of a grassy field.

Before her a woman stood staring into a large fountain. She was tall, with dark skin and hair knotted into braids that hung to her waist. She wore a red dress with narrow straps across her back and shoulders, revealing long arms ringed with four bracelets. She turned to gaze at her with eyes of pure silver.

Mally sank to her knees, the quilt block clutched in her hands. She bowed her head.

"Thank you, Mally Spencer. There are few who know me now, and even fewer who would bow at my feet. My name is Creo." She gestured at the quilt block in Mally's hands. "Do you know what you hold there?"

"A crown?" Mally guessed.

"In its most simplistic form, yes, that is a crown. But it is also much more. With that crown, you will be Queen of Quilst, ruler of a land that has nearly been destroyed by another. Are you sure you want this?"

Mally hesitated. She had no idea where she was, but something inside urged her to be honest. "I don't know. I just wanted to find my Grandma and fix everything at home, but it all went so wrong."

She looked down at the quilt block in her hands and noticed a streak of blood on one corner. The sight of the red stain slowly spreading over the fabric forced her to ask her next question.

"Will it hurt me? Menda said it hurt when I cut the quilt. She could feel it."

"Pain is a warning. When there is harm to your world, when there is damage to the quilt, you will feel it." The woman gently took Mally's hand and pressed her thumbs against the cuts on her palm. Pain shot up her arm and she gasped, trying to jerk free.

"But it will only ever be as much as you can handle." Creo released her grip and immediately the pain lessened to a dull throb.

The cuts were bleeding profusely now, but she noticed the woman's hands were completely clean. Mally's gaze traveled up to the bracelets circling her dark arms. The top ring was made of small stones, each a different color and carved into pieces that interlocked seamlessly together.

The next bracelet was made of dark metal. Half of it was pocked and pitted as if it had just been dug out of the ground. But along the bottom edge the metal had been polished so smooth Mally could see her face reflected in it.

A wide band of wood came next, a swirl of dark grain lines forming the only decoration over the surface. The last bracelet was dark red and woven from dozens of different threads. Mally's fingers itched to touch it, and she was surprised when Creo slipped it off her wrist and held it out to her with a smile.

She ran her fingers over the woven fabric, marveling at the soft texture. It was deceptively simple with each thread lined up in straight rows, but the different thicknesses of the fibers combined to make it the most beautiful bracelet she'd ever seen. *I could never make anything that pretty,* she thought.

"How can I be a queen?" she asked, giving voice to her fear. "I'm only ten and I've only just learned how to stitch. I'm not even that good."

"There are many ways to be a Maker," Creo said. "And they all begin with learning. Your greatest power will only come from mastering your craft." She opened Mally's hands again and gently touched the raw skin on her fingertips. "It is a goal you will never fully reach, but with effort you will make Quilst beautiful once again and from that world it will flow into all the other worlds." She gestured at the fountain behind her, but Mally was distracted by another worry.

"But what about Grandma and Ms. Bunny? We've all been missing for so long. What will we tell my parents?"

"You will find all the answers you need right here." She pressed a hand to Mally's heart and another to the crown in her hands.

"And Menda? What do I do about her?"

"Not all mistakes should be mended," Creo answered sharply. "If you accept this crown, you must be ready to do anything to protect your world. Remember Quilst at its best."

Mally was suddenly standing in the field, staring up at the Closed Door that had first carried her into Quilst. She wiggled her toes and felt the yarn grass slipping beneath her bare feet. She reached down to stroke her fingertips over a large rock and marveled at the delicate stitches that added texture to the surface.

"This is yours to rebuild and protect."

The ground under her feet instantly disappeared. She stood knee deep in fluffy white batting. The fabric forming the ground, hills, even half of the Closed Door had been ripped away. Piles of shredded fabrics littered the landscape. A high pitched whistle sounded and she ducked as a rope punched out from a nearby snarl. It caught the wings of the purple hawk that had gone searching for Grandma.

"Stop it! Don't hurt her!" Mally yelled, but her words had no effect. She was forced to watch as the monster ripped the bird's wings apart.

"With the power of the crown, you will be able to command anything made of fiber to do what you will." Creo gestured at the quilt block in Mally's hands. "The lesser creature that wore this before you barely used a stitch of her power, and see what she did with it. Imagine what you can do, Mally."

The world shifted again and they were standing before the Great Tree. The branches spread out around the base and warm light poured from the windows. She longed to run inside and explore the treehouse from top to bottom, to sleep in the swinging bed, and stitch by the window in the sewing nook.

"Use your imagination and your open heart as a guide, and you will make Quilst the most beautiful of all the worlds." Creo turned to face her and they were again standing in the grassy field, gazing into the fountain.

For the first time Mally looked at it properly. A massive golden hand rose from the middle of a glass dome. Water poured from the tip of the thumb and hit the center of the palm with a beautiful melodic sound. From there the water split into four chambers above the fingers. Simple symbols adorned each digit: a spiral, a curved hexagon, a simple tree shape, a set of woven lines.

Mally looked closer and realized the symbols matched the materials of Creo's bracelets: stone, metal, wood, and fiber. But for all the water rushing from the top of the fountain, only a trickle emerged from the tips of the fingers to rain over the glass dome. No, not a dome. It was a globe of the world, etched in exquisite detail.

"The power of creativity is a limitless flow, but the hands of men and women have become still. There are not enough Makers in the world to keep the fountain flowing." Creo turned the globe and Mally could see some of the surface was completely dry.

"What will happen if it stops?"

"You don't want to know," Creo said. A shadow crossed her face, then she turned her fathomless silver eyes on Mally. "I believe you have made up your mind, Maker, so I will ask again – Do you want this? Will you accept that crown in your hands and become the Queen of Quilst?"

Mally thought about all she'd seen and done since she'd accidently opened the door in the quilt. Her hand ached. *I just want to go home. I just want everything to go back to normal.*

But then she looked at the woman's woven bracelet and remembered what it felt like to run barefoot through soft yarn grass. She could feel the pull on her back as she soared out of the mountain room on wings she'd stitched with Ms. Bunny. *Do I really want things to be normal again?*

But Menda had done so much damage. Quilst had been perfect and she had ripped and twisted it into something almost unrecognizable. *What if I could fix it? What if I could bring everything back?*

The image of the Great Tree swam through her mind and she thought of all the other things she'd like to make and explore. The Cavern. The House in the Sky. There was so much she wanted to do in Quilst and so much to learn about sewing and quilting. *I want to make it beautiful,* she thought. *I want to make it amazing.*

"Yes. I want this," she said. The fabric in her hands shimmered. With the sound of ringing bells, it began to move. Around and around the fabric spun and as it did, it transformed into a woven ring of silver and gold threads. A single ribbon of red silk was braided through the middle.

"So you do not forget the price of malice." Creo ran her fingertips over the ribbon. "Or the weight of your responsibility." She lifted the crown to Mally's head and settled it in place. Then she leaned forward and planted a kiss on Mally's brow. A warm glow spread from that point through her whole body. Mally flexed her hand and found the cuts on her palm and the raw skin on her fingertips had stopped hurting.

"That will protect you until the moons rise to their highest point tonight." Creo's eyes were gentle, but she spoke urgently. "Heal Quilst as fast as you can. Anything left broken will echo back to you here." She touched Mally's temples. Pain seared through her skull for just a second, but that was long enough.

Creo stepped back and the wonderful music that pulled her to this place filled her mind again. "Good luck, Queen Maker."

*   *   *   *   *

In a swirl of color and ringing chimes, Mally was back in the mountain room. Patch was still squashing Menda onto the floor, yelling, "Mally? What's going on? Mally? Speak to me, little Maker!"

"I'm fine," Mally whispered. "Really, I'm fine." She pressed her hand against the wall as the crown began to spin. Images flashed in her mind. Mally saw broken seams, piles of ripped fabrics and a whole mountain of shredded thread. "Yes, I know it's broken," she muttered. "Stop it."

"What's going on? Who are you talking to?!" Patch roared. Distracted, his front paw slipped off Menda's shoulder. "Mally! Look out!"

With an ear-splitting shriek, the witch reared up off the floor. Mally shook her head. Her vision suddenly cleared, only to be filled again with Menda's twisted face.

"That's MINE!" the witch screamed.

Mally stumbled back. Her hands raised automatically in the air.

"Stop! Menda, stop!"

Miraculously, it worked. The Ripping Witch stopped dead, frozen in the middle of the room, her mitten hands stretched out to snatch the crown.

"Did you do that?" Patch asked. He cautiously pressed a paw to Menda's side. She rocked slightly on her pointy feet, but otherwise remained completely motionless. It was as if she'd been turned back into a stuffed doll. Her wide blue eyes stared straight ahead, her face frozen in a horrible expression of rage.

"I don't know. Maybe," Mally whispered. She heard a faint sound and walked around Menda's body, looking for the source. The noise was coming from the seams she'd cut on the witch's shoulders. The twelve scissors sewn to Menda's back had shrunk down to their normal size, but even in their smaller state, they were too heavy for the weak stitching holding the doll's body together. The seams opened wide, the threads screaming as they stretched out of shape.

"Three... two... one..." Patch counted down as the heavy blades dragged towards the ground, distorting the velvet until it split cleanly across the back of Menda's neck. Matted stuffing sprang free and the fabric ripped further, opening around her arms and down her side seams. With a clang of metal, the scissors fell to the floor in a heap.

"Remind me not to get on your bad side, little Maker." Patch said, patting Mally on the back.

Mally smiled weakly. Menda's stuffing littered the ground and continued to leak out in small clumps. She was losing her shape. A chunk of fluff dropped from her head and her mouth disappeared into a deep wrinkle in the fabric.

With the scrape of metal, her body pitched forward, then stopped. Many of the scissor blades had sunk point first into the floor. Still attached to the fabric on her back, they were now acting like tent poles, holding her lumpy body upright. But the weight of her upper body, even without the scissors, was too great for the velvet fabric to support.

RRRIIIPPPPP!

Her back fabric split along the bottom edge and Menda fell flat on her face. The room filled with a cloud of stuffing. Mally covered her face, coughing.

"Watch out!" Patch leapt in front of her, his wings spreading wide. Something hit the other side of his body so hard Mally was knocked off her feet.

"What's happening? Patch?!" Mally couldn't see anything, but the crown suddenly wrenched around her head and flashed horrible images of long slashes in orange fabric. Patch fell on his side, kicking more fiber into the air as his wings crumpled underneath his body.

Mally could just make out something large skittering across the floor to the window. Like a spider, the witch crawled up the windowsill with her hands and feet. She'd lost all the stuffing on her back and only the single layer of fabric forming her torso remained, loosely flapping against her legs. Her frayed inner seams were exposed, making it look like she'd been turned inside-out.

Menda's head turned slowly, all the way around so it faced backward on her neck. Her face had lost another chunk of stuffing so one eye was lost inside a deep dent, but the other bulged, glaring back at Mally with a look she would never forget.

"That's... my... crown!" The witch crouched low, her arms braced against the window frame.

"No!" Mally screamed, her hands rising protectively over Patch. "Go away!"

Menda's grip suddenly slipped. Before Mally could say another word, before she could even draw a breath, the former Queen of Quilst tumbled backward off the windowsill.

For a second it looked like the wind would carry her. The fabric of her stomach billowed out and she floated. Her wrinkled mouth opened wide and she let out a shriek that matched the rage filling her eyes.

Then a breeze caught her black velvet arms and the limp cloth twisted around her legs. Her body deflated rapidly, the fabrics bunching together.

She dropped like a rock.

Mally ran to the window and watched her fall in a screaming mass of stuffing and ripped fabrics. Menda disappeared beyond the edge of the mountain and her shriek cut off abruptly. Silence filled the air.

Chapter 12

A Great Mend

"You did good, little Maker," Patch wheezed from the floor. "Or I guess it's little Queen now?"

Mally shook her head, confused. "I'm not sure what happened. Do you think she's dead?" She surveyed the mountain room, her shoulders slumping. The cuts on her hand were bleeding profusely. She gripped her fingers in a fist, but blood still seeped out the sides.

"I don't think anything could survive that fall. She's gone. That's all that matters."

But at what cost? Mally thought, trying not to look at the bundle of brown fabrics scattered across the floor. She glanced out the window. Nothing moved on the landscape outside and Mally couldn't see any sign of Thimble or the animals in the field.

Massive snarls dotted the ground, many frozen in the middle of ripping things apart. Very little solid fabric remained in the field below. *How in the world am I going to fix this?* Mally thought. The crown sent her a simple image of a single line of stitching. The answer was clear: just fix one thing at a time.

She found her broken bookbag in the corner and awkwardly pulled out her sewing box with her right hand. She carried it over to Patch. He'd been slashed three times across the chest and his white

203

stuffing was leaking out all over the floor.

"I guess I need to stitch you back together again. It seems you can't go five minutes without splitting your stitches." Mally said, trying to inject some humor in her voice she didn't feel. Her hands shook as she clicked open the latch.

"Fix the rabbit first," Patch said. "You did it all for her."

"I'll need your help," she whispered. "Can we fix her together, please?"

Patch nodded and closed his eyes. Mally felt something soft touch her arm and she jumped, spilling the contents of the sewing box all over the floor. But it was only Goldie and the band of animals that had made it into the mountain with her.

"Mally Maker, the door sealed tight and we weren't able to help you." Goldie's eyes were fixed on the crown spinning over her head. "We tried everything to break through. Many were lost and it only strengthened the barrier."

"It's fine. The plan worked. We got the scissors so she can't hurt anyone else," Mally said distractedly, trying to collect the sewing supplies scattered across the floor. She pulled out a scrap of fabric and tried to wrap it around her bleeding hand, but the fabric kept slipping out of place.

She opened her fingers and the sight of the three deep cuts made her squeeze her eyes shut. The room spun sickeningly around her and she fought to draw breath. *How can I stitch Patch back together with my hand bleeding like this? How in the world can I fix Ms. Bunny?*

"Can we help?" asked a purple monkey with a white swirling pattern on his chest. "We can all stitch too."

"Please," Patch said, rolling onto his back. More white fluff flowed from his split seams onto the floor. "Just don't get any of that witch's stuffing mixed up with mine. I'd rather be dead than smell like her."

Mally looked around and found a dozen eager faces looking back at her. She lost control over her tears for a second as a hot pink bear took her hand gently.

"I don't want to bleed on you!" she cried, her voice breaking. "It might never come off."

"I don't mind, Maker, um, Queen Mally," the bear said, bobbing her head lightly. "Red is my favorite color, though I don't mind the pink I was blessed with. My name is Hoop and I daresay me and Lime here can put your hand to rights." She nodded to a green humming-bird hovering nearby.

Mally held her hand out and with that small gesture an enormous weight lifted off her shoulders. Hoop and Lime worked on her hand while three mice, the purple monkey, and a black and white cat repaired the slashes on Patch's chest. They took turns scooping up his white fluff and packing it back into his body. In the corner of her eye she could see several mice working on the bundle of brown fabrics. She looked around the room for Pattern and Pin, but couldn't find them.

"They were lost when the door sealed," Hoop explained sadly. "The spider web shredded their fabrics apart. We lost so many. I just hope…" But she trailed off as she caught sight of the look on Mally's face.

With so many helping hands, the work was finished quickly. Mally was surprised when Hoop clipped the thread tails from her palm. It hadn't hurt at all and Lime had fixed her hand with a line of tiny stitches that almost completely blended in with her skin.

"Thank you so much," Mally said, smiling at the little humming-bird. His wings were speckled with dark red from her palm, but it seemed to bring out the green color of his patchwork body. He hummed loudly which she took to mean he was pleased. Mally glanced over at the mice still at work on Ms. Bunny.

"Your friend is going to be fine," Hoop said, patting her on the shoulder. Her paws were also stained red, but it didn't look as flattering on her fabric. Bloody paws didn't suit hot pink patchwork bears. "It was an honor to help and I don't mind the stain, really."

On impulse, Mally gripped her paws. She hadn't thought about the crown since Menda's attack, but now she was curious. *Can I fix this?* she asked.

The crown sent her an image of Hoop's fabric clean and pretty once more. So yes, it could be repaired, but how? Mally frowned. Then words seemed to rise up from her heart and spill out of her mouth.

"Heal. Return to the way you were made, and…" Mally glanced up at Hoop and smiled. "Be the color you love best." Instantly the blood stains disappeared from Hoop's paws and with a slow shift her hot pink fabric darkened to a deep crimson red.

"Oh!" Hoop gasped. "Thank you."

"You said you liked red, so I hope you like your color better now," Mally said. The crown spun a bit slower and she felt it give a gentle nudge, right between her eyes as if it was saying, *Good job, keep going.*

Suddenly Goldie scampered up her leg, her tiny face creased in a frown. "Maker… Queen Mally… she is missing a substantial piece from her chest."

"Substantial? What do you mean?" Mally asked.

"She'll be fine, but do you have something we could use as a patch?"

"Um… let me see." Mally rooted through the pile of scraps still scattered across the floor. She'd packed a large collection of fabrics back at the Great Tree, but none of them felt right. She looked at her own red shirt. It was blood stained, wrinkled and torn in several places. Another hole cut into it wouldn't hurt.

Mally pulled out the little scissors out of her necklace and cut into the frayed sleeve. She sliced in a circular motion, but strangely when she pulled the piece away it had cut a perfect heart shape. She handed it to Goldie who raced off to the little crowd around Ms. Bunny.

Mally began gathering up all the sewing tools, fabrics, and spools of thread off the floor and arranging the materials neatly in her sewing box. Her damaged hand felt strangely numb, but at least the cuts weren't bleeding.

The animals working on Patch suddenly began clapping as he sat up and stretched. All the slashes across his chest had been repaired so neatly Mally couldn't see the new seams between his orange fabrics. Snaking a huge paw over, he pulled her in for a hug. Mally wrapped her arms around his neck and squeezed.

"I'm afraid Ms. Bunny won't be the same," she whispered. The cursed words Menda stitched on Sunshine still rang in her head and she could only imagine what this hole in her chest looked like.

"She probably won't be," Patch said flatly.

Mally pulled back, glaring at him.

"Will you be the same after all this?" he asked. "Are you still the girl who can't stitch a seam to save her life? Will you go home and cry all the time?" He skimmed a paw over her cheek, wiping away a stray tear.

"No," she said, looking down at her palm and the faint lines of stitching that ran through the middle. "But I don't want her to be different. She was perfect the way she was."

"She will be again, with some extra thread and fabric on top. Look at all the stitching you've added to me. I'm no worse for the wear. I think she would like it if you helped put her back together, though."

With a quick pat on the back, Patch stood and made his way across the room to watch the animals working.

"Hey now, that's not where that goes!" he said.

Mally jumped to her feet and ran across the room. "What?"

She had sudden visions of all the ways the doll could be stitched back together wrong. But Patch had obviously been joking. The animals pulled back as she lifted her friend from the floor and cradled her in her hands.

Ms. Bunny looked perfect. Her body had been repaired with her two long legs and segmented arms stitched securely to both sides. A red heart covered the left side of her chest. The stitches were so fine it almost looked as if it was woven into the original fabric.

Only a short line of stitching remained on one of her ears. A threaded needle dangled from the small seam.

"Thank you so much. You all did such a beautiful job," Mally said, sinking down to sit on the floor.

And they had. Their tiny paws had made even tinier stitches. The seams were almost invisible from the outside unless you knew where to look. Mally took the needle and finished the stitches holding Ms. Bunny's ear in place.

She remembered that night, it felt like months ago now, when Rose had ripped off this ear. Mally had never considered fixing it herself. Now she slid the needle smoothly through the fabrics, trying to keep her stitches just as small and even as the rest.

The crown spun around her head and sent her images of Ms. Bunny's ear fixed with no needle and thread. *I know there are ways to fix this quicker,* she thought. *But I want to stitch her by hand.*

She tied off the threads and reached for the scissors in her necklace, but the holder was empty.

"It's okay. I've got it, dear," a familiar voice spoke and a brown paw slid the tool into her hand.

Mally gazed into the eyes of her best friend. Ms. Bunny smiled, her thread mouth quirking up slightly in the corners and Mally finally lost the battle with her tears.

Ms. Bunny wrapped her arms around her and it was a long time before she let go.

* * * * *

Eventually Mally pulled away and Ms. Bunny handed her the ear she'd just stitched in place. She laughed and wiped her eyes with it, as she had every time she'd cried for as long as she could remember. She sighed deeply as Ms. Bunny stepped back, looking good as new.

"You're okay?" Mally asked.

"Yes, dear, of course I'm okay. You all stitched me back together." Ms. Bunny patted herself down, pausing briefly over the heart stitched on her chest. She glanced around the room at the crowd of animals watching. "It seems we have a lot to catch up on. But first..." she suddenly leaned forward to whisper. "Can you get me a new dress? I don't think my pink calico made it."

Mally almost laughed out loud. Ms. Bunny, the sweet, prim and proper little rabbit didn't seem a bit phased at being ripped to pieces and stitched back together again. But running around without clothes on? That was too much.

Lime buzzed over suddenly and dropped a bright blue cloth into Mally's lap. He circled twice around her head and flittered off again to join Hoop by the window.

Mally picked up the cloth and realized it was a beautifully stitched dress, perfect for Ms. Bunny. She held it out for her friend and helped her slip it on. It was a simply pieced sleeveless shift with a wide neck and gathers on both shoulders. It hung to just above her feet and made her look taller and somehow older as well.

"What about that missing piece?" Mally asked. "Are you sure you feel alright?"

"No worries, dear," Ms. Bunny said. "It will all come together in the end."

"I think blue suits you, rabbit," Patch said. He was stretched out in a warm sunbeam nearby.

Ms. Bunny turned on her heel and marched over to the massive cat. For a second Mally thought she was going to smack him, but then she leapt on his side and wrapped her arms around his neck in a tight hug.

Patch closed his eyes as Ms. Bunny whispered something in his ear. Mally could hear his purr rumble up, even from across the room. They had never gotten along particularly well, but it seemed now the cat and the rabbit would be friends.

Mally looked down and found she was still clutching her tiny pair of scissors. Seeing the cutting tool reminded her of the scissors on Menda's back. They were still piled up in the center of the room, under a large piece of velvet fabric and a heap of smelly stuffing.

Mally took a deep breath. It was time to start using the crown as Creo had instructed. She sank her hands into the fiber and thought hard. *Can I make this disappear?*

An image of a clean room filled her head. *Yes.* Now to find the right words. Mally bit her lip, trying to hold her breath against the overwhelming smell of lavender. When the words came to her, she nearly laughed at how simple it was. "Go make this world better in some way."

A strong wind blew through the room and picked up the stuffing. It swirled between the patchwork animals like a snowstorm, then blew out the window. The room was silent for a beat, as all the animals stopped what they were doing and stared. Even Ms. Bunny was awe-struck, her ears standing straight up in surprise.

"You've been holding out on us, little Queen. You could have had me stitched back together in a second," Patch said.

"I'm not sure I'm doing it right. Would you really want to be my first test subject?" Mally asked, wiggling her fingers and everyone laughed.

She pulled on the scrap of velvet, but it wouldn't budge. The scissors were weighing the fabric down, making it impossible to flip over. On impulse she pressed her hand to the cloth and said, "Release."

All the scissors fell to the floor with a loud clatter. Mally flipped over the velvet and gasped. Words were stitched across the surface in silver thread. It hadn't been visible with all the metal tools in the way, but now she could clearly read:

I loved you with my whole heart, and you died.
I gave you everything, but you died.
I will miss you every day, and you will still be dead.
Menda Amare – Mistaken Love
In memory of my husband David Wright
Grace Mallory Harrison Wright

Mally's heart plummeted. There was no denying the truth any longer. She snatched the cloth off the floor and bundled it up as fast as she could. She glanced around the room, hoping no one else had seen the words. She carried it over to her bookbag and shoved it into the very bottom.

Then she piled the scissors on top and covered them with her sewing box. The bag made a noticeable metallic clanking sound, but hopefully she wouldn't need to be sneaking around anywhere else.

There was a cry from across the room. Ms. Bunny's head had fallen back, her eyes staring up at the ceiling. Then she cried again, clutching her chest and collapsed to the floor.

Mally was across the room in seconds. She scooped the doll up and cradled her in her hands.

"Ms. Bunny! What is it? What's wrong?"

"Everything feels… broken."

"What's broken? Where does it hurt?" Mally looked around for Goldie. "She was stitched perfectly! What's going on?" All the animals clustered close, their wide eyes staring, as the mouse darted up Mally's knee.

"I have no idea." Goldie pressed her paws over Ms. Bunny's chest and shook her head. "It seems the missing spot is what's giving her pain."

"Not me… the quilt…" Ms. Bunny gasped. "I can feel… the quilt…"

"The quilt?" Mally didn't understand.

"Trust that witch to come up with a failsafe," Patch growled. "She's woven them together."

Mally rounded on him. "What do you mean? Woven *what* together?"

"I've seen this before." He sighed heavily. "The piece she ripped, she sent it into the landscape in a snarl. Told the fibers to weave themselves in deep. She tied the rabbit to the quilt and the quilt to the rabbit. It was one of her favorite games to play."

"So the pain she's feeling…" Mally looked down at her best friend.

"It's an echo from Quilst," Patch said. "Everything ripped apart, all seams frayed and split will be reflected in that spot."

"Echoes." Mally touched the crown on her head and pain split through her skull. It lasted only for a fraction of a second, but that was long enough. She flinched, fighting back tears. Ms. Bunny was carrying this pain and soon she would be too. What had Creo said? She had until midnight.

Can't I fix her? She asked the crown in her mind. It placed two images before her. The first was the heart shape stitched over the doll's chest. The second was Quilst, repaired and beautiful once again. The message was clear. She would be healed only when the quilt was fixed.

She stroked Ms. Bunny's soft ears and folded them across her chest for comfort. She set the doll into Hoop's hands and rose shakily to her feet. All the animals scooted out of the way as she walked to the door.

The remnants of the spider web barrier hung loosely from the frame. She could see dozens of thread colors, bits of ripped fabric, and a few pieces of a quilt block near the corner. It looked like a blue bears claw. Mally pulled it all down into a pile on the floor. She ran her fingers over the door frame and wall, checking that she got every bit of frayed fabric.

"What are you doing, little Maker?" Patch asked.

"I need to fix this," she said, rolling up her sleeves. "I need to fix all of it by midnight."

"Says who? How do you know this?" Patch frowned. "And why midnight?"

"A woman told me when I touched the crown. It's a long story, but this–" she gestured at the crown "–shouldn't spin. Quilst is broken and I'm the only one who can fix it.

She sank her fingers into the shredded material. *What do I say to mend everything?* She thought. She focused on the soft fibers sliding against her skin and the right words flowed seamlessly out of her mouth.

"Heal. Stitch yourself back together. Fix whatever was broken and become whole again."

For a second she didn't think it worked. The broken pieces of thread and scraps of fabric just sat in a motionless heap on the floor. Then with a *whoosh* that ruffled her hair, half the pile disappeared. Everyone gasped as a swirl of fiber flew across the room to the window.

She ran over in time to see blue and purple threads weaving themselves back together along the seams Menda had ripped. She touched the windowsill cautiously. It was perfect. The fabrics were restored and a line of decorative stitching edged the seams.

"Look at that!" an excited voice called.

Mally whirled around. A mini tornado had formed in the doorway. Blue threads and scraps of fabric twisted in midair and slowly wove themselves back together. A Bear's Claw quilt block slowly took shape in the center.

"It's Pattern!" Hoop called and all the animals in the room cheered. Mally bit her lip as the block changed and the giant blue bear was suddenly standing in the doorway, good as new. He gripped the wall, shaking his head as a dozen animals rushed up for a hug.

"Mally Maker? What happened? The door sealed and that's the last…" His eyes grew wide as he spotted the crown on her head.

"It's okay, we won. Menda is gone." Mally let out a breath she hadn't realized she'd been holding. "I'm so happy you're back."

A red and green quilt block swirled together next to him.

"That'll be the Christmas Gang!" Goldie called and all the mice cheered as the block transformed into a festive cat and four tiny mice. They all looked dazed, and even more so when they were engulfed by a crowd of animals, all hugging and squeaking and talking to them at once. More quilt blocks wove themselves back together and soon the room was filled with happy chatter.

"That's everyone we lost when the door closed behind you," the purple monkey said as Pin's green face appeared in the doorway. "Everyone can be remade once again!"

The little crowd of animals cheered. Mally felt the spinning crown slow very slightly. She returned to Ms. Bunny's side. The doll took a deep, shuddering breath.

"Better," she said. "It feels a bit better."

"I'm going to fix it, Ms. Bunny. I'll fix everything," Mally said. "Just hang on and I'll be right back."

She turned and found Patch right behind her, his wings unfurled and ready to fly. He bent down slightly and Mally raced to his side and leapt onto his back.

"Maker Mally, err… Queen Mally, how can we help?" Pattern called from the door. He was still being hugged around the knees by the black and white cat, but he looked ready to take charge once more.

"Search the mountain and collect all the broken pieces," Patch answered for her. "Pile them up so she can fix it quickly."

Mally caught his logic instantly. "As long as the pieces are touching, I only have to mend them once. We need to fix everything before midnight."

"We'll go on a scrap hunt and pile it all up for you." Pattern saluted her, then turned to the other animals. "Come on, Queen Company! Let's clean up this mountain!"

"We're going to start on everything ripped outside and work our way back here." Mally searched the room for Hoop. "Can you take care of Ms. Bunny until we get back?"

"It would be an honor, Queen Mally," the red bear said with a bow.

With that Patch whirled around and raced to the window. Mally flattened herself against his back and with a mighty leap, they were out of the mountain and soaring through the air.

The ground below was a gruesome mess. Tangled spider webs hung off the mountains. Menda's last set of snarls had eaten the fabric right off the landscape, leaving huge piles of shredded fiber next to wide channels of white batting. Mally searched everywhere for animals, birds, anyone who had survived, but nothing moved. In the distance she could see a strange brown lump. Her hands clenched into fists as she realized it must be all that was left of the Great Tree.

Patch landed at the base of the mountain where the purple fabric met the green landscape. The surface gave sickeningly under his paws. Mally lurched off his back and sank her hands into a small mound of broken threads. She said the same words she'd used before and *whoosh* the pile disappeared. In seconds the purple patch of ground became sturdy and stable as the missing fibers knitted themselves back into the landscape.

But it was such a small space repaired. Mally could see miles of destruction stretching out in every direction. She took a deep breath. "One down, a hundred million to go."

"Think of it like taking your first thousand stitches," Patch suggested. "Except it's your first thousand magical repairs."

"Good idea. That was number nine hundred, ninety-eight." She scrambled onto his back, and then leaned over his side so she could skim her fingers through another tangle as he took flight. With a sound like a gunshot, the pile of threads burst apart and Patch nearly fell out of the sky.

"What was that?"

"I guess the bigger the pile, the louder the noise it makes," Mally said, watching the fibers swirl off to their proper places in the quilt. "That makes sense. It's a lot of stuff flying in all directions."

"Just give me a little warning next time, little Queen."

They worked together for hours. Mally sank her hands into everything broken she could find and at her words, the threads and fabrics instantly swirled away to repair the quilt. Patch took to carrying her in his front paws so he could drop her off, then swing around and scoop her back up again as the quilt mended itself.

At long last, only the spider web wall circling the largest purple mountain remained. It sagged over the landscape, like a great soggy necklace. By some unspoken agreement, they had saved the biggest mess for last.

Patch set her down a few feet from the wall and Mally walked toward it. Thread, yarn, and bits of recognizable quilt blocks were tangled together in the mess that stretched nearly thirty feet high in places.

Twisted ropes stuck out from the surface and it was hard to believe they wouldn't whip back to life and suck her inside. Mally wrapped her arms around herself as she drew near. It was cold in the shadow of the wall. She pressed her hands flat to the surface and felt a tremor echo through the landscape.

"Heal Quilst. Stitch yourself back together. Fix whatever was broken and become whole again," she said clearly. The ground shook and a sound like thunder rumbled in the distance, growing steadily louder. She raced back to Patch as pressure built against her skin.

She reached his side as the wall exploded. The force of the shock wave threw them to the ground. The sky went black as every broken thread, every ripped fabric sought out its original place in the landscape. Patch unfurled his wings, shielding her from the worst of the storm.

Mally covered her mouth with her hands, struggling to breathe as the air became thick with cotton and wool fibers. Her ears popped painfully as the whistle of flying fiber grew to a roar. It was like being in the middle of the tornado once again, only this time she had created the maelstrom.

Quite suddenly, everything stopped. Silence rang in Mally's ears and she pushed against Patch's wings. He released her and she sat up, not knowing what to expect.

The landscape of Quilst stretched out before her, as perfect lush and green as the first day she'd seen it. The blue sky was filled with birds once again and all the patchwork animals she'd brought to the mountain were back on the hillside, looking a bit confused, but no worse for the wear.

"It's back," she whispered. Soft yarn grass reached to her knees and tickled between her bare toes. She bent down and ran her fingers over the perfect seams and tiny stitches Grandma Grace had made to create the world. The Great Tree stood tall in the distance, its branches stretching high into the sky.

The crown had changed as well. With a sigh of relief, Mally felt it slow down and nearly stop spinning around her head. She was able to reach up and touch the braided band, something she wouldn't dare do before.

"You did good, little Queen," Patch said. "One thousand repairs at least. But we might want to tell them what's going on." He nodded at the growing crowd of animals congregating on the landscape.

Mally stood up on his back to give herself more height and waved her arms to get their attention. "It's okay! We won!" she yelled and a cheer went up as the animals gathered around them. Everyone started asking questions at once.

"Is the Ripping Witch dead?"

"How did you defeat her?"

"Where are my ears?!"

That last call came from the middle of the group where Mally could see a handful of threads still zipping through the air towards a gray monkey.

"Be patient," she said. "You've just been repaired, but it may take more time for all your threads to come back to you. I'll tell the whole story tonight at the Great Tree. Right now we need to find anything still broken. I've fixed everything here, but I know there's more in the far reaches of Quilst. Fan out and search and bring anything broken, even a single piece of cut thread to the tree tonight and we will fix this world once and for all."

"And make it quick," Patch added. "Or your new queen will have a mighty headache around midnight tonight."

The crowd of animals immediately turned and ran in all directions. Mally sighed and sat down on Patch's back. She rested her forehead briefly on the green star between his shoulder blades. The crown stopped spinning momentarily and it was such a relief.

"Tired, little Queen?"

"No, let's keep going." Mally sat up and shook her head. They were just about to take off when a voice called from above. Mally whipped around to find a familiar orange and yellow bird soaring out of the sky.

"Mally! Mally! Mally! Did it work? Did the flying geese help you?" Sunshine called. She looked perfect, every stitch in place, her bright little body glowing like a fireball.

Words failed her so Mally just opened her arms and Sunshine flew straight into her embrace. They fell to the ground in a tangled hug. When they finally broke apart, Sunshine hopped back on her short legs and cocked her head to the side.

"Hey! You took the crown! Oh my gosh! Oh my gosh! You're queen? Really?"

"Oh Sunshine! What you did—" Mally's eyes brimmed with tears as she remembered the battle on the mountain and the bird's brave sacrifice. "Yes, we won, and it's all thanks to you. How did you know about the crown?"

"Lucky guess." Sunshine shrugged. "She never took it off and once when I bumped into her, it slipped and she really freaked out. I figured if she wanted it that bad, it must be special. It is, isn't it? Super special?"

"Super special," Patch said. "You're smarter than you look, bird."

"Oh Patchy Poo! Thank you!" Sunshine rushed at the cat and enveloped him in her wings. After a long hug, she squared her small shoulders and Mally knew what she was going to ask next.

"Ms. Bunny? Have you found her?" she whispered.

"Yes. We found her and the mice stitched her all back together," Mally said quickly. "But..."

"Did you see the witch rip her chest? Did you see what she did with the pieces?" Patch asked.

"Yes, it was awful. She sent them off with one of those snarly things and said 'You know where to hide them' but I didn't know what that meant." Sunshine trembled, her wings wrapping tight around her body.

"She's going to be okay. I promise, she's going to be fine," Mally said. "We just need to fix Quilst as quickly as possible, and then find her missing pieces. Can you help us?"

"Of course!" Sunshine said. "What do you need me to do, Queen Mally Maker?"

"Tell the birds to search for anything broken and spread the word about the meeting tonight at the Great Tree. I need to fix everything before midnight tonight."

"Got it! Broken stuff to the Great Tree. Check!" Sunshine nodded her head vigorously.

"But there's one more thing," Mally said, drawing close and lowering her voice to a whisper. "I need you to look for Menda. What was left of her body fell out of the mountain. She was in really bad shape so I don't think she could have survived, but… I'd still like to find her body just in case."

"I'm on it! I'll find her Mally, I promise!" With that Sunshine rocketed into the sky. Birds swirled around her, then began breaking off in smaller flocks, heading in all directions.

"Are we going on a witch hunt too?" Patch asked.

"Yes," Mally said. "And a Grandma hunt. We have to find them both."

Patch beat his wings against the ground and they rose slowly into the sky. Mally smiled as she saw the spots of white disappearing one by one. No more batting leaking through. No more rips in the landscape. She hoped it would be enough for Ms. Bunny.

*   *   *   *   *

Patch flew up to the mountains and wove between the peaks. They hadn't searched this area as thoroughly and Mally could see many seams had yet to be healed. She heard a faint noise from below and leaned across Patch's back to look down. They were at least a hundred feet off the ground, but she could have sworn she heard the neigh of a horse.

"There's something down there," she called to Patch, pointing at a spot between two mountains.

"Let's check it out." He angled his wings to take them into a steep dive. Mally spotted a long split in the ground between a purple and blue mountain. Batting filled the gap and there on the edge stood a massive brown horse. They landed awkwardly and Patch stumbled on the frayed ground.

"Oak?" he yelled suddenly.

"Patch? Is that you?" a female voice called back. The horse stepped cautiously into the light and Mally gasped. She towered over Patch, nearly twenty feet tall. Like the cat, she was a mix of many different fabrics, but her seams were all curved like the bark of a tree. Thick white hair flowed wildly across her shoulders, framing her beautiful face and huge gray eyes.

But it was the sight of her body that had caught Mally's attention. Her chest had been crudely ripped open. The hole stretched across her front, nearly two feet wide, the edges frayed and tattered. The cloth surrounding the cut had been badly distorted, and as Mally watched, small bits of stuffing and loose threads broke free and fell on the ground.

"Well, look who grew up and sprouted wings," the horse said, obviously pleased. "How long has it been, my friend?"

"Too long, old girl. Too long," Patch said gruffly.

Mally slipped off his back quickly and immediately Patch hugged the horse with both paws wrapped around her neck. Mally noticed he was careful to avoid the gaping hole in her chest.

"I see you've brought along a friend." Oak's large eyes were on Mally as they broke apart.

"Um... hi. My name is Mally," she said, stepping forward with her hand outstretched.

Oak pulled her head back with a snort. "She's a Maker. Patch, what are you doing? Did you learn nothing from our dealings with them before?"

"I'm sure... he has good reason... to be with this girl," came a soft, gasping voice. Mally looked around for who had spoken.

There came a rustling from inside Oak's chest. More white fiber rained down her front and a set of glittering red eyes suddenly gazed out of the torn hole. It was Mally's turn to step back as the fabric around the cavity bulged. A dark shape moved within the horse's body.

Oak's face contorted in obvious pain, but she quickly bent her head down and Mally caught her whisper, "Shh... don't wear yourself out now. It's our friend, Patch. Everything is going to be fine."

A soft, halting voice replied, "I know... I know. Don't... worry." More rustling came from the hole and the red eyes closed briefly, then opened to stare at Mally. "I am Shadow. Forgive Oak's... rudeness. She's carrying... a heavy burden. We have been... falling... for so long... and this is the first time we've seen... the sun in ages."

"What happened to you two?" Mally asked, pressing her hands over her heart. Just looking at the rip in Oak's fabric made her own chest ache.

"The Ripping Witch happened," Patch growled, but his voice softened as he asked the horse, "How has he been doing?"

"I'm right here... I may not be... whole... but I'm not deaf," Shadow said, and Oak gasped as the fabric over her shoulders and neck rippled. She lifted her head quickly, her ears pulled back and teeth bared as a small black owl emerged and perched on the edge of her frayed fabrics. His triangular face tilted to look up at Patch and Mally saw his wings were wrapped tight around his chest. Something about the way he gripped his body reminded her instantly of Ms. Bunny.

"You have a missing piece too," Mally reached out automatically to help.

"Stay back, Maker." Oak shied away from her hands. "Don't touch him!"

"Calm, Oak... let the Maker... speak," Shadow said in his slow, gasping voice.

The horse pulled her long neck back with a snort. Mally cautiously approached and peered down at the little owl. He slowly spread his wings and she flinched at the sight. His entire chest had been shredded. Ribbons of frayed fabric remained, but it wasn't enough to hold his stuffing inside. He had to keep his wings wrapped tightly around himself at all times.

"Menda did this? She took threads from you?" Mally whispered.

"Yes... it has hurt... ever since."

"Is there anything you can do?" Patch asked quietly.

Mally closed her eyes and lightly touched the ripped fabric. *How can I fix this?* she thought, but again the crown only showed her an image of Quilst fully repaired, just as it had for Ms. Bunny. Her shoulders slumped. "Did it get any better today? Is the pain less?"

The owl closed his eyes and swayed back and forth. "I am... talking to you. So yes... it's better today."

"Good. My friend has a missing piece too. We're going to fix it all, I promise," Mally said, but her words felt empty in the face of Oak and Shadow's obvious pain. The little owl shifted back inside the horse's chest and closed his eyes.

Mally's attention was suddenly caught by something fluttering in the breeze over Oak's back. There on the side of the mountain, looped through a long stitch was a strip of brightly colored cloth. "What is that?"

She ran over and pulled it down. It was a silk scarf. She slid it through her hands and watched the colors shift smoothly from red to orange to bright yellow. And there at the end was a big blue dot.

She dyed fabric and scarves with Grandma one sunny Saturday before her eighth birthday. She could still remember the hot sun on the back of her neck and the way sweat kept trickling down into her gloves, but Grandma wouldn't let her take them off. She had painted what felt like a hundred scarves that day, and this one was her favorite. Bright and cheerful with the colors of the sun. She'd painted it carefully and set it apart from the rest to dry.

But when she checked it later, she'd nearly cried. A single drop of blue paint had landed in the middle of the yellow section. It was ruined. In a split second she went from loving the scarf to hating it so much she never wanted to see it again.

But Grandma had loved it. She'd kept it and wore it almost every day. Mama had searched her house top to bottom looking for it, along with Grandma's favorite red quilted jacket. It had nearly driven her crazy looking for this scarf, yet here it was.

"Patch, this is Grandma's scarf." Mally held it up, stunned. Her eyes were brimming with tears as she asked Oak, "Where did this come from?"

But it was Shadow who answered in his labored voice, slightly muffled from inside the horse's chest. "The Quilt Maker... She was... falling... with us... When the white filled the darkness... she helped us... climb up..."

"The Quilt Maker? You knew my grandma?" Mally asked excitedly.

"A story for another day," Patch interrupted, and Mally saw a strange look pass from Patch to Oak. Before she could ask, the horse flicked her tail at the path curving around the base of the mountains.

"She wandered off in that direction. She didn't want to stick around for the Ripping Witch to catch her a second time."

"We need to find her," Mally said impatiently, turning to look up the path. Her bare feet itched to take off running, but a painful twist from the crown reminded her she still had duties to fulfill here. "She won't know what's happened and probably thinks Menda is still a threat."

"The crazy hag is gone, then?" Oak asked.

"There's a lot to catch you up on, my friend. The Ripping Witch is no more, and you have this little Maker, now the new Queen of Quilst, to thank for that," Patch said, patting Mally on the back with one huge paw.

"Queen? I noticed the crown. That's a dangerous amount of power for a Maker to carry."

"Menda wasn't a Maker, she was a monster," Mally said, clutching the scarf in her fist.

But Grandma made Menda, a little voice in her head reminded her. *What does that make Grandma?*

Mally shook her head, ignoring the thought. "I would never use this power to do anything like Menda. I'm using it to fix Quilst."

With that she marched past the horse to the gaping tear in the landscape. She sank to her knees and buried her fingers in the frayed fabric. The scarf was still clutched in her hand and one end blew against her face as she said the magic words.

Whoosh!

She opened her eyes and watched the broken threads weaving themselves together along the edge of the fabrics. Many pieces of cloth and fiber flew off to fix things further away. She smiled as the path became perfect once more. Thousands of French knots formed a gray path that snaked its way between the mountains.

The fabrics were no longer frayed, but crisply turned and decorated with a simple blanket stitch where the two mountains overlapped. She ran her fingertips along the seam and felt her eyes burn. *Grandma. If you'd only stayed here with Oak and Shadow, we could be going home right now.*

The crown twisted painfully around her head again and she caught herself. Even if she had found Grandma, there was still a lot of work to be done before she could go home.

The sound of flapping wings had her spinning around in alarm.

221

Shadow perched on the edge of the hole in Oak's chest, stretching one wing, then the other, a look of shock spread across his small face. He flew a short distance and landed on the horse's back. His tiny beak quirked into a smile at their shocked faces. "Thank you, Queen Mally. That was a great mend."

He bowed to her and Mally was momentarily distracted from her thoughts about Grandma as she caught sight of Shadow's chest. Apparently a lot of the broken threads between the two mountains had belonged to him because only a small hole remained on the left side of his chest, just like Ms. Bunny's.

Without pausing to think, she ripped a piece from her shirt sleeve and held it out. "Patch and heal, hold and seal. Make him as whole as I am able."

The crown spun around her head slowly and Mally watched as a tiny red heart formed on Shadow's chest, the ends of the fabric weaving into the edges of the hole. The owl stared at the spot for several seconds, then with a shrill screech, he took off. His black wings beat against the air, carrying him higher and higher into the mountains.

"Careful you don't strain your stitches!" Oak shouted from the ground, her four hooves dancing nervously. The hole in her chest gaped wider than ever and white stuffing littered the path around her.

"He'll be fine. You, on the other hand, aren't looking so hot," Patch said, holding out a clump of her fluff.

"You try carrying around a friend who can barely talk, let alone walk or fly! I've managed. Just pack it back in, Patch. You know how it goes."

The crown tightened around Mally's head and she knew what it wanted her to do. She approached the horse cautiously and held out her hands. "Can I help you too? That looks so painful."

Oak stared down at her and Mally could see fear in her eyes warring with desire to be free of the pain. She shared a look with Patch that Mally couldn't interpret and finally nodded her head in assent.

Mally held her hands out and with a few words, stuffing, thread, bits of cloth, and decorative yarns were speeding back to their rightful place. Shadow soared down and landed on Patch's shoulder just in time to see the last stitches lock together.

The effect was amazing. The fabrics repaired themselves seamlessly and this time no hole was left behind. Brown fabrics flowed over

Oak's chest in gentle curving seams, making her even more wildly beautiful than before. The horse suddenly reared, silver hooves flashing as she pawed the sky, then she took off galloping up the path.

"She didn't have a missing piece?" Mally asked, watching as Oak became a brown blur against the blue mountains.

"No. The Ripping Witch didn't make that hole," Shadow said with a sad smile.

"That was me," Patch said, looking down at one of his paws. "There are a lot of things we had to do back then that I'd never like to do again." He extended his sharp claws one by one and Mally shuddered.

"Why did you have to–"

But she was interrupted by Oak's return. The horse galloped right up to Mally. Her huge body towered over her and Mally fought the urge to step back. She'd always loved horses and Oak was magnificent, but also a little scary at the same time.

The horse stared down at her for a long second, then suddenly bent her front legs and bowed. Her long neck extended for several seconds before she lifted her head and spoke quietly, "I see now that I was wrong. You aren't a Maker, little one, you're a healer. Thank you."

She turned and nuzzled Shadow gently. The owl batted her face playfully with his wings and Mally could see a glimmer of what these friends were like before Menda had gotten a hold of them.

"We'd better get going," Patch said, arching his shoulders to knock Shadow off his back. "We have a lot more damage to repair before the day is done."

"And Grandma is just up the path. We might run into her along the way," Mally said excitedly, wrapping the scarf securely around her neck.

"Before you go, I'd really like to know how you took the crown," Shadow said, landing neatly on a nearby rock. It was strange to see the owl moving so easily after being critically hurt just moments before. "I can't imagine the Ripping Witch parted with it easily."

"No, she didn't. We're meeting tonight at the Great Tree," Mally said as she climbed onto Patch's back. "If you'd like to hear the whole story."

"We'll be there."

Chapter 13

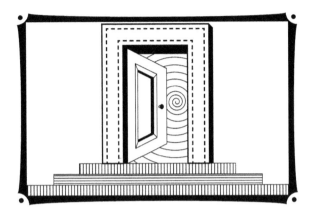

Maker of Menda

Mally kept her eyes peeled for any sign of movement as they flew through the mountain pass. She kept thinking she saw Grandma hiking up a slope or walking through the narrow spaces between the triangles, but every time they drew closer it was just a dead snarl or tangled bit of ripped fabric.

The suns had passed the highest point in the sky and the mountains cast shadows against one another, making it hard to see anything from a distance. Eventually they had to give up and fly back to the mountain room.

Patch angled his wings into a dive and Mally tucked herself tight to his back. They shot through the window and animals scattered in all directions as Patch's paws skidded across the floor.

"I need to make that window bigger," Mally said, climbing off his back with a laugh. "Maybe a balcony so you can land–"

Her words died in her throat as she took in the most amazing sight. At first she wondered if they'd come to the right place. The stark room was now filled with color and light. In the center of the floor, a pair of wings had been outlined in gold thread.

Mally recognized the shape and realized the mice had stitched along the pencil lines Ms. Bunny had marked around her on that horrible day they were trapped in this room. Delicate swirls of stitching in white, silver, and black spun around the elegant motif. In the corners, cream colored fabrics had been seamed together cleverly to look like Roman columns.

But the real masterpiece of the room was the story tapestry. Stretching from floor to ceiling, and wrapping around each wall, the story of Quilst was illustrated in brightly colored threads.

Mally's face burned as she saw a tiny figure in a red shirt standing before the Great Tree, racing away from a tornado, and wielding a small blade against a dark monster. Most of the details were just outlined, but she could see how beautiful the room would look when it was complete.

"Do you like it, Queen Mally?" came a tiny voice from the center of the room.

"I love it," Mally said in wonder. She tore her eyes away from a new set of doors stitched on the side wall and found a crowd of patchwork animals surrounding Hoop and Ms. Bunny in the corner. "It's just incredible."

"We all thought it could use more decoration in here. Too much purple," Goldie said, scrunching up her tiny nose. Lime hovered nearby with a threaded needle in his beak and Mally could see how they'd added stitching even to the ceiling.

"Ms. Bunny suggested adding the columns," sang a red and green mouse from the Christmas gang.

"We found your sewing box filled with thread and needles," Pin chimed in. "I hope you don't mind us using your materials."

"Of course not," Mally said, distracted. She'd just noticed that Ms. Bunny was still laying in Hoop's paws. The bear didn't meet her eyes as she bent down and asked, "How are you, Ms. Bunny?"

"Better... a bit better," the doll said, sitting up with difficulty. She kept both her paws tightly clamped over her heart and tried to lift herself with her elbows.

"Why is she still hurting?" Mally asked, looking at Patch. "I fixed everything broken I could find and it worked for Shadow. It should be much better now." The crown on her head was spinning so slowly, she couldn't believe the quilt could still be hurting her friend.

"But her missing piece remains," Hoop said solemnly. "I don't know how this will fare until all the threads taken from her are returned."

Mally took a deep breath. They had worked all day, scouring the landscape for broken bits of the quilt, but it wasn't enough. "I'll keep working, Ms. Bunny," she said softly. "I'll be right back."

She stood and swayed on her feet. The crown suddenly felt much heavier and the room spun slowly around her. She reached out to steady herself and felt Patch's solid body at her side.

"Queen Maker!"

"Mally!"

All the animals in the room rushed over in alarm.

"I'm fine. I'm fine." She rubbed her temples and glanced outside. The moons were just peeking over the edge of the landscape. Midnight was coming and if this was any indication, the quilt was much further from being fixed than she thought. The dizzy spell passed and she looked around for Goldie.

"Where is Pattern? Did he find anything broken for me to fix?"

"Yes," Goldie said. "He's collected it all in the throne room. Come see!"

Mally and Patch followed the mouse through an endless maze of purple hallways. It was impossible to tell anything apart, but Goldie somehow knew where she was going.

The passageway suddenly opened into a vast chamber. Purple was still the only color in residence, but Mally could see the animals had already started making improvements here as well. Outlines for three stained glass windows had been stitched into the dark fabric along one wall. Dozens of patchwork paws were busy stitching bright threads and fabrics to the surface.

Mally caught sight of a small pile of broken fibers in the middle of the room. She rushed over to mend the damage and it disappeared with a *whoosh*. A cheer went up around the room and she looked up to find Pattern, Patch, and a host of mice and the black and white cat watching her.

"That's better... but I can still feel more..." Mally frowned as the crown spun faster.

"This way, Queen Mally," Pattern said and led them to the next room where another mound of broken threads was piled up along one wall.

"Why didn't you just pile it all up in the main room?" Patch asked as he followed them.

"I decided to split it up so she wouldn't create another earthquake and tornado at the same time," Pattern replied. "I didn't think that was a good idea in the middle of a mountain."

"You saw that?" Mally asked.

"I felt it, along with everyone here," he said. "You rebuilt three mountains in a few seconds, or did you not notice?"

"Oh, I certainly noticed," Patch said. "It was like standing in a thread blizzard and just about as much fun."

*　*　*　*　*

Back in the room with the window, Mally was happy to find Ms. Bunny sitting up on her own, couching thick green threads to the wall. She stood and gave a little twirl, her blue dress fanning out around her skinny legs. Just like Shadow, she couldn't seem to resist celebrating being free of pain.

Mally scooped her up into her arms and her friend smiled. "I don't think I'm used to seeing you with a crown on your head, Mally dear."

"Neither am I," Mally whispered back. "How are you feeling?"

"Good enough to come with you and Patch. I hear we're having a gathering at the Great Tree tonight to fix the last of the broken pieces."

"I hope so. I asked Sunshine for help so…"

"She'll make it happen if she has to fly to every corner of the quilt herself," Ms. Bunny said with a laugh, hopping down from Mally's arms to join the mice stitching the floor.

Hoop smiled up from her stitching nearby. "The quilt is being healed so I think that's helped greatly as well." The bear was working on a small bag and had spread out the contents of Mally's sewing box on the floor. Needles, threads, seam rippers and scissors were neatly arranged in piles and the animals were helping themselves to the tools as needed.

Mally's heart picked up speed as she noticed her bookbag propped against the wall under the window. She hurried over and unzipped the bag quickly to check inside. The black velvet fabric cut from Menda's back was folded neatly in the bottom of the bag. She could have sworn she'd just stuffed it inside. *What if they find out Grandma made Menda?* she thought.

"Shouldn't I take the scissors back with me?" she asked, giving voice to another fear.

"The only creature with the ability or desire to rip this world has been ruined herself. We need at least a few blades to cut threads for this decorative stitching," Hoop said with a slight edge to her voice, gesturing at the walls and floor. Many of the animals around the room stopped stitching to watch their exchange.

"But what if someone cuts into the fabric again?" Mally asked. "I'm afraid Ms. Bunny will be hurt if the quilt gets damaged again."

"No one here wants that, little Queen, or they wouldn't be stitching their paws off just to make it pretty," Patch said dryly. "Take the biggest shears. They're too big for most of us to handle. Leave the rest."

"Can I trust you to keep these safe?" Mally asked Hoop.

The red bear rose slowly to her feet and held out the purple bag she'd just finished making. Mally scooped up the seven smaller scissors and placed them in the bag with a metallic clatter. Hoop held it up and spoke clearly, "I am Hoop, Scissor Guardian of Quilst, I will protect these tools and ensure they are never used to harm this world."

"Thank you Hoop," Mally said and the tension over the scissors eased out of the room. She let her eyes travel over the walls and take in the gorgeous embroidery and delicate patterns being added and she couldn't help but be happy the animals had made these improvements. She could only imagine how pretty it would look in a few days time.

"Well, it looks like you're all going to need a lot more fabric and thread," she said, placing the five largest pairs of scissors carefully into her bookbag, then topping them with her empty sewing box.

"As to that, we have several requests. We'll make a list for you and bring it to the meeting at the Great Tree." Hoop smiled.

"Speaking of that, shouldn't we get going?" Ms. Bunny asked. "The moons are rising so midnight can't be far off."

"Could we fix this window first?" Patch asked, frowning at the little square in the wall.

"I was thinking about a little deck," Mally said. "With a bigger doorway. The suns are so beautiful and that would certainly brighten up the space. But how can I cut the fabric without hurting the quilt?"

"I would hazard a guess," Hoop put in, "that if you asked nicely, Queen Maker, it would be done with no damage to anyone."

With that, the bear clapped her huge paws, "That's enough for today, Queen Company! We have a meeting at the Great Tree to attend so put your needles away and climb on!"

All the mice, monkeys, and cats stashed their needles in a make-shift pincushion by the door and raced over to the bear. Hoop gripped her scissor bag in her mouth and shifted to stand on all fours so the smaller animals could scamper onto her back.

"Yay! We're going to the Great Tree!" two mice from the Christmas gang sang. "We'd better hurry or Queen Mally will beat us there. Go, Hoop, go!"

The animals on Hoop's back waved as the bear turned and bounded for the door. Mally could hear the steady patter of paws moving through the mountain. Birds of all shapes and sizes filled the sky. All the creatures of Quilst were on the move and headed for the Great Tree.

Mally focused on the small window and altering it to be just exactly what Patch and the other flying animals would need to easily come and go. She considered her words as she walked over to the square cut into the wall.

She pressed her hand against the purple fabric and an electric jolt shot up her arm to the crown on her head. The band twisted in place, but it didn't hurt. She closed her eyes and imagined how she wanted the new doorway to look with a small deck outside surrounded by a braided railing.

RRIIIIPPPPP!

The purple fabric tore cleanly down the wall and curved over the window. She turned quickly to check on Ms. Bunny, but she was shaking her head.

"It didn't hurt. Not a bit. Let me see what you've made."

Mally scooped her up and turned to find the work nearly complete. The window had fashioned itself into a wide open door. Fabric ripped from the wall shifted outside to become a small balcony. She watched as threads braided together in midair to form a sturdy railing. It fit her imagination so perfectly it was almost scary.

"I'd say that's a job well done. Now don't go forgetting how to stitch something by hand, little Maker," Patch said, patting her on the back.

"Of course not." Mally said. Even now her fingers itched to add extra detail to the railing and color, any other color over this purple.

She stepped out to the balcony and gripped the railing as the wind whipped through her hair.

Quilst stretched below, and at least from this distance, appeared perfectly pieced. The light from the two moons shone silver over the curving landscape. A smile spread across her face as she searched for the glow of exposed batting and couldn't spot a single patch.

"It's in much better shape, dear," Ms. Bunny said with a sigh. "I can feel it coming back together."

"The crown is spinning so much slower," Mally said, running her fingers over the shifting band. "I think a few things are still broken, but far less than it was earlier today. I just wish this had never happened to you."

"I know, dear." Ms. Bunny took her hand and ran her soft paw over her stitches. "We'll just have to make the best of the scars we carry from this adventure."

"Well ladies, I do believe we have a date with more broken junk and several hundred patchwork pals," Patch said, stepping out onto the balcony with his colorful wings unfurled. "Shall we?"

He took flight easily from the little platform and immediately they were surrounded by a variety of birds. Triangular flying geese began diving around them, creating beautiful patchwork patterns in the sky. A handful of hummingbirds buzzed around Mally's head before speeding off for the Great Tree, closely followed by the swarm of honeybees.

Mally laughed as the birds formed shapes together in midair, so close Patch had no choice but to fly through an endless stream of circles, squares and stars created by the happy geese. They were passing through a particularly long spinning tunnel made by birds lining up side to side when a thunderous roar sounded from below.

The birds broke apart in a rush and Mally panicked, searching the ground for the source of the commotion. Animals packed the clearing around the Great Tree. Everyone was screaming, but she couldn't see anything attacking them. The roar of sound filling the air was so close to the rumble of a snarl she reflexively reached for the seam ripper in her pocket.

"It's okay. There's nothing wrong," Ms. Bunny said, pressing a paw against her hand. "They're just celebrating."

Indeed they were. Fluffy chicks bounced up and down on Thimble's back while monkeys and frogs did summersaults down the grassy hill. Pattern and Hoop were just bounding into the clearing with dozens of animals from the mountain riding on their backs. Mally spotted Oak's mane of white hair near the Great Tree as they circled the field.

Patch landed smoothly on the Nature Path to a storm of applause. He slowly walked up to the Great Tree while the crowd went wild all around them. Paws of every shape and size pressed against Mally's legs. She clapped and cheered along with them, so happy to see all their colorful faces restored.

But as they neared the tree, her crown began to spin. Mally suddenly pitched off Patch's back, her head splitting in pain. The crown sent her flashes of broken seams, frayed threads, and a pile of debris nearly as tall as the Great Tree. For the first time an intense electric shock accompanied each image. She glanced up at the sky. The two moons were nearly directly overhead.

The animals crowded tightly around her. Mally struggled to move against the press of their soft bodies. She could see the pile of broken pieces ahead but couldn't reach it, and the crown wasn't happy about it.

"Make way for the Queen!" Patch roared and blessedly the path cleared. She ran straight for the hill of broken fiber and sank to her knees. The animals were shouting questions, but she ignored them all as she shoved her hands, right up to her elbows, into the damaged material. A tremor rippled through the ground and the crowd went quiet in time to hear Mally say the words:

"Heal. Stitch yourself back together. Fix this world and make Quilst beautiful once more."

Immediately the pain in her head eased. She sat back on her heels and sighed as the crown finally stopped spinning. She barely noticed the ground shaking or the broken threads swirling around her. She sat in blissful stillness for a full minute as the last split seams of the quilt were repaired.

Mally got shakily to her feet and looked around in surprise. It was like walking through a door and suddenly realizing she was on stage. Everyone was staring at her, standing eerily silent and still.

Then as one, they bowed.

Every animal from the tallest bear to the tiniest bumblebee lowered their head and sank to the ground before her. The landscape shook as their movement spread across the field. Mally's heart squeezed. So many animals, so many beautiful creatures in this vast world. It was only just dawning on her what being the Queen of Quilst would mean.

"Thank you… Thank you so much," Mally said pressing her hands to her racing heart.

They were just raising their heads when a booming voice rang out from the middle of the field, "All hail Mally the Maker, Queen of Quilst!"

"Queen Mally! Queen Mally!" the crowd roared and she found herself scooped up by dozens of paws and carried to the Great Tree where Patch and Ms. Bunny waited.

"Ready to tell the story, little Maker?"

"Any chance you could do it for me?" Mally's hands shook as she climbed onto Patch's back. Ms. Bunny immediately scrambled onto her shoulder and she felt immensely comforted by her warm weight.

"Nope. Not part of my job description." Patch shrugged. "Just tell the story. You are wearing the crown and they clearly accept you as queen. They just want to know how it all happened."

So Mally told the story of the attack on the mountain and Menda's horrible spider web wall. She found Pattern in the crowd and thanked him for catching her when the ropes attacked. It seemed all the bears favored a larger-than-life size so the small group stood out, nearly ten feet taller than everyone else.

She explained how they ripped their way through the web wall, but were only able to get through because of the sacrifice of over one hundred flying geese, led by Sunshine. As they were mentioned, dozens of birds flew across the clearing, their triangles lined up perfectly side by side.

They soared towards the Great Tree and on impulse Mally held her hands up high in the air. She had only seconds to find the right words as the birds rushed towards her. She skimmed her fingers along their fabrics and as they swirled back into the sky, their wings were marked with a glittering gold ring.

"We would've been trapped without them," Mally declared and the crowd cheered as the flock returned to the sky. "Please carry a piece of my crown, and my thanks with you forever." The birds immediately began showing off, flying together, then splitting apart to create pretty patterns with their new wings.

But one very important bird was missing. Mally frowned, searching for Sunshine, but she couldn't find her. Ms. Bunny asked what was wrong and Mally just shook her head and continued with the story.

She explained how Goldie and her gang of mice led them through the tunnels and into the witch's mountain. Cheers went up as the smallest creatures of Quilst were picked up and applauded by the entire crowd.

The hardest part of the story was what happened inside the mountain room. Mally looked down at Patch who nodded, giving her permission to tell the whole story.

So she did. She explained how they tricked Menda into thinking Patch had betrayed them until the last second. A collective gasp went through the gathering as she described the witch's back ripping away and the scissors falling to the ground.

The greatest roar went up as Patch yelled, "And then the crown fell from her head. The Ripping Witch is no more!"

Mally felt the crowd's excitement and happiness flowing through the crown. She looked up to the sky and imagined fireworks bursting above them and suddenly they were there in the sky. Colorful threads burst in all directions and rained down in bright, glittery streams. It was quite awhile before the crowd calmed down.

Ms. Bunny tugged on Mally's sleeve. "We could still use some help finding your missing Grandma. Why don't you ask for help?"

Mally felt uncomfortable, remembering Oak's dismissive attitude and Shadow's cryptic comments. "What if they say no?"

"Why don't you ask and see?"

So Mally gathered her courage. She raised her hands again and the crowd gradually grew quiet.

"Thank you all for your help today. I know many were lost or broken in the attack. I never want that to happen again. Now there are two tasks left for us. We need to find Menda's body. It fell out of the mountain room, so it should be somewhere in that area. Also please continue collecting anything broken, any fabrics ripped or threads cut and bring them here. Everything can be repaired and all the friends we lost today can be remade!"

A large turkey stepped out of the crowd. Mally recognized it as Spool from the meeting the night before. "If Mally the Maker desires, I can take a squad of turkeys and begin the search around the mountain base."

"Yes, um… but there is one more thing." Mally squared her shoulders. "My Grandma, the Maker of this world is still missing."

A strange murmur ran through the crowd. Seam, the sentry of the Great Tree stepped forward, his dark body stretching nearly fifteen feet tall.

"We have learned today that this Maker you speak of is in fact the Maker of the Ripping Witch."

Mally froze. The crowd went silent, all eyes staring at her. She felt like she'd been slapped. Ms. Bunny shifted closer on her shoulder and whispered quietly in her ear, "They all know, Mally. There's no way to hide it. Best be as honest as you can, dear."

She squared her shoulders and took a deep breath. "Yes, my Grandma made Menda." A shudder rippled through the crowd. Bodies shifted around her, restless and agitated.

"I don't know the whole story. I don't know why she did it, but I still need your help finding her."

Seam crossed his arms over his chest, drawing his body up so he towered over her. Even on Patch's back she felt tiny.

"We will help. We will search, but when she is found this Maker must leave and never return. The Maker of Menda is not welcome here."

*   *   *   *   *

Hours later Mally rolled onto her back and stared up at the ceiling. She'd finally had a chance to tour the Great Tree and climb the beautiful woven spiral staircase. Multiple rooms were arranged on each floor, their walls curving with the shape of the tree trunk. It was exactly as she'd imagined it, right down to the tree shaped lanterns on the wall.

But she had always imagined being here with Grandma, sewing together in the little nook downstairs, reading in the sunshine and walking around the massive branches outside. So much of the fun in the imagining was thinking of how they would spend time together here.

She had argued against kicking Grandma out of Quilst last night. She'd asked for more time before an ultimate decision was made.

Maybe if they knew the whole story, Menda's existence would make more sense. But in the end, she had to acquiesce to their near unanimous demand.

The weight of her crown felt too heavy to bear as she proclaimed the words, "Please seek out and find my Grandma, Grace Mallory Wright. It's time for her to go home. The Maker of Menda must leave the world of Quilst."

She'd paused here, but Oak's head had risen from the crowd next to Seam. The horse glared across the field and Mally had no choice. "Forever," she added in a whisper.

*   *   *   *   *

This is Grandma's quilt! Mally thought, punching her pillow viciously. *Grandma made it. If anyone should be queen, it should be her! But where in the world is she?*

She picked up the silk scarf from her bedside table and ran the soft fabric through her fingers. In the dim light, she couldn't see the blotch of blue paint on the end. That mistake was only visible in the light.

Mally closed her eyes and focused on the light weight and silky texture sliding against her skin. She wished she could go back to that hot day painting in the sunshine with Grandma.

So much had happened. Everything had changed and she wasn't sure she really knew who her Grandma was now. How could she have made Menda? Why? The same questions swirled endlessly through her head until she finally drifted off to sleep.

*   *   *   *   *

Mally blinked and found herself standing in a strange place. Patchwork steps in a random mix of colors stretched out below.

She caught a sudden movement in the corner of her eye and turned quickly to find a dark shape crouched before an Open Door. Mally recognized the teal frame. This was the quilt block she'd used to replace the door ruined by Menda's tornado.

But the light in the door was flickering. It blinked out for a second, then came back on, then out again. Mally squinted, trying to make sense of what she was seeing. Then pain, more intense and immediate than she'd ever felt before split through her head.

She gripped her face with both hands as the crown wrenched this way and that. Tears clouded her eyes as she fell to her knees.

"Do I have your attention, Mally May? Can you see me, or do I need to do more damage?" The dark shape shifted. Menda's horrible white face was suddenly illuminated in the bright light.

However deformed she'd looked in the mountain room, nothing could prepare Mally for the sight of her now. She crouched on all fours, the fabric of her torso twisted so many times it formed a kink in her back.

She'd lost significant amounts of stuffing from her legs, arms and head. What little stuffing was left was shoved tight to the tips of her appendages, leaving her limbs disturbingly floppy.

Her neck couldn't support the weight of her head. It sagged between her shoulders like a deflated balloon. With a spastic jerk, she twisted her head all the way around, the velvet fabrics protesting with a sound like fingernails on a chalkboard.

"Yes, you must be here." Menda waggled her head from side to side, one of her mitten hands clutching the door frame. A small metal seam ripper was stuck in the teal fabric. Mally instantly recognized the little tool. It was the one she'd lost cutting Sunshine free.

"Well, just in case." Menda gripped the silver handle and pulled the tool out of the frame, then stabbed it back inside. She shoved the blade viciously through the cloth, ripping a gash at least four feet long. Mally felt the rip split through her skull. The light in the door began to flash on, off, on, off.

"What are you doing? Stop! Stop it!" Mally gripped her head. "No! I can't think!" The crown continued to spin, but the pain lessened to a dull throb.

"Mally? Mally!" Voices called out of the darkness. Mally shook her head, confused. Menda was speaking as if she hadn't heard her.

"You stole something from me, Mally. Something very, very special to me." The witch's voice was thick with tears as her head rotated in a freakish angle, looking up to the sky, then down to the ground. Then her emotions flipped yet again and she snarled. "So I've stolen something from you!"

She skittered back from the Open Door to a strange shape crumpled on the top step. The light from the door flashed on and off and with each blink of light, the figure slowly came into focus.

Flash! Wrinkled hands gripping the fabric.
Flash! White hair twisting in the wind.
Flash! A red jacket quilted with white thread in a diamond pattern.
Flash! Wide blue eyes ringed with thick glasses.
Flash! The face Mally had been searching for all this time.
"Grandma!" Mally shouted.

Chapter 14

The Queen's Regent

Mally jumped for the steps, but strong hands were gripping her shoulders, holding her back. She turned her head from side to side, but nothing was there.

"Let go of me! Grandma!" Mally yelled.

"Mally! Wake up!"

"You have to wake up!"

The voices were shouting now. Mally's body shook from side to side as if invisible hands were shaking her shoulders. She forced her way up the courthouse steps one at a time and reached out to grip Grandma's hand.

But something was wrong. Mally couldn't feel the soft fabric under her bare feet. She lunged, reaching for Grandma's arm, but her hand passed through her jacket as if she were made of smoke.

"Grandma! What's happening?" she cried, her hands clawing uselessly in the air. Dimly she heard Menda laughing.

"This is pretty simple, Mally May. I have what you want. You have what I want. I propose a trade." She turned and hauled Grandma up by the arm. The older woman struggled, and Mally screamed as the light from the open door flickered off, plunging them into darkness.

"Mally, please wake up!"

"Come on, little Maker, open your eyes!"

Mally ignored the voices as the light from the door blinked back on and glinted off the seam ripper in Menda's hand. The witch pressed the little blade to Grandma's throat.

"Bring me my crown, Mally May. Only you can save the day." Menda whispered and her visible eye bulged as she smiled. "Come alone and you'd better come quick or my hand may just slip." She pressed the blade closer and Grandma gasped.

"No!" Mally screamed, leaping at her. But again her hands passed through everything as if she was a ghost. Darkness filled her vision.

"She's going over!"

"Catch her, Patch!"

Mally's stomach plunged. She was falling from a great height. Branches whipped past her face as the ground rushed up to meet her. She held out her hands, ready for the crash when something caught her from above and jerked her out of the fall.

"If sleepwalking is a side effect of that crown, I'd advise not wearing it to bed," Patch growled. "Are you awake now or should I drop you again just to be sure?"

"Awake." Mally gasped for breath. She seemed to have left her lungs behind. "What happened?"

Patch landed softly and sat Mally on the ground. "Something's up. A chicken came to tell me Ms. Bunny was in pain, but on the way to help her I caught you doing the crazy pants dance right out of the top of the tree." Patch looked at her with concern wrinkling the fabric around his eyes. "You okay, little Maker?"

"I'm fine, but Grandma isn't." Mally got shakily to her feet, wrapping her arms around herself. "Menda has her. She's still alive and she still has a seam ripper, Patch. That one I dropped the night we saved Sunshine! She was holding it to her throat —" Her voice cracked as she saw the scene again in her mind.

"How do you know this? How did you see it?" Patch asked. But before Mally could answer, a crowd of patchwork animals found them in the darkness.

"Queen Mally! Are you okay?"

"We saw something fall from the tree."

"Mally, Ms. Bunny needs you!"

Mally had no choice but to let them guide her back into the Great

Tree. The crown spun slowly around her head, sending a constant throbbing ache down her face and neck. *The quilt is damaged. Menda has Grandma. What do I do?* Mally couldn't escape the thoughts circling her mind. *What do I do? What do I do?*

*   *   *   *   *

The first thing Mally saw when she stepped into the Great Tree was Pin carrying Ms. Bunny down the spiral staircase. She barely noticed the dozens of patchwork animals filling the wide circular room. Her eyes were riveted to Ms. Bunny's pain stricken face.

"Is she okay?" Mally said, holding out her hands. "What happened?"

"She collapsed, Queen Maker. I caught her as I was walking up the steps."

"Thank you. Thank you so much for catching her." Mally whispered. Ms. Bunny lay as still as the inanimate doll she used to be, both paws and her ears tightly wound around the hole in her chest.

"I'm so sorry, Ms. Bunny. She's ripped the quilt."

"I can… feel it… the Open Door… your way home." Ms. Bunny's words came out in short gasps.

"She has Grandma too," Mally said. The crown was sending her images in flashes, along with short electric shocks.

Curious fabric faces surrounded them on all sides. Behind, she heard the distinctive "clip clop" of Oak's hooves against the floor. The horse had shrunk in size considerably, but her voice boomed angrily through the room, "Shadow is hurt. How is this happening? I guess the witch isn't as dead as you thought she was."

There was a ripple through the Great Tree as many animals cringed in fear. A green fox fell off the windowsill with a crash and quickly scurried under a nearby cabinet. A dozen baby chicks lost their heads completely and rushed for the stairs. A yellow hen chased after them, but she was immediately knocked backward by a new commotion at the door.

Several flying geese were trying to fly through the opening at the same time. Their wide wings hit the door frame twice before they angled their bodies properly. In their clawed feet they carried another familiar bundle.

"Sunshine?" Mally fought back tears as the birds carried her over and set her gently in the middle of the big table. Sunshine was wrapped up tight, her wings doubled over twice around her tiny body. Mally ran to help, but her hands were already filled with Ms. Bunny.

"Let me take her, Queen Mally," Hoop said, scooping the doll gently out of her arms.

"Yes, let us help! Let us help!" A chorus of voices rang out all around.

"Quiet!" Mally yelled and the room went instantly silent. Her head felt like it was going to split in two, but her heart plummeted as she realized what she'd just done.

The crown gave her power over all things made of fiber. She'd experimented a bit before going to bed and asked a scrap of red fabric and silver thread to make a simple bracelet. It was a poor imitation to the one Creo wore, but it had made her happy to see the threads weaving effortlessly through the material.

Apparently that power extended to everything made of cloth, including her patchwork friends. All the animals in the room gaped at her, their mouths opening and closing, but no sound came out. With one word she'd effectively muted everyone at once.

Oak glared darkly at her and her look was mirrored on Patch's face as well. Mally took a deep breath. "I'm sorry, I didn't mean to do that. You can all speak again."

She thought fast, her heart racing. "I need a meeting with the First Made, if they're here. Menda is still alive. She's in bad shape, but she may still be able to make snarls. Can we send out patrols? If monsters are coming, the earlier we know the better. If you can't help with the patrol, please go to bed for now. We'll wake you when it's time... to go..."

"And what about Shadow?" Oak demanded, nodding at the swinging bed. Mally could see the owl's black feathers spread out over the pink patchwork quilt. "Should I have Patch rip another hole in my chest so I can take care of my friend, or are you going to finish that monster for real this time?"

Mally clenched her hands into fists, digging her fingernails into her palms to try to stop from crying. "I'm doing my best, Oak! If you'd just stop shouting at me, maybe I could figure out what we're going to do!"

"Shouting? I wasn't shouting!" Oak roared, her white mane whipping through the air. Patch's big orange body suddenly slid between them.

"As entertaining as it would be to see the two of you go toe to toe, I think we should leave that for another day. Let's go see Shadow and tell me how I can help."

Patch led Oak over to the swinging bed and Mally let out a long, shaky breath, forcing her body to relax. She watched the horse nuzzle at Shadow's limp form, her face drawn with concern. *She's just afraid, she thought, trying to let go of her anger. Menda is back and hurting the quilt and now everyone can be hurt too. What am I going to do?*

Hoop carried Ms. Bunny over to rest on the swinging bed with Shadow. Mally hugged her arms around herself and waited for the First Made to join her at the table. The flying geese that had carried Sunshine inside took off to follow her orders. Chickens and ducks flapped their wings, herding chicks and ducklings up the spiral staircase while the bears, monkeys, foxes, and cats left to patrol the field outside.

Finally the room began to clear and Pattern, Pin, Thimble and Goldie joined her at the table. Spool raced into the room last, his dark blue turkey face pinched with annoyance. Patch slipped into the chair on her right as Mally whispered. "Sunshine, I'm here. What happened?"

"Mally? Oh Mally!" The bird's head popped up and she stuck out her legs to stand. But she kept her wings tightly folded around her body. "I did what you asked and I found the Ripping Witch, but she wasn't dead. It was awful. She's so twisted and gross and what's up with her eyeball?"

"Focus, Sunshine. What happened? Why did the birds have to carry you inside?" Mally was surreptitiously checking her body for ripped seams and couldn't see any damage.

"I don't know how, but she had your Grandma." Sunshine shook her head. "I tried to hide and keep my wings shut like Patch taught me, but I couldn't get close enough to help her. I'm so sorry, Mally. I couldn't get her free."

"It's okay, Sunshine. You're here and safe and that's what matters now." Goldie said. "How did you get away?"

"Wait, that's not all. I watched and watched because that Menda sure is flippity floppity. One minute she's crying and the next she's screaming. But your Grandma was sewing something as if she couldn't hear a word. It was weird." Sunshine hopped from foot to foot. "She just sat there and stitched while Menda went bananas over and over. I kept watching because I figured something had to happen sooner or later, and then it did!"

Sunshine opened her wings with a flourish and everyone standing around the table flinched as her brilliant light flashed through the room.

"Oh, sorry, sorry, sorry! I always forget about that." Sunshine scooted over to Mally, pushing something small across the table. "Menda made your Grandma leave. She had a sharp thingy and she made her go. But your Grandma had stopped stitching. She left this behind and I think it's for you."

Mally looked down at a tiny black and white quilt block. It was less than three inches wide and pieced in a simple pattern that formed a strange shape in the center. She picked up the patchwork, turning it around to see it from another angle. A sudden gust of air blew through the room and the walls began to spin.

What's happening?" Mally gripped the table tight as Goldie and Pin tumbled off the surface. Pattern dropped to all fours, his claws digging into the floor as Thimble rolled onto her side, her trunk and ears flailing.

Pain lanced through Mally's head. It felt like she'd been shot through the temple with an arrow. The crown twisted, and she doubled over, trying not to throw up.

Hoop was suddenly at her side, Ms. Bunny's prone form cradled in her paws. The doll's dress had slipped from her shoulders and Mally could see the open spot on her chest gaping wide. She looked down at her shirt and found the sleeve whole and uncut, as if she'd never sliced out the heart shape to give to her friend.

The quilt block slipped out of her hands and spun to the floor. Another gust of wind blasted through the room as it rotated the other way, faster this time. Then it stopped so suddenly, Mally felt like she'd been slammed against a wall. The pain in her head disappeared instantly, but it felt like every bone in her body had been wrenched out of socket.

Patch glared at her from the floor where he'd flattened himself like a small orange rug. "Whatever you're doing, please stop."

"I'm not doing it! I don't know what happened! Ms. Bunny, are you okay?"

The rabbit lifted her head and shook it hard, her ears flapping. "I'm not sure anyone else could do that, Mally. For a second there, I felt every seam that had been fixed open up wide again. It was like we went back to yesterday."

"Yes, I could feel it in my crown too."

"But how? You were just sitting here," Spool said crossly. Blue feathers stuck straight up out of his tiny turkey head like he had a mohawk.

"Wait, what is that quilt block?" Ms. Bunny asked. She hopped up off the floor and ran over. It was shocking to see her back on her feet so quickly after being unable to move just seconds before.

The doll touched the quilt block gingerly, as if afraid it might bite and rotated it in her paws. As she did, the design suddenly became clear to Mally. "Hourglass. That's an hourglass quilt block."

The room didn't move as each animal played with the patchwork. They passed it down the table and everyone tried turning it this way and that, but nothing happened. Then Mally took another turn. She rotated it ever so slightly to the right. Nothing happened.

"That's clockwise. Try counter clockwise," Ms. Bunny suggested.

Mally turned the block just slightly counter clockwise and the wind blew her hair into her face and her stomach registered the slow spin. Patch padded to the window and looked out at the dark sky. "I'd say it's an hour earlier. I could have sworn it was getting light and now it's back to full dark."

"At least my crown stopped spinning." Mally reached up to touch the braided band resting still on her brow. She looked at Ms. Bunny. "Are you hurting?"

"Not a bit." Ms. Bunny smoothed her ears down her back. "I feel just like I did after you mended that last pile of broken threads in the field outside."

So…" Patch pressed a paw over the hourglass block. "You have the power to turn back time, little Queen. Question is, how do we use it?"

*   *   *   *   *

Mally took a deep breath and held it as she counted to ten. She crouched on the top of the Courthouse Steps block, hiding behind the new Open Door she'd stitched to the right edge of Quilst. This was where she'd seen Menda in her vision and it was surreal to be back in a place she'd never actually been.

Twelve colorful steps formed a small pyramid on the grassy landscape. The Open Door was perched on top like a strange monument to an ancient god. A single winding path had led them to this clearing through a thick forest of appliqued trees. Like everywhere else she'd visited in Quilst, Mally wished she had more time to explore and enjoy the area. But now was not the time for fun and games.

Patch pressed against her side, his body shrunk down to fit behind the door frame. She turned and met Ms. Bunny's calm gaze. The rabbit rode on Patch's back, the hourglass quilt block pinned to the front of her blue dress. Her ears were up, listening for any sound and Mally was suddenly struck by how different she looked. She could barely recognize the little doll she'd brought with her into the quilt only a few days ago.

A faint gust of wind at her neck was the signal. The birds had set up spotters in almost every tree between the Open Door and the mountain pass.

Menda was coming.

Mally heard her before she saw her. The witch was keeping up a constant stream of crazy commentary.

"That was MY crown. MINE! She coerced my pet and only with his help did she take it. She will give it back, she has no choice!" Her voice carried loud and clear up the patchwork steps to where Mally was hiding.

"What you think you had wasn't yours to begin with," a soft, gravelly voice answered. The sound made Mally's heart ache. It was Grandma.

"Not mine? Not mine?" Menda shrieked. "That was the only decent thing you ever gave me and your stupid brat granddaughter stole it!" There was a strange muffled sound, like a baseball hitting the center of a catching mitt, and a sharp cry split the air. Mally couldn't help herself. She peeked around the door frame.

What she saw changed everything. Light from the Open Door shone against Menda's contorted body. Half of her head had caved in and one of her eyes was completely lost in a mass of deep wrinkles. The other eye bulged three times larger than normal. She stood in the middle of the courthouse steps, her arms raised high into the air, her black mitten hands clenched into fists ready to strike again.

"No!" Mally screamed. She forgot the plan, she forgot about the animals hiding in the trees and she forgot she was queen. All she saw was Grandma crumpled on the steps, her white hair spread over the bright fabrics, a dark bruise already blooming on her cheek.

She flew down the steps three at a time. The witch had heard her shout and was just turning to look when Mally caught her in the back and shoved. Menda bounced down the steps and landed with a sickening thud on the ground.

"Protect Grandma!" Mally yelled and a massive flock of birds took to the air. Dozens of flying geese swooped out of the sky and surrounded Grandma, forming a thick ring of triangles around her body.

Mally kept her eyes fixed on the witch. Part of her torso had untwisted and her arms flopped uselessly in the air. With a thunder of marching feet, animals emerged from the trees.

"Come to finish the job, Mally May?" Menda slurred. The stuffing in her head had shifted again and only half of her mouth moved. "Ready to be a killer and Queen?"

"If that's what it takes, yes," Mally said, pulling out her largest pair of scissors from her back pocket. But she hesitated, shifting from foot to foot. Menda's mouth crooked up in one corner and she laughed softly.

"It's one thing to rip a creature when her back is turned. It's another thing to look me in the eye while you end me." Her head wobbled from side to side as she chuckled. "I've grown to enjoy those expressions. Your rabbit was especially fun. She was so sweet and innocent. Right up to the second I carved out her chest. I watched her eyes change. I warned you. She'll never be the same again."

"Stop it!" Mally shouted. She jumped down the last two steps and leaned over the witch, brandishing the scissors in her face. "What did you do with her missing pieces? Where are Shadow's pieces? How do I fix them?"

"Fix them, HA!" Menda barked out a laugh as she rolled awkwardly to one side. "You have no idea what it means to be queen. You're just a stupid little girl playing pretend. As I said… She will never. Be. The same. Again." She stretched out each word. The stuffing in her head shifted and her mouth suddenly bulged in a wide grin.

Without warning the witch lunged forward with shocking speed. She lashed out and the scissors flew from Mally's hand. The witch's contorted body wound around her in seconds, her long arms clamped around her neck. Mally felt the sharp bite of metal press against her throat.

"Back up! Back off!" the witch barked at the animals surrounding them. "You make one more move, you'll get to see a Maker turned inside out. And you —" She waved her seam ripper at the flying geese surrounding Grandma. "Take off. My Maker needs to see what she made."

The birds took flight at her command. Grandma rose shakily to her feet and watched as Menda pulled Mally up the steps one by one. The witch's arms were surprisingly strong and gripped her neck so tight she could barely breathe.

Mally struggled against her hold, but the seam ripper bit deep into her skin and she gasped at the sharp pain. The witch jerked her close as they neared the Open Door as she shouted at the top of her voice.

"Is this your queen? Did you really think a child could beat me?" She gripped Mally's hair in her fist and shoved her down, forcing her to sit on the top step so she could stand above her.

"Menda Amare, stop this. She doesn't have anything to do with you," Grandma called. "Let me take her home. We'll leave and you can have this world all to yourself."

"That's not good enough!" Menda shrieked. "I deserve to be worshipped! You will stay here forever and make me anything I want! And it all starts with me being Queen."

Mally felt the crown being lifted from her head. She could do nothing to stop it. Tears streamed down her face as the familiar weight disappeared. She turned and watched Menda lift the crown high into the air. Light from the door and the rising suns glinted off the silver and gold fabrics.

"I have the crown! Bow to me! I am your Queen!" The Ripping Witch brought the patchwork ring down and settled it around her lumpy head. She threw out her arms and screamed. "Bow!"

But no one moved. Row after row of mice, turkeys, monkeys, frogs, cats, foxes, chickens, and bears all stood still as statues, staring up at her. There was a ripple through the crowd as a few animals crossed their arms or turned their backs.

A band of glittery ducklings suddenly raced around the bottom of the courthouse steps, giggling madly. The laughter rippled through the crowd and suddenly everyone was laughing. Bears slapped their knees as the flying geese nearly fell off their branches, doubled over with mirth.

"I said bow! Why aren't you obeying me?!" Menda shouted. She looked on the verge of screaming again when the crown on her head suddenly exploded. Four silver and gold birds burst from the center and attacked her mitten hand. Her last weapon flew in a wide arc and disappeared into the Open Door.

Menda stumbled backward. She caught herself on the door frame, shaking her head from side to side. The light in the door wrapped around her dark body. Even from several steps away, Mally could feel the pull of the real world sucking her inside.

"It would help if you knew your quilt blocks," Grandma said. "Menda Amare, you should've known the difference between a Chimney Swallows and Coronation block."

"What? How could you trick me like that?" Menda cried, her voice suddenly high and pleading as she clung to the door frame.

"I found a book of quilt blocks in the Great Tree," Mally explained. "That block was listed by both names, but once I made it, the birds were more than happy to help out." She waved to the chimney swallows as they flashed around the steps, then soared off with a glimmer of gold and silver fabrics.

"No! I am the Queen of Quilst!" the witch shrieked, but her velvet hands slipped on the soft fabric. She was sliding into the door frame, one inch at a time. Her eyes fell on Grandma. "You did this to me! You made me what I am! This is MY world! MINE!!!"

Her last shriek stretched out long and high. Then the sound cut off abruptly as her body disappeared into the bright light of the Open Door.

Ringing silence filled the air and Mally let out a great sigh of relief. "She's gone," she whispered. Then she turned and lifted her arms high and yelled the words. "She's gone!"

The shout was taken up and soon turned into a roar as everyone in Quilst celebrated. Something tickled her bare leg and she looked down to find Ms. Bunny scrambling up to her shoulder. She scooped her friend into her arms and hugged her hard.

"We won," she whispered. As she pulled away she noticed Ms. Bunny wasn't smiling, but there wasn't time to ask what was wrong. They were immediately engulfed by a crowd of animals all laughing, talking, and cheering at once.

A trumpet blast sounded and Thimble appeared at the bottom of the steps with Hoop and Pattern at her side. The elephant carried the real crown balanced on her long trunk. Mally had left it with her just in case their plan didn't work.

The crowd around Mally hushed as the three animals walked slowly up the steps. Hoop lifted the crown and placed it back on her head, then hung her scissor necklace back around her neck.

"Thank you," Mally said with a sigh of relief. The crown rested still and steady on her brow. Quilst was whole once more.

"Thank you, Maker," Hoop said, then whispered, "I'm sorry."

"Sorry for what?" Mally shook her head, confused as another voice rang out over the crowd.

"The Maker of Menda has been found."

The crowd parted to reveal Oak standing at the foot of the Courthouse Steps, her long mane blowing in the wind. Shadow was perched on her back, the red heart stitched on his chest clearly visible even from a distance. A few animals Mally had never seen before clustered around the horse, their eyes wide and wary.

Mally didn't have a chance to wonder about the new creatures as Oak shouted, "Grace Wright, step forward."

A murmur ran through the crowd as Grandma moved into the open space. She walked up the steps slowly, her head bowed. When she reached the top, Mally couldn't help herself. She threw her arms around her. "Grandma!"

"Mally, oh my Mally May," Grandma said with a gasp. "I am so sorry." She turned and looked out at the crowd of patchwork faces and raised her voice. "I am so sorry for what Menda did. I am so sorry she hurt you. It was never my intention… I never meant for any of this to happen."

"Intention or not, you are the Maker of Menda. The harm she inflicted on Quilst may never be fully healed and you are responsible," Oak said. "As proclaimed last night by the Queen of Quilst herself, 'the Maker of Menda must leave the world of Quilst forever.'"

"Wait, right now?" Mally cried. She glanced from face to face and found many animals were avoiding her gaze. "Menda's gone. I thought we would have a day together at least."

"No, she's right. It's for the best," Grandma said softly. She turned to gaze out over the landscape she had made, one stitch at a time. "I loved it here. It was such a surprise the first time I came. Well, you must know what that's like." She smiled, glancing at the crown on Mally's head, then she spotted Ms. Bunny sitting on her shoulder and chuckled softly. "This is an incredible world, isn't it?"

"But where have you been this whole time? Why didn't you come home?" Mally gripped her wrinkled hands. Her heart squeezed tight at the sight of Grandma's thick knuckles and paper thin skin.

"Ah, I'm afraid that's a very long story. Much too long to begin right now. Let's just say if I could have come home, I would have... I never meant for anyone to know I'd even been gone."

"But what are you going to tell Mama?" Mally asked. "She's been looking for you for months. She's... changed. And Daddy. He might have seen me leave the last time. What will you tell them?"

Grandma smiled. "Did you get that quilt block I left you? I saw a pretty bird sneaking around and figured she would get it to you."

"The hourglass? Yes, that's how I was able to turn back time to save you, but how did you know it would work?"

"Menda Amare let a lot slip. She happened to mention there were lots of new animals loose in the world and I put two and two together. I figured if you could bring a Monkey Wrench block to life, an hourglass might just turn back time."

"It should have worked for you too." Mally was confused. "I brought all of the animals to Quilst when I was just a Maker, before I was queen."

"Didn't you notice yesterday was a lot longer than it should have been?" Grandma winked. "I might have stretched things out a bit. But I'm ready to go home now, Mally May."

"What do you... Oh." The crown planted an image in her mind. The hourglass block tossed in the middle of the Open Door. "Do you think it will work?"

"Only one way to find out." Grandma gave her one more hug, then turned to face the Open Door. "You're making something new here, Mally. The only thing you can know for sure is you have a lot to learn."

Ms. Bunny unpinned the quilt block from her dress and held it out. Mally took it, being careful not to rotate the cloth as she pressed it between her hands and focused on what she wanted. *What do I need to say to send Grandma back so she never went missing?* She opened her mouth and let the words flow.

"Stitch this Maker back to the hour she first left home. Preserve the quilt, this world of Quilst, exactly as it is today so everyone can live here and flourish."

Mally threw the hourglass into the door. A strong wind kicked up instantly, blowing her hair into her eyes. All around her animals crouched low, digging their paws into the fabric on the steps. Instead of sucking inward, the rush of air now pushed outward. The white space in the door frame changed. Black, silver, and white threads swirled together creating a vortex of color in the center.

Grandma turned, her hair swirling crazily around her head. "You'll be coming home soon too?" she asked, but her tone wasn't really a question. She planted a soft kiss on Mally's cheek, gave Ms. Bunny's ear a tweak, and without another word she stepped forward and disappeared into the Open Door.

Mally sighed as the light in the door dimmed. The rushing wind died down, but the swirl of colors remained, beckoning her to return home. If the hourglass block worked, Grandma would be back and it would be as if she'd never gone missing. Would Mama be okay? Would everything be back to normal?

I want to go home, Mally thought. For the first time since she'd stepped inside Quilst, she wanted to leave. She took a step towards the Open Door, then another. She was just one step away when a familiar voice called her back.

"You're not leaving us without saying good-bye, little Queen?" Patch asked. He'd shrunk down to the size he'd been when they met and was stretched out, sunning himself on the top of the steps. "Hardly like you to stitch and run."

Mally turned and found all of the creatures of Quilst watching her. Baby chicks flittered between patchwork legs while monkeys and frogs bounced happily up and down the steps. Hoop and Thimble gazed at her from the grassy landscape along with all the new friends she'd made over the last two days. But the pull to return home was overwhelming.

"I'm sorry. I need to go home too," she said. "I want to make sure Grandma returned safely and if my Mama is… well again. I miss my family."

"Aren't we your family now too?" Goldie asked. She was perched on Seam's shoulder and her triangular face drooped sadly.

"Of course you are!" Mally said quickly. "I just need to make sure everything is okay back home. If the hourglass block worked properly, then I'll never have to worry about spending time here again."

"But what about us? Who will lead us?" a baby chick yelled from the back of a pink rooster. Everyone turned to look at her and she rushed to hide under his legs.

"I… um…" Mally was at a loss for words. "I don't know."

"She needs to go home, immediately," Oak called. "With the Ripping Witch gone, we don't need her here. The trouble only started when the Makers came."

"Be nice, Oak," Shadow said in his quiet voice. "Before the Makers came, we didn't exist. There are a lot more animals in the quilt now. We will need a ruler."

"She must return. She's missing school," Hoop added. She must have sent a bird back to the Great Tree for Mally's bookbag because she was suddenly carrying it up the steps, slipping the largest pair of scissors back inside. "And we need to check if this time change thing is working."

"Thank you," Mally said quietly, slipping the straps over her shoulders. Her head spun as more animals begged her to stay and two mice from the Christmas Gang ran up to wrap their little arms around her ankles.

"But we're going to miss her! It won't be fun without Mally the Maker inside Quilst!" Sunshine cried. In seconds she had a crowd of flying geese chanting 'Stay! Stay! Stay!' which pretty much drowned out all other argument.

Mally pressed her hands over her ears and tried not to command everyone to be quiet. Thankfully they all caught on within a few seconds and quieted down on their own.

"What about a regent?" Spool called from the middle of the steps. His blue feathers still stuck up on his head like a mohawk. No one seemed to want to tell him about it. "Someone or several of us could help while she is beyond the Open Door."

"Like that council of the First Made?" Oak tossed her head. "You know, you were only the first made by THAT Maker. The Originals need a say too. There are more of us than you know."

The debate heated up again, but Mally ignored them. She caught Patch's eye and held out her hands.

"Would you take care of this world for me?" she asked.

"Not on your life," the cat said, lazily stretching his paws over the steps. For the first time in several days he looked like a normal tabby cat. "I'm destined for a decade long cat nap in the sun after this adventure." It was clear he was joking, but her heart twisted. If Patch wasn't willing to be her regent, there was really only one other choice.

Ms. Bunny slipped down from her shoulder. She pressed her paw into Mally's hand, against the stitches that were still tender. They both knew without speaking exactly what she meant – this is going to hurt.

"You want to stay?" Mally whispered. "Don't you want to come home with me?"

"It's not that I don't want to, dear." Ms. Bunny said, pressing her other paw to her chest. "I don't think I can leave. I'm tied to this world now."

Mally's eyes filled with tears. "I thought kicking Menda out would fix that. But it didn't, did it?

Ms. Bunny shook her head.

Thick tears slid down Mally's cheeks as the doll wrapped her arms around her neck. "I'll take care of things here. I promise. I'll keep that horse in check."

Mally laughed in spite of her tears, but wanted to cry all over again as Ms. Bunny lifted one of her ears to dry her eyes. The soft fabric slid over her face and Mally knew she would miss this most of all.

She gave her friend one last hug and set her on the ground in the middle of the tallest step where everyone could see her. Then Mally smoothed her ears around her little chest and adjusted her dress so it hung just right, as if she was still the cloth doll she liked to play with.

The crowd went quiet as Mally lifted the crown off her head. A pulse of electricity shot up her arms and she saw three images in her mind. She followed their direction and pressed her hands together on either side of the crown.

Blinding light burst from the center of the braided ring. As her hands moved, she considered her words. Only when she had it just

254

right, did she raise her face to the crowd and speak.

"I, Mally, Queen of Quilst, have selected a regent to be my eyes, my ears, my voice, my hands and my heart in this world at all times when I am beyond the Open Door. Ms. Bunny, will you accept this duty?"

"Yes," Ms. Bunny replied solemnly. "I will do my best."

Mally pulled her hands apart and in a flash of light the crown split into two pieces. In one hand she held the crown and in the other dangled a woven necklace of silver, gold, and red threads, the perfect size and shape for Ms. Bunny to wear.

"Please show my best friend the same love and loyalty you show to me," Mally said, kneeling down to clasp the necklace around her neck.

Suddenly Hoop bounded to the middle of the steps and let out a shocking roar, "All hail Mally the Maker, Queen of Quilst! All hail Mistress Bunny, the Queen's Regent!"

The crowd replied with a storm of clapping, stomping, and squawking. The collective roar was deafening. Mally sat back on her heels and bowed her head to her friend. The ground trembled as every animal in Quilst followed suit. Mally glanced to the side and saw that even Patch had risen from his nap and pressed his nose to the ground.

"Oh my," Ms. Bunny said in a shaky voice. "Come on now everyone, that's quite enough of that." A chuckle rippled through the crowd and Mally laughed along with them as they all rose to their feet.

"Looks like you're in for a lot of bowing and groveling from here on out, rabbit." Patch said, patting Ms. Bunny on the back with a paw bigger than her whole body. "Careful you don't get a fat head. It won't fit between your cute ears."

"She'll never have a head as fat as yours, Patchy Poo." Sunshine swooped down and wrapped her wings around Ms. Bunny in a warm hug. "She'd have to grow like a million, billion times bigger to even get close to the size of your head."

"As long as I have you both around to keep me in check, I think we'll be just fine." Ms. Bunny laughed, then she asked, "Queen Mally, do you have anything you want us to do while you're away?"

"I have only one request," Mally said, gripping the bookbag straps as she rose to her feet. "This message came from Creo, who I believe is the Great Maker of all the worlds. She asks that we make Quilst as beautiful as we can. Can you help me with that?"

"Only if you can bring us more thread!" Hoop shouted.

"And more fabric!" Thimble added and the crowd erupted in laughter and more shouts for different sewing supplies followed.

"I promise to return as soon as I can, and I'll bring you as much fabric and thread as I can manage. Please help yourself to everything in the Great Tree and work together to make Quilst as pretty as it can be."

With that Mally turned and faced the Open Door. Colors still swirled wildly together within the door frame and the wind picked up speed as she stepped closer. She looked back one last time at Ms. Bunny, surrounded by Patch and Sunshine and all the animals of Quilst.

"I'll be right back," she whispered, then turned and stepped through the Open Door.

About the Author

Leah Day grew up in Asheboro, North Carolina teaching herself to sew, crochet, and knit. She slept and played under many quilts made by her grandmothers and great grandmothers and was always fascinated by the magical ways the pieces fit together.

Leah made her first quilt when she was twenty-one to celebrate her wedding. That project was a total disaster, but she stuck with it and went on to become an award winning quilter and well known quilting teacher.

The inspiration for Mally the Maker came from her experience growing up sewing and crafting and spending time every weekend with her grandma. Ms. Bunny was a real doll Leah was given when she was four years old, but she was unfortunately lost on a camping trip.

Leah lives in the foothills of North Carolina with her husband, son, flock of chickens, two cats, and one lazy dog in a house filled with fabric, yarn, beads, and of course, lots of quilts.

Acknowledgements

The experience of writing Mally the Maker has been such an adventure from start to finish and I have many people to thank for helping me create this novel.

My husband, Josh, was instrumental in this book becoming a reality. From long talks about how things come alive in Quilst to ways to fix the time issue, Josh was my writing buddy, mentor, and occasional taskmaster. He patiently edited the text three times and is still trying to teach me how to properly use commas. The reason you're holding this book is entirely thanks to his help and encouragement.

I'm very thankful for my son, James, who was the very first kid reader of this book. Even though it was "about a girl" he enjoyed it and that made me very hopeful kids would enjoy it as well as experienced quilters.

Thank you Dad for inspiring me to make Menda smell like rancid lavender. I never smell that scent without thinking of you!

A shout out to my early readers: Leah, Laura, Janet, Jan, Marsha, Stephanie, Dianna, Rhonda, Riley, Nicolle, Elizabeth, Jen, Jenedel, Stephanie, and Marsha. I really appreciate all your kind feedback, typo catches, and suggestions to make the book better for all ages.

Thank you to all the listeners of my Hello My Quilting Friends podcast and your nthusiastic support and interest in the book. It's impossible to quit when so many quilters are excited to see the finished book!

I'm extremely grateful to my writing buddy Kati and our weekly writing check-ins which helped keep me motivated when things got tough.

A big hug from across the pond to Joanna Penn, the wonderful host of The Creative Penn podcast. I'd been carrying around this idea of Mally and a magical quilt world for years, but it was listening to this podcast that encouraged me to try fiction and to develop a habit of writing every morning.

All the blocks mentioned in this book are traditional quilt blocks and can be found in Jinny Beyer's The Quilter's Album of Patchwork Patterns. This amazing resource stayed by my side throughout the writing process and is a continual source of inspiration. Who knew traditional pieced shapes could have the power to turn back time?

I'm also immensely grateful for my parents who didn't buy a new television after ours broke when I was around seven years old. I know I wouldn't have learned how to sew, crochet, or knit at such a young age if I'd had anything better to do.

How to Piece a Four Patch Quilt Block

Would you like to make quilt blocks and hand stitch like Mally? Follow the instructions below to make your own Four Patch Quilt Blocks like Mally and Audrey from the book. Remember what Patch said - it will probably take you one thousand stitches for it to feel comfortable.

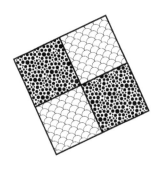

- Materials -

4 – 5-inch squares of 100% cotton fabric
Cotton thread
Package of needles - #9 sharps recommended
Pencil, ruler, scissors, and pins

- Instructions -

Arrange the four pieces of fabric to create a checkerboard pattern. Fold the upper left square over the right so the fabrics are right sides together. Mark a straight line ¼-inch from the edge of the fabric with a pencil.

Cut off a length of thread as long as your arm, then thread the needle. Hold the thread tails together and make a loop, then pass the ends of the thread through the loop to make an overhead knot on the end.

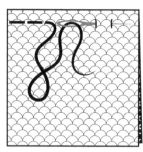

Starting on the left edge if you're left handed or the right edge if you're right handed, insert the needle on the marked line. Make sure the two squares of fabric stay perfectly aligned along all the edges.

Slide the needle through the fabrics to the back, then back up to the front to form a stitch. Pull the needle through slowly so your thread doesn't tangle.

If it does tangle, gently pick it out or clip the knot and start again.

Aim to keep your stitches consistent (the same size) and on the marked line. As you make more stitches and the needle becomes more comfortable to hold, your stitches will naturally become smaller.

When you reach the end of the marked line, take a backstitch. Insert your needle backwards into the stitch before, then slide it through and bring it back out the end. This reinforces the seam and stops it from coming apart. Tie another overhand knot and clip your thread.

Repeat stitching the two remaining squares together the same way.

Spread the pieced squares on your table so the right side faces down. Press the seams from the top two squares to the left and press the seams from the bottom two squares to the right. Now arrange the pieces right sides together again, and place a pin in the middle to line up the center seam.

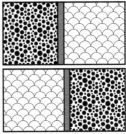

Mark another line ¼-inch from the top edge of the patchwork. Stitch along this line carefully. It will feel different because the piece is much bigger in your hand. Don't give up!

Make another backstitch in the center of the block where the seams come together to help reinforce that spot. Make one last backstitch on the end of the seam. Tie a knot and press this seam to the left.

Your Four Patch Quilt Block is now complete! It should measure 9 ½ inches square. Isn't patchwork magical?

I bet you can't make just one Four Patch quilt block. I hope you'll teach your friends how to make magical quilt blocks too.

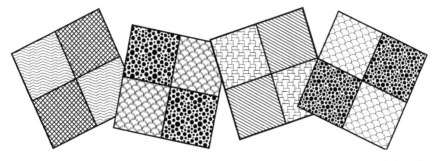

Find a free video tutorial on how to hand piece a four patch block with Leah Day at: **MallytheMaker.com/FourPatch**

Did Mally manage to turn back time and
fix everything back home?

Find out in the next book in the Mally the Maker series,
coming soon in 2019! Learn more about Mally and
find fun projects to make from the book at:

MallytheMaker.com

CPSIA information can be obtained
at www.ICGtesting.com
Printed in the USA
BVHW06s1125221018
530870BV00032B/2530/P